Marvi Lacar

About the Author

ZOE FISHMAN lives in Brooklyn, New York, with her husband. This is her first novel.

balancing acts

A Novel

zoe fishman

HARPER

NEW YORK • LONDON • TORONTO • SYDNEY

HARPER

This book is a work of fiction. The characters, incidents, and dialogue are drawn from the author's imagination and are not to be construed as real. Any resemblance to actual events or persons, living or dead, is entirely coincidental.

BALANCING ACTS. Copyright © 2010 by Zoe Fishman. All rights reserved. Printed in the United States of America. No part of this book may be used or reproduced in any manner whatsoever without written permission except in the case of brief quotations embodied in critical articles and reviews. For information address HarperCollins Publishers, 10 East 53rd Street, New York, NY 10022.

HarperCollins books may be purchased for educational, business, or sales promotional use. For information please write: Special Markets Department, HarperCollins Publishers, 10 East 53rd Street, New York, NY 10022.

FIRST EDITION

Library of Congress Cataloging-in-Publication Data is available upon request.

ISBN 978-0-06-171180-0

10 11 12 13 14   OV/RRD   10 9 8 7 6 5 4 3 2 1

For Ronen,

my eternal subway crush

PRANAYAMA

(Sanskrit: pranayama)
lengthening of the breath

Comprised of four parts:

PURAKA: *inhalation*
ANTARA KUMBHAKA: *retention (lungs full)*
RECHAKA: *exhalation*
BAHYA KUMBHAKA: *retention (lungs empty)*

Part 1

....

Puraka

chapter one

Charlie

In one swift, graceful movement, Charlie was up from the floor—
following behind her students, adjusting the pile of blankets
and neatening the mound of blocks. She smiled to herself as she
watched them zip themselves back into their jackets and prepare
for the frigid blast of winter, happily noting the contrast between
their newly relaxed faces and the tense, jaw-clenched bunch that
began her class just an hour ago.

She never stopped marveling at the restorative powers of yoga.
She loved opening up her students' hearts and weary, New York–
trodden minds with each stretch and flow. Turning to face the
wall of windows overlooking the bustling Brooklyn street below,
she surveyed the now empty studio and smiled.

To think that this belonged to her, that she was truly the cap-
tain of her own destiny . . . it was something. Sometimes she still
had to pinch herself. She turned out the light and glanced at the
clock on the front wall.

Five fifteen! Damn it! she thought. She had only forty-five minutes to make it into midtown, and she was in the far-out Brooklyn
neighborhood of Bushwick. *Please let the train be in a good mood*

today. With no time to shower, she gave her underarms a quick sniff and surmised that a spritz of her perfume would have to do the trick.

"Classy!" she heard behind her. She turned around, smirking already.

"What, you've never seen someone inspect their pits, Julian?"

"Yeah, gorillas do it all the time." He looked up from behind his post at the front-desk computer and gave Charlie a grin. "Do you pass inspection?"

"As fresh as a mountain spring! What's cooking on the Web?"

"In today's news, another former teen star has checked herself into the psych ward and Scientology has claimed another closeted leading man," answered Julian, shaking his head as he scrolled through his favorite gossip website. "I swear, I think the bad weaves are to blame."

"What are you talking about?" asked Charlie, as she changed clothes in the adjoining bathroom. She pulled her favorite red sweater out from her gym bag and gave it a shake.

"All of these teen starlets, losing their minds . . . I think it's the toxic glue from these rat-nest weaves seeping into their skulls. Maybe we should develop our own line of weaves and organic glue. I'm sure Felicity has a formula to share. We could sell them here and make billions of dollars!"

"Oh yeah, that makes perfect sense. Yoga and weaves. We might as well offer Botox, too," she said as she pulled her boots on over her jeans.

Julian laughed and got up from his chair. He stretched toward the ceiling. "I think we might be on to something here. A yoga studio for the new millennium!" He glanced at Charlie as she pulled her honey-colored hair into a huge bun on top of her slightly sweaty head. "Where you goin', hot stuff?" he asked.

Charlie paused as she pulled out her lip balm. "Why, to my pseudo ten-year college reunion, of course," she responded.

"Say what?" asked Julian. "You lookin' for an old boyfriend to reignite the passion? To carry your books and hold your hair while you puke? Honey, you know Big Man on Campus is now balding and married to some hooker with three kids. Oh, and his pants are pleated." Charlie cringed at the thought. "Wait, why is this a pseudo reunion and not a real one?" asked Julian. "Are you too cool for name tags and a catered dinner of iceberg lettuce wedges and Hamburger Helper? Maybe a Jell-O dessert and a little dancing to Black Sheep and Biggie Smalls at the end of the night?"

Charlie laughed. "Good Lord, Black Sheep? That's a blast from the past. No, it's not that I'm too cool at all, I just think that the alumni association wanted to do a little something in New York, since a lot of the Boston University graduates live here now, especially the old ones. Ten years out. I can't believe it, actually." She paused to reflect. *A decade. Damn.* "All I know is, I got an e-mail, and I decided to go. I have zero interest in rekindling any sort of long, burned-out flame, by the way. I only have one goal in mind for tonight."

"To show off your yoga abs?" asked Julian.

"Um, no. I'm going to spread the word about Prana Yoga. Surely, some of these people are looking to make good on their New Year's 'get in shape' resolution. The timing couldn't be better."

"That's not a bad idea, Lil' Miss Business Sense," answered Julian. "But show off your abs anyway. A little eye candy always works."

"What are you, my pimp?" asked Charlie with a snort. "That's rich. Seriously though, we all have to start pounding the pavement to get our memberships up. Including you, mister."

"Hello, earth to Charlie! Duh."

Charlie, Julian, and Felicity were co-owners of Prana, and since their opening two months ago, they had been on a serious mission to pack classes. Guerilla marketing had so far proved mildly successful, but they were still far from target. Running a business was not an easy gig, even if said business was based on Zen principles and faith in the universe. All of the *om*s in the world couldn't pay their electricity, mortgage, and heating bills. Not to mention gas and water.

They had all realized this coming in, of course—Charlie was a former Wall Street wiz, Julian had made a small fortune in the real estate market, and Felicity had even owned her own yoga studio at one point. Still, with all the brain power and know-how between them, it was a struggle to keep their dream afloat.

"Where have you been spreading the word?" asked Charlie.

"I've been hitting all the coffee shops and holier-than-thou hipster boutiques in Williamsburg and Carroll Gardens," Julian replied. "Handing out flyers and posting them on bulletin boards. I hit Flatbush Avenue this morning before I came in. And then, of course, there's my ultimate marketing coup," he pointed to the dog's bed behind the desk. George and Michael, the much-adored pugs of Julian and his partner, Scott, looked up at Charlie warily. Their tight little tummies and haunches were bound in Prana Yoga onesies—one in orange and the other in baby blue. Charlie laughed.

"Those poor little nuggets!" she exclaimed, walking over to give them a love pat.

"Are you kidding me, they love dressing up! Don't you, babies? Seriously Charlie, people on the street are constantly oohing and ahhing over these guys, so I figured, why not make them walking billboards?"

"Pretty genius. Although they don't look entirely enchanted by their wardrobes, I have to say."

"Oh, that's just George and Michael. Being fabulous is a way of life for them. Expressing any sort of enthusiasm for anything is so bourgeois."

Charlie laughed again as she zipped her jacket. "Okay, I'm off to midtown!" she announced, as she slung her bag over her shoulder.

"Oh gawd, you poor thing." He hopped up to hug her. "Good luck and try not to come back with a washed-up frat boy clutching your ankles."

"Will do," she replied as she breezed out the door and down the stairs. The cold air smacked her in the face. She inhaled sharply and pulled her hood up around her hair.

She wondered who would be there tonight. She had lost touch with almost everyone since college. She shook her head with a slight grin as she imagined what they would make of the "new" Charlie.

She was a far cry from the money-hungry, raging type-A tycoon of yesteryear. While all of her peers had been smoking pot out of downy tubes and laminating their fake IDs, she had been color-coding her note cards and watching C-SPAN.

She had been bound and determined to make it in New York among the other cash sharks, and knew that her humble beginnings would make her journey that much harder. But as her wise Pops had always said, "It's all about the journey, baby." That little pearl of wisdom had never been truer than it was right now, considering her imminent return to her past. Thank goodness it was only for one hour.

Okay, two hours! Charlie reminded herself begrudgingly. A trip into midtown warranted at least a two-hour stay, as that would probably equal her travel time on the godforsaken subway. Charlie swiped her fare card and eased through the turnstile.

Making her way down the damp platform, she was surprised

by the nervousness she felt. *Who would be there?* She mentally Rolodexed her very short list of college paramours. She rarely had made time for them, but occasionally she had broken her stoic reserve and engaged in the typical two- to three-week dating ritual. She marveled at the length of those entanglements, but three weeks in college seems like four years—or at least they always did to her. Especially if the guy was a total dufus, which they almost always were.

As the train approached, Charlie laughed to herself, remembering Russ, the strapping football player with a penis the size of a jujube. Said jujube was a steroided mess, and even after rolling out her tried and true tricks, that candy was just never going to unwrap. After surrendering and submitting herself to an awkward snuggle, Russ had made no mention of the "incident" and had instead asked her which kind of sports car was her favorite. The next day, Charlie was back in the business school library, plotting her eventual world takeover. If Russ was any indication of what was out there in terms of distraction, she was all too happy to maintain her focus.

Charlie switched to the 6 train at Broadway-Lafayette. She thought about what it would feel like to explain herself to these people she knew once upon a time. She had run into the occasional person from her Wall Street past and just shrugged off the noticeable difference.

"Where did you go?" a former colleague had asked incredulously during an awkward Saturday Starbucks run-in. "One day you were there, and the next day—poof! No one had any clue what had happened to you." She had adjusted the strap of her Birkin bag as she said this, one hand juggling her nonfat, nonsugar mocha grande and the other nervously smoothing her Japanese-straightened and lowlighted hair.

"Oh, I just had a—" Charlie frantically searched for an explanation that would reveal just enough, while at the same time, slam the door shut on any further questions. "I had a quarter-life crisis, you know? It was just time." Charlie tried to look dramatic and mysterious. The woman, whose name Charlie couldn't remember for the life of her (Sasha? Natasha? Nicole?), nodded her head as if she understood, the whole time thinking (Charlie was sure), *Bankrupt lesbian chops up her bodega guy and stores him in the fridge. The full story at eleven.*

"Got it," she whispered, obviously uncomfortable. "Well, glad to see that you're still alive!" she said, making her way away from Charlie and into her afternoon of Bergdorf and ball-busting.

Charlie smiled, remembering. She looked up. *Oh shit! How are we at Forty-second Street already?!* She rushed out of the car—her canvas shoulder bag just barely escaping the jaws of the closing door. The crowd surged forward and Charlie was more or less carried up the stairs and planted above ground, right in the thick of New York City mania. She took a deep breath as she began heading toward the bar.

Here goes nothin', she thought.

chapter two

Sabine

*S*abine pressed SEND and rubbed her temples. Violet was not going to be pleased about her five pages of edits. Not at all. But what could she do? Violet's book was about vegan romance and, sorry, there were only so many ways to make an impromptu quickie in the co-op bathroom sexy.

Sabine's editor in chief was on a mission to expand their readership and somehow she had determined that organic vegetables and soy cheese were a recipe for sexy. Hence, their new line of vegan and eco-friendly romances.

At a publisher best known for Fabio-covered bodice-rippers, this was a departure, to say the least. And as a senior editor, Sabine had to make these new titles work . . . or else. *Or else, what?* she often wondered. *Would getting fired be such a bad thing?!* Sabine sighed. She supposed that some days she did like her job, and even found herself strangely turned on by editing page after page of passion-fueled romps, but today was not one of those days.

She looked up to find Jasmine, her assistant, lurking in her doorway. "Um, is there anything else you need, Sabine?" she asked hesitantly, her hope that the answer was no and that she could go home decidedly apparent.

"No, no, go home!" answered Sabine. "Start your weekend, already!"

Jasmine smiled with relief. "Thanks, Sabine," she answered, practically running out of her doorway. She heard the distinct zip of Jasmine's jacket and then her sneakered feet bounding toward the elevator. She wondered what Jasmine's weekend entailed. Jasmine was twenty-three, fresh out of college, and living in the East Village with four other struggling friends. Jasmine had confided in Sabine that "really, she wanted to write" one night as Sabine treated her to wine and appetizers at a nearby bar. *No shit,* thought Sabine. *Good luck with all that.*

Sabine, too, had started in book publishing with the sole intention of writing, and here she was, ten years later, spell-checking *quinoa.* She stretched her arms high above her head and rotated her neck counterclockwise as she shut her computer off. The kinks in her body were so textbook "office kinks" that she wanted to weep. Work had been a bear lately. When was the last time she had gone to the gym? August? It was January. Ugh.

Sabine's cell phone rang. She picked it up to inspect the culprit. MOM it read, the shrill ringing eerily reminiscent of what she was sure to hear the moment she pushed TALK.

"Hi, Mom," she answered.

"Hi, Saby," she replied. "Are you wearing lipstick?"

Sabine laughed as she involuntarily grazed her lips with her fingers. They were so chapped by winter's unrelenting cruelness that they felt like beef jerky. And there was not a speck of color gracing their flesh. "Oh sure," she replied. "I've got a full face of fake on. Not to mention a push-up bra, a miniskirt, and stilettos. You know, just another day at the office."

"Your attitude is for the birds, Sabine," her mother replied.

"Being such a smartass is going to land you on your couch with that dumb cat for the rest of your natural life."

"Don't call him dumb!" Her cat, Lassie, was a huge bone of contention with her mother, who, as soon as Sabine had adopted him, had told her he was "the feline equivalent of a locked chastity belt."

"Well, I hope you're over penis," her mother had gone on to say in one of her more vulgar, martini-induced moments. "Because you'll never see it again in that apartment." Sabine had laughed at her audacity.

"Mom, keep your pants on, I'm on my way to that ridiculous ten-year reunion night," Sabine said.

"Oh good!" her mother shrieked. "I have a good feeling about this." As much as Sabine hated her mother's involvement in her personal life (or lack thereof), she was a glutton for punishment. She couldn't help herself from sharing and her mother was a particularly entertaining sounding board.

"What's the good feeling about?" asked Sabine. "Washed-up divorcés desperate to spread their seed?" Sabine reached into her bag and pulled out her makeup case. She had been staring at a computer screen under the brutal glare of fluorescent lighting all day. She didn't even have to see a mirror to know that she looked like a corpse.

"Listen, I have to dash," her mother said, cutting Sabine off. "I'm meeting the girls for movie night. Don't act like a jackass, and put on some lipstick and mascara. You're a beautiful girl and I love you."

"Thanks, Mom," replied Sabine, her eyes tearing up against her will. "Love you, bye."

"Love you, too, honey. Call me tomorrow. For chrissake, don't sleep with anyone! Not yet, at least."

"Roger that, Mom," Sabine replied, laughing. She hung up

and wiped her eyes. She couldn't believe she had teared up. Had it really been that long since someone had called her beautiful? She whipped her magnifying mirror (the mirror responsible for Sabine's ever-changing eyebrow arch) out of her desk to survey the damage.

See, you're pretty, she said to herself. And she was. With her big hazel eyes and wild chestnut locks, she was a classic, Mediterranean beauty. When Sabine wanted to, she could turn on the charm and snag more than a few second looks from appreciative men—it's just that she seldom wanted to. Men seemed to require a lot of energy, and she just couldn't muster it up these days.

She sighed as she pulled out her concealer and rubbed it into the circles underneath her eyes, remembering her last suitor—the constant checking of her cell phone (did he call? is it working? should I call him?), the uncertainty of their future, the good but not great sex, and then his eventual disappearance. It was a lot of anxiety and heartache for very little reward. She closed her eyelashes into her curler, counted to two, and then released. *Amazing what a difference this torture device makes.*

She resolved to push her negative thoughts about men out of her mind and refocus on the possibility of meeting someone who exceeded her ten years of dating in New York expectations. They couldn't all be cads. There had to be at least one who broke the mold.

She surveyed her face one last time and swept the mirror back into her desk drawer. She stood up and stretched, her back and neck cracking like Rice Krispies. "I need a massage," she said aloud to her empty office. She piled her manuscripts for the weekend into her bag and zipped herself into her coat.

"Go Terriers!" she sarcastically whispered, paying tribute to her college mascot. She flipped off her light and made her way out into the madness of midtown.

chapter three

Naomi

Mama, where are you going?" Noah asked suspiciously. "How come you have that stuff on your lips?"

Naomi laughed. She couldn't get anything past her son, or the Inspector, as she liked to call him. Noah needed to know everything, all the time. "Who is that? How does this work? What is milk made of? Why is your tummy sticking out?" This last question had come quite recently, when Naomi had attempted to squeeze herself back into a pair of jeans that had last seen the light of day in 1998. She had gotten them on, by the grace of God, but zipping them had been a different story entirely. She had lain across her bed and pulled with all her might, half expecting the metal teeth of the zipper to rip off entirely, but then—victory! The zipper had miraculously completed its journey upward and she had even managed to button them.

She had laughed, or, rather, wheezed appreciatively, wondering how she was going to get up. Awkwardly, she had made her way to a standing position—kind of like a baby calf's first steps—and wobbled to the mirror.

Just then, Noah had wandered in, surveying every detail of

the scene before him, but naturally zeroing in on the fact that his mother seemed to be encased in some sort of denim torture device on the lower half of her body.

After he asked her the stomach question, Naomi had promptly removed (very carefully) the denim relic of her past and placed the jeans in the Goodwill pile. Now Noah was her personal Tim Gunn as well as her inspector. Two for one.

"I'm going out, lovey," she replied, zeroing in for a hug. Noah tensed when she put her arms around him.

"Where out?" he asked again. "And who is staying with me?"

"I'm going to see some old college friends in the city." She cringed a little at the thought of what lay ahead of her. Since Noah had been born almost eight years ago (eight years ago? What?!), she had been a virtual recluse—and happily so.

This year she had vowed that she would make more of an effort to have conversations that didn't revolve around dinosaurs or the virtues of orange juice with pulp. And just like that, the Evite for this ten-year college reunion night had landed in her in-box. This was especially strange because Naomi had spent only one year at said college, and certainly couldn't legitimately be considered an alumna. It had seemed almost predestined somehow, even though Naomi didn't believe in that kind of thing. But still, it had been eerie.

"What college friends?" probed Noah. Naomi paused. That was a good question from the Inspector, and one that she wasn't entirely sure how to answer. She had spent most of her one college year skipping class and trying unsuccessfully to turn Boston into a smaller version of New York. She had barely made any friends at school, truth be told. She wouldn't be surprised if she didn't know a single soul tonight.

"Just some people I used to know," she answered.

"Oh," answered Noah. "Are they nice?"

"Sure," she replied, as she slid her gold hoops through her lobes. *I hope so,* she thought.

"Am I going to college?" he asked.

"Yes, you most certainly are," she replied, scooping his warm body into her arms. He was getting so big! Despite herself, her uterus lurched in response to this little man who just yesterday was a cooing baby. "But that's not for a long time. Oh, and Cecilia is going to come hang out with you tonight while I'm gone."

Cecilia lived in their building and was Naomi's lifesaver. Whenever Naomi had to dash out for the occasional work meeting or sanity-keeping emergency (the denim disaster of last weekend came to mind—it had been a wake-up wardrobe call that she had to heed), Cecilia was more than happy to watch Noah. She was getting her psychology Ph.D. at NYU and was always up for taking a break from her dissertation for a couple of hours. Naomi also suspected that Cecilia was analyzing the hell out of her for kicks, but she supposed that was okay. Trusting someone enough to let her take care of her son was a rarity.

"Okay, cool," replied Noah, as he de-pretzeled himself from their embrace and returned to his dinner at the kitchen/living room/everything table.

Naomi surveyed herself in the mirror. *Not too bad,* she thought. She had done a little shopping in preparation for her reentry into the adult universe and liked what she saw. Her neighborhood in Fort Greene had really reinvented itself over the past couple of years, and she had boutiques boasting a ridiculous array of enticing clothes at her disposal. She had flinched when purchasing her new pieces—visions of Noah washing dishes to pay for his college tuition ran through her head—but she knew it had to be done. Wearing jeans from the nineties was not going to win her any new friends, even if they were left over from her modeling days.

Naomi ran her fingers through her short Afro, tousling it just so. She wondered if anyone at this alumni night would recognize her. In college and for many years afterward, her long dreads had been her trademark. She had chopped them off in a hormonal fit of epic proportions when she had been pregnant with Noah, and luckily the short do suited her just as well, if not better.

"Knock, knock!" Cecilia yelled from outside their apartment door.

"Who is it?" she heard Noah ask.

"It's a land shark!" Cecilia replied, causing Noah to erupt into a fit of giggles.

"Sharks don't live on land!" he shrieked, excited to have his playmate just outside the door.

"Oh, okay, then it's a brontosaurus." Noah, still laughing, opened the door and Cecilia enveloped him in a hug.

"Hey Naomi!" she said, smiling broadly—her dazzling white teeth contrasting beautifully with her silky curtain of ebony hair. Just then, Naomi wanted nothing more than to grab her camera and capture that moment of pure light. She pushed the thought out of her mind.

"Hey Cee," she answered.

"You look hot!" exclaimed Cecilia, giving Naomi the once-over. "I wish I could wear skinny jeans. And with flats, no less!"

"It's okay?" Naomi asked nervously. "It's not too much? It doesn't look like I'm trying too hard?"

"No way," answered Cecilia. "You look annoyingly effortless."

"Perfect answer," replied Naomi, smiling. "Okay, Noah is finishing up his dinner and then maybe you can watch a movie, or—"

"Yeah, yeah, yeah, I know the drill, Naomi," interrupted Cecilia. "Get moving!"

Naomi glanced at her watch. If she didn't leave now, she would go from fashionably late to last call. The commute into the city from Brooklyn was less than speedy. "Okay, okay," she answered. "Noah! Give me a squeeze, please!"

Noah ran to her, his blue eyes dancing. "Bye, Mama," he whispered, as he pressed his compact frame into her willowy legs.

"Bye, baby boy," she whispered back.

She grabbed her bag and let herself out. She hit the street and took a deep breath in. The cold air was refreshing. She had been in the house practically all day, except for her walks with Noah to and from school.

She had finished up a huge Web design project a week ahead of time, and although that had meant long, grueling hours hunched over the computer, it had been worth it. Now she could enjoy her weekend with no guilt. That was the funny thing about freelancing—even though her schedule was her own, the lines between her personal and work life were criminally blurred.

She made her way down the subway stairs and swiped her card through the turnstile. It felt so strange to be out by herself, without a bag full of snacks and juice boxes. Strange, but good. She was ready to enter the non-Mommy world again, even if it meant revisiting her past to do so.

chapter four

Bess

So, do you think it's coke bloat or is she prego?" asked Rob. They both peered intensely at the photo on Bess's computer screen.

"Well, if we zoom in on her eyes, you can see she's wearing those ridiculous colored contacts again," answered Bess. "Which would corroborate the coke bloat theory."

"What do you mean? Can pregnant women not wear colored contacts?" asked Rob, confused. "Are they made out of nicotine and mercury?"

"Nooo," answered Bess. "I just have this theory that really fucked-up starlets wear those heinous contacts to conceal the fact that their pupils are the size of platters."

"Wow!" exclaimed Rob. "I never even thought of that! Bess, you are a genius."

"Tell me something I don't know," she answered.

"Okay, run a pill-popping caption. Stay away from any mention of coke or heroin though. Last time we specifically labeled her habits her PR bitch came in, guns blazing."

"Got it," answered Bess, thinking for the 998th time that day that her job was absurd. She got paid heaps of money to point out celebrities' flaws to a rabid, regular public. Sometimes, very rarely, she actually did some work with a hint of substance—like the time she traveled with a certain celebrity–cum–U.N. spokesperson to Africa to research a story on her efforts there—but most of the time it was the same old story over and over again: talentless teenager falls facedown into a pile of coke and makes a sex tape. Or something like that.

She captioned the picture with her trademark snarkiness and e-mailed her pages to the managing editor. She had no articles running in this week's issue, so it was a relatively easy Friday, considering.

"What are you up to tonight?" asked Rob. "Is Dan flying in on the love shuttle?"

"I wish," grumbled Bess. Dan was her boyfriend. Technically, he was her long-distance boyfriend, but it felt strange to think of him that way. He had moved to Los Angeles three months ago, and the coastal separation had proved to be more of a strain than Bess had been anticipating. A screenwriter at heart but a Wall Street banker by trade, he had taken a huge risk and applied to USC's film school last year. Bess had known he would get in— he really was talented—but was still shocked to find out that he would, indeed, be leaving her to do so.

They had been traveling back and forth on weekends here and there, but not having immediate access to each other was hard. Very hard. "He's staying in LA this weekend, working on a script," she explained with a sigh.

"No nookie for you then, huh?" asked Rob, as he squirted lotion from a freebie tube that retailed for $80 an ounce into his palms. As senior editors and reporters at the most popular celebrity tabloid magazine in the country, they were forever getting the best swag imaginable. This, of course, was highly unethical, but then again, everything about their job defied any sort of ethical code.

"Zero," replied Bess. "And the next time the word *nookie* comes out of your mouth, I am going to strap you into your time machine and send you back to the year 2000."

"Clever girl!" replied Rob, clapping his hands. "Point taken. So you're just going to lay low this weekend?"

"Yeah, for the most part." She had been planning to research story ideas for three weekends in a row now. Her New Year's resolution had been to break out of her ridiculous job to actually do some real reporting. Something that had nothing at all to do with weight fluctuation, hair highlights, or Botox, which were the usual topics of the freelance work she did for a couple of the major women's magazines around town.

Every time she would sit down to brainstorm, however, she was about as focused as a puppy with a bowl full of Red Bull. She found herself daydreaming about Dan, wondering what he was doing and fantasizing about seeing him again. She had become a cliché, much to her chagrin. She knew it was okay to be in love, but to shelve your own goals while doing so was a huge mistake— one she had seen too many people make.

"What are you doing this weekend, Robbo?" she asked, ready for his usual spiel: work out, see a movie, hang with his girlfriend. Rob was nothing if not predictable.

"Eh, nothing much, actually. Amelia had to go out of town for work, so I guess I'll just have a dude weekend."

"And what does that entail?" asked Bess.

"Pizza, clothes strewn all over the place, not putting the toilet seat down, and porn."

"Sounds thrilling!" replied Bess, laughing.

Rob smiled. "I know, right? It all sounds so good in theory, but I'll be honest, it gets old in about four hours, tops. Hey, are you busy tonight? Maybe we could grab a drink or twelve? "

"Oooh, crap, I can't," said Bess. "I have to go to my ten-year college reunion."

"Huh?" asked Rob. "Since when are you the school spirit type?"

"Good question," answered Bess. "The only reason I'm going is because of this story idea I have. I think this might be the perfect way to get my rusty wheels in motion. At least, I'm hoping so."

"Oh yeah, what's the idea?" asked Rob.

"Not to be a bitch, but do you mind if I keep it to myself for a while? Just until I have a firmer grasp on it? I'd hate to jinx myself."

"Not at all, m'lady," said Rob. "Keep it close to the vest as long as you like."

"Thanks, Rob." She looked at her watch. "Oh shit, I have to go! I'm just going to freshen up my tired mug and then I'm out the door. I hope your dude weekend is all that you have been dreaming of."

"Thanks, Bess. Have fun tonight. Be sure to take note of how big the homecoming queen's ass is now."

Bess made her way to the bathroom. She dropped her coat on the couch in its foyer and faced the mirror. As she reapplied her makeup, she thought about the story idea that had been marinating in her head since the reunion e-mail had landed in her in-box. She wondered if she could pull it off. She withdrew the wand from her mascara tube and brushed it through her lashes. *Maybe. But you have to focus, Bess. Really focus.*

Her phone rang. She glanced at it—Dan was calling. She shoved it deeper into her bag, even though she was dying to talk to him. *No distractions tonight!* she reminded herself, as she zipped into her jacket and headed out the door.

chapter five

Ten Years

"Hi, welcome to ten years ago!" greeted an over-caffeinated woman.

"Um, hi," replied Charlie.

The woman handed her a blank name card. Charlie hated those things, they always made her feel like a geek. *When in Rome,* she reminded herself. She filled out her name and stuck it to her chest. *Hi, these are my breasts and my name is Charlie.*

She thanked the woman and moved past her into the bar, hesitantly searching the small crowd for a familiar face. No one was registering. She approached the bartender, suddenly feeling the need for a very large glass of wine.

"Could I have a glass of pinot noir, please?" she asked as she plunged into her bag for her wallet.

"Charlie?" she heard a raspy voice next to her say. She looked up and into the smile of a pretty woman with blond hair pulled into a severe ponytail. *Wow, hello cheekbones,* she thought.

"I'm sorry, do I know . . ." Charlie paused. "Bess!? Oh my God!" She moved to embrace her.

"Hey!" Bess replied. "You look great! How are you?"

"I'm well, thanks. You too. You haven't changed an ounce. It's ridiculous."

"Well, I hope I'm dressed a little better than the last time you saw me," said Bess as she laughed, obviously pleased by the compliment.

"Well, I guess anything's an improvement over flannel pajama pants and a hooded sweatshirt forty-seven sizes too big," agreed Charlie.

"Very true," said Bess. "Remember those Sunday breakfasts in the café? What I wouldn't give now for a waffle station and an endless supply of Lucky Charms at arm's length."

Charlie laughed. "Seriously. Did we ingest anything but sugar for four years or what?"

"Barely," said Bess. "I'm lucky all of my teeth haven't fallen out."

Charlie and Bess had lived in the same dorm for two years and on the same floor their freshman year. Charlie remembered Bess's luxurious blond ponytail—always piled on top of her head. Bess remembered Charlie's long legs. No matter what the season, Charlie had always walked the considerable distance to and from class. Even in the depths of winter, Bess would gaze out from the T window and see Charlie loping down Commonwealth Avenue, bundled up beyond recognition except for those long, denim-wrapped legs.

"So what are you doing now?" Charlie asked Bess. "You were in the journalism school, right?"

"Yup," answered Bess. Charlie settled up with the bartender and turned to face Bess for her explanation. "I'm working for a magazine now."

"Oh, which one?" asked Charlie.

"*Pulse*?" Bess replied timidly. It sounded more like a question than an answer.

"Ooh, I know that magazine!" said Charlie. "That's the one that lambastes all the celebrities, right?"

"The one and only," Bess answered wryly.

"Do you like it?"

"Eh, it's okay. I do some freelance work on the side, so hopefully I can break out of that place soon enough." She moved on quickly; the last thing she wanted to do was talk about her job. "What about you? Weren't you a finance major? Have you taken Wall Street by storm?"

Charlie laughed. "Believe it or not, I'm a yoga instructor."

"What!? Get out of here! That's amazing. How did you end up doing that?"

"Long story. In a nutshell, I just got sick of the rat race."

"I hear that," said Bess. "Seriously, I think that's incredible. To have the balls to make a career switch like that . . . that's something that I dream about all the time. Where do you teach?"

"I actually have my own studio out in Bushwick. You should come check it out."

"Oh, that sounds good," answered Bess. "But I'm a complete novice. I've taken yoga only once and I was terrible at it."

"Yoga is not about being good or bad at it. You have to let go of that mind-set. You should absolutely come by, I'd love to have you." Charlie reached into her bag and handed Bess a flyer. "And I know Bushwick seems like a long way to go for yoga, but it's only about forty minutes from midtown, door to door."

"Thanks, Charlie, maybe I will," answered Bess, thinking about her story idea. The premise was pretty simple actually, but based on more of a vague idea than any concrete evidence. Bess was hoping to meet women tonight who naturally fed into her hypothesis. Charlie was actually the antithesis of the type of women Bess had planned on profiling, so she wasn't sure if yoga had any promise for her on that front. On the other hand, she could use more stretching in her life.

Charlie searched the crowd. "I was hoping to pass out a ton of fliers tonight, actually. We've only just opened our studio, so I have to get the word out."

"I'll help you! It will give me something to do besides drown my workweek sorrows in vodka. Let's take a lap."

"Nice! I really appreciate it." They both slung their bags back over their shoulders and turned to face the room.

"Here, give me a bunch of fliers," said Bess. "I'll go this way and you go that way. We'll meet in the middle. Whoever has handed out the most fliers buys the other a shot."

"Good deal," replied Charlie, with a grin.

As Bess plunged through the crowd, she thought about her article. She had come to the reunion wanting to write about the washed-up dreams of thirty-plus women; maybe a "then and now" sort of exposé about the aging female's shifting priorities. In a way, she was taking her concerns about her own life and projecting them onto a group of virtual strangers. Since she struggled with maintaining any sort of creative drive, she figured her former classmates had to as well. Right?

But then, what about Charlie? She completely turned Bess's entire quasi-hypothesis on its head. Instead of turning into a Wall Street power-bot, Charlie was now a yoga guru. Bess panicked for a moment. What if every woman here had managed to turn their dreams into reality and she was the only one drowning in a sea of complacency? Yikes. She handed a flier to a group of leering bald men, one of whom she was sure she had taken six-foot bong hits with at a house party junior year. She avoided his hopeful gaze and kept moving. That was not a reunion she was the least bit interested in.

Charlie scanned the crowd as she made her way around the

bar's perimeter. She noticed a familiar face. Who was that? She scanned the recesses of her brain. Was she in Statistics with her? No, she didn't think so. Did she take lifeguarding with her?

Charlie smirked remembering that class. Much to her horror, the teacher had flunked Charlie after she failed to properly turn over a facedown victim in the water. She blamed her summers of retail hell solely on that teacher. Had she been a little less rash, Charlie could have been tanning on the beach in Cape Cod instead of folding T-shirts at J. Crew.

Suddenly, the woman locked eyes with Charlie and smiled. She approached her. Watching her gracefully meander toward her, it struck Charlie. Naomi! The impossibly chic, camera-toting, supermodel look-alike who had lived in her dorm freshman year.

"Naomi!" Charlie exclaimed, as she went in for a hug.

"Hey, Carrie?" Naomi asked uncertainly. "Is that your name? I was trying to rack my impossible brain . . ."

"It's Charlie, actually."

"Yes! Charlie! I knew it. Please forgive my horrendous memory. The good news is at least I remembered your beautiful face."

Charlie blushed. Naomi, the queen of chic, actually thought she was beautiful? She suddenly felt fourteen again. "Oh please, it's fine. How are you, Naomi?"

"I'm well, thanks. How are you?"

"The same, more or less. Mostly less. Hey, did you transfer out after freshman year or something? I feel like I never saw you again."

"I did, actually," replied Naomi. "I actually sort of, well not sort of, what am I saying? I flunked out. My parents were less than pleased naturally, so it was back to New York for me."

"You grew up in New York? I never knew that. But that explains your sophistication."

"What do you mean? I was far from sophisticated in those days."

"No way, you absolutely were. We were all hanging around in ripped jeans and North Face puffy coats, but you had your look together. And you were so elusive. Whenever I saw you, you were with that pack of skateboarding artist types. They didn't go to BU, right?"

Naomi laughed, remembering. "No, no. They went to Emerson. God, it was so long ago! So much has changed. It's really unbelievable. We're old!"

"Tell me about it," agreed Charlie. Over Naomi's shoulder, she saw a dark-haired woman with an incredulous look on her face approach. She mouthed 'hello' to Charlie and tapped Naomi timidly on her arm.

"Naomi?" she asked.

Naomi turned around. "No way! Sabine! Hi!" The women embraced as Charlie looked on. Sabine looked familiar to her, too.

"I'm sorry, Charlie, do you know Sabine?" asked Naomi. "She was my roommate freshman year."

"You know, you do look familiar," Sabine said, as she extended her hand to shake Charlie's.

"So do you," answered Charlie. "I think you lent me laundry detergent once."

"Wait! Yes! Now I remember. You had like, seventeen loads or something, and you ran out!"

"Yep, that was me," answered Charlie. "I was always so busy cramming for school that my laundry would pile to the ceiling before I realized it was time to hit the machines."

"Sabine, how are you?" asked Naomi. "It has been forever!"

"It really has," agreed Sabine. "I was convinced I wouldn't know anyone here, but I am so happy to be running into you. I always wondered where you went.

"Naomi was the best roommate ever created," Sabine explained to Charlie. "She was hardly ever home, number one. And number two, when she was, she would lend me clothes and straighten my hair for me."

"And remember 'the smoky eye'?" asked Naomi, laughing. "You always begged me to give you 'the smoky eye.' "

"Yes!" Sabine exclaimed, clapping her hands with glee at the memory. "No one could do it better than you. And then you would take pictures of me!"

"Hey, Charlie!" crowed Bess as she broke through their circle. "I got rid of all of my fliers. I'll take a shot of Patrón, thanks!"

Charlie laughed. "We were just talking about the good ol' days," she explained to Bess, including her in the circle.

Sabine smiled in greeting and continued her conversation with Naomi. "Are you still taking pictures?" asked Sabine. "You were so talented. You even made me look like a model, and that is an impossible task for mere mortals."

"Excuse me, Miss Modest," replied Naomi. "It was not an impossible task at all."

Sabine smirked. "So, are you still photographing?" she asked again.

"Um, no, not anymore," explained Naomi dismissively.

Charlie, sensing an opening, turned to Bess. "Ladies, this is Bess. Bess, do you know Sabine and Naomi?" she asked.

Bess peered at them inquisitively. Naomi's obvious discomfort about her photography had struck a chord with her. This was the kind of stuff she had been looking for. "Are you the girl who somehow made dreads look chic?" she asked Naomi.

"Oh, I don't know about the chic part, but my hair was dreaded back in the day," answered Naomi.

"Yes, I know you then! You were 'Lisa Bonet,' " said Bess, pleased to have made the connection.

"What?!" asked Naomi, laughing.

"Yeah, that was my name for you. Is she or is she not a dead ringer for Lisa Bonet?" she asked Sabine and Charlie.

Before they could answer, Bess pointed at Sabine. "And you, you were in some of my English classes! Shakespeare, junior year?!"

"With Professor Gottlieb!" exclaimed Sabine. "Of course, I remember you now."

"What are you doing with your English degree these days?" asked Bess. "Writing bestselling novels?"

"Oh please. Not at all. I'm just an editor at a publishing house."

Bess sensed some sadness in Sabine's tone. It looked like she had found another shelved dream in tonight's crowd. Bess was reinvigorated. Her article did have legs after all.

"What fliers were you talking about, Bess?" asked Naomi, changing the subject.

"Charlie owns a yoga studio in Bushwick. She's here to spread the word about it, so I told her I'd help out. Besides, it gave me something to do besides standing around and looking lost."

"You own a yoga studio, Charlie?" Sabine asked. "That's tremendous. I wish I were a yogi. I've always wanted to get into it, but just haven't made the leap from the treadmill to the mat yet."

"Why not?" asked Charlie. "You don't have to abandon running for yoga, you know. They're actually very complementary."

"I can barely get out of bed for the gym, much less double time it between that and a yoga studio," Sabine explained. "Or at least I've been convincing my lazy ass of that in order to make it feel better."

Naomi laughed. "I know, it's amazing how we can persuade ourselves out of something before even attempting it," she said. "I was doing yoga pretty religiously while I was pregnant and then, well . . . I stopped. I'd love to get back into it."

"Ladies, helloooo!" said Charlie. "Come to my studio. Let's get a Saturday workshop going. If you all commit to six weeks, I promise you that you will never think of a reason not to do yoga ever again. Once you're in, your whole life changes."

"Yeah, Charlie left piles of Wall Street money behind after she got hooked on it," Bess explained to Sabine and Naomi. Bess was not the slightest bit interested in yoga, but if she could encourage Naomi and Sabine to join, she would be golden on the article front. She could probe them for details about their unrealized dreams and get to know Charlie's motivation for turning her former life on its ear. It was a win-win-win.

She turned to Charlie. "You know what, Charlie, I'm in! I might have to miss a Saturday or two because of travel, but I am in."

"How far is Bushwick from the East Village?" asked Sabine. The thought of a subway commute first thing Saturday morning was mind-numbing.

"Not that far, maybe a half hour?" answered Charlie. Sabine thought of her Saturday mornings lately. Her, her cat, an unread paper, and *That's So Raven* on the television. Then she thought of spring's imminent arrival and the way that her upper arms jiggled.

"I'm in too!" she said.

"Well, I'm in Brooklyn already, so for me to bow out would just be sad," said Naomi. "I could have my neighbor watch Noah I suppose. I'm in too, Charlie."

"Fantastic!" exclaimed Charlie, beaming. She handed them each a flyer. "Here's the address and the directions. Should we start tomorrow?"

"Erm, no," replied Bess. She needed to simplify her thesis before jumping in. "Let's allow ourselves one more week of stationary existence."

"Yeah, I agree," said Naomi. "I wouldn't be able to get a sitter on such short notice anyway."

"You owe me a shot, Charlie!" Bess interjected.

"Let's all do a shot!" said Sabine. She sidled up to the bar. "Four shots of Patrón, please." The bartender complied, filling each glass to its rim and providing plenty of limes and a salt shaker. Sabine passed around the various ingredients and poured the requisite salt on each wrist.

"To yoga class!" Bess cheered.

"To yoga class!" Charlie, Naomi, and Sabine repeated.

Part II

·········

Antara Kumbhaka

chapter six

Charlie

Charlie loved this time of the morning, right before day-break, when the city felt like her own. The streets were silent, yet she could still feel the energy beneath her feet, just about to burst forth into another day. Before, when she would wake early for her job on Wall Street, she would transform immediately from sleep to robot—shower, suit, subway, coffee. Now her pace in the morning was decidedly different. She still awoke with a sense of purpose—she had a studio to run after all—but the purpose felt considerably more her own.

She smiled to herself as she ducked into the bodega beneath the studio for her banana and espresso. Inside, Mario was reading the paper with a steaming cup of oatmeal resting beside him on the counter—his spoon partly submerged in its warmth.

"Good morning, Mario," she said softly, not wanting to disturb his ritual, even though by now he knew to expect her at the same time every day.

"Charlie!" he exclaimed eagerly, his brown eyes sparkling. "Good morning, beautiful."

Blushing slightly, Charlie replied, "Hello, Mario. What's happening in the world today?"

Mario put down his paper and shook his head. "You know, the usual. Politicians with their hands caught in the honey jar, a war with no end, drug busts in New Jersey. Same shit, different day."

"Good to know that you can count on something, ay?"

"Yeah, I guess so. Thank God for faces like yours—makes a man forget his troubles."

Charlie laughed off his advances. "Could I have my usual, please?" she asked.

"But of course. When you going to start letting me fix you a proper breakfast, huh mami?" he asked, as Charlie selected her banana with care. "This banana business is not enough. You are too skinny. Let me whip you up my famous egg and cheese with hot sauce. You will be running like a champ all day."

"No thanks, Mario. How many times are we going to have this conversation? Teaching class with an egg-and-cheese tummy would have me passed out mid-cobra. You know I'm going to get into something more substantial before noon. I like to work my way up."

"Like a little squirrel, you are," said Mario, laughing. He put a lid on her espresso and handed it to Charlie with a sly grin. Despite herself, Charlie felt her insides warm with that grin. Either Mario was sexy, or she was desperate. He wasn't Charlie's typical crush material—she tended to go for the bespectacled hipster type with elbow patched sweaters and haircuts that cost more than her own—but his rugged good looks and manliness couldn't be denied. About six feet tall, with a broad chest and forearms the size of most emo-Brooklyn boys' thighs, Mario stood out. Charlie couldn't quite figure out how old Mario was, but the endearing crinkles around his eyes and the subtle salt in his dark hair suggested late thirties. Maybe early forties.

"Thanks, Mario," said Charlie as she paid and turned for the door. "See you later."

"As you wish, lovely. Maybe I'll come up later and check out one of your classes?"

"I wish you would!" said Charlie over her shoulder. "Basics at noon! Perfect for you!" Every day Mario talked about coming up for a class, but he had yet to follow through. Charlie had a hard time imagining him in the tree position, but it was clear that he knew his way around a gym.

She unlocked the front door to the studio and bounded up the stairs, simultaneously unpeeling her banana and sipping her espresso. Inside the studio, she flipped on the lights and surveyed the space. It felt so good to know that she shared this haven with so many others. When she, Julian, and Felicity had been looking for just the right property, it had felt like an impossible mission. They knew they couldn't and really didn't want to afford Manhattan, but the places they saw all over Brooklyn just didn't feel right either. Too much work needed to be done, or the space wasn't big enough, or it faced the wrong direction and the sun blinded them. They had begun to feel like a three-headed Goldilocks.

But then, this place. They had almost given up. Mario owned the entire building and Felicity, who lived nearby, had been commiserating with him about real estate in the area one afternoon as she bought some much-needed dark chocolate for a pick-me-up. Mario mentioned the units upstairs, and asked her if she wanted to have a look. Felicity begrudgingly agreed, figuring that this would be just one more dead end. Once upstairs though, she knew their luck was changing. It was the very definition of "diamond in the rough," with huge windows and a view only partially obscured by the standard city culprits. Not wanting to alert Mario to her jubilation, she calmly asked if she could make some phone calls to her partners. Mario complied and returned to the bodega to give her some privacy.

It was all she could do to contain herself once on the phone with Charlie and Julian. "I found it!" she had practically screamed. "I don't care what you're doing, get your asses down here pronto!"

Thirty minutes later, they had a deal—much to their own delight and astonishment. They had sat in the empty space that evening as the sun set, envisioning the layout of their dream studio and sipping celebratory champagne. George and Michael had been skittering around, their toenails tip-tapping on the wood floors as they pirouetted in delight.

"To never giving up!" Julian had raised his red plastic cup and toasted, referring to their seemingly endless and fruitless search.

Charlie smiled, remembering, as she wandered through the studio, flipping on the lights, straightening the mats, and rearranging the blocks. She took a seat in the empty room as it slowly began to fill with the sun's dappled light. She closed her eyes and focused on the stillness, mindful of its gift before the inevitable clamor of the day ahead.

As she stretched her legs, she took note of the way her body felt—slightly stiff and unwieldly as she willed her tight muscles to unfurl. Slowly, she began her practice. Down to the floor and up to the sun she went, resisting the urge to fight the wandering of her mind while simultaneously nudging it back to that illusive center of stillness.

In tree pose now, with her foot resting on the inside of her knee, she breathed in deeply and felt her spine straighten and reach for the sky. The exhale released her tension, and for a moment she felt the exquisite pleasure of her body's balance. This was why she loved yoga. In its purest form, it was merely appreciation for the intricacies of the human form—mind, body, and spirit.

But just as her mind found peace, an image of Neil danced

through her mind, causing her to tense up; an involuntary re-action that was always the product of his virtual presence. She could see him, sitting on the floor of his tiny studio apartment on Ludlow Street, his legs folded neatly into the lotus position as she scrambled to get ready for work.

"Charlie, come down here and join me," he had demanded, as he began his morning's meditation.

"Neil, come on, you know I can't. I'm going to be late for work," she had explained.

"Oh, right, work," Neil replied, his eyes still shut. "Hurry up and get to that soulless rat race with all of the other little rats. Go go go!"

Charlie hated the fact that she always took the bait when Neil started ribbing her about her priorities, but this time had been no exception. "Oh, I'm so sorry, Obi-Neil," she had retorted, her voice dripping with sarcasm and beneath that layer, hurt. "While you're meditating, someone has to make a living."

Neil was silent, which further enraged Charlie. She had stomped angrily around the apartment as she finished getting ready, but he was as unresponsive as a statue. He always did this—slammed her with his judgments and then shut off. It enraged Charlie, but her anger was always tempered by her insecurities. In the back of her mind, she often felt like the rat Neil made reference to, going around and around on a meaningless corporate wheel. She had left the apartment that day like most days at that time in her life—frustrated, insecure, and consumed by all things Neil.

Charlie opened her eyes and noticed that her fists were clenched. She exhaled and unlocked them, shaking her head in silence. Still, he consumed her on some level. Why couldn't she shake his ghost?

She pulled herself up from the now sun-drenched floor.

"Good morning, Charlie," she heard behind her. She smiled.

No one had a more soothing voice than Felicity. Julian called her Syrup. Her voice would no doubt cascade seductively down pancakes if it was in liquid form.

"Hey, Felicity," Charlie answered, as she glided into the studio's foyer. Her body felt so much lighter than it had just an hour before. "How's your morning so far?"

"Not too bad, all things considered." Tall and strong, Felicity was the very definition of regal. Her skin was the color of expertly polished mahogany and her salt and pepper dreads were piled in a gigantic mass on top of her long neck. To call it a bun would be an insult to its sheer magnitude. It was more like a basket of hair.

Felicity was fifty-five, but didn't look a day over forty. Her smooth face gave her away only slightly, with a refreshing crinkle at her amber eyes and laugh lines that disappeared into her blinding smile. They had met at a yoga retreat upstate three years prior. Charlie had still been a relative novice—in the middle of getting her teaching license—and Felicity had been one of the instructors. Her no-nonsense attitude had soothed Charlie from the beginning. In jest, Charlie often told her that she wanted to be her when she grew up. At thirty-two, Charlie was an adult by all standards, especially considering the fact that she owned and operated a yoga studio, but she felt miles and miles away from Felicity's sense of self and authentic wisdom.

"Did I tell you about the class I've started up?" Charlie asked her.

"No, you did not," answered Felicity as she took a gulp of her coffee, her eyes twinkling with enthusiasm. "Do tell."

"So, you know how I went to this reunion night in Manhattan last week?" she asked. Felicity nodded. "I went to recruit naturally, not thinking that I would run into anyone from my past—"

"You ran into your college boyfriend!" shrieked Felicity, interrupting Charlie's story.

"Um, noooo. I think he's married with two kids in Westchester."

"Oh. Go on, go on—sorry for my big mouth."

"Anyway, I ran into three women from my year—women I was friendly with," said Charlie.

"How nice!" said Felicity. "Were you close and lost touch?"

"Oh no, nothing like that. We were more like acquaintances, although two of them were roommates freshman year. You know, we lived in the same dorm and would see each other around—that sort of thing. They were all cool girls."

"And are they now cool women?"

"I think so," answered Charlie. "It was a trip to see us all grown up," she added. "Same faces and all, but we carry ourselves differently now. Not in that cliché Manolo Blahnik bullshit kind of way—more in an organic, time passing kind of way."

"Good. Because if I see one more idiot lady teetering around this neighborhood in five-inch heels, remarking on the architecture, I might not be accountable for my actions. It's an insult to us all, really. Who are these girls?"

Charlie laughed. Felicity had a low tolerance for bullshit, which is why she was the epitome of cool. "Too true," she replied. "Anyway, to make a long story shorter, these women have agreed to take a six-week introduction class here on Saturday mornings. I am really excited about it—I think it'll be great for business."

Felicity was quiet. "How many women did you say there were?" she inquired, a hint of something less than thrilled in her voice.

"Three."

"I don't want to be an asshole, but three women do not a class make—especially on Saturday, our best day for business. Charlie, how are we ever going to make money if we treat this place like the ice cream and not the cake?"

Charlie tensed. "The cake? What? You know your food analogies always confuse me."

"What's to be confused about? We need to run this like a business, not a sorority."

"Felicity, don't worry. They're all paying a lump sum up front—at an escalated cost. These are essentially private lessons, after all. I raised the cost substantially, and they've all agreed to it."

"You have their approval in writing?" asked Felicity, still doubting Charlie.

"Better than that, I actually have their credit card numbers and I'm running them through this morning. I've been e-mailing with all of them."

Felicity's brow unfurrowed as she listened to Charlie's explanation. "Oh, okay then," she said. "Charlie, I'm sorry I'm being such a hard-ass, it's just that with this nasty recession, the maintenance fees, the bills, and the renovations we have in mind, we have to look out for the bottom line."

"Felicity," said Charlie, as she put her hand on top of hers. "Bottom line is my middle name. Don't forget where I come from."

"My little Wall Street tycoon," said Felicity with a grin.

Charlie grinned back. "You know it. Prana Yoga is going all the way. I'm not living in la-la land here, Felicity."

"I know you're not. I'm just a bit stressed out lately. Our bills are no joke and we need more students. That's all I'm saying. I just don't think there's enough traffic in here, and I don't see the economy turning around any time soon."

Charlie moved behind the desk to join Felicity. "I agree. We really need to get our website up and running."

"I know!" said Felicity emphatically. "I've been riding Malcolm to get it done, but he always has an excuse as to why it's not a priority."

"Is he busy with school?" asked Charlie. Malcolm was Felicity's son. He was finishing up his senior year and waiting to hear from colleges. His first pick was Cornell and most days it was all Felicity could do not to drive up to that campus herself and hack into the computer system's admission logs. Surely they had to know by now but they insisted on keeping them all in limbo.

"He is," answered Felicity. "Senior year is no joke these days."

"Senior year of high school," Charlie echoed. "That feels like a hundred years ago." She shook her head with a smile.

"Since Malcolm is a wash, do you have any friends who might be interested in building one for us?" asked Felicity.

"I really don't think so, but maybe I can make one," Charlie answered, smiling at her students as they ambled past the desk.

chapter /even

Bess

"What are you wearing?" Dan asked.

Bess surveyed herself, splayed on top of her gray Calvin Klein duvet cover. Her sheets set had been a splurge, but Bess had sworn to herself that when she finally was making decent money and lived in an apartment with a legitimate living room, she would spring for the luxurious thread count. It had been worth it. Her bed was like a cloud. "A white, spaghetti-stained tank top and my navy sweatpants with the gigantic hole in the crotch," she answered in her best mock-sexy voice.

"Ooh, easy access."

"You know it, big boy."

"Bess!" chirped Dan. "I miss you again."

"You missed me already today, you get only one shot," replied Bess, smiling to herself. She rolled herself to an upright position and transferred herself down to the floor. The fact that Dan missed her so openly, without any of the cool-guy bullshit that she so often encountered, was almost enough to rid her of her trademark cynicism. Almost, but not quite.

"Rules are made for breaking. How was your day?"

"Good. Kind of boring on the work front though. Ever since rehab became the new overdose, it's been pretty dead. No one does anything interesting anymore."

"Yeah, rehab has really ruined it for everybody. Hey, should I get tacos or a burger for dinner?"

Bess, in the middle of attempting to touch her toes, grunted in response.

"What's that? Are we communicating monosyllabically now? Like cave people?"

Bess laughed, "Oh sorry, no. I was stretching and 'tacos' came out like 'blurgh.'"

Dan laughed. "That's a painful stretch. 'Tacos' and 'blurgh' aren't even in the same family. Careful you don't pull something—like your spleen."

"Roger that, doctor. I told you about that yoga class I signed up for, right?"

"Oh yeah, the one in Brooklyn with your old college peeps?" asked Dan.

"Yep. Saturday is our first class and apparently I have the flexibility of balsam wood. Seriously, my hamstrings are like two slabs of marble."

"Oh marble hammies, you exaggerate. I happen to know that you are quite flexible where it counts."

Bess blushed. "This is true. But you and I aren't exactly downward dogging together."

"Yet!" replied Dan gleefully, happy to exploit Bess's yoga reference.

Bess laughed. "I walked right into that one, I guess."

"Slammed face-first into the wall!"

"So, did I tell you my real reason for becoming a yogini?"

"Ooh, look at you with the fancy, gender-appropriate terminology," teased Dan. "I dunno, Madonna biceps? It's okay to use faux spirituality to mask your body dysmorphia, Bess. If rehab is the new OD, yoga is the new anorexia."

"No, it's not about my biceps, although I guess that would be a nice by-product. I'm actually working on a new story idea."

"Oh really?" asked Dan, excited for Bess. "Awesome. What's the story?"

"Well, I was looking for some sort of divine inspiration to get me out of my slump, and it all sort of fell into place at that reunion thing."

"How so?"

"Seeing these women and how they've changed since college really got me thinking. I mean, these were all creative, driven women, you know? Women who had dreams and goals that weren't yet affected by the hustle of the real world. Now all of them seem to have sold out and given in to society's rules about how to make a living." Dan was silent. "You know what I mean, Dan?"

"Um, I guess so," answered Dan—a note of wariness in his voice.

Bess decided to steamroll over his lack of enthusiasm. She got up from the floor and walked out of her bedroom, into the living room. She plopped down on her chaise and stared out the window of her twenty-third-floor apartment. Turn one way and she experienced the serenity of the twinkling city lights and the Hudson just beyond. Turn another and she was basically inside the kitchen of the apartment across the way. Even living large had its limits in New York City. She continued her explanation. "I'm going to write an article about just that. How these creative women all changed what they wanted out of life to fulfill somebody else's idea of success."

"But how can you make that call at this point? You don't even know these women yet."

"True, but I have a pretty good idea that what they're doing now is not what they dreamed of. That's the thing, it happens to almost every woman—this sort of universal sellout."

"You think these women are going to agree to be the subjects of such a mean-spirited article? Who are you to call them sell-outs?"

"They don't know that I'm writing it. I figure I'll act as sort of a spy—finding out when and where everything went south for them in terms of their creativity. And I'm not planning on labeling them as sellouts per se, Dan. Just painting as accurate a picture as I can of a very real phenomenon. The reader can make any judgment they like." Dan didn't respond. Bess continued on, "Although one of the women, Charlie, seems to defy my hypothesis. She started out as a sort of money shark with a master's in finance and is now running the yoga studio. I can't help but think there's more to the story there though—I don't think her life change was as inspired as it seems to be. A one-eighty-degree switch like that has to have at least some sort of less than noble background, don't you think?"

"Bess, I think this is a bad idea," Dan finally said. "I don't like it at all. It's unethical."

"Oh my God, give me a break! When did you become the spokesperson for ethical? Reporters have to work behind the scenes all the time."

"Not to be an ass, but I wouldn't call this reporting."

"Oh really?" asked Bess. "What would you call it then?"

"I would call it a thinly veiled attempt to reconnect with your own creativity at the expense of others. It's a glorified puff piece, with nothing 'feel good' about it. These women are going to hate you if the story ever goes to print."

"Jesus, tell me how you really feel." She wanted to reach through the phone and scratch his smug eyeballs out. "A puff piece? You don't know what you're talking about. This is a significant female issue, and one that is almost never researched in an urban setting.

What's interesting about it to me is that by all standards, these women are living independent, self-empowering lives. They're in New York, they all are in some sort of artistic field, and yet they're really not that different from typical suburban housewives. All of them have sacrificed their dreams on some level. It's important that society know that all women wrestle with this dilemma." She flipped on her flat-screen television and muted it. Anderson Cooper soothed her, even if she couldn't hear him.

"Even if that is the case, why couldn't you just be open with them about your article? That way, there's no bad blood."

"Are you kidding me? There's no way I would get the kind of juice I need if it was all aboveboard. They would all censor their conversations with me and the article would have no heart."

"Oh, that's funny."

"How so?" snarled Bess. He was really pushing her buttons now.

"The way you've explained this article to me, 'heart' is the last thing that comes to mind."

"Real nice, Dan," said Bess. "Now I'm heartless because I want to fulfill my own dream and get the hell out of my stupid tabloid job? I'm heartless because I'm looking out for me for a change?!"

"You're twisting my words," Dan argued.

"I don't think so," Bess said as she held back tears. She couldn't believe how worked up she was getting. Why was Dan behaving like such an assface? "I have to go. Maybe we shouldn't talk for a while." And with that, she hung up her phone and tossed it onto the floor. She turned off the television. Not even Anderson could soothe her now.

chapter eight

Sabine

ʃabine grimaced as her alarm shrieked rudely in her ear. Eyes still closed, she scrambled to silence it. She turned from her side onto her stomach and buried her face in the warmth of her pillow. *You have to get up,* she thought. *No excuses. Get upppppp.* Her blanket cocoon was so warm. . . . *GET UP! NOW!* She forced herself into an upright position and switched on her bedside lamp. Through squinted eyes, she made out the distinct image of Lassie staring at her accusingly from the foot of her bed. She stuck out her tongue at him.

She got up and pulled her sweatshirt, pajama pants, and socks on before blearily stumbling into the kitchen for a glass of water. Well, really, she walked to the refrigerator, which—technically speaking—was in her living room. There was an island separating the appliances from the couch, but it wasn't much of a divider. This was New York. If your toilet was in your apartment, you were supposed to consider yourself lucky.

She gulped down half the glass and eyed the clock on her microwave. It was 6:03 AM. This was Sabine's first attempt at pre-work writing, since her after-work writing was a joke. Switching into writing mode after a day of editing and weaving her way through the various minefields of bureaucratic bullshit felt like a mild form of torture. Sabine hoped that reversing the process would yield better results. Any results would be nice, really. She had always been a gym-rat in the morning kind of person when she was so inclined. By the time she fully woke up, she was half-way through her workout. Why shouldn't the same kind of miracle occur here? Two cups of coffee in, and she would be a third of the way through her novel. She set up the coffee maker and moved into the bathroom to plunge her tired face into a freezing cold washcloth. "Gahhhh!" she shrieked into its folds. It was official now. She was awake.

Sabine filled her coffee mug and meandered into her bedroom, where her laptop sat on her half-a-desk, which was pushed up against the wall. She grabbed it and moved toward the bed, planning on propping it on top of some lap pillows as she typed. Just then, Lassie leaped onto the bed from the floor and gave her a judgmental glare.

"Damn you, Lassie!" yelled Sabine, pumping her fist toward the ceiling in mock anger. The cat was right, though. No writing of any value would get done in her bed. Two minutes in, she would pass out. It was a sure thing, as Lassie could attest.

She placed her computer back on her desk and pulled her folding chair out from its storage spot under her bed. She unfolded it, placed it in front of her desk, turned her computer on, and sat down. She opened Word and drew up a blank document. The stark white cyber-page stared at her accusingly.

Sabine coached herself: *No pressure, just start typing—see where it takes you.* Her mind flitted about like a pinball as she flailed internally. She was so consumed by the idea of writing with purpose that she couldn't just relax and let it flow. That was the problem with not writing regularly—it paralyzed your confidence and sense of ease. Sabine liked to call it creative constipation. She closed her eyes and breathed deeply.

She decided to write about a particularly absurd conversation she had had with her boss the day before. She began free-writing, just depositing the details onto the page the way she would a check at the bank. Three sentences in, she stopped.

"Should I go ahead and use the quotation marks now?" she said aloud. *That would save me a lot of time and maybe some confusion later,* she thought. She inserted punctuation where necessary and, in re-reading what she had just written, became doubtful.

"Ooh, this is bad," she whined. Lassie, stretched out on the bed, lifted his head as Sabine's doubt filled the room. "This is really bad." She pressed DELETE and watched the cursor steamroll through the past ten minutes of her life. She sighed deeply and turned to pet Lassie.

"Lassie, don't judge me," she whispered. "I just can't do it this morning." Sabine wondered if she even wanted to write anymore. Maybe she was just holding on to it out of habit.

Sabine felt like a failure, but somehow vindicated at the same time. It was her life, and if she didn't feel like writing, she didn't feel like writing. The question was, If she really wasn't into it anymore, how come it haunted her all day? Why, when she closed her eyes and visualized the rest of her life, did she see herself typing away ferociously?

She closed her computer and got up, crossing over to her bureau. Atop its cedar surface sat a huge magnifying mirror. She switched on its light and was immediately fascinated by the depth of her pores and the stray eyebrow hairs that needed attending to. Nothing was more satisfying than plucking those little guys. Sabine hummed to herself as she cleaned up her arches.

"Sabine, no!" she reprimanded, as she moved to pluck a hair that had no business being removed. Sometimes she went a little nuts and ended up looking like Drew Barrymore circa her boob flash on David Letterman. In college she had actually removed the entire interior corner of each one in an attempt to eradicate her monobrow. Her mother had called her Comma Face for the entire summer she had been home, and had even taken her tweezers from her.

"It's for your own good, Comma Face," she had said over their glasses of chilled box wine.

Sabine smiled, remembering. She put down her tweezers and shut off the mirror's light. It was 6:54. She could squeeze in another hour of sleep, no problem. She crawled into her bed, nestling herself carefully between Lassie and her plethora of pillows. She eyed her computer, which seemed to mock her from its post a few feet away. She took a deep breath and closed her eyes.

When she opened them again, it was 8:45. "Shit, shit, shit!" she cursed, jumping out of bed. She had neglected to reset the alarm. She had twenty minutes to shower, get ready, and head to the subway. Lassie smirked as she ran through the apartment like a madwoman. She emerged from her body shower—no time for anything hair related—and surveyed her closet. She grabbed her picks with zero consideration. *Were these pants always so tight?* she asked herself as she sucked in to zip. Good thing she was starting yoga. She did a quick concealer/mascara/lip gloss swipe in the mirror, noting that her eyebrows were still a bit red from her earlier descent into tweezing madness, grabbed her jacket and bag, and flew out the door. On the street, she looked at her watch: 9:10. *Not bad.*

At her subway station, she swiped her pass through the slot and moved through the turnstile—only to be stopped by the cold metal arm. Annoyed, she glanced over to the card reader.

"Insufficient fare?" she read aloud. She sighed deeply. She extricated herself from the small mob forming behind her and approached the card machine. She dug through her purse aggressively.

"Where the hell is my wallet?" she mumbled to herself.

Just when she was about to convince herself that her wallet had been stolen, there it was. She bought a new card and returned to the turnstile. Her second swipe successful, she continued on with her morning, already feeling like she needed a nap.

She walked down the platform, thinking about her outfit. It was not a good one. Sometimes, when she left for work, she felt like a somewhat together thirty-something with good taste. Not too much, not too little, but just right.

And then there were the days like today, when she was running late and ended up looking like a bank teller. Exhibit A: ill-fitting pants in a polyester blend, an empire waist shirt, and pointy flats from the late nineties. She had no one to blame but herself; certainly there were other options in her closet, but sometimes an extra five styling minutes was too much to bear so early in the morning. Sabine liked to excuse herself from judgment by saying that if she looked like a million bucks every day, she would never appreciate the occasions when she did. The occasional misstep into bank teller territory kept her humble.

She stopped and rested her bag full of manuscripts on the ground. She stretched to the sky, hoping to release some of the Monday tension that was already building. It started Sunday, late afternoon, this tension. Just thinking about the five days ahead of her was enough to knot up her entire back. Coming down from her stretch, she looked to her left. There he was. Subway Crush.

Her heartbeat sped involuntarily and she felt a blush spread over her face. He was standing about two people over, listening to his iPod.

God, she thought to herself. *I love him.*

For about two years running, she had been seeing him on the

subway. Not every morning, but maybe once a month or so. He was adorable. Tall, dark, and lovely. Black hair and a five-o'clock shadow, even at nine in the morning. A lean frame with hands that looked like they could do things: hang a picture, hammer a nail, maybe make turkey meatballs.

Her crush on him was epic. She had rehearsed what she would say to him maybe a thousand times, but every time she went to open her mouth, she went blank. Completely blank.

He looked over suddenly. His eyes were dark brown, but they twinkled like little raisin jewels. She had described them that way to her friend Karen over drinks one night and she had burst out laughing.

"Sabine, really?" she had said. "Raisin jewels? You've got it bad." Sabine had agreed, and taken a huge gulp of her gimlet in response.

"What's the big deal?" Karen had continued. "Just say hi! Jesus. What's the worst that can happen?"

She was right, of course. The worst that could happen was that he would ignore Sabine, or worse yet, brush her off unapologetically, but still—she just couldn't do it. Realistically, she knew that the odds of him being a complete dick were slim, but the thought of approaching him paralyzed her. This was New York, after all. If a guy wanted to say hello to you, he did. Sabine had been approached by enough clowns to know that.

Wait, is he looking at me? she thought, as she stared intently at the tracks. She could feel the raisin jewels burning a hole into her skull, but she couldn't be sure if that was just a product of her overactive imagination. The train approached and she snuck a glance back at him. Nothing.

They got on the same car. He was exactly four people over. Still listening to his iPod and also now reading a book. The double-whammy combo of the two screamed "leave me alone."

Sabine took a seat, once again reminded of her bank teller ensemble. Even if she wanted to, she couldn't say hello today. Her outfit was a disaster and he . . . well, he was perfect. She sighed. She pulled a manuscript out of her bag and pretended to read.

"Hey, Sabine!" she heard beside her. She looked up. Great. There was Michael, the Close Talker. He was a friend of a friend and he had zero respect for physical boundaries.

She turned to face him, nervous already about the proximity of his mouth to her nose. She knew from past experience that it would hang open, dangerously close.

"Hey, Michael," she replied, her discomfort obvious to anyone except Michael. She wondered if Subway Crush was watching. She cringed and hoped that wasn't the case. The Bank Teller and the Close Talker did not a good impression make.

"Soooo, what's new, Sabine? Last time I saw you, you were pretty wasted!"

Is this guy for real? wondered Sabine. *How old are we? Twelve?*

"Sorry, I don't remember that," she replied, with as much composure as she could muster.

"I bet you don't!" guffawed Michael. "We were at Carrie's birthday."

"Oh righttttttt," said Sabine. "I wasn't wasted, I just had a killer sinus infection. I was doped up." She thought back on that night. She had been so miserable and then, naturally, Michael appeared. They had had some horrible conversation that she couldn't even hear in between her head feeling like a balloon and the loudness of the bar. By the end of it, she literally felt like her skull was on the verge of exploding.

Michael started jabbering on, but Sabine could not even pretend to be interested. The train pulled into the station and she realized that she had only three more to go to freedom. She made a mental note never to sit in this car again. But wait! Subway Crush.

She couldn't sacrifice the chance of seeing him just to escape from the clutches of the Close Talker. She craned her neck around a giant backpack to get another glimpse of him.

Wait, what!? Her heart stopped. He was craning his head around the backpack, trying to get a look at her. Or was he? Sabine looked around her for a supermodel or maybe a former president. Nothing. She realized that Michael was still talking. As a matter of fact, he was the only person talking in the entire car. Of course he was that guy. Sabine looked back. One of Subway Crush's iPod buds was hanging from his ear. Was he trying to overhear their conversation? Really? He was back to his book, but the bud dangled—the only proof that maybe Sabine wasn't hallucinating. He was looking at her. Or wait, maybe he was gay and looking at Michael.

She turned back toward Michael. *No, not possible.*

"You know what I mean?" he asked breathlessly. He had been talking the entire time. Sabine had not heard a word he had said. No wonder he always thought she was drunk.

"I do, Michael," she replied. The train pulled into her station. "Well, this is me!" she announced. "See you!"

She gathered her bag and pushed her way out of the train. She glanced back to mentally say good-bye to Subway Crush. He was looking! He was definitely looking!

They locked eyes and Sabine froze in her tracks.

"Hey lady, give us a break, will ya?!" a burly guy yelled in her ear. She willed her limbs to work and turned to exit the train.

Through the turnstile, up the stairs, on the street. Finally, here, Sabine could take a moment to digest what had happened. An eye lock with Subway Crush! It had really happened. She smiled and straightened her shoulders as she marched down Sixth Avenue.

Next time, she would say hello. Well, maybe not. No, she would. She was going to and that was final. No excuses.

chapter nine

Naomi

That one kind of looks like a robin, don't you think, Noah?" asked Naomi. She looked at her son, walking beside her—his long eyelashes all she could see peeking out from the insulated hood of his down parka. It was a brisk afternoon, but they had decided to take the long way home from school. Naomi loved these walks with her boy. Sometimes, his little paw would drift into hers and her heart would melt as they ambled through the park, looking at birds and trees—talking about the pleasures and perils of an eight-year-old's life.

Noah's hand in hers was so warm and small. Naomi knew all to well that these were her last chances at Noah hand-holding. Soon, he would think that gesture too babyish. It was the circle of life.

"Mmm, not really, Mom," answered Noah. "It's not even red!"

"Good point. Maybe I just want it to be a robin because that would mean that spring was on its way."

"Mommmm, it's not even February yet! We have a long winter ahead of us." Like his mother, Noah was very matter of fact about most things. But about winter they differed. He never started climbing the frozen walls of April like Naomi did, praying for leaves on trees and warm sun. Whenever Naomi had a hissy fit, which happened like clockwork around the last week of April every year, Noah would pat her on the head and tell her, in sweet little-boy speak, to get a grip.

"Spring is in May, almost June, Mom," he would say. "That's just how it is." Then he would grab a cookie and saunter back into the living room, leaving Naomi shaking her head and mumbling, "You're right, Noah. I know you're right."

Here again, she found herself adhering to Noah's season-coping strategy. "I know, Noah. Spring is many, many miles away. Point taken. How was school today?"

"It was okay," answered Noah, as he stopped to try to make a ball out of some slushy snow. Rolling it proved impossible, so he stopped midway with a sigh. "This snow sucks."

"Hey, hey," reprimanded Naomi. "I don't like that word."

"What, *snow*?" asked Noah, with a lopsided grin.

"You know what word I mean," said Naomi. "There are so many words to use, why use—"

"An easy one that requires no thought," finished Noah. "I know. This snow is . . ." he searched his mind for the appropriate word. "Useless!"

Naomi laughed. "Much better. It is pretty useless. It's more like slushy ice."

"When Dad and I were out last weekend there was some good snow. We made a snow cat."

Naomi fought to keep herself from making a face. Whenever Noah mentioned his dad, she reflexively tensed up. Gene had come back into Noah's life in the past year. Even acknowledging it mentally made her angry and defensive. She knew that having him around was good for Noah, but she couldn't help but feel as though she were waiting for Gene to mess up royally. She didn't trust him for a minute, and she fought with herself internally every time Noah expressed happiness about their newly formed relationship.

"Oh yeah?" she asked, battling the urge to make a sarcastic remark. "What's a snow cat?"

Noah took her hand again, instantly calming her down. Even though she tried hard to maintain a neutral front, Noah somehow knew, with wisdom way beyond his eight years, that Gene made her nervous.

"It's what you make when there's not enough snow to make a man," Noah explained.

Naomi laughed. "That's resourceful. What did you use for whiskers?"

"Straws! That was Dad's idea. It looked pretty cool. We took some pictures."

Gene was a photographer. That was how he and Naomi had met, so many years before. They had both been somewhat big shots on the New York underground photography scene. Now Naomi could barely pick up a camera and mostly felt zero connection to what had once been her biggest passion.

Gene, on the other hand, had turned his skill into a full-blown career as a fashion photographer. When his photos first started appearing in magazines, Naomi had not been surprised. The perks of that job—young, beautiful women, drugs, and a jet-setting lifestyle—all seemed like perfect matches for a man with eternal Peter Pan syndrome.

While Naomi had been changing diapers and wrestling with strollers on subways, Gene was screwing his way through Milan. Now, only when Noah was more of a buddy than a baby, was Gene back in his life. Gene had missed so much, and willingly at that. Naomi wasn't sure if she could ever forgive him or take him seriously. The mere mention of his name made her want to scream.

"I can't wait to see them," said Naomi, regaining her composure for Noah's sake. "Hey, what do you know about yoga?" she asked him, eager to change the subject.

"Oh, yoga is cool," said Noah. "We did it at school once. It's when you stretch and think about stuff," he added knowingly.

Naomi smiled. "Think about stuff?" she asked.

"Yeah, you know. You close your eyes and are quiet on the inside," he explained.

Wow, thought Naomi, *my own little Zen master.* "Good definition, monkey," she said. "I'm going to start taking a class on Saturdays for a while."

"Cool!" answered Noah. "Can I do it, too?"

"Mmmm, I don't think so," said Naomi. "This is something that I'll do myself." Noah's face crumpled a bit as he turned to face Naomi. Her heart smushed, seeing him look so forlorn.

"Don't worry," she said as she squeezed his hand.

"What about Saturdays at the park?" asked Noah, a slight whine creeping into his voice.

"We'll still go to the park. My class is early in the morning. I'll be home by noon and then we'll go. You won't even know I'm gone."

"Who's going to stay with me? Dad?"

Naomi tensed involuntarily. "No, Cecilia will come over and fix you cereal. She'll hang out for a bit and then, before you know it, I'll be back."

Noah digested the information as they walked. "Okay. Will she watch cartoons with me?"

"Maybe. Or you can watch them yourself while she does some of her work."

"Okay, Mom," said Noah, agreeing to the setup. "That works." He dropped her hand. "Will you show me some of your stretchy moves?"

Naomi laughed. "Yes, I will show you all of my new stretchy monkey moves."

"Monkey moves!" repeated Noah, laughing. "I like that." They were almost home now—the wind whipping a bit faster and colder as the sun set.

"Mom, can I get a cupcake?" He gestured ahead of them toward his favorite bakery. Two blocks from their apartment, it had the most amazing vegan confections. Naomi had winced originally at the mere thought of sweets without the sweet, but even she had to agree that the cupcakes and cookies were delicious. Naturally, she and Noah were not alone in their love of these confections. It appeared as though every Bugaboo-pushing mother in a fifteen-mile radius had also gotten the memo. Every time Naomi and Noah went or even just strolled by, the front door was always swarming with what seemed to be hundreds of them, talking about the merits of breast-feeding. Naomi didn't smoke, but she often fantasized about lighting up a cigarette in the middle of the swarm, just to witness the mass mayhem.

"Sure, you can eat it after dinner. I'll get one, too."

"You get chocolate and I'll get vanilla," demanded Noah, skipping ahead of her a bit to part the sea of strollers first. His brown curls bounced out from underneath his wool cap with each stride. "We'll split 'em!"

"Deal!" answered Naomi, quickening her pace to keep up with her boy.

chapter ten

Class One

"Luuuuuucy, I'm hooooome," bellowed Julian as he entered the sun-dappled studio. George and Michael scampered in in front of him, their tiny nails skittering over the hardwood floors.

Charlie peeked her head into the front room. She had been at the studio for a couple of hours—first running her Sunrise Class at the crack of dawn and then preparing for the first installment of her Saturday class with Naomi, Sabine, and Bess. After her discussion with Felicity, she had decided to push it back an hour earlier, to 9 AM.

Luckily, the women had all agreed—Bess and Sabine half-heartedly, as they had to commute from the city. As much as Charlie had been comfortable defending the class's financial viability to Felicity, she did have a point. Naomi was occupying their most profitable day with a tiny class. Better to make it as early as possible.

"Hey, Julian," answered Naomi.

"Good morning, my love," said Julian, as he unzipped his lean frame from a long, puffy coat and hung it in the closet. "It is cold as a witch's tit!"

"What does that even mean?"

"I have no idea. But my Gramma always used to say it. Gramma Joan. She was a firecracker, God rest her soul. Used to sip a glass of bourbon every night during the winter. She would pour herself up a cup and talk about witch's tits while I sashayed around the house in her pearls."

"No way! Really?"

"No. At least, not the pearls part. I always like to say that though." Julian kneeled and unzipped George and Michael from their respectively ridiculous coats. "I wasn't aware enough to know that I even wanted to wear the pearls, truth be told. But maybe I did sashay a bit instinctively."

Charlie smiled, envisioning a mini, gawky Julian. She looked at the clock. It was ten to nine. "My ladies should be here in a minute."

"Oh right, your BU class! Felicity told me about it."

"Was she freaking out? She wasn't so jazzed on the idea when I told her."

"She wasn't freaking out really. Just concerned about the time and the size."

"I know. But I promise that this class is a good thing. They're forking over a nice chunk of change and the class is early enough that it doesn't cut into the day really."

"Hey, I trust you," said Julian, sprinkling some flaxseed into his yogurt. "You know what you're doing. I am glad you pushed it to an earlier hour, though."

"Thanks, Julian."

She heard footsteps on the stairs. Sabine walked in, her mass of dark hair concealed beneath a gigantic, rose-colored knit cap. She pulled it off and smiled nervously at Charlie.

"Hey!" Charlie greeted her warmly.

"Good morning, Charlie." She giggled nervously. "Don't they

say that in *Charlie's Angels*? You know, when they gather around the phone and talk to the mysterious voice?"

"They do!" agreed Julian. "I never thought of that."

"Hi," said Sabine, extending her hand. "I'm Sabine."

"I'm Julian. Welcome to Prana!"

"Oh thanks, I'm excited to be here." Sabine unzipped her coat and Charlie showed her the closet.

"You can hang it here," she explained. "How are you?"

"I'm good. A little nervous."

"What's to be nervous about?" She put her arm around Sabine's shoulders. "This is going to be fun and relaxing," she said. "No nerves."

Sabine smiled at Charlie. "No nerves," she repeated. She couldn't help but envision her terrible flexibility ruining the entire class. She had tried to touch her toes the night before in an attempt to limber up, but she hadn't even made it to her knees. It wasn't pretty.

"Hey!" they heard behind them. They turned to see Bess and then Naomi as she appeared behind her. Both were ensconced in their urban winter gear—only their bright eyes and chapped lips peeking out from gigantic, fake fur–rimmed down hoods. They unzipped themselves as Sabine, Charlie, and Julian greeted them—the studio suddenly abuzz with laughter and electricity.

Despite her original intention of merely running a Saturday class, Charlie already felt herself warming to them. It was like freshmen year all over again, except Charlie had always been too focused and consumed by her schoolwork to reciprocate her classmates' kindness. She paused, remembering how lonely she had felt in those first months, choosing—instead of making friends and hitting the requisite Landsdowne bars with abandon—to hole herself up in the library. If she could go back in time and change her behavior though, would she? Would she be here today if she had taken a different turn at an earlier point in her path? She thought so—her life had never felt so refreshingly "hers" and ultimately, so right—but she couldn't be sure. Inevitably, she thought of Neil.

"Hey Charlie, where do we get our mats?" asked Naomi, shaking her out of her nostalgic coma.

"Oh, in the classroom there's a pile of them against the wall," she answered, leading the way. She pointed to the wall. "Just grab one."

Bess and Sabine followed behind her, each one of them selecting a mat from the wall.

"Wow, what a gorgeous studio," said Bess, taking in the stark white walls, the huge windows, and the waxed wood floors. "I really like how spare it is. It's soothing."

"Oh thanks," answered Charlie, pleased by the compliment. They had taken great pains to create a soothing atmosphere—ripping up the floors, knocking down walls, and painting over years of city soot on the walls. It was a labor of love, no doubt, but it was definitely labor.

"Okay, if you have a seat, we can get started," said Charlie. Bess, Sabine, and Naomi were all standing awkwardly in the middle of the studio, clutching their mats with apprehension. Charlie was suddenly sure that they hadn't looked much different fourteen years earlier, arriving at college with their suitcases and shower caddies—their clothes smelling of Mom's detergent. Their nervousness was endearing, but Charlie had to nip it in the bud now, if she expected them to get anywhere in that morning's class. They had only six weeks, after all. They had to let go.

Bess spread out her mat carefully and sat at its edge. Yoga had never held an iota of interest for her before. She preferred running. It wasn't a workout for her unless she felt like she might die around the halfway point. She thought about her article and closed her eyes, pretending to relax although her mind was racing. She would try to take the subway back in with Sabine after class. That way, she could start gathering some information for the article. Six weeks felt like an impossibly short amount of time to get to know these women inside and out, but she didn't have a choice. She had to make every minute count.

"Hey Bess," whispered Charlie, "ease up honey." She took Bess's hands, which were balled into fists by her side, and unfurled them. "Don't think right now, just be." Although Bess's eyes were closed, she rolled them. Already, yoga annoyed her. Such was the sacrifice she had to make though. She took a deep breath.

Naomi perched on the end of her mat. It had been so long since she had truly acknowledged her body. She couldn't remember a time postpregnancy that she had given it her undivided attention like this. She looked down at her belly, slightly protruding over the waistband of her pants as she sat, cross-legged. And there were her breasts, firmly contained within the impenetrable shield of her sports bra but considerably less perky than they had been before Noah. She straightened her spine and took a deep breath. *This is not about perky breasts,* she reminded herself. Her brief experience with prenatal yoga had been refreshingly devoid of any physical insecurities, but Naomi suspected that had to do much more with maternal celebration of the baby growing inside her than with the state of her self-confidence.

"I want to take a moment to welcome you all here," began Charlie. "I am honored to introduce you to yoga. I know you must all be slightly intimidated by the idea of moving your bodies in new ways. Maybe you're a bit apprehensive about the idea of letting your minds go and of connecting with a much more interior sense of being. All of that is completely normal."

Sabine listened intently to Charlie, somewhat entranced by the soothing nature of her voice. Already she felt her tension subsiding.

"Before we begin, I want to talk a little bit about the type of yoga we will all be practicing here. We will be practicing vinyasa yoga, which is a technique that focuses on connecting our postures, or asanas, with our breath. Vinyasa is all about achieving balance through this connection." Charlie paused, acknowledging the furrowed brows of her pupils. She was losing them. "This all sounds horribly technical, I know, but once we begin, it will seem far less textbook and, hopefully, much more organic. Eventually, to maintain our asanas, we'll be incorporating some of the blocks, blankets, and straps you saw against the back wall when you came in."

Sabine turned her head to examine the wall of props. This was sounding far less enticing than it had at alumni night. She had been seduced by the thought of sinuous arm muscles a la Gwyneth and now, finding out that she would be strapped into some kind of yogic torture device for the next six Saturdays, her own floppy triceps were sounding much more like something she could live with. She sighed deeply.

"Sabine, I hope that's a sigh of extreme excitement," joked Charlie. Sabine blushed. Subtlety was not her strong suit.

"I want you all to close your eyes, please," continued Charlie. "Connect with your bodies. Feel the way your neck sits on top of your shoulders and your shoulders extend into your arms, and your arms into your outstretched hands."

Bess unclenched her hands, which were rolled into tight fists again, despite Charlie's unfurling of them just minutes before. *Take it easy, Bess,* she said to herself. She wondered if her nervousness was just a natural product of her covert intentions, or whether she was just wound up beyond repair by nature.

"I'd like to start class in what is called Vajrasana, or thunderbolt," said Charlie. "Sit on your heels with your knees and feet together and your arms above your head," she began.

God, this feels gooood, thought Bess, surprised. Knots she didn't even know she had unclenched as she stretched toward the ceiling.

"Okay, now exhale and lower your arms with your palms facing down," said Charlie, as the women all released collective *whooshes* of relief.

"Let's do it again," said Charlie, taking the women through the second of four of the stretches.

She circled the room, cognizant of how tough the class would be for Sabine, Bess, and Naomi just because of the nature of yoga. It wasn't something that you reaped the benefits from physically until you were relatively comfortable with the process. It was nearly impossible to relax when every movement was new and challenging. She hoped that their six classes together would be enough to establish a true level of comfort for all of them.

"Throughout class, I would like you all to be as mindful as possible about your breathing—inhaling and exhaling fully and deeply," Charlie explained. "I know it can be difficult to move through these foreign positions and keep track of your breath, but I also know that the flow of the two into each other will become more comfortable for you as time goes on." She smiled reassuringly.

Sabine opened one eye quizzically. She could barely walk and chew gum at the same time, much less be mindful of her breathing while she contorted herself into pretzel-like positions. She thought of her mother in a yoga class and stifled a laugh. When she had mentioned the yoga class to her, she had given Sabine her standard advice: "Wear lipstick, for God's sake. There could be a young man there, you never know." Sabine envisioned bringing Julian home and giving her mother a heart attack. "I met him in yoga class, Ma!" she would exclaim, as Julian pirouetted into the living room—George and Michael trotting in beside him.

"We're now going to move into Tadasana, or mountain pose. This is the basic standing pose," said Charlie. The women stood up from their mats, following her direction. "Keep your spine straight and your feet together. Your heels and big toes should be touching each other. Keep your stomach in, Bess," Charlie chided gently.

"From here, we move into Vrksasana, or the tree pose." As she demonstrated the pose, she noticed Sabine struggling to maintain her balance. As she wobbled, her brow furrowed in obvious frustration. Charlie moved across the room to help her.

"Sabine, try to let go," encouraged Charlie.

Sabine shook her head in frustration. "I'm sorry, Charlie," she said. "I just can't get this." Tears welled up in her eyes, much to her own horror.

"Hey," whispered Charlie. "It's okay. Don't be so hard on yourself. Comfort here takes time and practice." She wanted to go on to say that the pressure Sabine was putting on herself was the very thing preventing her from "getting it," but her instincts (and the fact that Sabine was very near tears) told her that this was not the time.

"Stay for a few counts in this pose, breathing deeply," instructed Charlie, moving from Sabine's side to address everyone. "Lower your arms and separate your palms. Straighten your right leg and stand again in Tadasana."

The women looked at Charlie, clearly puzzled. "Mountain pose," she translated. As if to say, "Oh, right!" they all relaxed into the now familiar pose.

"Now, repeat the tree pose on the opposite side," said Charlie.

She moved to Bess's mat, watching as she, too, struggled with her balance. She had been noticing Bess's impatience since the start of class. It emanated from her like a toxic glow.

"Everything okay?" asked Charlie, as Bess wobbled wildly.

"Yeah yeah," she replied. "This isn't so hard!" she puffed— her breath coming in short bursts.

Yeah, because you're plowing through it at the speed of light, thought Charlie. "I know, right?! It might be good for you to take things a bit slower though," Charlie said instead, assuming the patient teacher role. Sometimes it was difficult to censor herself, but a student's first couple of times on the mat required relative teacher sweetness.

"Oh, okay," answered Bess. "Slow and steady, huh?" she asked.

"Yes, slow and steady," echoed Charlie. She smiled at Bess and moved Naomi's mat on the other side of the room.

Bess took a deep breath. *Slow and steady, my ass,* she thought to herself. The time in the studio couldn't go fast enough for her. She had been compiling a list of questions for Sabine, ranging from innocent to loaded, to ask on their subway ride home.

I wonder if Sabine will think I'm too nosy? she thought. As she struggled with her tree pose, she thought of ways to make her line of questioning seem less like the Spanish Inquisition and more like a Cosmo quiz.

She grinned, imagining giving Sabine A., B., C., and D. options with her questions. *Which is your idea of a better date? A. a hot balloon ride; B. a steamy hot tub session and chocolate-covered strawberries; C. a foreign film and burned coffee; D. all of the above.* Those quizzes were always ridiculous, yet Bess always felt compelled to take them. It was a secret she would take to the grave.

Charlie observed Naomi, pleased by what she saw. Her movements were graceful and her mind seemed clear. Whereas Sabine's brow had been furrowed in frustration and Bess's eyes had that vacant "out to lunch" look, Naomi seemed focused and calm.

"Hey Naomi, looking good," said Charlie.

Naomi paused and smiled at Charlie, her thousand-watt teeth momentarily blinding her.

"Really?" she asked, obviously pleased by the compliment.

"Thanks, Charlie." Charlie smiled and made her way back to the front of the room.

"Okay everyone, from here, we move into Virabhadrasana I, or warrior I. You all look great," said Charlie, adjusting the women's angles as they held the position. "Beautiful."

As they transitioned to warrior II, Naomi was embarrassed to find her legs quaking from exertion. *I guess I'm more out of shape than I thought.* It had been a long time since she had exerted herself physically, but instead of her muscles crying out for mercy, they felt heavy and unresponsive. It took all of her will to maintain her balance. She took a deep breath, searching for a clock to let her know that not much time remained in their hour and a half session. Naturally, there was no way to mark the passage of time, which wasn't really a surprise considering the very definition of yoga. There was no way to simply be in the moment with a clock tick-tocking in your vicinity. Naomi shifted and it felt as though her muscles released a bit. The truth was, every so often lately, she had felt this same heaviness when she overdid it. Climbing her four flights of stairs with heavy bags of groceries that week, her legs had felt as though they were made of lead. If she didn't know any better, she would think she was pregnant, but save for immaculate conception, that was an impossibility. She had chalked the sensation up to typical New York single mom exhaustion and brushed it off. Now, here it was again. *You're just exhausted,* she thought. *Out of shape, that's all.* She vowed to sign up at the new gym in her neighborhood. *Some strength training is what I need. And maybe the treadmill.*

Charlie looked at her watch as she guided the women. How was time almost up? She hadn't taken them as far as she had wanted to today—not by a long shot. There was no way she was going to get them into sun salutations this morning. Next Saturday she would have a better idea of what she was working with and manage their time more effectively. All she could squeeze in now was Parsvot-tanasana before taking them into cool down.

"Okay, we're about to launch into our last standing pose for the morning," Charlie informed them. A look of relief washed over their flushed faces. "This is called Parsvottanasama—a fancy word for what is basically an intense chest stretch."

Owwwww, thought Bess, following Charlie's instructions. Her shoulder blades felt like they were on fire.

"Very, very nice, ladies," said Charlie. "Now we're going to take it to the floor." As Sabine sat cross-legged and walked her fingers toward the wall, her back felt like it was bursting into a giant smile. It was as though her muscles had been made of granite prior to class.

"Walk yourself out of this stretch and sit up straight," said Charlie. "Our last sitting move is my favorite. It's a spinal twist in essence, but its yoga name is Matsyendrasana," Charlie explained.

Naomi nodded in response. Naomi did a spinal twist every morning. Few things were more gratifying than hearing her contorted spine crackling back into place.

Charlie walked them through their twists to horizontal positions on the mats.

This is definitely my favorite part of class, Sabine noted. She smiled, imagining a hot shower.

Naomi tentatively shook out her legs. The heaviness seemed to have disappeared. She sighed in relief. Despite her tiredness, there was no denying how cathartic yoga was. As she lay there, she vowed to reconnect with her body more often. She rolled her eyes, realizing that the very sound of that was a little woo-woo and out there. *What does that even mean, reconnect with your body?* she asked herself. But she knew. She had gotten so caught up with being a mom that she had forgotten who she was outside of that role—body and soul. Maybe her body was simply reminding her how important it was for her to remember more often. Yoga was perfect for that, and the strength training on the side would only help matters. *Maybe I'll buy some free weights and forego the gym, though.* The idea of a gym, with all its Lycra-clad members going round and round on treadmills and bikes, was unappealing, to say the least.

"When you're ready, come up to a comfortable seated position," Charlie said, after a few minutes had passed.

As the women reluctantly returned to the upright world, Charlie began again. "I want to thank you all for coming today," she said. "I know class was difficult, and that it may seem that you'll never fully feel comfortable on the mat"—Sabine grimaced here, convinced that Charlie was speaking directly to her—"but comfort only really comes when you think of yoga as a journey rather than a destination. Be patient with yourself." She smiled warmly at the women before continuing.

"At the end of class, it is customary to say good-bye with Namaste, with your hands placed in the prayer position over your heart like this." Charlie put her palms together to demonstrate. "*Namaste* simply means 'The Divine in me salutes the Divine in you.' Beautiful, huh?"

The women nodded in agreement. Even Bess, despite herself, was moved by the power of the sentiment.

"Namaste," Charlie said.

"Namaste," Bess, Sabine, and Naomi repeated in unison.

Naomi attempted to pull herself up off the floor with the sole aid of her core muscles. She laughed as this attempt rendered zero results.

Feeling a bit overconfident, ay? she said to herself, using her hands to lift herself up.

"Naomi," said Charlie, approaching her with a half smile.

"Hey Charlie. Thanks for such a great class."

"Oh, thank you. You look really good on the mat, Naomi. You really seem at ease."

Naomi blushed. "Oh!" she replied, pleased and surprised by Charlie's compliment, considering the difficulty she had been having. "Thanks! I forgot how much I love yoga, you know? How good it makes me feel."

"Have you done it before?" asked Bess, overhearing her exchange with Charlie.

"Well, sort of," answered Naomi. "Prenatal yoga. But I think that's really a whole different ball game in terms of exertion. The same basic principles, though."

"True," agreed Charlie. "But you really seem present in class."

"Wait," interjected Bess. "Prenatal yoga?! Naomi, are you a mommy?" Bess's mind salivated wildly as she thought about the unexpected perfection of this detail in terms of her article.

"Actually, yeah. My son's name is Noah."

"Oh, I love that name," said Sabine. "I bet he is a beautiful boy. How old is he?"

"He's eight now," answered Naomi. She watched the women string beads on their internal abacuses. *Thirty-two minus eight equals twenty-four.*

Having a baby anywhere else in the country at twenty-four was pretty normal, but in New York you might as well be making moonshine in your trailer basement with Uncle Jeb. Twenty-four was the new fourteen in terms of urban, career-woman baby making.

"Wow, a young mama," said Sabine comfortingly. "I like that. By the time I get around to having a kid, I'll be lucky if there will be only one set of diapers to change in the house."

"Eww, Sabine!" exclaimed Bess. "That's gross."

Sabine lifted her hand to her mouth as if to cover it. "Oh, I know. My bad. Sometimes, without warning, I turn into Jackie Mason. Forgive my bad joke."

Naomi laughed, grateful for the new direction of conversation. It wasn't that she didn't like talking about Noah—she could go on and on about how incredible he was—but she was always aware of how the mere mention of him around women with no kids sent them into a tension-filled spiral of either feigned interest or bad jokes about the state of their uteruses.

The three of them piled their mats back against the wall.

"So, Naomi, are you married?" asked Bess.

"Jesus, Bess, that's a pretty personal question, don't you think?" asked Sabine.

Naomi put her hand on Sabine's back to comfort her. "It's okay, Sabine. No, Bess, I'm not," she answered, staring her directly in the eyes and daring her to ask anything else. Bess got the hint.

"Okay," she mumbled. "Hey, I'm sorry if that was out of line," she added, looking first at Naomi and then at Sabine. "I mean, I'm a reporter, you know? I just ask a question without thinking of its impact. Forgive me." Bess felt bad for going for Naomi's jugular with the husband question, she really did, but a huge ticking clock loomed large over this six-week period.

Bess hoped that this hadn't ruined her chances of probing Sabine. Now she would have to be a bit less direct if she expected any answers. This was not great news, as tact had never been Bess's strong suit.

"That's okay," answered Naomi. "It's a pretty standard question."

Bess looked at her, expecting more of an explanation about her lack of husband, but she got nothing. The conversation was over. Bess could respect that. She would think of a way to open that vault more effectively in the future.

They shuffled out of the studio. Sabine felt uncomfortable. She had a habit of absorbing tension whenever it arose, and now she was pulsing with it. Her mom would say that Bess had some chutzpah for being so unapologetically nosy, and she'd be right.

"How was class, ladies?" asked Julian. He and Charlie were sitting behind the desk. Charlie was rubbing a satiated-looking George behind the ears and smiling.

"Awesome," answered Naomi. "Charlie, thanks so much. I'm looking forward to next week."

"Me too," agreed Sabine. "This class is really good for me."

"Me three," chimed in Bess, anxious to erase the black cloud that she had created with her big mouth.

"Good," said Charlie, pleased by their enthusiasm. "Me four."

They moved to the coat closet and zipped themselves back into their winter cocoons and boots. Winter was such a production.

"See you next week!" Charlie yelled after them as they made their way down the stairs.

"Bye, Charlie! Bye, Julian!" they yelled. Naomi pushed open the door to the street. The cold air blasted them angrily.

"How are you getting home?" asked Bess.

"Oh, I'm just gonna walk," answered Naomi. "It's not that far. See you guys!"

"Bye, Naomi," said Bess and Sabine simultaneously, as Naomi waved and began her trek.

"What train are you taking, Sabine?" asked Bess.

"Oh, I'm gonna take the L. You?"

"Me too!" answered Bess. That would mean a bit more of a hike for her, but the time on the train with Sabine was a must. She had to redeem herself and hopefully get a little juice. She could tell that Sabine was not her biggest fan after the Naomi hiccup.

"Hey, let me buy you a coffee," said Bess, motioning toward

Mario's bodega. The best way to make amends was something free.

"Okay," replied Sabine somewhat hesitantly. She wasn't psyched on taking the train back with Bess, but who was she to turn down a free beverage?

Bess pushed open the deli door and held it for Sabine. "How do you take your coffee?"

"Skim milk and half an equal."

"Me too!" exclaimed Bess. "We're the perfect pair. One equal for two. What's that song from that musical, a bicycle built for two?" Bess cringed at her own incessant rambling. The look of discomfort on Sabine's face confirmed her overcompensation. She needed to take it down a notch. It was unlike her to be such a ham, but the time constraint on the article was turning her into a maniac.

"I think it's *Oklahoma!*" said Sabine. "But I could be lying. Actually, I have no idea."

"Do you know?" Bess asked Mario, who was watching them quizzically from behind the counter.

"Know what?" he asked. *Two white girls ordering skim milk coffees. They have to be coming from Charlie's place*, Mario thought to himself.

"Musicals?" asked Sabine.

"Oh no," he replied, splitting the blue package of sweetener between the two cups. "Not my forte," he expanded, winking at them. "You girls coming from yoga?"

"Yeah, how did you know?" asked Bess.

"Just a hunch," he replied. "Who's your teacher?"

"Charlie," replied Sabine. "She's the best."

"You got that right," agreed Mario, nodding his head in approval. "She really is."

Bess picked up on his appreciation. "You like her, huh?" she asked as she handed him the money for the coffees.

"What's not to like? A beautiful woman running her own business? She's really something."

Bess and Sabine looked at each other with giddiness. It felt like a middle school moment. Somebody had a crush!

"That she is," said Bess. "Thanks for the coffees. Have a good day . . ."

"Mario," he said. "I'm Mario."

"I'm Sabine and this is Bess," said Sabine with a smile. She found herself blushing. This was not your typical deli guy. He was actually sexy as hell, with his olive skin and salt-and-pepper hair. Sabine giggled to herself, imagining him cradling Charlie on one of her romance novel covers. *Yoga Heat* would be the title.

"Hi, Sabine, hi, Bess," Mario replied. "Tell Charlie I said hi."

"Will do," Bess promised with a coy smile as they made their way out of the deli.

On the street, Bess glanced mischievously at Sabine. "Hellooooo, handsome," she whispered.

"For real!" agreed Sabine. "And he is hot for Charlie!"

"*En fuego!* She could do worse than a hot piece serving her free coffee for the rest of her life!"

They burst out laughing and made their way toward the train.

chapter eleven

Subway

O oh, this coffee is like nectar from the heavens," declared Sabine, after swallowing her first sip.

"Yeah," agreed Bess. "Looks like hottie deli dude is quite the barista."

They were sitting in the subway station, waiting somewhat patiently for their train back into Manhattan. Sabine stretched out her legs and rested her head against the wall.

"Why is the MTA so evil?" she asked Bess. "Every weekend is like a pie in the face. They run so slowwwwwww."

"No kidding. About a month ago, we took the train back from JFK," explained Bess. "We figured out that it took us, between the slowness and the transfers and the inevitable bullshit, almost as long to get back to my place as it did for Dan to travel a quarter of the way across the entire country."

Sabine laughed and shook her head in disbelief. Just then, the tunnel lit up with the lights of the approaching train.

"Sweet! Seats!" exclaimed Sabine moments later, as she plopped herself down with gusto.

Bess dropped down beside her. "First of all, my legs are like Jell-O! I am so out of shape! That yoga kicked my ass!"

"I know!" agreed Sabine. "My muffintop hurts. But I guess that's a good thing. I am not opposed to beating it into submission."

Bess laughed. Despite her article anxiety, there was something about the day that felt very collegey to her—even excluding the fact that she had just spent time with her classmates from that very era. There was something about the comfy clothes, the no makeup, the early morning chatting, and the 'nowhere to be' vibe that made Bess feel eighteen. It had been so long since she had spent any real time just shooting the shit. Between work, her career aspirations, and weighing the pros and cons of her long-distance relationship with Dan, she was a bundle of fried nerves.

"Wait, so back to our conversation," said Sabine. "Why the hell were you taking a train back from the airport? I mean, yeah, the taxi fare is absurd but come on! Cut yourself a little bit of a break."

"Please, I always do, but my boyfriend is frugal as hell."

"You guys took a trip together? A little lover's retreat?"

"I wish," answered Bess. "He lives in LA right now. He came in for the weekend."

"What's he doing out there?" asked Sabine, wrinkling her nose in distaste.

"He's getting his master's in screenwriting at USC," explained Bess.

"Nice! I hear they have an amazing program."

"Yeah, definitely. Hey, are you dating anyone?" she asked Sabine, eager to switch the focus back to her. She wished Sabine was less likeable. On one hand, Bess could classify her questions as just innocent, getting to know you kind of queries, but on the other, she did feel slightly guilty about her motivation. The image of Sabine's head juxtaposed on top of a kitten's neck briefly popped into her head.

"Who, me?" asked Sabine. "Noooo. Nobody."

"Really?" asked Bess. "But you're so pretty! Every time I saw you in college you were being hit on by a different guy."

"Oh wow, that is too funny. I did have a lot of luck in college, you're right. I'm afraid that's where I peaked, however." Sabine laughed. It was funny that Bess remembered her as some sort of campus vixen. "Where did you see me with guys, though?" she asked Bess. "Just around class and stuff?"

"Yeah, but also around the student union. You always wore this teal fleece."

Sabine clapped her hands with glee. "Yes! I loved that thing! God, I was such a pseudo-hippie. Maybe I should incorporate some fleece back into my wardrobe. It certainly worked for me back in the day." Sabine often wondered why her college dating life had been so much more exciting than her current one. She suspected that it had a lot to do with weed, which she and her various paramours smoked mass quantities of. She had been a lot more relaxed back then, to say the least.

"I doubt college was your peak," said Bess. "You've just got a lot more on your plate now than you did back then. And let's face it, guys in their twenties and early thirties are almost worse than they are in college in terms of commitment issues. Trust me, I know the drill. Dan and I have been together for only a little over a year. Before him, it was the Sahara—and not necessarily because I couldn't get a date. I just didn't feel like dealing with the bullshit."

"Exactly!" agreed Sabine, sitting up in her seat and rattling her neighbor out of her iPod trance with her excitement. "That's really what's happening with me, too. I mean, I go on dates you know, I just have a really hard time getting excited about guys anymore. For the most part, they're just lame."

"And predictable," said Bess.

"Yes! Completely predictable. It's like they all read this hand-out on how to behave like an affected moron." Sabine took a breath. "Forgive me, I sound like a bitter old hag. I don't hate men, I just . . . am largely unimpressed by them these days."

Bess nodded. "I hear you. Dan is an exception to the rule, but even he can be a pain in the ass." She racked her brain for an easy way to segue into questions about Sabine's job. How could she slip out of this conversation without jolting Sabine out of an already established comfort zone?

"How did you meet Dan?"

"I met him at a random party actually. You know, the typical drill. It was a Friday night and I was in the middle of a serious funk. I was on my couch, watching a *Hills* marathon. A green mask on my face, a full belly of sushi, two glasses of wine in."

"I love those nights!"

"Me too. But when it's the sixth Friday in a row, the love kind of dies, know what I mean?"

"Amen," agreed Sabine.

"At any rate, my friend called me and literally pulled me off the couch with the most annoying pep talk I have ever received. It was straight off of *Dr. Phil.*"

"Ooh, I hate that man," said Sabine. "He truly is a massive tool."

"Yeah, a massive tool that fooled Oprah all the way to the bank."

"True enough."

"I got up and put my clothes on, bitching the whole time, knowing it would be the same crowd of postcollege frat boys turned bankers who were sleeping their way through New York," continued Bess. "I don't even think I put makeup on. I knew it would be a lame night and that I'd end up home, in bed, in two hours. I just wanted to prove my friend wrong, you know?"

"So what happened?" asked Sabine, thinking of her own un-willingness to go out these days, for the very same reasons. It was just so much effort. And for what?

"I showed up to the party, completely uninterested in anything other than saying 'I told you so' to my friend. And wouldn't you know it—there he was."

"Naturally," said Sabine. "Unreal! Who approached whom?"

"He came up to me and just said, 'Hi, I'm Dan,'" answered Bess.

"No bullshit," said Sabine. "Gotta love that."

"Nope. Nada." She smiled and put her hand over Sabine's. "And it's been rainbows and kittens ever since!"

Sabine laughed. "Really?"

"Hell no," answered Bess. "Relationships are not easy. Espe-cially when you're already bona fide adults. At least, age-wise."

"And what are you gonna do about the long distance thing? Would you move to LA?"

"No way. I can't give up everything for him. Moving out there would erase all of my hard work here. Plus, don't forget that my move would automatically give him the upper hand. I would al-ways be the one who sacrificed everything for him. Pathetic, really."

"I mean, I wouldn't know because I've never been in a long-distance relationship, but I feel moving to LA isn't like moving to the South Pole or something. I'm sure you could get work out there, doing what you want to do. You could make it work. Don't be so hard on yourself."

Bess knew Sabine was just trying to help, but her argument might as well have been delivered by a singing Shirley Temple on the Good Ship Lollipop. "Sabine, thanks. I just . . . I think that might be a naïve way of looking at the situation."

"Maybe . . . but I really don't like the idea of thinking about 'upper hands' in terms of relationships. Seems to me that once you start going there, the magic is already long gone," Sabine said before looking up suddenly. "Oh shit! I missed my transfer!"

Bess panicked. She'd been blabbing about herself the whole time and had gotten zero personal details from Sabine.

"Um, stay on the train, we'll uh . . . we'll grab lunch!" said Bess. Time was super limited and she had just blown a chunk of it by jabberjawing about her own troubles. What was happening to her?

"I wish I could," answered Sabine, getting up as the train pulled into the station. "But I have two manuscripts to read this weekend and I have to chain myself to my apartment."

The doors opened. "Well, are they good reads at least?" asked Bess.

Sabine moved toward the door. Looking back over her shoulder she shook her head.

"Terrible. But what can I do? See you next week, Bess!" And with that, she breezed through the subway doors and was gone.

Bess felt a headache seize her temples. How was she ever going to pull this off? These women were so refreshingly cool and down-to-earth. And smart. That comment Sabine had made about relationships was spot-on. They were almost impossible to not like. Or to judge, for that matter. She looked up to find the man across from her reading the *Times* intently.

Almost, thought Bess, *but not quite.* This story had all the right ingredients for success. She wasn't going to sabotage her ticket out of tabloid magazine hell because of some girl crushes.

No excuses, Bess, she said to herself as she got up from her seat. The train pulled into her station and she exited, her magenta hood bobbing through the crowd like a buoy.

chapter twelve

Sabine

Sabine lumbered up the subway stairs thinking about Bess. She wasn't so bad, just a little bit of a big mouth. There was something refreshing about that. *And plus, she thinks I'm pretty.* Sabine laughed. She was such a sucker for compliments. "Oof, my dogs!" she mumbled under her breath. Her quads were on fire from class. Yoga might be a bitch to master, but at least you knew it was working something.

Once on the street, she eyed the grocery store up ahead warily. There was something about picking out her food under the glare of fluorescent lighting and navigating aisles that felt like—and probably were—two feet wide that made her feel depressed. On the other hand, watching her money swirl down the drain every time she ordered takeout made her feel even worse. She took a deep breath and entered the store, tabulating a list in her head and strategizing the quickest way to get what she needed and get out.

The best part about this is that once I get it over with, I don't have to think about it again for the whole week, Sabine reminded herself. Once inside, she made a beeline for the vegetables. After that, a quick swipe of some milk, some cereal, veggie burgers, cheese . . . she was almost done. She made her way to the chicken, thinking about grilling some up for dinner. Out of the corner of her eye, she spotted the premade rotisseries, glistening seductively. For a moment, she hesitated.

Premade rotisserie does not count as cooking, Sabine, she reprimanded herself. She continued to eye it. *But chopping vegetables for a salad does!* She put down the chicken breasts and grabbed the ready-made bird, along with some vegetables.

She surveyed her cart. It was missing her favorite low-cal ice cream bars. She circled back around and tossed a box into her cart. She glanced at her phone. Less than fifteen minutes. Record time! Now, she only had to make it through the checkout line and—the worst part of the entire ordeal—walk the four blocks home carrying her cumbersome bags. Luckily, nothing was too heavy. She couldn't count the number of times she had been convinced that her forearm was going to snap off under the weight of poorly packed grocery bags. Living in New York was filled with gigantic obstacles every day, not the least of which was carrying home your damn groceries.

As Sabine pushed her cart to the checkout line, she noticed a very nice tush on a tallish guy standing by the vegetables. High and tight. She attempted a subtle once-over of the rest of him. *Wait, is it!? Nooo. Oh shit! It is!* The purple hooded sweatshirt peeking out from the top of his jacket gave him away. Her heart plummeted into her shoes. It was Subway Crush. But not on the subway. The very notion that he could exist somewhere outside of the underground tunnels of Manhattan was wild.

Sabine attempted to quiet her racing heart with some yoga breathing. She closed her eyes and tried to breathe in for five counts. *One, two, three, four, five,* she instructed herself, as her rib cage contracted. Now let it out. *One, two, three, four, five.* Sabine exhaled deeply. She did feel better.

She opened her eyes. He was gone! Noooooooooooo! She wanted to scream. She looked around, hoping that maybe he had just darted down an aisle to grab something before checking out. Nothing.

Sabine pushed her cart to the line, feeling defeated. She had closed her eyes for only ten seconds! Literally, ten seconds. *Maybe Subway Crush is just a figment of my imagination,* she thought. *What if he doesn't exist at all, and is just a reminder of my lameness?*

She began to pull her groceries out of her cart and place them on the belt. As she reached in for the chicken, a voice behind her asked, "Are those any good?"

"You know, I think they're pretty delicious," she answered, not turning to face the questioner until she had released the bird.

Holy shitttttt! Holy shit cowballs shit gahhhhhhhhh! she thought to herself, as she subtly tried to avoid collapsing in disbelief. It was him. He had a voice. He could speak. He was talking to her. To her!!! She tried desperately to compose herself.

He smiled at her, somewhat nervously. Up close, his face looked different. Better different, but not in any weird, supermodel way. He looked like a human being. She could see that he had missed a spot shaving, and that he had the beginnings of a pimple on the left side of his nose. His eyes, however, were just as amazing as she had always imagined from afar. *Raisin jewels, indeed.* They sparkled like diamonds.

"Well, I'll take your word for it, then," he answered. His voice was low, but seemed to have a bit of a twang. She wondered where he was from. Could it be that he was a Southern boy in the city?

"I saw one in your cart and it looked so good," he explained. "I went and grabbed one for myself. I copied you."

Jesus, his smile is blinding, thought Sabine. For a moment, she forgot the English language.

"I believe that's a copyright infringement," she finally replied. She couldn't believe it. She was actually managing to be clever! It was a miracle.

He laughed. "Please, don't sue!"

"Miss?" interrupted the cashier. "Are you going to pay or what?"

"I'm so sorry," she replied. "How much?"

She got out her wallet. She had approximately three minutes to lock down the man formerly known as Subway Crush and was now officially called Raisin Jewels. He was flirting with her. Even she, self-deprecating Sabine, could not deny that. Should she ask him if he wanted to walk home together or was that too desperate?

"Hey, do you mind waiting a minute?" he asked, beating her to the punch. "We can walk home together."

Sabine's smile threatened to break her jaw. "Sure, that works."

The cashier watched their interaction with a bemused expression. "I see this girl on the subway all the time," Raisin Jewels explained. "I can never get up the nerve to talk to her though. She always looks so busy, you know?"

The cashier smiled as she scanned his groceries. "The train is hard," she agreed. "Everybody's busy gettin' somewhere."

"Exactly."

"You never exactly looked open either," countered Sabine. For a moment she had considered playing dumb, as though she had never seen him before, but then she just couldn't hold back. She had imagined this happening for so long that playing any games to suggest otherwise seemed a gigantic waste of time. He had been looking at her! Unbelievable.

He paid and gathered his bags. "Do you have a name?"

"Sabine. I would shake your hand, but my bags . . ."

"Of course, no worries. Here, let me take one for you." He looped her heaviest bag around his wrist. Sabine was speechless. Beautiful, charming, and a gentleman? With good shoe taste!? He was the very definition of an urban legend.

"I'm Zach."

"Oh wow, what an ass I am!" replied Sabine. "I was going to ask you for that, honest."

"It's okay," he answered, laughing. "It's not every day you get steamrolled in the grocery store by a virtual stranger."

Sabine laughed. "Yeah, I came in here for some cereal and I'm leaving with a dude. I had no idea there was a special going on! Buy one box of cereal, get one man free."

Zach smiled. "So where do you live?"

"Oh, just a couple blocks up." Sabine stopped herself from telling him that he didn't have to escort her anywhere, she could take care of herself. Of course she could, but this was Subway Crush slash Raisin Jewels for chrissake. And he was carrying her groceries! If there was ever a time to accept the damsel in distress role, it was now. They began to walk.

"So, where do you go on the subway every morning, looking so determined?" Zach asked.

"Do I really look that scary? God, I don't mean to, I swear. I guess it's just my New York bitch face. After you live here for ten years, the city gives you one. It's kind of like a badge of honor."

Zach laughed. "Beautiful and funny, huh? What are the odds?"

Did he just call me beautiful? Sabine wondered if she was dreaming. Maybe she went straight home after yoga and passed out in exhaustion. She looked up to see Zach's eyes sparkling at her—his face only inches away, her bag of chicken looped around his wrist. This was no dream.

Sabine dismissed his compliment. "I'm a book editor," she explained. "I work for a publishing house in midtown."

"Aha! I thought you might be. I've seen you reading manuscripts once or twice." He paused, a little embarrassed by his candor. "I guess I've been watching you pretty closely. I hope that doesn't creep you out. Not in a stalker way or anything, but just in a 'There she is! It's Subway Girl!' kind of way."

"Wait, I'm Subway Girl to you?" Sabine asked, smiling broadly. "That's amazing."

"Really? Why so amazing?"

"Because you were Subway Cr—Subway Guy!" *Wait, did I just admit that out loud? To him? At least I left out the 'crush' part.* Sabine cringed.

"No way!" he responded, clearly pleased by the confession. "Why didn't we ever speak to each other?"

"I guess we were both chickenshit. I always wanted to say hello, but it's such a crapshoot in general, you know? And then, the morning commute element only further complicated things."

"Exactly. It's the sacred time before the grind. Interrupt someone who doesn't want to be interrupted, and you could lose a hand."

Sabine laughed. He was funny, too. Who was this guy? "Where do you go in the mornings, Zach?"

"I'm an environmental lawyer, so I go off to save the world." He rolled his eyes. "There are some good parts of my job, but it's definitely not as idealistic as I had originally imagined. There's a bit too much bureaucratic red tape for my taste."

"Ah, the man is keeping you down. We deal with a lot of red tape BS at my job too. How long have you been there?"

"A little over three years," Zach answered. "How long have you been at your company?"

"I've been there since the dawn of time," Sabine replied. "It was my first gig out of college. I've been there about"—she paused to do a mental calculation—"nine years, give or take."

"Wow, that is a long time. Especially by New York standards. But I've heard about the ridiculous publishing ladder. It sounds like a beast."

"Yeah, you're basically on welfare for your first five years, and you always bring work home on the weekends. Then you finally get the promotion, only to realize that you never liked the job in the first place."

"Yikes, is that what's happened to you?" asked Zach.

"Maybe. A little. Oh, I dunno!" *Look at me,* she thought, *already being Debbie Downer, not fifteen minutes into her very first, nonimagined conversation with Subway Crush.* She needed to snap out of it, stat.

"So," she began, changing the subject, "do you live close by?"

"Yeah, just over three blocks on Seventh Street. It's pretty nuts, right?" asked Zach. "I mean, we could have never seen each other not on the subway conceivably. Thank God for poultry."

"And neither of us would have ever spoken," Sabine added. "God knows how many more years this would have gone on!" She smiled and then immediately panicked as she realized that they were at her apartment. What did she do now? Ask him up for chicken?

"This is where I live," she offered.

"Oh," Zach replied, handing her her bag. They gazed at each other with goofy grins.

"Thanks for carrying my bag," said Sabine.

"Oh, no problem," said Zach, avoiding her gaze suddenly and examining the pavement.

Sabine racked her brain for ways to ask him out. Should she be aggressive here, or just wait for the next time she saw him in the morning? Her mother's voice rang in her ears: *You're not getting any younger, Sabine! Carpe diem!*

"So, would you maybe want to get dinner sometime?" Zach asked, his words tumbling out in a nervous avalanche.

"Yes!" Sabine replied, her face lighting up like the Chrysler Building. "Yes, that would be great," she repeated, hoping to appear relatively calm. Her insides were exploding like firecrackers.

"Great," said Zach, his face relaxing into a grin. "Next Saturday?"

Sabine racked her brain. Did she have plans next Saturday? It seemed light years away. She decided that if she did, she didn't give a shit. "Sure, I'm free."

"Cool. I wish it could be sooner, but I've got a crazy case that I'm working on."

"That's okay, I have a crazy week, too," replied Sabine. *Not!*

"I'll pick you up here then? At eight?" asked Zach.

"Sure. You'll remember where I live?"

"C'mon now. Me, forget where Subway Girl lives?! Impossible."

"Take my number just in case," said Sabine. If for any reason this date didn't happen, she wanted to be prepared. Standing alone on her stoop and freezing to death as she was stood up was not an option. She gave him her number.

"So," said Zach.

"So," replied Sabine.

"It was really great to meet you finally."

"I know," agreed Sabine. "Who knew that you could talk?"

Zach laughed. "See you in a week." He moved toward her for an awkward, bag-and-coat-laden embrace. Sabine leaned into him, feeling like a cumbersome sea lion.

"Yep," she replied. "See you!" She smiled one last time and turned to climb the stairs. It was all she could do not to turn around. *Play it cool, Sabine.* As she put her key in the lock, she allowed herself one peek. He was still there, watching her go.

With a final wave, she slipped inside. Up the stairs, quick, quick, quick, and into her apartment. Lassie greeted her with an expectant meow. She dropped her bags and unzipped her cocoon, scooping the confused cat into her arms.

"Lassie!!" she whispered. "I met Subway Crush!" Lassie gazed at her, unfazed.

"I. MET. SUBWAY. CRUSH," she said—slower this time. As Lassie wriggled out of her arms, Sabine sat in awe on her couch. Did that really just happen? Did she honestly have a date with Subway Crush/Raisin Jewels/Zach!?! What if she saw him on the train before then? How bizarre that would be. Speaking to him instead of ogling him from a safe distance.

She closed her eyes and hugged a couch pillow tightly. The phone rang, breaking her out of her revelry. She eyed the ID. Her mother! Perfect. Her timing was uncanny.

Sabine picked up the phone. "Hellooooo," she sang.

"Wow, you sound happy as a clam. To what do I owe this pleasure?"

"Mom, I met him!"

"Who? George?!" Her mother's George Clooney crush was epic. As far as she was concerned, he was the only bachelor suitable for Sabine. She would tell Sabine to "go out to one of those clubs I read about in the papers" in order to meet him. "He likes normal girls," she would explain matter-of-factly when Sabine laughed off her ridiculousness. "That girl he was with? She was a waitress. Give me a break. Put on some lipstick, show off the girls, and get out there."

"Um, no. Not George."

"The guy from the Bond movies? I just rented that last one the other week. He is a gorgeous young man, Sabine. He's not even my type really—a bit too Aryan—but there's something about him . . . I think it's the accent."

"Mom, no one famous! I met Subway Crush."

"Really!?" she squealed. "Oh Sabine, this is even better. How did it happen? Tell me everything."

Sabine relayed the story. "So can you believe it? We have a date!"

"Of course I can believe it. I told you that he was checking you out. Who wouldn't be? You're the whole package."

"He came up to ME," Sabine said dreamily. "I didn't have to do any work at all."

"It is nice that he did the approaching. Men these days are such, well Sabine, they're not like they used to be. We have to do all the work. And for what?"

"Tell me about it," Sabine agreed. "But he seems like a mensch."

"Sure. What's this mensch's name?"

"Zach," Sabine replied, savoring the syllable.

"Ohhhh!" replied her mother. And then, in a whisper, "He's Jewish!"

"Mom, how do you know that?"

"Who names their kid Zach if they're not Jewish?"

"Plenty of people," Sabine answered—her mind suddenly flashing back to the character Zack Morris on *Saved by the Bell*. He was definitely not Jewish. Although he was a fictional character on a television show. She couldn't really rely on him as an example.

"I don't know what he is, actually."

"You don't know? Well, I guess it doesn't really matter. As long as you're happy. And he's rich."

"I am happy," said Sabine. "But I don't think he's rich. He's an environmental lawyer."

"Oy. Well, at least he has a job. Mindy was telling me that her daughter was dating a homeless person."

Sabine laughed. "Mom, please! To Mindy, *homeless* just means he pulls less than a six-figure salary. Mindy is the worst. And Nicole, the daughter? Don't get me started." Sabine had been forced to go on a friend-date with Nicole when she had first moved to the city. At Nicole's suggestion, they had met at a bar filled with men drenched in copious amounts of hair gel and girls with tiny Louis Vuitton bags. Nicole fit right in. Needless to say, there was no second "date."

"Fair enough," agreed her mother. "Anyway, you sound happy, Saby. I'll take happy."

"Thanks, Mom. I better run. The day is getting away from me." Sabine glanced at the clock. How was it already three thirty? And why was it that the work week inched by like molasses, but the weekend went at the speed of light?

"I know! I have to get to my Pilates class. Bye, honey, love you."

"Bye, Mom." Pilates?? To name a class her mother hadn't taken was impossible. She eyed the grocery bags on her kitchen counter and smiled. *Zach.* Best Saturday ever.

chapter thirteen

Naomi

Mama, can I have more syrup?" pleaded Noah as he pushed his pancakes around his plate with his fork. "These aren't gooey enough anymore."

Naomi glanced over at his plate. "What happened to that syrup ocean I saw earlier? I could barely make out pancakes floating around in there!"

"Mooooooonm," bellowed Noah. "It wasn't an ocean." He smiled. "And the pancakes soaked it all up."

"Like delicious sponges?" asked Naomi, as she squirted more syrup out of the bottle. Usually she was pretty strict about Noah's sweet tooth—which was a monster—but today was Sunday. Everybody should be cut a break on Sunday.

Noah laughed. "Yeah! Like delicious sponges!" He speared a pancake morsel with his fork and lifted it, dripping with syrup, to his mouth.

God, I love this kid, thought Naomi. The force of her love for her son often shocked Naomi. Nothing else had ever affected her like motherhood. Not being in love, not taking photos . . . it was the most amazing feeling in the world. Sometimes, when she thought about the fact that Noah almost didn't happen, tears sprang to her eyes. It was a little sappy, she knew, but it was how she felt.

"Mama, are you still sore?" he asked, spearing another pancake piece and eyeing her, his amber eyes twinkling.

"Ugh, I really am! Everything hurts. It feels like I was run over by a Mack truck or something." Yoga had really done a number on her. She had left class feeling much better than she had during her heavy leg moment, but by the time dinner rolled around, she was stiff as a board and completely exhausted. Where was the Zen in that?

"Yikes," said Noah. He dropped his fork and Naomi watched it sink beneath a golden syrup pool. He moved around behind her and put his sticky hands on her neck. He began to knead her skin, hoping to help. Each contraction of his hands felt distinctly unhelpful though, as his technique was more reminiscent of karate than massage therapy.

"Baby, that is very sweet of you to want to make me feel better, but that's not really helping so much."

"Okay," said Noah, returning to his plate of syrup. "I was just trying to help." Naomi could see his lip quivering a bit.

"Hey, I didn't mean to make you feel bad. It's just that I hurt so much that any touch at all is bad news right now." She got up from her chair and moved behind Noah's body, scooping him against her from behind. He was a sensitive little bugger. Sometimes she worried that the fact that he was mostly dad-less might be turning him into a mama's boy, but most of the time she was pretty confident that she was doing a decent job of exposing him to sufficient levels of testosterone. Whatever that meant.

"Okay," he said, settling back into her scoop.

"What's cooking at school lately?" she asked, releasing him with one last squeeze and collecting their plates.

"Did I tell you about Mini-Noah?"

"No! Who's Mini-Noah?"

"It's so cool!" he replied. "Mrs. Lynch read us this story at school about a little boy named Flat Stanley. He's this little cardboard boy that gets to do all sorts of cool stuff because he's flat."

"Like what?"

"He goes to California in an envelope! He doesn't need to take a plane even!"

"Cool!"

Noah nodded excitedly, his curls bobbing. "We get to have Flat Stanley's, too, except for us it's mini-us! Get it?"

"Mmmm, not really," answered Naomi. "Tell me more, please." She cringed a little inwardly. The last time Mrs. Lynch had given an assignment that had evoked such excitement from Noah, Naomi had been the one up until 2 AM the night before, pasting cutouts on a three-dimensional poster board for the science fair. Not fun when she was eight and definitely not fun when she was thirty-two.

"See, we drew little mini versions of ourselves at school and cut them out," Noah explained. "Here, let me show you." He ran from the table into the other room. She heard him unzip his backpack and rummage around in its depths.

"Here he is!" Noah said triumphantly as he ran back into the room. He held up a cutout of himself, complete with his mop of brown curls. "See!"

Naomi laughed, charmed by his excitement. "I see! He looks just like you!"

"He's wearing my favorite shoes," Noah said, pointing to its tiny cardboard, Stan Smith sneakers.

"It's you!" agreed Naomi. "So what now? What do you do with him?"

"I'm going to send him on trips and take pictures of him. And then I'm going to write about them." Naomi breathed a sigh of relief. Thank God no poster boards were involved. The picture thing she could handle, especially since she would be taking them with Noah. It might actually be fun.

"Where are we going to take him?"

Noah guiltily gazed at the floor. "Well, I had an idea," he said, adopting the tone he used when he was asking for something that wasn't going to warrant an immediate yes.

"What?" asked Naomi, envisioning a ferry ride out to the Statue of Liberty. Although sort of a pain in the neck, it was certainly doable. She would just have to get the bulk of her work done during the week and free up a weekend day. Not a big deal.

"I wanted to ask Dad if he could help me," answered Noah.

Naomi fought back the urge to yell. *Be calm,* she said to herself. *Calm.* She thought about yoga. *Breathe.*

"What?" she asked, as pleasantly as possible.

"Well, I know Dad's going to Paris in a coupla weeks," explained Noah. "And I just thought it would be really cool if Mini-Noah got to go. Dad could take cool pictures of him in all these French places. Places that the other kids aren't going to get to use."

"What's wrong with Brooklyn?" Now she really felt like she had been run over by a Mack truck.

"Nothin', Mama. It's just that Paris is different, ya know? I think it would be awesome to have my mini at the Eiffel Tower and stuff."

Naomi took a deep breath, searching desperately for her center. She made a mental note to ask Charlie about the proper utilization of yogic breathing when in full-on panic mode. It wasn't just that her feelings were hurt, although Noah's decision to involve his father rather than her certainly stung. It was more that she was certain that Gene would let Noah down.

The version of himself that Gene presented to his son was

undoubtedly very different from reality. Noah thought his dad would take his mini to the Eiffel Tower, but Naomi was visualizing his true trip: Mini-Noah hoovering lines of coke at a model party. Mini-Noah passed out in front of the minibar. Mini-Noah asking some fourteen-year-old Estonian supermodel for her number.

Gene was a fashion photographer, and if his life was anything like what it used to be, he was going to the Eiffel Tower only if he was meeting his dealer there. Gene had told Naomi that he was clean when he reentered Noah's life, and hadn't indicated otherwise when he picked him up for their weekly visits, but still Naomi didn't trust him. She so wanted to warn Noah of his father's inability to do anything for anyone other than himself, but she knew she couldn't. Noah was a little boy and this was his dad. It was that simple. Noah would have to find out the rest for himself.

"Honey, if that's really what you want to do, then I think you should ask him." She tried to smile while saying it, but her smirk was made of steel.

"Really, Mama? Thanks!"

"Well, thanks for asking me what I thought about it," answered Naomi. "You didn't have to do that."

"Yes I did," answered Noah, pressing his warm body against hers in a hug. He released her and smiled. "I'm gonna ask him today when I see him, okay?"

"Okay," answered Naomi. Sunday afternoon was Noah's day with Gene. It had been ever since Gene had reappeared, after eight years of nothing, in her in-box. Just seeing his name on-screen had made her want to throw her monitor against the wall. She had ignored the e-mail, and the four more that followed, knowing that if Gene wanted something, he didn't give up.

Sure enough, she was right. Coming home from the Laundromat one morning last spring while Noah was at school, she had found him on her stoop. He wanted to meet his son, he had told her. It hadn't been pretty. Naomi resisted until her conscience had gotten the better of her.

Noah did need to know this man, as much as she couldn't stand or trust him. She had let Gene back in tentatively. What began as walks in the park—Naomi at a distance behind, watching fearfully, had bloomed into Sunday afternoons. So far, Gene hadn't screwed up, but Naomi was always braced for his disappearance.

"Thanks, Mom," cooed Noah in her ear.

"You're welcome, peanut," she answered. She squeezed him as tightly as she could.

chapter fourteen

Charlie

Charlie climbed her stairs slowly. She was exhausted. It had been a hectic day—five classes plus a money meeting with Julian and Felicity. A money meeting as in "we don't have any." They certainly had their fair amount of students, but not enough traffic to get them fully out of the red.

Really, there was only one way to increase their visibility: a website. Charlie had immediately thought of Naomi. She designed websites for a living. Charlie had promised Julian and Felicity that she would ask her about designing a site for Prana.

Part of Charlie regretted even mentioning Naomi's day job to them. She had learned many times in her previous life as a Wall Street drone that mixing business with pleasure was almost always a gigantic mistake. But in this case, when the business was yoga and the pleasure was teaching it, it seemed like it was safe for Charlie to bend her own rules a bit.

She unlocked the door to her apartment and breathed a sigh of relief. She had taken great pains to make her home her haven, and it showed. It wasn't much—really just a studio with a tiny alcove for her bed, but the walls were painted a pretty, delicate shade of eggshell blue and her sparse furniture looked expensive but actually wasn't, thanks to Charlie's flea market and stoop sale obsessions.

Her couch was a chocolate brown, cushiony work of art with a few orange and white patterned pillows strewn across it. A small, honey brown table hugged the corner of what was her eating area and a Persian rug in rich shades of maroon, navy blue, and gold lay on the floor. A smattering of framed black-and-white photos adorned the walls. Small lamps perched on a few wooden tables throughout the space and a towering bookshelf was filled with her favorites. Her bed was a vision in white—fluffy and inviting, with pillows piled high. It was perfect.

"Honey, I'm hooooome," she called to no one, as she dropped her bag and struggled out of her jacket.

Mmm, it's warm in here, she thought. She changed out of her yoga gear and put on her favorite pajama pants and her old BU hooded sweatshirt. There were few things in life that felt as good as changing into pajamas after a long day.

Charlie opened her refrigerator and surveyed its contents. She was starving. She could make a salad and sizzle up some tofu. She wrinkled her nose at the thought. Tofu and wilted vegetables were not going to cut it tonight. She was hungry. She closed the door and moved to her cabinet.

"Yes!" she exclaimed. Macaroni and cheese. The old-school kind—filled with preservatives and ingredients that no one could pronounce. Most of the time she ate healthfully, but every once in a while she had to break out of the box. The box in this case being filled with dry noodles and powdered cheese.

As she filled a pot with water and placed it on the burner, she smiled, remembering her mac 'n' cheese birthday. Neil had been in between bartending jobs and pretty strapped for cash, but she had come home from work to find their dingy, Lower East Side apartment transformed into a cozy bistro, complete with flowers and a tablecloth. He had served macaroni and cheese and red wine, and had saved up to buy her a delicate gold giraffe charm necklace that she had been eyeing at one of the boutiques down the block. It had been the best birthday of her life. Sweet, romantic, thoughtful . . . all the things that Neil had been before he became somebody else entirely.

Charlie sighed and poured the noodles into the boiling water. Sitting at her table, which pulled double duty as a desk, she switched on her laptop.

"Ads, ads, ads," she said aloud, as she deleted them with the click of her mouse.

Ugh, what is the story with Facebook? she wondered, as she saw three more invites from people she hadn't spoken to in a good five years in her in-box. Over the past couple of months, she had gotten countless requests from various names that rang a faint bell in the caverns of her mind. Part of her was intrigued, but a much larger part just couldn't be bothered.

Just then her phone rang. She picked it up, eyeing it warily. Sasha! Sasha was a friend from one of Charlie's very first yoga retreats. She, too, had left a well-paying corporate drone existence to open her own studio in Queens. Honest, funny, and smart as a whip, Charlie really liked her. As new studio owners however, they were both so busy that they barely had time to see each other.

"Hey stranger," answered Charlie. She envisioned Sasha on the other end—in a borough that was really only a subway ride away but felt like Mars in terms of destination reality. Charlie barely even made it into the city these days. She got up to check on the status of the water's boil.

"Helloooo! What's new in the world of Charlie?"

"Oh, you know, same shit, different day." She ripped open the box of noodles, her phone cradled between her jaw and neck, and poured them into the bubbling water.

"Tell me about it. All I do is work."

"How's everything going with your studio?" asked Charlie. She loved hearing about Sasha's experiences, as they were always very close to her own.

"It might end up sending me to an early grave. Our pipes burst last week. Total nightmare."

"Cha-ching!" said Charlie, cringing at the thought of that unplanned expense.

"You ain't kidding. But what can I do, I love it too much to back out now."

"Yes, me too. When it's good, it's really good and when it's bad . . ."

"It blows," said Sasha, finishing her sentence. "And you're broke. It's like a relationship with someone who has no money and never has sex with you."

"Remind me what the good parts are?" asked Charlie, laughing. "I'm making macaroni and cheese," she confessed. "I am a bad yoga teacher."

"Ooh, the boxed kind that's filled with garbage that rots your insides?"

"Yep, the one and only."

"Yum! That sounds really good right about now. Too bad the only thing in my kitchen is a can of chickpeas."

"Yuck," said Charlie. She returned to her computer. "Hey Sasha, are you on Facebook?"

"Yes! I am a Facebook geek and I am not even ashamed to tell you that."

"What's the story with it? Aren't we too old to join?" She glanced to her stovetop to find the water bubbling out of her macaroni pot. She got up quickly and removed it from the burner. As she poured the noodles into the strainer, the steam flushed her face with its warmth.

"What do you mean, what's the story? It's like high school except without the pressure to interact. You can be friends with hundreds of people you never speak to."

"So it's like being a single, thirty-something woman in New York?" asked Charlie. "Only in cyber-form?"

"Ha! Good call. But no, it's more fun than that. The best part about it is the ex factor."

"What do you mean?" asked Charlie, as she poured the powdered cheese, milk, and butter into her noodles. She began to stir.

"Well, my friends and I have actually developed a tag line for Facebook that pretty much sums up its appeal. Or lack thereof, as the case may be," Sasha explained.

"What is it?" Charlie finished stirring and scooped a portion of her macaroni and cheese into a bowl.

"Take your vagina back in time with Facebook," answered Sasha.

"Wait, what?!" Charlie almost choked on the gigantic spoonful of macaroni she had just consumed.

Sasha laughed. "Charlie, let me tell you. Everyone I have ever slept with has sought me out on this thing."

"No wonder you have hundreds of friends."

"Oh, snap!" said Sasha, laughing. "Very funny. No, but seriously. It's actually kind of hilarious. You get this invitation from someone whose name looks kind of familiar. One click later, you realize that it's the guy from 2004 who disappeared after a month."

"So these men are still alive?! I thought they all died when they pulled crap like that. Or at least that's what I hoped." She took another bite.

"Me, too. But guess what, they're all alive and well and more than happy to engage in cyber-friendship. They might not be able to tell you why they left you at that party in Green Point, with no way to get home at four in the morning, but they are more than willing to wall post with you."

"Unreal! This is hilarious. Wait, you didn't accept this Green Point asshole as your friend, did you?"

Sasha was silent.

"Did you!?" yelled Charlie. "You are such a sucker!"

"I know. But I couldn't see his profile otherwise. I wanted to see if he had gotten fat, since that is what I wish on all of the assholes that have come and gone in my life."

"Did he?"

"No, but he is totally bald," answered Sasha.

"Nice!"

"Seriously, it's fun. Vagina past or no vagina past."

"All right, maybe I'll check it out. My vagina might not necessarily want to go back in time, but lord knows she needs to go somewhere."

"That's the spirit!" exclaimed Sasha. "Good girl. Ooh, my sushi is here. I have to go. Find me on Facebook!"

"Will do. Bye." Charlie hung up and returned to her computer, plopping down in her chair with a thud. *Vagina back in time,* she thought to herself. She wondered if Neil was on Facebook. Most likely, yes, as the entire world seemed to be on board. She was the sole remaining survivor of the cyber-networking apocalypse.

Do I stay the course or sell out? she asked herself—her cursor poised on top of the 'Sign Up!' link. "Sell out!" she yelled, clicking on it with abandon. She wondered if Facebook would have held any appeal if Sasha hadn't pitched it the way she did. The moment she had explained it to be a link to lovers past, Charlie's Neil-meter had gone into overdrive.

Spooning the rest of her now slightly cold mac 'n' cheese into her mouth, Charlie filled out the required fields. She realized she didn't have a picture to upload. That was okay by her. No need to get nuts.

She saw the search button in the upper right corner of the screen. Should she? She hesitantly moved the mouse toward it. Her fingers hung over the keyboard, ready to hit the N key.

No, she said to herself. *Not yet.*

Maybe, just maybe, Neil would look for her, just like Sasha had said. She would give it a week. No, two weeks. It was a test. She wasn't sure why she wanted to see him—even if it was only in cyberspace—but her need for some sort of redemption was palpable. He had been the love of her life and had consequently smashed her heart into a million pieces. She hated herself for still giving a shit about him after all this time, and after all the pain that he had caused her. That said, as long as her longing was mostly private—save for the occasional drunken ramble to Julian or friendly commiseration with Sasha—who was it really hurting? *After all, obviously I have some will power about it. If I was really psycho, I would search for him.* She switched off her computer, the irrationality of her pseudo pep talk embarrassing her a bit. She knew who she was hurting—herself. Despite that knowledge, she couldn't move past him. It was somehow infuriating and comforting at the same time.

Speaking of will power, she thought, and scraped the rest of the macaroni into the trash.

chapter fifteen

Bess

Bess sat at her desk, her requisite evening cup of coffee steaming beside her. She was struggling to write a caption about an unfortunate photo of Courtney Love in a bikini. At least she had been told that this was Courtney Love. The disfigured, plastic bobblehead staring at her bore no resemblance to the Courtney Love she had grown up with.

"Rob, is it my imagination or does Courtney no longer have a belly button?" she asked. Rob got up from behind his desk, which directly faced Bess, to have a look.

"It's not your imagination," he replied. "Jesus Christ, that's creepy."

"Yeah, that's one word for it. Did the doctor just say to himself 'Eh, she won't miss it'?"

Rob laughed. "I'd be surprised if she knew it was gone."

"Yeah, except now her super secret prescription pill hiding spot has been erased by medical science. Ooh, that's my caption!"

"Nice!" encouraged Rob. "That's why they pay you the big bucks." He returned to his seat.

Bess noticed her instant messenger dock blinking. She clicked on it. Dan! She beamed involuntarily, all thoughts of certifiably insane celebrities temporarily shelved. They had moved past their argument by basically agreeing to disagree about the article. Dan wouldn't ask and Bess wouldn't tell. Part of Bess knew that this was the equivalent of putting a Band-Aid on a broken leg, but she had decided not to focus on it. Besides, she missed the hell out of him.

DAN: Hey hot stuff. What are you wearing?
BESS: Nothing. I never wear clothes at the office. They're
    too constricting.
DAN: That's it, take a stand! How's your day?
BESS: Sort of blah. I miss you.
DAN: I miss you, too! I can't wait to see you in the flesh.

Dan was coming in three days. Bess had a countdown going.

BESS: Our itinerary is almost finalized.
DAN: Oh really? Does it go something like this:
    Morning: Sex, Breakfast. Noon: Sex, Lunch. Evening:
    Sex, Wine, Dinner.

Bess's grin threatened to crack her jaw as she read Dan's plan.

BESS: That sounds about right. One thing though, I can't
    get out of yoga on Saturday morning
DAN: What?!? Yes you can. I'm not going to forfeit a
    morning together for yoga!
BESS: Don't worry, it's a very early class. I'll be back
    before you're awake. You won't even know I'm gone.
DAN: Why do you have to go to yoga? Your boyfriend is

flying a zillion miles specifically to wake up with you
in the morning and you can't miss one class?
BESS: I'm sorry, Dan, I really can't. You know that time
is of the essence with this article. The class lasts only
six weeks. That's very little time for research.
DAN: Oh, come on! You're not still going through with
this article, are you?
BESS: What the hell does that mean?

Her fingers pounded into the keyboard like nails.

DAN: Listen, I'm sorry. I just don't think this article is a
good idea.
BESS: No, you just don't want to wake up alone on
Saturday, and you're being a big fat baby about it.

Her entire body was coiled to spring. It was all she could do
not to put her monitor in a half nelson. She couldn't believe Dan
was being such a condescending asshole. And all because he
would have to brew his own coffee on Saturday. Men really were
transparent.

DAN: Sorry to get all heated over IM. I know that it's
a lame way to argue. You know how I feel. I guess
beating my point to a pulp isn't going to help anything.
BESS: Guess not.
DAN: I'll call you later, ok?
BESS: K.

Bess clicked out of IM. The thought of continuing this asinine
conversation gave her a headache. She and Dan should just stick
to their plan of agreeing to disagree. There were plenty of times

that Bess had read Dan's screenplays and cringed inwardly. Had she always been kind in her critiques? Yes. Okay, except maybe once, when she laughed out loud at a premise that Dan considered to be avant garde but was really just obnoxiously pretentious.

She knew her article was no Pulitzer Prize contender, but she did think it had potential. It wasn't just a puff piece. And all of Dan's talk about the unethical nature of "betraying" these women was horseshit. Ugh, just thinking about Dan and his smug judgments from LA—the capital of unethical bullshit—made her want to scream.

"Hey Bess, you okay?" asked Rob, breaking her out of her head space.

She looked up to answer him. "Uh, yeah, why?"

"Because your face is the color of a tomato," he answered. "And you're crouched over your keyboard like a prize fighter."

"Oh," said Bess, attempting to straighten her posture. She so wanted to tell Rob about Dan's asshole-like behavior, but she couldn't. She wanted to keep her article idea to herself. She couldn't stomach another opinion at this point.

"Yeah, I'm fine. Just trying to figure out what I'm going to do with Dan this weekend." *Besides drown him in the bathtub,* she added to herself.

"He's coming?" asked Rob. "Awesome. You must be psyched!"

Bess laughed. "Yeah. It will be great to see him." And it would be. They just couldn't talk about the article.

Rob switched off his computer. "Looks like it's closing time," he said. "Time to slide down the dinosaur's tale and into the night." Bess looked at her computer clock. How was it already seven?

"Don't stay too late," he warned, as he stood up and slung his bag over his shoulder. "Courtney Love will still be a mess tomorrow. There's no need to break your neck over today's caption." He patted Bess on the head as he headed toward the door.

"Truer words were never spoken. Bye, Rob!"

Bess stood up for a moment, stretching her arms toward the ceiling. She had to loosen up and move on from the Dan disaster if she wanted to get any work done.

She sat again and faced her computer screen. She couldn't shake the feeling that maybe she wasn't that different from these women at all. She too had sold out in order to make a living in this city. She worked at a tabloid magazine for chrissake. That was a far cry from Christiane Amanpour.

No! she reprimanded herself. She had shelved some of her dreams, but only temporarily. After all, here she was still doggedly pursuing them. Inevitably, her mind shifted gears to Dan. What would continuing their relationship do to her dreams? If he was already pulling rank about her article ideas, what was to stop him from sabotaging her entire future with his negativity? And what if he wasn't even legitimately unconvinced about this article, after all? What if he was more concerned about her free time being sucked up by her outside interests instead of him? His overreaction to the fact that she couldn't miss her yoga class was pretty telling, after all. Maybe beneath his sensitive, writer's facade he was just a selfish, chauvinistic pig. Should she just break up with him now?

She clicked into her photos and pulled a picture of them up on the screen. She studied his face, wondering if evil lurked beneath its handsome surface. She had a look at herself as well, cringing slightly at the smitten, love-soaked grin plastered across her face. Was that the smile of a serious career woman?! No. She sighed heavily and closed the picture.

She had to focus. No doubts and no man (*Dan, are you listening!?!?*) was going to veer her off track.

chapter sixteen

Class Two

G ood mornin', ladies," greeted Charlie, as Sabine, Bess, and Naomi sat on their mats, watching her as expectantly as Saturday morning at 9 AM allowed.

"So, I was searching for a way to open class today," said Charlie. "The perfect quote or frame of mind to launch you back into this new world of yoga. On my bookshelf was a dog-eared copy of Aristotle's *Nicomachean Ethics*. From college, no less. Have you guys read it?"

Sabine nodded. "Yep, in college. Humanities. Pretty epic stuff."

"Indeed," answered Charlie. "I had completely forgotten. Anyway, I was particularly moved by what Aristotle has to say about moral virtue and balance." She paused, noticing Bess's discomfort.

"Bess, stay with me here, I promise this will make sense in a minute." Bess laughed nervously. She really had to be more careful about her facial expressions.

"He talks at length about how moral virtue is about striking a balance—'hitting the mean between two extremes,' " Charlie continued. "He then goes on to say, more or less, that everyone's balance is relative to themselves. There is no universal, inarguable mean that everyone should strive for. The best we can do is be conscious of what *extreme* means to us and always lean back toward the middle to regain our balance." Charlie paused for emphasis.

"On some level, this same premise can be applied to yoga. Sabine, your sense of balance is not going to be the same as Naomi's. And Bess, yours is not going to be the same as mine. The best we can do is connect with our inner equilibrium and encourage it. Here, in class, and beyond—in our everyday lives."

Charlie smiled. "Sorry to ramble on, but I tend to get a bit nerdy when old school thoughts are so incredibly applicable, you know?" Sabine, Naomi, and Bess nodded in agreement.

"Okay, let's begin," said Charlie, as she took them into breathing.

As they moved through their mountains, trees, and triangles, Sabine struggled to maintain her positions. Her mind was elsewhere. Subway Crush to be exact. Tonight was their date and she could barely contain her anticipation. They hadn't spoken all week, which worried her. What if he stood her up tonight and she could never take the subway again? Inevitably, she was also worried about the real Zach vs. Subway Crush. How could he possibly live up to the standards she had set for him? It was practically impossible. By the same token, what about the real Sabine vs. Subway Girl? Were they already doomed from the get-go?

"Hey Sabine, you okay?" asked Charlie, suddenly by her side and attempting to lengthen her back and adjust her hips. "You seem a little tense today."

"Who, me?" asked Sabine, clearly flustered by Charlie's critique. "I just," she paused and released her position in defeat, "I just don't think I'm very good at this."

"What? 'Good' at this?" Charlie laughed, shook her head and

lowered her voice. "Honey, there is no 'good' or 'bad' in yoga. You have to stop thinking that way. Your sense of equilibrium is inherently your own, remember? Just aim for that connection here."

Sabine looked at Charlie quizzically. What she wanted to say was, "Okay, Yoda, thanks for the tip," but what she said aloud was, "I know, I know. On paper that makes sense but on the mat it's a bit more difficult." She motioned to Naomi, who was moving through her positions like Mikhail Baryshnikov. "I mean, when you're up against that . . ."

"But see, you're right back to that way of thinking!" scolded Charlie, her voice rising in frustration. "You're not 'up against' anyone! C'mon, Sabine, work with me here. Really try to connect with yourself. Humor me."

"Okay, I'll try. I have to switch the natural flow of my brain to get to the natural flow of my body I guess. Or something."

Charlie clapped and smiled. "That's exactly it," she whispered. "Exactly that." She moved away from Sabine to continue her loop around the studio.

Bess's grin stretched from ear to ear, like a demented jack-o'-lantern. Dan's arrival had catapulted her into a universe of elation. They hadn't mentioned her article once since he had arrived. They hadn't really done much talking at all, actually. She took a deep breath, relishing the lingering tingles of last night's events.

Sex, she thought. *Really good sex.* It was all she could do not to hump the door frame of the studio in excitement. All the stress of that week, all the doubt about her relationship with Dan and her independence . . . poof! Gone. She assumed tree position and marveled at the elasticity of her post-romp muscles. She had crawled out of bed that morning like a cat burglar, quietly gathering her things and even waiting until she was outside in the hallway to zip her jacket and climb into her galoshes.

Of course, she knew why she was escaping her apartment with

such unnecessary skill, but she didn't feel like thinking about it then. Although she had told Dan ahead of time about her yoga class—memories of their IM blowout still haunted her—she hadn't exactly reminded him the night before. *Why ruin the moment?* she had thought to herself. She had left a note on the bathroom mirror with the promise of bagels upon her return, but she couldn't be sure how Dan would react. Hopefully he was over his high-and-mighty ethical stance and had just accepted her decision. If not, well . . . she would cross that bridge when she came to it. For now, she would continue to marinate in her postcoital bliss.

Charlie turned her attention to Bess. Bess was a strange one. She seemed to be the very definition of tightly wound. Charlie had seen her rolling her eyes on more than one occasion, so why was she here? Maybe she wanted to change those tendencies within herself. Or maybe she wanted Madonna arms—which was usually the case with the less than spiritually inclined. Either way, Charlie was glad to have her. She loved watching the ones like Bess learn to open their minds through yoga.

It reminded Charlie of her own initial struggles with the practice. She was so busy doubting it that she had consistently missed out on its benefits. It was only after a huge fight with Neil and an ensuing yoga retreat to "prove" to him her openness that she had let herself go and surrendered to yoga's powers. The rest, as they say, was history.

Charlie circled Naomi, watching her with satisfaction. She really was a natural. Naomi, however, was battling evil thoughts about Gene and Mini-Noah. She was also hypersensitive to her body's reactions to the poses. Last week's sensations had thrown her for a loop, even though she was relatively back to normal now. Her body felt familiar again, but still unnaturally fatigued. It was becoming harder and harder for her to get out of bed in the morning.

It's just the winter blahs. Plus, the whole Mini-Noah thing, which I really need to just chill out about. It's a freakin' doll for chrissake. But why didn't Noah suggest that I take his mini to yoga class? That would have been cool. Or to . . . wait, where else do I go? To my desk to work on lame websites? Naomi envisioned the sad Mini-Noah album she would produce.

She could just see Noah in class, showing it to his peers, mumbling through it in an effort to mask his embarrassment: "And here's Mini-Noah watching *The Hills*, despite himself. Here he is going to the grocery store with his coupons. And here he is coveting a bag in the window at one of the ludicrously overpriced boutiques on my block." Naomi giggled to herself, but mostly she was a bit horrified by the lack of variety or spice in her life. Did her son think she was boring?

"Hey Naomi," said Charlie, who was suddenly beside her, "take it easy. Slow and steady."

Naomi broke out of her thoughts. "Oh, right! Sorry, I lost myself for a moment." She attempted to regain some sense of Zen, but her doubts were working themselves into a frenzy.

"Today, we're going to segue into Surya Namaskar, or sun salutations," explained Charlie. "The sun salute is a series of twelve vinyasas, or postures, performed in a single flow. Most of these postures are going to be new to you, so we'll take it slow."

The tips of Naomi's fingers grazed the floor as she followed Charlie. She was still trapped by thoughts of Mini-Noah, only now, she had moved from self-doubt to raging anger.

Boring!?! I'll show him boring! she thought. Naomi tried to breathe deeply in an attempt to escape from the boiling cauldron of her mind. She wasn't boring per se, but her life was admittedly "small." It revolved around Noah for the most part. She knew that it was time to let go of him a little, to return to her ideas about her own happiness pre-Noah, but it was not an easy feat. He was her baby boy.

God, how did I get here? Naomi asked herself, exhausted by her interior wrestling match. *From Mini-Noah to my boring existence to my resentment of Gene's freedom to my realization that I need to get a life to utter exhaustion to the tips of my toes? All in less than an hour?* She breathed deeply. Yoga was a workout in more ways than one. No wonder she was exhausted.

Oh, so this is what downward facing dog is, thought Bess as her blood rushed to her head. Before this class, it was the only yoga position that she had heard of.

Charlie walked over to Sabine and placed her hands under her lower back, lifting her gently. "Just a little further," she coaxed. "Nice, Sabine."

As Charlie then led them into plank pose, Bess's arms quaked from the pressure. *I hope the next move involves sitting on my ass,* she thought, as a bead of sweat wobbled precariously on the edge of her nose before falling to its demise on her mat below.

"From here, we move into Ashtanga Namaskara, or the knees-chest-chin pose," said Charlie.

Enough already with the yoga names! thought Sabine. *Like we're going to remember them, anyway!* Her triceps felt like Jell-O. She wanted to inflict pain upon Charlie. Smug, yogi Charlie, with her ropy arms and what looked like a six-pack underneath her shirt.

"Exhale and bend your knees to the floor. Next, lower your chest and chin to the floor as well. Keep your chest open and your elbows close to the side of your rib cage. That's it, Naomi, nice work! From here, we move into Bhujangasana, or cobra. Everyone, focus on pulling your tummy up and toward the back of your spine. Good, very good," she encouraged. "Now, let's repeat it on our left sides."

Nooooooo, damn you, evil womannnnn, thought Naomi. Her arms felt like limp noodles, as she begrudgingly followed along.

Please, please let this be the last part of class, thought Bess. *I promise I'll be nice all week,* she added. Her postcoital happiness seemed like a distant memory. She looked over at Sabine and Naomi. Their faces registered the same sort of frustrated exhaustion. *At least I'm not alone here,* she thought, before plunging her left leg back.

When they had finished, Charlie led them into child's pose on their mats. With their knees bent and their torsos extended over them as far as they could go, they all relished the release.

Ahh, I love this one, thought Sabine. The stretch was so comforting and restorative. Sabine wasn't sure what came first, the posture or its name, but they were the perfect match. It reminded her of nap time in first grade—that feeling of being sweaty and tired from recess. Mrs. Wheeler would dim the lights, Sabine would drift off to what couldn't have been more than a half hour's sleep, and she would wake up to iced animal crackers and apple juice. Heaven.

Charlie led the class through their seated stretches and into corpse pose on their mats. As they all cooled down with their eyes closed, she circled the studio and ran her fingers from the bridges of their noses to the tips of their foreheads, her fingers forming a *V.*

Holy cow that feels good, thought Naomi, as Charlie completed her caress. All of her tension seemed to evaporate under the pleasant pressure of Charlie's fingers. Amazing.

As they returned to their seated positions, Charlie returned to the front of the studio.

"Thanks for being here today," she said. "I hope that you can take a sense of your own balance through the week. Remember to strive for it, even when the hustle and bustle of New York makes you want to scream." She smiled.

"Namaste."

"Namaste," they repeated, smiling back.

chapter seventeen

Post–Class Two

G ood morning, ladies," greeted Felicity as they streamed out of the studio. She was setting up her various jars and pomades in a neat formation on the front desk with studied concentration.

"Does this look tacky, Charlie?" she asked, a note of doubt in her usually confident voice."

Charlie surveyed the somewhat large pyramid she had assembled. "Hmmm, not tacky. But maybe a little much."

She picked up a jar of Felicity's hydrating crème and eyed it. "Cool label, though! And the name is pretty damn clever." The fat, glass jar was filled with a gelatinous goo that promised to relax even the most rebellious frizz. Felicity had called it "SHHH-Hut up and Curl." Charlie unscrewed the lid to take a whiff of the faintly lavender scented pomade. "Mmm, it smells good, too."

"Really, you like it? I experimented with a whole slew of scents. In the end it was between this and tangerine."

"Well, if something is supposed to relax, better it smell like lavender than tangerine," remarked Naomi, overhearing their conversation. She joined them at the desk and picked up the jar herself for a sniff. "Wow, this smells pretty delicious," she added. "Are all of these yours?" She motioned to the now dismantled pyramid of jars and tubes.

"Yep," answered Felicity with pride. "I've been working on this hair care line since before you were born, I bet. Just tinkering with different ingredients until I got it right."

"Remember that shampoo from a few months back?" asked Charlie, laughing at the memory. "That was not one of your best works."

"Oh! The one that promised volume but instead delivered instant dreadlocks?! I still don't know how that happened. A little bit too much of something."

"What? Elmer's Glue?" teased Naomi.

"At any rate, my point is that you have come a long way. Just the other day some woman at the grocery store told me my hair was super shiny and asked me what I had done to it," said Charlie.

"She did!?" exclaimed Felicity with glee. "What did you tell her?"

"Well, I told her all about you, naturally. But when she asked me where to buy it, I was sort of at a loss."

"Asked you where to buy what?" interjected Bess as she came out of the bathroom. She was in a hurry to get home to Dan, but didn't want to miss any potentially juicy nuggets of conversation.

"My hair line," explained Felicity. "I haven't been able to get around to marketing the products like I want to. Between the studio and my kids, I barely have time to make them in the first place."

"You have kids?" asked Sabine, joining the group as she twirled her scarf around her neck.

"Oh yeah, two. Malcolm and Dionne. Although, *kids* seems to be a strange word for them these days. Malcolm is a senior in high school and Dionne is a freshman."

"I can't believe your kids are that old," said Naomi. "You have the skin of an infant. It makes me sick."

Felicity smiled. "Thanks, love. But you're in for the same fate, Naomi. I really do think that black skin wears well. My sisters look about ten years younger than they actually are."

"Really?" asked Naomi. "Even if I'm half and half?" She smiled mischievously.

"There's enough cocoa there to serve you well," answered Felicity. She reached out and rubbed Naomi's shoulder as she smiled back.

"Yeah, and meanwhile us whities are practically born with crow's feet," said Bess with a sigh. "The other day I looked in the mirror and screamed."

Naomi laughed. "Bess, please. You are an ivory goddess."

"Felicity, do you have a website at least?" inquired Sabine. "I would think that would be an ideal place to sell your stuff. You could link to other websites and voilà! Instant fan base."

"Yeah, Malcolm and Dionne keep bugging me to get one up. I see their point, I really do, but I am embarrassingly ignorant about the World Wide Web. I can barely e-mail."

"But who designs the website for Prana?" asked Sabine. "Why don't you just sign them up for your hair products?"

Felicity cocked her head and looked at Charlie. "Charlie? Want to answer that?"

Charlie fidgeted nervously. "Yeah see, we don't exactly have a Prana website."

"What!?" shrieked Bess. "What is this, 1942? Hello? Without a website, you're toast." Bess made a mental note to include this information in the article. Even Charlie, who seemed to be an anomaly to the rest of the group (well, besides herself, of course) was half-assing her way through life. How seriously did she take herself if she couldn't even announce her web presence with confidence?

"Hey, take it easy, Bess," reprimanded Charlie, annoyed by

the intensity of her outburst. "I just haven't had time to find a web designer yet. It's the next thing on my endless list of shit to do." She scowled at Felicity. "Why can't Julian get it done? I don't see why I have to take care of every damn detail around here."

The group was temporarily silenced by Charlie's tantrum.

"Hey Charlie, sorry to jump down your throat," replied Felicity, placing her hand over hers on top of the desk. "I was out of line."

Charlie relaxed. "I know we need a website. I just honestly haven't gotten around to it yet. I'm pretty web-ignorant, too, and the idea of spending more money to set one up is a bit daunting."

"Hey, Naomi is a graphic designer!" announced Sabine. As soon as the words were out of her mouth she wanted to take them back. She had an annoying habit of volunteering other people's services without asking them first. She glanced at Naomi to gauge her reaction.

"I am indeed," said Naomi. Sabine couldn't tell by her voice just how pleased she was to make herself known. "I design websites all the time," she added. "I'd be happy to try to get one up for you."

Bess wondered if Naomi would quote a price. Any man in that position clearly would. Why was it that women were so willing to undermine their worth? Obviously, Prana Yoga wasn't exactly swimming in cash, but surely they could pay her something.

"Really?" asked Charlie. "Are you sure? That would be amazing, Naomi."

"Completely amazing!" echoed Felicity. "I'll keep you in hair products for the rest of your life."

"Speaking of, I could also showcase your stuff on the Prana site, just to get you started," said Naomi. "Two birds with one stone, you know?"

"Ooh Naomi, will you take pictures?" asked Sabine.

"I dunno," she mumbled uncomfortably.

Sabine, oblivious to her discomfort, continued. "Naomi is the best photographer. I mean, the stuff she used to take in college. Her half of our dorm room was like a photography exhibit. She has the most amazing eye, seriously. She took a picture of me once, late at night in our room, and I still use it as my go-to photo to this day." She paused. "Well, no, that's a lie. I had to retire it last year. College was a long time ago."

"Ten years ago, to be exact," added Bess.

"Anyway, Naomi, sorry to blow up your spot, but I've never forgotten how talented you were," explained Sabine.

"Yeah, 'were' as in past tense," replied Naomi. She sighed. "I just don't really take pictures anymore. It's not the same to me."

"Why not?" asked Bess. "You grew out of it or you just don't have time for it?" She was anxious for Naomi's answer. This kind of information was the fuel her article needed to run on.

"I'm not exactly sure why," Naomi answered. "I just don't do it anymore, okay?"

Sabine felt terrible. "I'm sorry for opening my big mouth, Naomi. I didn't realize."

"It's okay," answered Naomi, slightly embarrassed by her defensiveness. "I'm happy to design the website, but I think you guys might need to supply me with the images, Charlie."

"Oh, no problem!" answered Charlie. She wondered why Naomi was so adamantly against her own God-given talent, but she knew better than to push. Everyone had their reasons for things. "Julian is a decent photographer," she volunteered. "I'll ask him to take some shots."

"Yeah, and so is Dionne," added Felicity. "Naomi, we are so thrilled about this. Honestly, I can't even tell you." She got up from behind the desk and wrapped Naomi in a warm hug.

Naomi, flustered by Felicity's sweetness, detached herself from the embrace and smiled. "Oh please, it's my pleasure. Everyone should know about this place! It's about time for you to hit the Web. I'll try my best to get something together for you in a couple of weeks or so."

"That would be amazing," said Felicity, her warm brown eyes glowing with excitement.

"Okay, girls, I need to run to the restroom before my next class," said Charlie. "Today was wonderful. I'm looking forward to next week already." She smiled warmly and trotted off.

Bess looked at her watch. She had to run—no time for dawdling if she wanted to make it home before Dan woke up. "I have to dash! Bye, Naomi, bye, Sabine, bye, Felicity!" She waved goodbye and practically ran out the door.

"Be careful on those stairs!" called Sabine after her. "Jesus, she sounds like a herd of elephants. I wonder where she has to be?" She glanced at Naomi guiltily. She felt terrible about her faux pas. "Hey Naomi, really, I am so sorry about before. I went too far."

Naomi smiled at Sabine. Ten years might have passed since college, but Sabine was still as sweet as the day they met, offering to share the giant bin of animal crackers she had brought with her to school. "Oh, it's okay. I overreacted." They smiled at each other.

"Hey, want to get some breakfast at this diner down the street?" she asked Sabine. "I am famished!"

"Yes! Only if you promise to split some hash browns with me." Sabine ignored the manic prom queen inside of her. She wasn't seeing Zach for ten hours. There was only so much hair removal one woman could do. Besides, hanging out with Naomi alone sounded really enticing.

"Done," replied Naomi, her stomach already growling in anticipation.

chapter eighteen

Bess

B ess sat on the subway, thinking about the power of sex. She had been an irritated ball of amplified estrogen just days ago—wanting to murder her boss with a chainsaw each time she presented her with yet another asinine story idea, wanting to pour Rob's soup bowl all over his keyboard while she listened to him greedily slurp its contents at lunch, even cursing an elderly Chinese woman under her breath as she blocked her path hobbling along Ninth Avenue in her plastic slippers. Even thinking about Dan's imminent arrival hadn't helped to quell her unmitigated evilness. Since their IM argument, they hadn't really connected on the phone—it was all pleasant jibber-jabber about their days, but no real meat to the conversation.

It was only when Dan called her to tell her that he was in a cab, on his way to her apartment, that the tide had started to turn. The mere thought of seeing his scruffy face and putting her arms around his broad, boy back brought a smile to her face—the first smile that face had seen in weeks. Bess was almost embarrassed by her lust. It seemed silly somehow, especially in contrast to how rational she usually was. It was only when Dan walked through the door, and the warmth flowed through her body like blood, did rationality pack its bags and take a much-needed vacation.

They had tumbled right into bed, hungrily groping at each other and laughing with giddy glee. Afterward, Bess had showed him the itinerary she had crafted for his visit. Dan had smirked and taken it from her, ripping it in two and throwing it on the floor.

"I just want to be with you," he had said, hugging her close. "No fancy plans necessary. As far as I'm concerned, we never have to get out of bed." Bess had hugged him back fiercely, surprising them both with the ferocity of her grip. Having Dan in her bed—in New York—made her deliriously happy.

At least for the first, sex-filled twelve hours, she reminded herself. If only they could truly section themselves off from all forms of reality, including her doubts about the durability of their relationship for the long haul. This morning's reality had delivered itself as Bess's yoga class. She really hoped that Dan had come to the realization that his opinion about the article was better left unsaid. She would hate to taint their very limited time together with a pointless argument. Maybe a surprise bagel and lox ambush of deliciousness would head off any of his rumblings at the pass.

Once off the subway, she went to her bagel shop and picked up Dan's favorite: toasted everything with scallion cream cheese, onion, and lox, and the same for herself. *If his breath is going to reek anyway, I have nothing to worry about,* she told herself. This was one of the gigantic benefits of coupledom: you could eat anything offensive that you wanted to and you never had to worry about not getting kissed. Well, maybe that was true almost always. It was certainly true if you both ate the exact same olfactory nightmare.

The warm brown paper bag clutched firmly in her hand, Bess bounded up the stairs to her apartment. She looked at her watch: 11:45. She really hoped that Dan was still in bed. That way, she could just offer up her yoga explanation casually when he inquired as to her whereabouts, and hopefully his grogginess would overwhelm any judgments.

I can't believe I'm sneaking around to go to yoga class, thought Bess. Even though she considered this in ironic terms, part of her was wary about the concept. To have to lie about anything to your boyfriend, or even belittle an experience so as not to evoke anger, was not a happy foreshadowing. Her excitement about seeing a sleepy Dan began to wane as reality—this time in the form of resentment—crept in.

Bess shook it off as she opened her apartment door. She peeked around its corner into her laughably small living room. To call it a "living" room was a joke. It would have been better described as the "couch" room as that is really all that fit inside of it. It was empty—no signs of Dan.

Yes! she thought to herself. *I can make like Martha Stewart and bring him bagels in bed.* She wondered if she had anything that could pass as a tray.

"Mornin', beau-tee-full," she heard from the kitchen. Happiness flooded her body at the mere sound of his voice.

I really am a sucker, she thought. Dan shuffled into the room and smiled broadly at her—his face still creased from the pillow's imprints and his hair matted into a roosterlike approximation.

"Hey sleepyhead. I have bagels!" she exclaimed, holding the bag out in front of her and rattling it excitedly. "Your favorite!"

"You are the best," replied Dan, moving toward her and scooping her into a hug. "Bagels are against the law in LA. Anyone who even thinks about one gets life at fat camp."

Bess laughed as he took the bag into the kitchen. She unzipped herself from the confines of her down prison.

"It is no joke cold outside. Sometimes I become convinced that winter never actually ends—that summer is just a myth."

"It does last forever here," agreed Dan from the kitchen, putting their bagels on plates. "I made coffee. Want some?"

"Yes, please." She wondered if she should get out of her yoga gear and take a shower before eating. She did feel a bit grubby, but not grubby enough to trump the promise of food. That was the thing about yoga: she never really sweat her brains out the way she sweat when she ran at the gym, but her muscles still felt pleasantly exhausted afterward—perhaps even more so.

"Here you go, madam," said Dan as he handed Bess her bagel on a plate. "These look so delicious. Thanks so much for getting them." He plopped down beside her and took a giant bite of his bagel.

"Mmmm, blurgh rerr boo meeve?" he asked, his mouth full. Even this was adorable to Bess. She chewed back at him, her eyes sparkling.

"What?" she asked after she swallowed.

"Sorry. Forgive me, I was raised by wolves." He took a sip of his coffee. "Where were you this morning?"

Bess took a deep breath before answering. "Yoga," she explained, refusing to meet Dan's eyes. *Please, please, please, no argument.*

"Oh," answered Dan, as he examined his bagel for the next best bite. "That's cool." Bess noticed that he wasn't meeting her gaze either. "How was it?"

"It was good. Really good. My muscles are aching, but in a good way, you know?"

Dan nodded in response as he chewed. Bess moved closer to him on the couch and laid her head against his warm chest. How was he always so warm? It was incredible.

"I'm so glad you're here," she said, partly to change the subject and partly because that was really how she felt: incredibly happy to be sitting next to him on the couch, eating bagels.

"Me, too," he replied, snuggling into her. "You know, if you moved to LA, you would never have to deal with this winter crap."

"Thanks, Al Roker," she replied, already slightly defensive. They had talked about the idea of her moving once or twice before, and Bess was always adamantly opposed. Not only because she had grown up in southern California and had a hard time with the idea of settling there as an adult, but because she didn't like the idea of turning her entire world upside down for the sake of a man. It felt too fifties housewife to her.

"Dan, I know the weather rules in LA." She sat up straighter beside him. "But you know how I feel about leaving my life completely behind for you. I don't like what that sacrifice entails. It sets a tone."

"Jesus, when you start spewing that 'setting a tone' bullshit, my arm hair stands on end. What does that even mean?"

"What do you mean, 'What does it mean?'" Bess shot back. "It means that I would be giving up everything I've worked for to follow you across the country. And for what?"

Dan placed his cup on the tiny coffee table with studied concentration. "First of all, you are using this bullshit explanation as an excuse. You wouldn't be leaving shit behind, really. You could transfer to the LA office and you would have a much better chance of getting your freelance stuff published in LA newspapers than here. You even have a hook-up there that you refuse to utilize." It was true; Bess had gone to high school with the head of the *Los Angeles Times* Metro desk, but she barely knew him. She felt like Dan was grasping at straws.

Bess tried to remain calm. "I have come too far in New York to turn back now. And I'm really excited about this article. I really think it has a shot at being picked up by a major publication."

Dan was silent as he eyed her with disdain. Bess could tell that he was holding something back. "What?! Go ahead and say it," coaxed Bess.

"You know how I feel about the article. There's no point in bringing it up again."

"You know, it's interesting that this article upsets you so much."

"How so?"

"I think its premise scares you. I think its premise scares every man," she explained.

"Bess, no offense, but what the hell are you talking about?"

"This idea that women no longer have to feel as pressured to push their own dreams and goals aside for someone or something else. It's not like it used to be. Men are like accessories now. Women don't need them to thrive."

"What the hell does that have to do with your article?" snarled Dan angrily. "Your article is about the groundbreaking idea of 'women working at jobs that they don't love—to survive in one of the most expensive cities in the world.' Wow, what a novel concept! Give me a break. Your article has nothing whatsoever to do with men and whether or not they're accessories. And what's with the word *accessories*? Who are you? Gloria Steinem or Paris Hilton?! I don't even know what you're talking about! You're making no sense, Bess."

Bess felt the anger rushing through her body like a sandstorm. Part of her was outraged by Dan's arrogance and part of her—a tiny, boiling part—knew that what he was saying was true. Lately, she had been paralyzed by the thought that maybe this article had no legs at all to stand on. That, ironically, she was just as guilty as Sabine and Naomi of selling out.

That was the thing though—writing the article was her ticket out of that same classification. She had to complete it just to prove to herself that she did still have a creative vision—that she did crave a life beyond her mundane nine-to-five one. That she wasn't going to stop striving just because she had gone and done something stupid like fall in love with a man who lived across the country.

All of her thoughts, reservations, and anxiety had swirled into one giant mass of confusion in Bess's head. She had been avoiding this tornado of emotion for a good week and a half, and here it was, touching down in her living room. Too bad she couldn't hide under the couch until it passed.

She held back tears of frustration. "I am going to take a shower. I can't talk about this anymore right now. Nothing is making sense and you are being an asshole." Dan opened his mouth to argue against the moniker, but thought better of it as he saw a tear roll down Bess's face and betray her tough facade.

"Okay," he answered, fighting the urge to take her in his arms. He hated arguing, too, but he couldn't be a no-opinion doormat. It just wasn't his nature. "I'm going to go for a walk."

"Fine," she replied over her shoulder as she walked toward the bedroom. She closed the door and flung herself on the bed in a heap of emotional exhaustion. What if Dan was right? What if this article was nothing but a sad attempt at greatness with something that wasn't even good? Facedown on her bed, she couldn't see the door open, but she felt Dan's presence instinctively. She tensed up, like a threatened snake ready to strike.

"Hey, Bess," whispered Dan. She didn't answer.

"Bess," he repeated, moving to sit on the bed beside her. He put his hand on her back. Instantly, Bess felt warmth radiate up her spine. She relaxed against it, damning the power of physical chemistry. It was impossible to fight.

"Listen, I'm sorry I'm being so hard on you about LA and this article."

Bess turned over to look at him. "You should be sorry. I feel like you're giving me no room to breathe on either subject, Dan. You're backing me into a corner."

"I just, well . . . I guess I'm just worried about the future."

"Really? Why?"

"I mean, I look at our dreams as easily intertwined, you know?" explained Dan. "I just don't see us as having to strive for such separate goals. We can both strive for creative fulfillment together, you know?"

Bess fought back tears. "Oh Dan," she said, sitting up and enveloping him in a bear hug. "I know you're right, but it's hard for me. I've been single for so long that I never really thought that I could have everything I wanted. Career fulfillment and love? How can you have one without sacrificing the other?"

"Wow," he said, stroking her hair. "That's crazy to me. You are so someone who deserves everything in life. The fact that you see love and personal fulfillment as two separate entities makes me sad." He kissed her cheek. "I know you can have both."

"But at what cost? I mean, something's got to give."

"Maybe you'll fall behind on your fruit canning," teased Dan. "Or your embroidery. Come on, Bess, you're not giving yourself enough credit. I know you can make your life as full or as vacuous as you want it."

Bess laughed. "I have the power to live a life completely devoid of meaning! The power is within me!"

Dan squeezed her tightly as he laughed with her. "You know what I mean. I just want us to do this together. I don't want to lose you to your insecurities about your independence or lack thereof."

Bess stroked his scruff. "And I don't want to walk away from what we have because of those insecurities, either. But it's not just the insecurities. I mean, what are we doing?"

"What do you mean?"

"LA . . . New York . . . what's happening? Who's going where? Are we really going to do this thing or are we going to live in long-distance la-la land forever?"

Dan sighed heavily. "Every time I bring up LA, you shoot it down."

"Why hasn't the possibility of you coming back to New York ever really been discussed? Why is it just *assumed* that I'll be the one to make the move? That's the kind of shit that really gets under my skin, you know? The whole male-female dynamic. Naturally, the woman has to pack it up to follow her man. God forbid it's the other way around."

"Whoa, whoa, whoa! Take it easy, anger management. Jesus. You know why I can't come back to New York anytime soon. I'm getting my master's in screenwriting for chrissake. That's sort of LA-centric, at least for the first couple years or so, wouldn't you say?"

"I know it is," she conceded. "I just don't think I could leave New York to be with you and not resent the hell out of you if we didn't work out. You can spin it however you want it—I could easily get a job in LA, my family is from LA and my dad's not doing too hot lately, LA is cheaper, blah, blah, blah—but the fact of the matter is that I would really be going only because of you. That's a lot of pressure to put on one relationship."

"I know it's a lot of pressure. It's pressure for me too, you know. True, I wouldn't be the one having to move, but I would be the one having to take at least a bit of responsibility for your happiness. And us living together would take things up a whole other level." He paused. "Hey, how is your dad, by the way? You haven't brought him up in a while. How's the pacemaker working out?" Bess's father had had a heart attack when she was in high school, and had been lucky to survive. Although he was still as robust and active as ever, he was operating on only two thirds of his heart. Because of who he was, you would never know that he felt the repercussions of that loss on a daily level, but his basket full of medications and his defibrillator told a different story.

"He's hanging in there. You know, he's the last one to say that he feels weak or unwell. I'm worried about him," said Bess. Dan brushed her hair off her face. "I really need to go see him, and my mom. Maybe I can do a double trip or something—see you and my parents." She paused. "Would you want to meet them?"

"I would love to meet them," he answered, not skipping a beat. "That's some 'next level' stuff, Bessie. I like it." She smiled at him. Her parents hadn't met a boyfriend of hers since high school.

"Listen, I want to give us a real shot," said Dan. "Of course I understand your hesitancy and doubts about moving west, believe me. If we have to continue the long-distance thing, we'll make it work. I don't want to lose you . . . or us. I love you, Bess."

Bess inhaled sharply. Dan had never said that to her before. It was huge. Involuntarily, tears sprung to her eyes. *Who knew I was such a chick?* she thought. "I . . . I love you, too. I really do."

"Holy shit! We're in love!" exclaimed Dan. He wrestled Bess onto her back and smiled down at her.

"I know! What a world!" She reached up to stroke his hair. "Now that this part is established, maybe the rest of the details will just work themselves out on their own."

Dan shook his head and laughed. "Yeah, of course. Like in the movies." He lowered himself down on top of Bess and she encircled him with both her arms and legs. *Mmmm, nice. Just me and the man who loves me, snuggling.* She couldn't help it. The girly girl genie deep within her had been summoned by the three magic words: *I love you.* Bess would shove her back into her bottle soon, but for now, she could live a little.

"Bess, I'm sorry I'm chapping your ass about your article. I'm going to shut up about it now, okay? This is your journey and I don't want to put my stink all over it."

Bess wrestled Dan onto his back and crouched over him, pinning him down with her hands. "To be honest, this article is starting to not make as much sense to me, either, but I'm just not done with it yet. I have some more wrasslin' to do with it."

"I'll give you something to wrassle," replied Dan with a smirk as he broke out of Bess's hold and reversed their positions. "But first, I must brush my teeth."

"Yeah," agreed Bess, wrinkling her nose in mock disgust. "That lox, onion, and garlic combo is not doing you any favors."

Dan exhaled deeply into Bess's face. She screamed in delight. "Gahhh! You just exfoliated all of my nose pores!"

Dan laughed and got up. "I'm hitting the shower, too," he announced.

Bess lay on the bed, pleased with the way they had worked through their argument. *Look at me,* she thought. *In an adult relationship. With someone who loves me. With someone who lights up when I mention him meeting my parents instead of disappearing into the ether.* She would get to work on her own reservations about the sacrifices being in a relationship entailed, but for now she would just relish the bliss of being open enough to admit she was in love with someone who loved her back. *Who said it first.*

She sat up and grabbed her laptop off her bureau. She decided to e-mail Sabine to set up a hang. She wasn't exactly sure where her article was headed, but she figured that a glass of wine with her might point her in the right direction. It certainly couldn't hurt.

chapter nineteen

Sabine & Naomi

Is Brooklyn singlehandedly responsible for the soy movement?" asked Sabine, as she sat with Naomi at a coffee shop in her neighborhood. She had asked for a regular latte and their waitress had looked at her like she was speaking Swahili.

"What do you mean, regular?" she had responded, exasperated by Sabine's assumption of a universal "regular."

"Um, with milk?" Sabine had replied meekly.

"Full soy, light soy, chocolate, vanilla, hazelnut, what?" the waitress had replied, rattling off the list with practiced disinterest. Sabine had looked to Naomi for help.

"She'll have vanilla soy," she volunteered. The waitress left and Naomi laughed, putting her hand over Sabine's. "Welcome to Brooklyn, Sabine! Milk is déclassé here, in case you weren't aware." She laughed nervously. "I apologize. This place just recently changed owners. The owner is supposedly a dairy nazi, but the coffee is just too damn good. I hope you don't mind the aforementioned additive. It's actually very good in coffee. And cereal, for that matter."

"Oh, I know," said Sabine. "It's not that I haven't had it before, it's just that I wasn't prepared for the waitress's soy sass. No worries."

" 'Soy sass'!" echoed Naomi. "That's the perfect way of describing what just went down." She paused for a moment. "Aren't you a writer?"

Sabine sighed. "In my dreams, I'm a writer. In my reality, I'm an editor at Rendezvous Books. I edit romance novels."

"No way! That must be fun—reading steamy sex scenes all day."

"Mmm, not so much." The waitress appeared with their lattes and set them on the table. Sabine cradled her mug between both hands, savoring its warmth. "It pays the bills, but other than that, it sort of sucks."

"Really? I'm sorry to hear that. How did you end up there?"

"Oh, typical story. Young, naïve writer with big dreams comes to New York thinking that a gig in publishing will lead to novelist status. Cut to ten years later and the only thing I write are e-mails." She sighed heavily. "I miss writing, I really do, but I just don't have the time for it. Or the drive, obviously."

"I can relate to that," said Naomi, taking a sip from her mug. "I used to take photos and now all I do is design websites."

"Well, surely your designs are based in the same sort of artistic sphere?" Although she meant it as a statement, it came out more as a question. She didn't have the first idea about web design, other than what she surfed through every day as a means of procrastination.

"Mmm, not so much. I basically plug someone else's ideas into a template, throw in some rollovers and call it a day. When I first got into it, I would spend hours laboring over the exact placement of even the most mundane detail, but now it's a pretty robotic setup. Plug in, link to this, roll over that," she said, her voice shifting from its normal tone to one of a C3PO-like intonation.

"But at least it's YOUR company. You might be a robot, but at least you're your own robot."

"Okay, that I will give you," conceded Naomi. "It is a gift. If only for pure wardrobe reasons. Most days I don't get out of my pajamas until I have to pick Noah up from school."

"That's right!" exclaimed Sabine. "Your son. How old is he?"

"He's eight. Even as I say that, I can't believe how old he is. He was just a baby, like, yesterday."

"What's he like?" Sabine wanted to probe Naomi about his father but thought better of it. She was pretty sure that Naomi was a single mom, but she wasn't positive.

"Oh, he's a love. The sweetest, smartest, funniest, handsomest boy in the whole wide world. I don't know how I got so lucky."

"Probably because you're an amazing mother. I highly doubt it's a coincidence that he's so great."

"You're sweet, Sabine. Thanks. I try. It's not easy though, especially doing it myself."

Sabine did a little mental calculation. Eight years ago would have made Naomi twenty-four. Twenty-four. What had she been doing at twenty-four? She searched through the caverns of her mind and could come up with nothing as life-altering as deciding to bring a child into the world.

"Did you not plan it?" she asked, although the answer was clear.

"No way. Not even close. I was taking pictures in Manhattan and Brooklyn, enjoying the good life, living like a rock star. A baby was not even in the realm of my imagination. Alas, my uterus had different ideas."

"I wanted to ask you something," said Sabine shyly. "I hope you don't mind."

"Ooh, this sounds serious. I'm glad I'm sitting down." Naomi's blue eyes sparkled at Sabine over the rim of her mug.

"Were you a model in some Calvin Klein ads around nine years ago?" Sabine blurted out the question in an excited rush. She had been dying to ask Naomi since, well, since she had seen them so long ago.

Naomi laughed. "I'm afraid that the answer is yes."

"I knew it!" said Sabine, practically yelling. "I knew that was you! I kept looking at those ads and wondering. I mean, it was you from behind, right? You could just barely see a hint of your profile."

"Yep, that was me, all right. How funny is that?"

"You looked amazing! A total supermodel. How did that happen?"

"How did what happen?" asked Naomi. "The modeling part?"

Sabine nodded eagerly. "Yeah, of course! Were you discovered in a shopping mall, just like Paulina Porizkova?"

Naomi laughed. "Paulina Porizkova!? God, Sabine, you are a riot. Actually, no, nothing that dramatic. I was actually a fairly successful photographer in those days. I had some photography shows in Manhattan and Europe and was kind of on the scene, you know?"

"What scene?"

"Oh you know, the bullshit downtown, club and drugs scene. My boyfriend at the time, well, actually, Noah's dad, was a huge fixture. He was a photographer also, but he was much more successful than I was."

"Why?"

"A tiny part talent, a large part schmoozing capability, and an even larger part good looks and drug-snorting," replied Naomi. "He created a huge name for himself."

"So you guys were like, a contemporary Studio 54 or some shit?" asked Sabine incredulously.

"I guess so. It was a wild lifestyle. Gene, that's his name, was on this crazy rocket to stardom and I just hopped on for the ride." She paused to take a sip of her now lukewarm latte. "Anyway, he met Calvin at an art opening and immediately became his muse. Calvin met me shortly thereafter and asked us to be in his fall campaign. Voilà, instant stardom. We were both so high during those shoots. I can barely remember them."

"Really? You couldn't tell. But I guess that was the height of heroin chic, right?" Sabine remembered the first time she had seen the ad—on a huge billboard at the corner of Lafayette and Houston. She had literally shrieked in surprise and awe, so certain she was seeing her former college roommate blown up to gigantic proportions on one of the busiest intersections in the world. It had amazed her.

"I know her!" she had bragged breathlessly to her friend, pointing excitedly up to the billboard in the sky. "I went to college with that chick! She was my roommate!"

Her friend had eyed the billboard and said, "She could use a burger. Jesus." Sabine agreed but was thrilled by the very idea that Naomi, the same girl who had given her a smoky eye in her dorm room of all places, was now a famous model.

"Yeah, it was," said Naomi. "Thankfully, I only dabbled a bit in drugs. I could never fully give in to their allure. Gene, on the other hand, he was a mess."

"I'm sorry. That must have been tough. Is that why you broke up?"

"More or less. I got pregnant and he left. He couldn't deal. I thought about giving up the baby or an abortion, but I just didn't want to. I thought the baby was a sign. Finally, someone or something other than my parents telling me to get it together. So I did."

"What happened to your photography?"

"I just kind of fell off the art world map at that point," said Naomi. "When Gene and I were no longer a couple, nobody really gave a shit about me or my work. It was him they wanted."

"Really? I always remember you being so talented, even as a freshman."

"Well, thanks. But my stuff just didn't work past a certain point. And for me, photography became intertwined with a lifestyle that I didn't want to lead anymore. I hung up my camera, as they say."

"I'm really sorry," said Sabine.

"Oh my God, don't be sorry! I have a beautiful baby boy and a sense of self and independence that only comes from going through the ringer. Please! Nothing to be sorry about here."

Sabine laughed. "Too true. What an interesting story you have, though. I kept hoping I would run into you after I saw that billboard. Never did I think that I would actually be sitting with you drinking soy lattes in Brooklyn, though."

"Who knew that that goofy reunion would pay off so handsomely?" Naomi laughed. "I feel terrible, Sabine. I've been blathering about myself and you've barely gotten a word in edgewise. I want to hear about your writing. And we haven't even talked about class!"

"Oh please. We talked plenty about my writing. I don't do it, so it's only appropriate that our conversation was so short." She laughed and looked at her watch. "I can't believe it's noon! I have to go!" Zach was picking her up in T-minus-8 hours and she hadn't even begun the cosmetic overhaul that she had planned. From the depilatory cream to the exfoliating scrubs to the nail polish and beyond, she had just about spent half a week's pay at Duane Reade in preparation.

"Noon! No way! Cecilia is going to kill me. I was supposed to be home an hour ago."

"Who's Cecilia?" asked Sabine, as Naomi motioned wildly for the check.

"Oh, she's my neighbor. She babysits for Noah while I go to yoga." The women paid and zipped themselves back into their winter suits of armor, preparing for the face-biting cold outside.

"This was so nice," said Naomi, giving Sabine a hug on the street.

"I know," agreed Sabine. "Hey, would you be into getting drinks one night this week? I was thinking about inviting Charlie and Bess, too."

"Definitely. That's a great idea. There's no reason we have to confine our hangs to Saturday mornings."

"Exactly! Cool, I'll send an e-mail around."

"Okay, bye!" said Naomi. "Get home safe!" She waved and took off at a quick clip down the block.

Sabine headed toward the subway, smiling. Naomi was a former Calvin Klein model! What a trip. *Ooh, I should get some water for my ride,* she thought to herself as she passed a deli.

Her entrance was blocked by a gaggle of teenage boys. Tall and lanky, with noses too big for their faces and unfortunate cases of varying acne, they were all wearing shockingly light jackets considering the frigidity of the weather and barking at each other.

"Yo, you stupid," said one Asian boy.

His white counterpart mumbled something back that sounded like "pussy." Sabine couldn't be sure. She always noticed how most teenage urban kids talked like washed-up rappers. She wondered if this was the way in which they addressed their parents, who no doubt owned brownstones down the street and summered in the Hamptons.

As she prepared to go in, the door of the deli blew open and two more boys emerged in a fog of addled testosterone. In their hands they clutched brown paper bags. Sabine couldn't believe that they had just bought forties. There was no way they could pass for even sixteen, much less twenty-one. And it was only noon!

One of the boys reached into the bag. Sabine braced herself for the inevitable bottle of Olde English. To her surprise, he pulled out a carton of . . . soy milk!?

Could this really be happening? She looked around, hoping someone else was there to witness this.

"Yo, that mess tastes like garbage," said the Asian boy.

"Yo, this shit is mad good son," answered the soy-milk lover. And with that, he twisted off its cap and began drinking it straight from the carton. His other brown-bagged friend followed suit.

Sabine, barely able to contain herself, pushed past them into the fluorescent-lit deli and burst into laughter. *What!? You cannot write this shit! Soy-guzzling Brooklyn gangsters!?*

She ambled over to the refrigerator and pulled out a bottle of water, shaking her head at what she had just witnessed. Sometimes stories just wrote themselves. She smiled broadly, pleased by the universe's unexpected inspiration.

She couldn't wait to get home to put it on paper. It was too good.

Part III

Rechaka

chapter twenty

Sabine

$\int$ abine uncorked the wine and poured herself a glass. She made a mental note to brush her teeth before she left the apartment. Nothing was worse than red wine mouth. Well, maybe Kool-Aid mouth. Thankfully, there was no danger of that happening. Orange Crush mouth, maybe. It was a guilty pleasure of Sabine's left over from childhood. Sometimes in the summer she would buy a can and relish the syrupy sweetness as it coursed down her throat. It always made her feel six again.

Tonight was her date with Zach. *Breathe.* She had almost fully convinced herself that their meeting was a figment of her overactive imagination thanks to the fact that they had not spoken—cyber, textually, or otherwise—since last Saturday. But then, as she was walking home from the subway after brunch with Naomi, her phone rang. She rabidly dug in her suddenly bottomless bag, hoping that it was him but expecting to see her mother's digits. To her great surprise and embarrassing joy, her ID displayed a 212 number that she had never seen before. *Zach?* She briefly considered not picking it up, but in the end, she couldn't help herself.

"Hello," she answered, as nonchalantly as possible.

"Um, Sabine?" asked Zach. His voice sounded better than she remembered, but not too smooth. That was a good thing. The last guy Sabine had gone out with had a voice like butter, and he had ended up being an asshole of massive proportions. Zach's voice was manly, but it also had a hint of boyishness to it.

"Hi!" replied Sabine, revising her plan to play it cool. Life was too short.

Zach laughed. "Hey. It's nice to hear your voice."

Sabine's smile threatened to tear through her cheekbones and boomerang around the room. "Yours, too," she agreed. "What's up?"

"I just wanted to make sure that we were still on for tonight," said Zach, sounding a little unsure of himself. Sabine liked his vulnerability. It made her feel less self-conscious about her own.

"Of course," she had replied. "Eight o'clock, right?"

"Yep, eight, your doorstep, be there or be square." He laughed. "Jesus, I can't believe I just said that."

"It's okay," replied Sabine. "I am a huge fan of nerdy catch phrases. See you later, alligator!"

"I'm not going to dig myself any deeper into the nerd hole," said Zach, refusing to go for the obvious crocodile closer. "I'll see you soon. I'm . . . I'm really looking forward to it, Sabine."

"Me, too." She had hung up and stomped her feet like an excited toddler before breaking into a sprint back to her place.

Now, just over a half hour before Zach's arrival, she was completely ready. There was not one stray eyebrow hair left to pluck, or any tendrils left to be expertly mussed. All appropriate parts were shaved and she was moisturized head to toe. She had even rubbed the tinted moisturizer that her mother claimed was "God's work, in a bottle" all over her face before painstakingly applying the small amount of makeup she usually wore.

Her text alarm went off. She picked it up, her heart pounding in her chest at the thought of Zach, canceling.

"Speak of the devil," she said aloud, as her heart resumed its normal pattern. It was her mother. She had just recently learned to text—her friend's seven-year-old granddaughter had given her an expert tutorial, including a brief session on texting jargon.

"Hey gurl!" her mother had typed. Sabine cringed. "What RU up 2? Ready for your hot d8? Don't forget to wax! LOL."

Kill me now. Nothing was more cringe-inducing than a sixty-five-year-old woman trying to kick slang. Except maybe a thirty-two-year-old woman uttering the phrase *kick slang.* Sabine made a mental note to follow her own advice.

She put down the phone and surveyed herself in the mirror. She looked good. Pretty even. She smiled at her reflection and took another sip of her wine. Just then, the buzzer rang shrilly, wrenching her out of her composed state and directly depositing her into a state of panic.

She flew around the apartment like a crazed bird. Wine corked, check. Glass in sink, check. Quick brush of teeth to avoid red wine mouth, check. Lip gloss reapplication, check. Nothing on fire, check. Jacket, check. Door locked, check. She took a deep breath outside her apartment door. This was it.

She bounded down the stairs, careful not to take them too quickly. It would be typical for her to break her ankle now. Safely at the bottom, she peered out the glass partition on the door. There he was, in all his Subway Crush, Raisin Jewel glory.

"Hey," she said, her voice quivering in excitement.

"Hey!" He moved to hug her.

I'm touching him! His shoulders felt so strong and warm. She fought the urge to lick his neck.

They disentangled and looked at each other, both of them with huge grins plastered across their faces.

"You look pretty," said Zach.

"Thanks," answered Sabine, feeling uncomfortable under his gaze. "So do you."

"I always wondered what color your eyes were," he continued. "It was impossible to know from the other side of the subway car. They're not quite green," he said, peering in closely for a thorough examination, "and they're not quite brown."

"They're hazel," Sabine explained. Jesus, he was cute.

"Hazel," he repeated. "They look like tiger eyes."

Sabine laughed. "Thanks, Zach. And your eyes are chocolate brown. I always knew that, somehow."

"Should we go? Tiger and chocolate, out on the town?"

"Yeah, let's."

"Make a left here," Zach instructed. "I thought we'd get a drink and then eat some Mexican food. Wait, do you like Mexican food?"

"Love it. If I could bathe with avocado, I would."

"Oh good. Walking over here, I realized that I didn't have a Plan B. If you hated Mexican food, we would have been screwed."

"If I didn't like Mexican food, I would be screwed, period. A person without love for soft tacos is a person without a soul."

"I'm putting that on my tombstone," said Zach. Sabine smiled. Their chemistry was palpable. "Listen, I'm sorry that I didn't call you all week," he offered nervously. "Not that you were expecting it or anything. I mean, I was definitely thinking about you, I just had this monster case at work. . . ."

"Hey, it's okay. I figured as much. I had a crazy week, too." Sabine was impressed that Zach had brought up his absence himself. Who was this guy? He was almost too perfect. She kept expecting some douchey Ashton Kutcher look-alike to jump out of a moving taxi and tell her that she was being punk'd. As if on cue, Zach grabbed her hand.

The conversation continued to flow effortlessly as they hopped over slush piles the color of thunderclouds to get to the bar and then the restaurant. The physical contact increased organically as well—a laugh turned into a thigh grab; the tasting of each other's entrée; Zach's hand at the small of Sabine's back as he followed her out of the restaurant.

Walking home, Sabine pretended to be entranced by the activity on the street. Inside her head, however, she was quickly weighing the pros and cons of inviting him in.

Pro: good sex. Con: bad sex. Valid pro: having sex with Subway Crush! Subway Crush!!! Valid con: blowing any chance of a real relationship because she was so quick to hop into bed.

Do I even want a real relationship? She pondered the inevitable decline of her independence as a result of said relationship and wondered.

"Hey, whatcha' thinkin' about?" asked Zach, putting his warm, strong hand over hers and breaking Sabine out of her thoughts.

"Oh, nothing." *Well, actually, I'm wondering if fucking you is a good idea.* They arrived at her apartment, unclasped hands, and faced each other awkwardly.

"I had a great time with you tonight," said Zach. "You're just like I thought you would be and more." He laughed nervously. "Jesus, that sounded goofy. But hopefully you know what I mean. So, next weekend, are you around?" he asked.

"What?" she answered, shaken out of her pro/con game of sexual roulette.

Zach looked slightly puzzled by her confusion. "Zach, I am so sorry. My brain was out to lunch a couple of minutes ago. I'm afraid I missed everything you said."

"What were you thinking about?"

Sabine decided to tell the truth. She had a feeling that Zach would get it. They were both adults. To pretend that sex wasn't on either of their minds was futile.

"I was wondering whether I should ask you up or not," she explained, feeling bashful.

"Oh yeah?" said Zach, with a coy smile. "What did you decide?"

"I couldn't come to a unanimous head decision. Naturally, I would love for you to come up, but I just don't want to do anything stupid, you know?"

"I do," answered Zach, taking her gloved hands in his. "That's actually what I was telling you while you were in la-la land. I want to come up more than anything, but I think I'm just going to go home instead. I dunno, I . . . I don't want to rush things."

Sabine smiled. "I agree. Let's use our brains and not our . . ."

"Other things," said Zach, finishing her sentence. "I really want to see you again. That's why I was asking you if you were around next weekend. Saturday night, maybe?"

"I am."

"Good." Zach pulled her close and kissed her lips. A long, lingering peck. His lips felt like heaven: plush, soft, firm.

"See you," said Sabine, pulling away before she wrestled him to the ground. "Thanks for tonight."

"See you."

Sabine turned and went inside.

In her apartment, she unzipped her jacket and cuddled a confused Lassie. "Lassieeee," she cooed, "he's perfect." Lassie was unimpressed. He wriggled out of Sabine's grasp.

Lying on her couch and looking up at her ceiling, Sabine smiled broadly. Was it possible that she had finally met a decent guy? In New York?! Talk about an urban legend.

She undressed and washed her face, realizing that the margaritas she guzzled at dinner were stronger than she had thought. She winced at the idea of her inevitable tequila hangover and the manuscript she had to edit. Not a fruitful combination.

She turned out the lights and hopped into bed, relishing the heavy warmth of her down comforter. Her phone beeped on her bedside table.

"Good night, Subway Girl," it read.

Underneath her comforter, Sabine did a mini victory jig and rolled her head back and forth in extreme happiness. Urban legend or not, she was downright giddy.

"Good night, Lassie," she whispered, opting not to text back. She placed her phone back on the table and rolled herself into a blanket burrito, drifting off to sleep with a huge grin plastered across her face.

chapter twenty-one

Charlie

T his is so good," Charlie announced appreciatively. She swallowed the rest of her ambitious bite of beet salad. "Wow. Beets are my new favorite vegetable."

Sasha nodded in agreement. "Yeah, they are really delicious. My salad isn't half bad either." She took another bite as Charlie sipped from her glass of wine. "So, how's Prana?" she asked, after swallowing. She and Charlie were out for their annual March 14 dinner. Annoyed by the concept of Valentine's Day, they had been treating the same day a month later as their big middle finger to the Hallmark-inspired establishment for three years running. Sasha had introduced the tradition during a romantically bleak time in their lives—calling it an excuse to celebrate themselves. In reality, it was more of an excuse to indulge in yummy, overpriced food and drink too much.

"The same, really," answered Charlie. "Some days are great and some days are a pain in the ass. Like electric bill day for example."

"I hear that. We are raped by Con Ed every month. I can't wait for spring. That's at least three months of no heat and blessed sunlight."

"Spring! I want it so badly. Winter always stretches on for eternity. Did I tell you about my newish Saturday class?" asked Charlie as the waiter cleared their salad plates.

"No, what's the deal?"

"You know that BU reunion thing I went to a few weeks back?"

"Yeah, the one that you were dreading?" asked Sasha, with a sly smile.

"Yep, that's the one. I ended up running into three women I used to go to school with. We started talking and I turned on the charm. Next thing I knew, they all agreed to start a Saturday beginners' intensive."

"Awesome! But wait, there's only three in a Saturday class? Aren't you losing money with such an exclusive class? Three students—"

"Well, on paper I know that it sounds a bit small, especially for such a potentially busy time slot. But it works out, you know? The class is early and they're paying a bit more for my undivided attention."

"Oh, I get it. Cool. So, do you like the class?"

"You know what, I really do." Charlie took a piece of bread from the basket on the table and dunked it in some olive oil. "They're all really interesting women."

"Are you guys buddies now?" asked Sasha.

"Well, we're all very friendly. But I can't really be friends with them if I'm their teacher. I think that blurs the lines a little too much."

"You and your lines. You know, it's okay to push boundaries sometimes, Charlie. If you like these women, you can be friends with them. I think friendship might actually be a good thing in such a small class. Their comfort around you would probably filter right into a more pronounced sense of their comfort with yoga."

"You think so?" She considered Sasha's argument. The truth was, she did want to open up a bit more to Bess, Sabine, and Naomi—to be a person outside of just their yoga instructor. She just wasn't sure that it was such a good idea. The idea of mixing business with pleasure and letting down her guard was always a scary one for her. There were too many risks involved. But maybe Sasha was right. Charlie's rigidity often was her worst enemy. Even though she was aware of this, it was hard to break the habit. There was a sense of safety in it.

"I do," answered Sasha. "Change is not always a bad thing, you know."

"I know." The waitress returned with their entrées and placed them on the table with a smile. "Speaking of change," said Charlie, happy to maneuver her way out of the conversation, "what's new with you? Anything to report?"

Sasha smiled coyly, looking down at her lobster ravioli. "Actually, yes."

"Do tell!" exclaimed Charlie. It wasn't like Sasha to hold anything back.

"I met someone," she whispered, a broad smile lighting up her face like a halogen lamp.

"No way!" exclaimed Charlie. "That's tremendous. Give me details now, you minx!"

Sasha laughed. "I met him in class."

"What? Talk about blurring the lines! Jesus, Sash, what happened?"

"I know, I know. I didn't plan on it happening, it kind of just did." Sasha took a bite of her ravioli.

"Hurry up and swallow!" Charlie practically yelled. "Oh wait, I guess that's a pretty appropriate line given the context of our conversation."

"Dirty mind! Very funny. He started coming to my advanced

class on Tuesday nights. I noticed him right away, of course, but I was determined not to fall pray to the typical 'yoga guy' charms. I figured he was there to ogle some chicks in tank tops, you know?"

"Do I ever," answered Charlie. She had encountered many yoga guys in her time. All about small shorts and tribal tattoos, they would fumble through the classes with their roving eyes, anxiously awaiting the postclass hang, whereupon they would pounce on the first taker.

"Anyway, a couple of weeks passed and there was none of that. He would come in, set up his mat in the back of the studio, and then, as soon as class was over, he would leave. No hanging around, no nothing," Sasha explained.

"How's his practice?" asked Charlie.

"Really graceful. He knows what he's doing. And completely unobtrusive, you know? Humble."

"Humble, hot, and quick to leave?" asked Charlie. "Sounds like a dream."

"Tell me about it. Anyway, I guess about the third week in, my curiosity got the better of me, and I asked him what his name was before class."

"What's his name?" asked Charlie. "I'm imagining something tantalizingly exotic, like Rafaelo or something."

"Not quite," said Sasha. "Unless you consider Adam exotic."

Charlie laughed. "Well, maybe it's exotic in some country. So, he told you his name and the next thing you know, you guys are in love?"

"Not exactly. He told me his name and then it was just a gradual thing, you know? Over the next four of five classes, we just started opening up a bit to each other. It started very quietly, with a hello and then just kind of innocently led to a coffee one afternoon after class. That coffee date led to a movie, and then the rest is history I guess."

"Wait, so you guys started dating while he was taking your class? Isn't that a bad idea? Did the rest of the class catch on?"

"We went out two or three times before things became romantic," explained Sasha. "Sure, I had reservations about bending the constraints of my professionalism. But I wasn't about to let the first guy who had interested me in months slip out of my fingers because of some antiquated notion that didn't even apply to our situation. I mean, this isn't Psych 101 in college, you know, where I'm the professor and he's the young, naïve student. These are two consenting adults in a very physically oriented environment."

"That is true," agreed Charlie. The ferocity of Sasha's defense told her that this was not the first time she had had to explain their romance. "But still, I would be wary."

"Well, I was. When it became apparent that we had romantic feelings for each other, he noticed my hesitation about taking things to the next level. He asked me if it would make me feel better if he stopped coming to class. I told him that it would, so he stopped. He takes Gil's class on Tuesday nights now."

"Wow, that was easy enough to work out," said Charlie. "How long have you guys been seeing each other?"

"Since December," answered Sasha, smiling bashfully.

"What? You've been seeing him since December and you're just telling me now? It's March!"

"I know, it's sort of wack, Charlie, but you have to understand—I haven't told anyone until only very recently. There's something amazing about keeping something like this to yourself for a while. Then it's just the two of you. It's yours and nobody else can penetrate the bubble. It's nice."

Charlie shook her head. "I guess I can see your point, Sasha. But I can't help but be a little hurt. All of those weekends when I asked you what you had been up to, you never once mentioned his name. You were lying to me."

"I know, and I'm sorry about that. I just really wanted to keep it to myself for a while. We planned on telling our friends sooner obviously, but life kind of got in the way."

"Fair enough," said Charlie. She guessed she could see where Sasha was coming from, despite her hurt feelings. "I can see that you're crazy about him." She smiled at Sasha. "When you talk about him, your eyes crinkle."

"They do?" asked Sasha. She smiled. "It's true, Charlie, I'm in love with him. He is an amazing guy. I never thought I could feel this way again, after Nick." Nick had broken up with Sasha around the same time Charlie's heart had been annihilated by Neil. They had bonded over their mutual heartache.

Thinking back on those days, Charlie's heart melted a bit. Now that Sasha had healed, who could she turn to when she had a Neil relapse? She suddenly felt very alone. She took a deep breath, determined not to let her self-pity steal her friend's thunder. "Sasha, I am so happy for you!" she exclaimed. "I can't wait to meet him."

"Thanks, Charlie. I really think you'll dig him." The waitress returned to clear their plates. Charlie refilled her glass of wine. She needed a sip, badly.

"Hey, are you seeing anyone new?" Sasha asked.

Charlie almost spit her wine out. "Sasha, come on now, you know I'm not." Despite herself, her thoughts drifted to Mario. She considered bringing him up, but decided against it. Confessing her burgeoning lust for the deli guy seemed silly somehow.

"What about Facebook?" asked Sasha. "Any fresh meat there?"

Charlie thought about their previous conversation about Facebook being a porthole to your sexual past. So far, the closest she had come to reuniting with a former conquest was her middle school boyfriend, Jason Healey, who she had maybe pecked on the lips once during a particularly humiliating game of spin the bottle. Jason now lived in Hartford and had four kids with his wife, Misty.

"Unless you count being super-poked as foreplay, no," Charlie replied.

Sasha laughed. "Just wait. If you build it, they will come. You've been on there for only a couple of weeks, right?"

"Yeah," answered Charlie. "I haven't really had time to mess around with it yet." She didn't tell Sasha that she had had to bribe herself not to search for Neil. Just last week, as she hovered over her keyboard about to enter his name into the search engine, she had promised herself a new pair of boots if she refrained from doing so. The boots had won out, but she wasn't sure how long she could afford to ignore her instincts.

"Has Neil contacted you yet?" Sasha peered at Charlie with her gray eyes, her concern and judgment palpable. Sasha knew all about their relationship, ugly breakup, and ever-lingering aftermath. Sometimes she indulged Charlie and listened to her wax poetic about her unhealthy connection to him and her desire to see him again, but sometimes—and certainly much more in the past year or so—she wasn't having it. She had begged Charlie to talk to a therapist about her inability to move on, but Charlie had brushed her off, saying that she would get over him in her own time. Sasha had reminded her that four years was about three years too much of her own time. Charlie had stormed out of the restaurant that night in a blaze of anger and resentment. They hadn't spoken for two months afterward, at which point Charlie's loneliness had gotten the better of her. She missed Sasha terribly when she wasn't around. They could be friends; Charlie just wouldn't bring Neil up in conversation. Another boundary imposed of her own accord. It was easier that way.

"No," Charlie answered. "I'm sure he won't."

Sasha nodded, obviously holding back. "I hope he doesn't,

Charlie," she said, as carefully as possible. "The last thing you need is him back in your life, even in cyber-form."

Charlie nodded her assent, suddenly feeling very full. Her waistband dug into her stomach. "Hey, we should get going," she said, motioning for the check.

"No dessert? I was saving some room for tiramisu."

"No, not for me," answered Charlie. "That gnocchi was enough to keep me full for weeks. Besides, I bet you and Adam have plans later."

Sasha blushed. "I'm meeting him out actually. He's with some friends of his at a bar in Brooklyn. You should come!"

"No way. You're nuts. I'm too full to speak properly. Another time, though. I really want to meet him."

Sasha smiled as she paid her half of the bill and handed it to Charlie for her portion. "Fair enough," she said.

They got up from the table and made their way out into the blustery night. Snow from that week's dumping was piled high in the street corners, melting slowly into its inevitable gray, trash-filled slush mounds.

"Happy March fourteenth, Sash," said Charlie, enveloping her in a hug. "I am so happy for you and Adam. No one deserves love more than you do."

Sasha hugged her back. "Except maybe you. Thanks, Charlie. Get home safe!" The two women broke from their down-jacket embrace and headed off in separate directions.

Charlie ducked her head low against the cold as she walked away. Despite herself, she fought back tears. She wondered if Neil had ruined her forever. She couldn't even imagine loving again. As if on cue, she passed one of their favorite bars. They had come here all the time when they were first together. She stopped and looked in its window. Exactly the same. Same bartender even. She decided to go in for a drink.

"What can I get you?" he asked, staring at her blankly. Charlie wondered why she expected him to remember her, four years after the fact. The guy probably met dozens of new people every night. She ordered a Scotch on the rocks and slowly sipped the amber liquid. She knew she would regret the hard alcohol the next morning, but it was that kind of night.

Why had she decided to come in here? The last time she had set foot inside this place, her life had come crashing down all around her. She and Neil had been fighting all the time. He had suddenly become an aggressive super-guru of sorts—filling his days with meditation and yoga on her dime because he didn't have a job. She would come home after a full day of work to find him meditating in their tiny studio apartment. He would ask her to join him and she would refuse. She just wanted a bit of space and time to herself, and if that involved *Access Hollywood*, then so be it. They would hiss at each other and, inevitably, he would leave in a huff, and she would cry into her Lean Cuisine. Charlie sighed heavily, remembering.

Her Lean Cuisine nights had become more and more routine as Neil began to avoid her altogether by never being home. She began to miss him, and then her paranoia set in. If he wasn't with her, where the hell was he? How many meditation workshops could one man take? He certainly wasn't working anywhere. Her account balance told her that much.

She had set out one night on a walk through their neighborhood, peering into their haunts hoping to catch a glimpse of him and disgusted by her own desperation. Suddenly, she had found him. At this bar. Their bar. She had walked in, hoping to sidle up to him and tell him she missed him, when she had seen that he was not alone. Beside him sat a woman—the term *woman* loosely applied, as she didn't look a day over nineteen—batting her eyes at him coquettishly. Charlie's stomach had dropped into her shoes. Instinctually, she knew that this nymph was trouble. As she approached, Neil turned, his eyes conveying shock and then, quickly, fright. Trouble indeed.

"Charlie!" he had exclaimed overzealously. "Hey! This is Luna. She's in my yoga class."

Luna!? "Hello," she murmured.

Luna looked Charlie up and down with contempt. "Hi," she answered. No guilt, no nothing. Just two yoga friends out for a drink. *Yeah, right.* Charlie had wanted to rip Luna's blond braids out of her head. The conversation between the three of them had been stilted and awkward, with Neil attempting to cover his tracks and failing miserably. Luna had proved to be as annoying as she appeared, talking incessantly about her spiritual awakening in Starbucks months earlier. *Starbucks.* As she droned on, Charlie knew. She knew that either Neil was fucking her or wanted to fuck this dumb little girl. It was over. Neil had left with Charlie that night, but their walk home was a silent one. There was nothing to say. A few weeks later, when Neil announced that he was leaving Charlie for Luna because "they had more of a spiritual connection," Charlie had not been surprised.

She finished her drink, wondering if they were still together. She hoped that Luna had left Neil's ass in the dust as karmic retribution. She took a deep "woe is me" breath for good measure, and shook her head back and forth, reeling a little from the combination of heavy food, drink, and her walk down memory lane. She paid up and walked outside into the wind, stumbling slightly. The subway entrance seemed miles away suddenly. She raised her hand to hail a cab. Tonight, she deserved door-to-door service.

chapter twenty-two

Naomi

"Mommmm! Where's my backpack?" shrieked Noah.

Naomi, lying on her bed with a cold washcloth over her eyes, cringed at the decibel of his voice. She pulled her self-made compress from her face. Last night had marked her second monstrous headache that week. They had both appeared from out of nowhere and knocked her sideways. Thankfully, the first one had struck at night, when Noah was in bed, but last night, it had hit in the early evening just as she was making him dinner. Heavy and merciless, it had crept up from the top of her neck and lodged itself in the right side of her brain. Somehow she had been able to get Noah's fish sticks cooked and out on the table, but that was about all the energy she was able to muster. She had told Noah that she didn't feel well and taken refuge in her dark bedroom. Lying on her bed, the pain in her skull seemed to pulse into the mattress, making the entire room vibrate. Noah had come in to comfort her, his fright apparent. He had put his warm little paw on her forehead and snuggled in beside her for a few minutes. Virtually incapacitated, Naomi had asked him if he could put himself to bed. He had nodded solemnly that yes, he could. This morning, after half a bottle of Motrin, a heating pad, and maybe two hours of sleep tops, she could barely function.

Noah, however, had been operating at full speed since 6 AM—barely able to contain his excitement about Mini-Noah going to Paris. Naomi was trying with all her might to just go with the flow and support her son's unbridled excitement, but part of her—with or without her headache hangover—dreaded the outcome. Try as she might, she just couldn't see Gene upholding his end of the bargain. Visions of his return without Mini-Noah danced through her brain—the mad scramble of redesigning the tiny paper cutout and dragging him all over the city would inevitably fall to her.

"Noah, we talked about screaming in the house," she replied as calmly as possible, suppressing the urge to scream back at him and thereby setting exactly the wrong example.

She got up to find Noah lying on his bedroom floor, peering under his bed with a look of utter panic on his face. "Sorry, Mom. I just . . . I just can't find my backpack. Do you know where it is?" His voice wavered as tears pooled in his big blue eyes.

"When was the last time you had it, baby?" she asked, extending her hand to pull him up. "Let's retrace our steps. I'll bet you a hot chocolate from Fannie's that it's right where you left it."

Noah rose to his red-sneakered feet. "I came home with it on Friday," he ventured, walking hand in hand with Naomi out to the living room. "It was on my back."

"Yes, that's usually where backpacks live."

Noah looked up at her, annoyed by her casual attitude. "Mom, this is serious!" he reprimanded. Naomi fought back a laugh at Noah's sudden sternness.

"I'm sorry, of course it is, Noah. Okay, so it was on your back. And then you took it off and dropped it where?"

"I took it off and dropped it right here, next to the coats," he replied, motioning to the floor beneath the coat rack.

"And that was the last time you saw it?"

Noah's brow furrowed as he tried to remember. "No. Yesterday I had it. While you were at yoga, Cee Cee and I read about the plate tectonic theory."

"The plate tectonic theory?" she asked, experiencing a burst of nostalgia. How long had it been since she had heard that phrase? She paused for a moment, trying to remember when she had learned about it herself. Fifth grade, maybe? Noah was in second. *Well, at least the education system is advancing,* she thought to herself, looking for the silver lining on a cloud that made her feel really old.

"Yes, Mom," Noah whined, clearly attuned to her lack of investment in the task at hand.

"Okay, so where did you guys talk about that? In the kitchen?"

Noah ran ahead of her to investigate. "We did talk about it in the kitchen. Cee Cee made me pancakes for breakfast while we talked about it." He got down on all fours to investigate. "Here it is!" he exclaimed triumphantly, holding the small, black bag up with the flourish of a winning prizefighter. "Mom, we found it!" His eyes lit up like little Christmas trees.

"See, baby, I told you it was here," Naomi replied, happy to have caused her son such unmitigated joy. Gene might be taking Mini-Noah to Paris, but she was still the mama. Small victories like this one were her specialty.

"Thanks!" he cried, running at her like a ram and hugging her waist. "That was a close one. Mini-Noah is in here!"

"Oh, I'm so glad he's safe!"

"Me, too. Dad's picking him up for Paris today," he explained, even though Naomi was all too aware of his plan.

Naomi looked at the clock over the stove. "Speaking of, you better get your jacket on. Your dad is going to be here any second." She dreaded the pickup. There was always an awkward hello as she battled years of repressed resentment and passed Noah over to Gene. It took everything she had not to make some snide remark about Gene's hipster jacket or the new tattoo that peeked out of its cuff. The man was spending hundreds, if not thousands, of dollars in an attempt to stay young and current while Naomi was buying peanut butter and Flintstone vitamins. The disparities in their lives made her want to scream. And scream she would have if Gene was not paying child support. Thankfully, he was. Not always on time, of course, but he was.

Just then, the buzzer rang. Naomi froze. "Okay, get your jacket on," she told Noah, "and your scarf and hat and gloves." Noah frowned at her. He hated wearing a hat, saying his "head couldn't breathe" every time she crammed it on top of his curls. "No arguments! It's freezing out. Even Mini-Noah needs a hat today."

The buzzer rang again. Noah wasn't moving. He gave Naomi a look of discomfort. "What's the problem?" she asked him, exasperated.

"Mom, I have to go to the bathroom," he whispered.

"Okay, fine, go pee, honey."

Noah shook his head. "No, number two," he said, with a pained look on his face.

Naomi took a deep breath. It was like clockwork with Noah. Inevitably, whenever they had to be somewhere, he had to stop everything and go to the bathroom. He was cursed with Jewish bowels.

"Okay, go ahead. I'll have your dad come up and wait." Noah took off for the bathroom and she surveyed the apartment. It was a mess.

Oh well, I guess Gene should see how the other half lives. She buzzed him in just in time to realize that she was in her pajamas. *Great,* she thought, as she made an attempt to smooth down the cowlick that she knew was roostering off her head.

She could hear Gene's big man boots (designer, no doubt) bounding up the stairs. *Clomp, clomp, clomp* and then the knock. It was a hesitant knock. *Good. Some registered discomfort being on my turf.* She took a deep breath, noticed that she had not brushed her teeth, and opened the door.

"Hey, Naomi," Gene said. As much as Naomi disliked him, there was no denying the power of his looks. If the term *rugged, hipster handsomeness* were embraced by *Webster's*, there would be a picture of Gene immediately following it.

Tall and sinuous, he reached about six foot three in his boots. His brown hair flopped lazily around his ears and curled against the back of his neck. Olive skin, blue eyes, and dazzling white choppers finished off the picture. For someone who had lived a life that was decidedly unhealthy in all the predictable ways, Gene was distressingly perfect.

Naomi wondered if he still spent late nights snorting various substances with models young enough, at this point, to be his daughters. She had no idea, actually. Today, as he stood in front of her preparing to take their son on a Sunday adventure, she certainly hoped not.

"Hi, Gene. Sorry you had to come up, Noah's in the bathroom. Come on in." She extended her arm stiffly into the apartment, inviting him to cross the threshold. Gene's eyes darted around the interior as he gingerly stepped in.

"He's in the bathroom, huh?" asked Gene, with a knowing smirk. "That kid has the bowels of a fifty-year-old man. At least we know he'll always be regular, huh?" He smiled then, at Naomi, who was fighting back the urge to scream, "What do you know about my son's bowels!? You know nothing! He's MINE! Those bowels are MINE!" but thought better of it. To end up in a wrestling match about an eight-year-old's digestive tract was a bad way to start her Sunday.

"Yeah, can't take him anywhere." She paused. "Sorry for the mess. I was going to clean up today, while you guys were hanging out . . . you know, the apartment and well, me." Her headache returned, subtly pulsing behind her temples.

"Oh please, this place is clean as a whistle," said Gene. "If Maribel didn't come once a week to my crib, it would look like Armageddon."

Naomi reeled at both the fact that Gene referred to his apartment as his "crib" and the fact that he could afford a maid. She made a mental note to be more of a bitch when he was late on his Noah payments.

Gene took a seat on the couch and sat awkwardly. "You're looking good, Naomi," he said, his head cocked in appraisal.

Naomi blushed involuntarily. "Gene, give me a break. I look like hell. I haven't even had a chance to brush my teeth yet."

"No, you look cute. You always looked best in the morning. No makeup suits you."

What do you know about me in the morning!? Naomi screamed at him in her head. Aloud she said, "Thanks, I guess," as graciously as she could. She sat in the chair diagonal from the couch. "So, I hear you're going to Paris."

Gene's eyes lit up. "Yeah, I'm going to shoot a campaign for Catherine Malandrino. Do you know her clothes?"

Naomi thought of her store in SoHo. She had gone in once and stroked the fabrics like a lovelorn teenager. The price tags had almost made her weep. "Oh yeah! She does some beautiful work."

"Yeah, it's really nice, right?" agreed Gene. "She's a cool lady, too."

Just then, Noah burst out of the bathroom like a rocket. "Dad!" he cried, running to the couch. He stopped short, noticing Naomi sitting opposite his father. "Hi, Mom, hi, Dad!" he said, sizing up the visual. It dawned on Naomi that her son had never seen his parents inhabit the same space so casually. She hoped he wasn't getting any ideas. She had been very careful not to bad-mouth Gene in front of him, but if Noah started in on her about more three-way "family" hangouts, her carefully crafted facade would crumble.

"Hey, champ!" replied Gene, leaning over to envelop Noah in a gigantic hug.

"Well, I think we're gonna take off," offered Gene, standing up from the couch. "Put your coat on, Noah," he added. "It's like Siberia out there."

Noah ran to the coat rack and pulled his jacket from one of its hooks, his excitement causing an avalanche of various coats and sweaters. He looked at Naomi, alarmed.

"Noah, don't worry, I'll pick those up," she replied to his guilty gaze. "Have fun today," she added.

She looked to Gene. "Please make sure he keeps his hat on," she said. "He hates it, but he needs it."

"You got it. You know what, I'll wear mine, too." He reached into his jacket pocket to produce a knit cap. Noah's eyes lit up. Hats were officially cool again.

"Bye, Mom!"

"Bye, Noah!"

"Dad, have you really been to Siberia?" she heard Noah ask as the door shut behind them.

Naomi sank down on the couch and exhaled deeply. Seeing Gene was always hard, although not for any lovelorn reasons. His mere presence took her back to those last, awful days they had spent together before he took off, on his lame Vespa, of course, to leave her behind with their very tiny baby growing inside her. After days of trying to break through the drug-addled fog of denial that Gene had been living in, it was glaringly apparent that she was going to have that baby on her own. There was no room in Gene's life for any sort of responsibility, much less a human life.

Thinking back, Naomi was still surprised at her decision to keep their baby, despite all the odds stacked against her. For her, Noah had been a gift—a wake-up call in the form of a baby. Naomi had never been very religious, but it was the closest thing to divine intervention she had ever experienced. She had been lost, and now she was found.

Gene didn't want to be found, so he had left her in their giant, unpaid-for apartment in Dumbo, to pick up the pieces. Naomi's parents had swooped in, reserving judgment until she was safe, and cleaned up the mess. They had somehow managed to sell her apartment, get her home to the apartment she had grown up in on the Upper West Side, and prepare her for two new lives—hers and Noah's. She smiled, thinking about their selflessness. To rescue their hot mess of a pregnant, alone, and adult daughter like that . . . Wow. She teared up at the thought.

Naomi picked up her cell phone to call them, realizing suddenly that she and Noah hadn't seen them in more than a month. It was amazing how Brooklyn and the Upper West Side could feel like two separate continents, mass transit be damned. She dialed the number and looked at the clock. It was 11:00. They would no doubt be reading the paper—her dad waxing poetic about Maureen Dowd and her mother concentrating intently on the crossword, a scooped-out bagel on a plate in front of her.

"Hello," answered her mom.

"Hi, Mama. It's me."

"Hi, baby," she answered, her voice dancing with delight. "How are you? We miss you."

"I'm well," Naomi answered, her eyes suddenly tearing up again. What was it about hearing your mother's voice when you were down? Tears were a Pavlovian response, even now, at thirty-two. She wondered if Noah would have the same, eternal reaction to her concern.

"You don't sound well, Naomi. Are you okay? Is Noah okay? Do you want to come up here for some turkey chili tonight?"

Naomi laughed, moved by her mother's breathless questions and inevitable invitation. "Mom, I'm fine. A little moody this morning, that's all. Noah's off with Gene for their play date." Her mother's silence followed. She and her father had been outraged by Gene's reentry into their lives, and still had a hard time accepting Naomi's decision. It had been a bone of contention between them, but eventually her parents had surrendered to her explanation of his child support and Noah's need for a male role model in his life.

"Gene might be an asshole, but he's Noah's father," she had explained. "He's back and he's grown up a lot. He wants to be involved. As long as we keep his presence to a minimum, I really don't see what the problem is. It would be unfair to deny Noah this happiness."

Her father had shaken his head in frustration. "He's not a good man," he had said to Naomi. "I don't like it, but what can I do? This is your child and your life. Please just promise that you won't forget what he did to you. Don't get caught up in his bullshit." He had paused and taken Naomi's hand in his own. "And if he misses a payment, you tell me, and I will kill him."

Naomi had laughed at the thought of her sweet father taking a hit on anything besides a tennis ball. One look into his eyes had shut her up though. He was serious. In that moment, Naomi understood the gravity of their sacrifice for her so many years before. Although they had never been anything but accommodating, it had strained them beyond belief. And now, looking at the wrinkles and creases in her father's kind face, she could see that it had aged them as well.

"Okay, Dad," she had replied. "Okay."

"Oh," Naomi's mom finally replied. "I hope they have their jackets and hats on. It is freezing out!"

"Yes, they do. Everyone is bundled into their little igloos, don't worry. Hey Mom, have you ever gotten a migraine?"

"Noooo, thank goodness. I rarely get headaches, knock on wood. Why?"

"I got this horrible headache last night. It was awful. Felt like a sumo wrestler was sitting on the right side of my head."

"Baby, that doesn't sound good. You don't normally get headaches do you?"

"Well no, except this is my second one in like, a week," answered Naomi. Her voice trembled a bit from the sudden frog in her throat. *I'm scared,* she thought.

"Oh honey, that sounds painful. Do you have your period?"

"No, Mom," answered Naomi, laughing at the predictability of her question. Ovulation or menstruation was the answer to almost all of her physical ailments according to her mother.

"You're not pregnant, are you?" her mom asked, lowering her voice to a whisper.

As if on cue, her father picked up the other phone. "What's all this whispering?" he asked.

"I am definitely not pregnant," answered Naomi. "Unless I am giving birth to the next messiah."

"Oh, thank goodness," answered her mother. Naomi rolled her eyes. Technically, Noah was an "accident," but it wasn't as though she hadn't been involved with his father at the time. Nevertheless, her mother seemed convinced that Naomi had never seen a condom or a package of birth control pills, which annoyed Naomi to no end.

"Ruth, of course she's not pregnant, come on now," her father interjected. "What's the problem, Nay? You feeling okay?"

Naomi teared up again, despite herself. What was it with her inability to accept concern? "I've been having these crazy headaches," she explained. "And my body has been feeling a bit off lately."

"What do you mean, off?" asked her mother. "You didn't mention that before."

"Give her a break, Ruth," said her father. "She's telling us now. Go on, Nay."

"Well, in yoga the other day my limbs just felt really heavy. Just to stretch my arms above my head seemed to take a ridiculous amount of effort."

"Maybe you're just out of shape," said her father.

"Maybe," answered Naomi. "I thought about that. But it feels different from just being out of shape. I can't explain it. And then, a couple of times, on and off, my legs have gotten this weird tingling sensation. Not too extreme or anything, just this slight vibration for what seems like no reason." *Wow, it feels good to say this out loud.* Without meaning to, Naomi had kept all of this to herself. It was as though she were ashamed by her physical limitations. *God forbid I need help.*

"Mom, Dad—hello? You're not saying anything! What?!"

"I don't know, Nay, this sounds kind of serious. Tingling is never normal in my book, especially if it's accompanied by painful headaches. Have you called your doctor?"

"No, not yet," answered Naomi. There it was, the lump in her throat again. *Why am I so scared of the doctor? I gave birth for chrissake! A physical should be a cakewalk.* Even as she tried to reason with her fear, she knew why she was so disinclined to go. Instinctively, whatever it was that was going on inside of her felt serious. Something that would require more than one doctor appointment serious.

"Why not?" asked her mom, slightly panicked. "How can somebody not call her doctor when her body is vibrating?"

"Mom, please, take it easy. I just haven't had time."

"You don't take care of yourself like you should." She paused before continuing. "Nay, I'm sorry. I'm just worried. The last thing I should be doing is yelling at you."

"Listen, my friend Bill is a neurologist at Mount Sinai," said her father. "I want you to see him. I'll set it up. He owes me a favor."

"Whoa Dad, take it easy! Shouldn't I see my GP first?" *A neurologist? What?*

"Honey, your father is right. The headaches and the tingling sound like brain stuff to me. Your GP will just send you to one anyway, once you describe your symptoms. This will make your life easier."

"And Bill is a nice guy," added her dad. "Don't worry. You know what, I'm going to call him now to set it up."

"But Dad, I—"

"Nay, it's not such a big deal. Don't worry. He's a good doctor who can tell you what, if anything, is going on. We love you, honey."

Naomi sighed deeply. Ten minutes ago she was just someone who had a bad headache last night. Now she was going to see a neurologist. "Okay, guys. Thank you. I love you, too."

"I'll call you back as soon as I set it up," said her father.

"Nay, go lie down," her mother added. "With Noah out of the house, you should get some rest."

"Okay, I will. Bye. Talk soon."

She hung up the phone and put her head in her hands. *What's going on in there?* she asked her body. The idea of her brain being in trouble made her want to cry. A sick brain was never a good thing.

Feeling the need to be with someone, Naomi decided to pop down to see Cecilia. She brushed her teeth and searched for something to bring down to her. Her eyes rested on a tube of styling cream that Felicity had given her. Naomi knew it would sit in her bathroom cabinet, unused, for months on end, despite her best intentions to try it out. She grabbed it, closed her door, and bounded down the stairs.

She knocked on Cecilia's door and realized that just getting out of her apartment after the heaviness of her conversation with her parents made her feel better. *Normal.*

The door opened and a frazzled Cecilia poked her head around its edges. Upon seeing Naomi, she smiled and then, immediately, blushed—her snow white skin enveloped by a pink cloud. If Naomi didn't know any better, she would think she had a fever. Wait, maybe she did.

"Hey Cee! Are you sick?" she instinctively put the backside of her hand against Cecilia's forehead.

"No, no, not sick." She pulled the door closed behind her.

"Can I come in, then?" asked Naomi, oblivious to her awkwardness. "I brought you a present!" She waved the tube in front of Cecilia's face.

"Uh, actually, no," answered Cecilia. She smiled coyly. Understanding struck Naomi like a lightning bolt.

"You have a man in there!" she whispered excitedly.

Cecilia nodded in response, her eyes twinkling.

"Oh my God! Okay, when he's gone, you come tell me everything!" She kissed Cecilia on the cheek and raced back up the stairs—her energy rejuvenated by Cecilia's conquest.

Back in her apartment, she collapsed on her bed, her heart racing. She was so happy for Cee! She was having sex! What a wonderful, unexpected turn of events on an otherwise dark day.

Sex. Sweet, wondrous sex. Naomi thought back, happy for the distraction. *How long has it been for me?* She cocked her head, pondering her libido or lack thereof in her pajamas. *Oh shit, I can't even remember!*

It couldn't have been . . . Wait, was it? Gene!?!? Have I really not had sex in eight years? She considered Noah's birthday. *What!? Have I not had sex IN ALMOST A DECADE!?* She raked her hands through her hair in amazed frustration. *Oh wait, that*

guy! Thank God. What was his name?! Michael? Mark? Mark!
She breathed a heavy sigh of relief, remembering him.

Her parents' friend, Cindy Carpstein, had set her up on a blind
date with Mark when Noah was almost two. Naomi had seen her
at a party and she, a single mother herself—two kids in college—
Lauren at Wesleyan and Andy at Princeton, thank you very much—
had insisted that Naomi return to the dating world.

"With this face," she had said, touching her cheek, "ya can't
sit inside all day watching *Sesame Street*. I have someone for you."
She had nodded wisely and brushed off Naomi's attempted re-
fusal. "He's my friend Shelia's son." She paused here for emphasis
and whispered, "A doctor." With that, she had sauntered off to
refill her wine spritzer at the bar. A week later, true to her word,
Cindy had come through.

Mark, clearly used to being set up by everyone his mother came
in contact with, had called Naomi to ask her out, and Naomi had
begrudgingly agreed. They had gone to the River Café in Brooklyn and Mark had been perfectly acceptable—for someone who
wasn't Naomi. Relatively funny, well-mannered, a good conver-
sationalist, with nice eyes and a receding hairline. Naomi drank
three glasses of Riesling on an empty stomach and then, seized
by the moment, she had gone home with him to his ridiculously
spare bachelor's loft in TriBeCa. The sex was forgettable as a result of her wine fog and Mark's less than skillful technique, but she
was determined to reclaim her vagina as something other than a
birthing canal. She doubted that that was Cindy's intention when
she set her up, but that's what the blind date had meant for Naomi.
A reclaiming.

She had snuck out of Mark's apartment under the cover of
night, satiated only by the fact that she had done what she needed
to do, and returned to her asexual existence with great fervor.

Naomi rolled onto her belly. She flexed her fingers and toes.

Maybe her body was just telling her to slow down, to take it easy for a change. Her anxiety about Mini-Noah was silly. What was there to worry about? It was a paper doll. And if Gene screwed up, so what?! It was time for her to release her grip on things that were out of her control. To be kinder to herself.

Do I buy that? she wondered, as she closed her eyes and burrowed beneath her blankets. *That the tingling and the headaches are just wake-up calls from my body and nothing else? I want to believe it. More than anything. But I don't think I do.*

chapter twenty-three

Drinks

$\int$abine sat at the bar, halfheartedly attempting to edit a manuscript about a female werewolf with a raging libido. How this
was a bestselling series, she had no idea, but fans had gobbled up
the two previous novels with gusto. The writing was fine, but the
premise . . . well, what could she say? What seemed ridiculous to
her was obviously a winner with the book-buying public.

She rubbed her temples and wondered, for what had to be the
eleventh time that day, why she couldn't just bite the bullet and
pen her own novel about some sort of skin-puncturing, horny half
mammal. She certainly knew the winning formula by now, after
years of finessing manuscripts.

Sabine knew the answer went far beyond the obstacle of
her own taste. She just didn't have the drive. Novels like this one
might make her eyes roll in constant frustration and disbelief,
but she had to hand it to the authors—their commitment to their
craft was impressive. Sabine considered her own lack of follow-
through and shook her head in disgust. She just didn't want it
badly enough.

"That bad, huh?" a voice offered from behind her left shoulder. She turned to see Bess.

"Hey!" she exclaimed, jumping off her stool to give her a hug. "How are you?"

"Good. Just another day at the mines, shoveling salt." Bess pointed to Sabine's heavily marked-up manuscript on the bar. "Looks like you're having the same kind of day."

"Yeah," she agreed. "It's pretty bad."

"At least I can leave my salt at the office," Bess said. "You have to bring this mess home, huh?"

"Most of the time. I just don't have time to do any actual editing at the office, you know? Between all of the other stuff going on, there aren't enough hours in the day."

"Isn't it ironic that the one thing that concretely fits your job description is the very thing that you don't actually do at your job?"

"Indeed," answered Sabine. She shuffled the papers together and collected them in a rubber band.

"What kind of manuscript is that? I saw you shaking your head in frustration when I walked in." Bess hoped that she was successfully masking her nervousness. She had secured her tape recorder tightly around her rib cage, feeling like an inept James Bond in the process. Her previous attempts at remembering verbatim what Sabine, Charlie, and Naomi revealed were only mildly successful at best. Tonight she had to kick it up a notch. Relying on her memory was not an option at this point.

"Oh, it's a werewolf romance, what else?"

"Oy," replied Bess, commiserating. "That sounds fun." Bess settled herself on the stool beside Sabine. "Could you ever write a romance?" she asked Sabine. "I mean, I know that's probably not your bag on a personal level, but you could probably do it with your eyes closed, huh?"

"I don't know if I could write anything anymore." Sabine sighed heavily before continuing. "I mean, the other day, I was finally inspired—after months of dormancy—and when I got home to write it down, I couldn't even get past the first paragraph without being distracted."

"Distracted by a guy?"

"Guilty as charged." Sabine laughed. "But regardless, it's so weird. I mean, do I even want to be writing anymore?" asked Sabine. "Or do I just think I do?"

Bess gazed at her thoughtfully. "I know what you mean. It's hard to know. I try to sniff out leads for interesting stories that have nothing to do with the idiotic monotony of my day job, but my follow-through is pathetic," she confessed.

She thought about her article. This time was different, obviously, but it also came with a hefty price tag—the cost of her blossoming friendships with three pretty amazing women. On the flip side, it didn't have to be a scathing exposé about the passive state of the female drive.

Even as she tried to reason her way out of her guilt, Bess knew that she was betraying these women on a personal level. She was invading their privacy without their permission and then, adding fuel to the fire, judging them cold-heartedly. Bess cringed a bit at the thought, although she hoped not visibly.

"It's reassuring to hear that I'm not the only one struggling," said Sabine. "Most of the time I'm beating myself up for being such a slacker, but I guess it's hard for anyone trying to hold down a nine-to-five, you know? I mean, could you imagine if we had families right now? Taking care of babies and trying to juggle the day job with the other stuff? I have no idea how Naomi does it."

Bess nodded. "I know. I can't imagine, either. Speaking of, she and Charlie are coming, right?"

"Yeah, they are. I'm glad we finally found a time for all of us to get together, outside of class."

"A group adventure is perfect. I thought maybe Naomi would be busy with Noah and Charlie would be teaching." Initially, Bess had thought that she would like to get one-on-ones with all of them, but Sabine was right actually—there was something about the group dynamic that encouraged full disclosure. And with their class time almost halfway over, Bess was all too aware that her access to all of them was limited.

"Hello, ladies!" they heard behind them. They pivoted on their stools to find Naomi and Charlie, beaming brightly.

"We just ran into each other walking in," Naomi explained. "Perfect timing."

They all moved to greet each other with warm hugs.

"Should we get a table?" asked Charlie. She was a bit nervous to be hanging out with Sabine, Bess, and Naomi outside of the studio. It was hard not to adopt the teacher role, despite her best intentions. She thought of her conversation with Sasha. This was as good a time as any to practice blurring her carefully constructed lines. Why couldn't she show a little vulnerability? Just thinking about it made her tense. She hoped the women wouldn't pick up on her discomfort. She needed a drink.

"Sure," answered Sabine. "There's one over there in the corner." She and Bess gathered their things, and they all made their way to the table.

"Winter is such a drag!" moaned Sabine after they had all struggled out of their jackets and stowed them on the various hooks behind them. "I cannot wait for no-jacket weather."

"Seriously," agreed Charlie. "Just to walk freely, without these gigantic down prisons on top of us."

The waitress approached the table. "What do you guys want to drink?" asked Naomi.

"Red wine sounds good to me," answered Bess.

"Me, too," agreed Charlie.

"Sabine, is that cool with you?" asked Naomi.

"Oh yeah, of course," she answered. Naomi picked a bottle for the table and the waitress retreated. "I hope you guys are all okay with a Syrah," said Naomi. "I figured it was safe. And it's one of the cheapest bottles on the menu," she added.

"Now you're talking," said Bess. "Isn't the markup nuts?" she asked. "You can get the same thirty-dollar bottle here for, like, eleven ninety-nine at the store."

"I know," agreed Charlie. "Have any of you guys bought milk lately, by the way?" she asked in mock horror. "The price is insane!"

"This economy is in the shitter in a really scary way," added Naomi. "Buying food for two these days is killing me. With what I spend every month, I could take a weeklong trip to Tahiti."

"How's Noah?" asked Sabine.

Naomi smiled. "Oh, he's great. He is really great. We had a long talk about how sometimes it's okay for me to go out by myself at night. He had a tough time with it at first, but then he reluctantly saw the light. After pouting for a half hour or so, he gave me a big squeeze before I left and told me I looked pretty. He's perfect."

"Isn't it crazy how little men change?" Sabine asked. "I think I dated that guy a year ago, except leave out the telling me I'm pretty part."

Bess laughed. "Seriously. It's not too hard to see the little boys they once were, is it?"

"Not at all," Charlie said. "Especially if they are denied something they really want. I've seen some man tantrums in my time, believe me."

"Charlie, do you have a boyfriend?" asked Naomi.

Charlie shook her head. "Noooo. I honestly don't think I

would have time for one right now, even if it was an option." As
the words came out of her mouth, Charlie wondered if that was
even true. She looked at the women surrounding her and thought
about opening up about Neil and her inability to move past him.
Surely they could commiserate and offer advice. She just couldn't
step over the line, though. There was too much to lose—namely,
their respect. To find out that their together yoga teacher was a
mess? Unthinkable.

"How are things at the studio?" asked Bess. Getting Charlie
to open up was like prying steel bars apart. The woman was a
vault. Subtly, Bess adjusted the tape recorder. The band was digging into her ribs.

"Oh, the usual. The classes and the people are terrific, but the
day-to-day bullshit is a drag."

"Like what?" asked Naomi.

"Oh you know, bills, money, plumbing, blah blah blah. All of
the unglamorous stuff behind the scenes."

The waitress returned with their bottle, pausing to display the
label before uncorking and pouring a splash for Naomi to taste.
Naomi took a sip and nodded appreciatively.

"How did you decide to open your own studio?" asked Bess,
when their glasses were filled. This was the money question.

Charlie blinked rapidly, a nervous twitch she'd always had.
Should she reveal the way she came to such a monumental decision or should she give her usual answer? She decided to play it
safe.

"I got into yoga about five years ago, and it just changed my
life," she explained. "I started to lose any sense of fulfillment at
my finance job, you know?" The women nodded in response. "I
had worked so hard for what felt like forever at something that
provided minimal enjoyment. It was time for a change, and thankfully, the timing was right. I met Julian and Felicity and we de-

cided to pool our resources. Voilà—Prana Yoga." Charlie smiled. This wasn't a complete lie. In fact, it was almost completely true, except for a vital detail or two.

"Weren't you scared to do it?" asked Naomi. "What if the studio had tanked and you had lost all your money?"

"Well, never say never," said Charlie, taking a big gulp of her wine. "That could still happen. I just figured that I had to take that chance. Worst case scenario, we do tank, I can always go back to Big Brother and work for some giant money machine. I have the skills."

Bess nodded. "True," she added. "But still, it's impossible not to respect your ballsiness and commitment to your dream." She really liked the direction this conversation had organically taken. Maybe the article wasn't dead in the water after all. She surveyed the table, waiting for one of the other women to expound on her point. As if reading her mind, Naomi spoke.

"I agree with Bess," she said. "And don't forget the points you get for even knowing what it is you want to do. Most days I feel like I've completely forgotten why I ended up doing what I do."

"How so?" asked Sabine.

"Well, obviously I ended up designing websites somehow," answered Naomi. "It just didn't fall in my lap randomly. I used to take pictures, you know? That was my great passion. And when that wasn't working out the way I had always envisioned it would, I left it behind to focus on a more lucrative venture. I mean, photography and web design are related, sure, but there's a lack of passion and interest in what I do now that I can't ignore."

"But you had to pursue something that paid more money on a more regular basis," said Sabine. "You're a single mom in New York. Talk about bills—yours must be astronomical."

"Very true. And I would never take back Noah. He has made my life one hundred percent better in ways that I would never have the time to explain. But even when I take photos of him, just for us, there's a hesitancy on my part that I never experienced while I was photographing full time. It's like I'm scared of taking pictures now. A couple of clicks, the joy returns, and then what? I can't quit my day job." She paused and took a sip of her wine. "Ugh, listen to me, going on and on." She felt so comfortable with these women. *Should I tell them about the tingling?* she wondered. *Maybe they could help. Or maybe they'll ask too many questions and freak me out.* She had already made the mistake of Googling her symptoms. What she had found online was terrifying. She decided not to say anything. Speaking about whatever it was that was happening to her made it real—too real for a drinks night with her yoga friends.

"No, I get what you're saying," said Bess. "I mean, obviously I don't have a child, but Sabine and I were talking about exactly this before you guys joined us. Even though I know rationally that I could make the time to cover the sort of stories I want to cover, I always think of a million reasons why I can't. You know, I have to go to the gym, I have to go to the grocery store or pick up my dry cleaning, I have to hang out with Dan. Sure, I do have to do all of these things, but I could find the time to pursue my dreams if I really wanted to. The question is, do I really want to, or do I just think I do?" Bess thought of the tape recorder strapped to her rib cage. Did she want to do this? What a hypocrite she was. These women were just like her.

"Wait, hold up, who's Dan?" asked Charlie. "You didn't tell us you had a boyfriend, Little Miss Secret!"

Bess suddenly felt trapped beneath the expectant stares of Charlie, Naomi, and Sabine. Should she open up? Would that further her betrayal by really making them feel like her friends? She decided to go for it, hoping that she could volunteer just a little more to open up the conversation even further. They hadn't even touched on men yet.

"Dan is my boyfriend, yes," replied Bess, suddenly timid. She could feel a blush spreading over her cheeks.

"Who is he? What does he do?" asked Naomi excitedly. "How did you meet?"

"We met here in New York, at a random party," answered Bess. "You know, typical story: I didn't want to go at all, but forced myself off the couch after days of self-imposed, glorious isolation. I showed up and there he was. It's been about a year since we got together."

"Wow, do you guys live together now?" asked Charlie.

"I wish. He actually moved to LA. He's getting his MFA in Screenwriting at USC."

"How do you guys pull off the long-distance thing?" asked Naomi.

"Not very well. It's hard, you know? Not having that immediate access can change the dynamic incredibly. But we try to see each other at least once a month."

"How long is the program?" asked Naomi.

"Two years. But when it's over, Dan will probably need to stay out in LA for work. It's hard to land a screenwriting gig in New York, at least in comparison."

"Really?" asked Charlie. "What will you do?"

Bess reached for the now practically empty bottle. How did the conversation become all about her? "I don't know. I love him, but I don't want to leave everything I have worked so hard to create for myself behind. I mean, ten years of blood, sweat, and tears in the magazine industry is no joke. Not to mention the fact that I just moved into an apartment that has actual, legitimate space. To give that up just seems really naïve, you know?"

"But you love each other," said Charlie, quietly. "That counts for a lot. If you overlook that by focusing on the size of your apartment, I think you're doing yourself a disservice. I mean, you could work in LA, couldn't you? Doesn't your magazine have a West Coast office?"

Bess nodded. "Yeah, they do. Lots of silly magazines do. But that's just the thing. I'm trying to break out of silly and segue into substance. You can't say *LA* and *substance* in the same sentence. They're oil and water."

"What about the *Los Angeles Times*?" asked Sabine. "Your New York credentials would probably be much more impressive outside of New York. You could break in with them and then expand your empire."

Bess shook her head in frustration. "Newspapers are dying and, even so, I would be following him. Giving up my entire life—my dreams!—for a man. That sounds terribly archaic to me. Not to mention the resentment I would feel toward him, and the fact that I'd be returning to the place I grew up. I spent half my life wanting to get out of there." She thought guiltily of her parents, and her dad's illness. *I have to get home to see them soon.*

Naomi spoke up. "See, I think you're looking at this the wrong way. You're seeing it as an end rather than a beginning."

"Excellent point, Naomi," said Sabine. "I tried to tell her the same thing before."

"If you're in love with Dan and he's in love with you, moving to be together as a unit is just a natural next step. Your dreams used to be just about what you wanted in a very individualistic sense, but now that you have someone else to consider, your dreams can just as easily evolve to envelop two." Naomi paused, seemingly impressed by her own wisdom. "Wow, I don't even know where that came from!" she exclaimed. "Must be all the yoga, Charlie."

Charlie laughed. "No doubt! But Naomi, what you're saying is truly right on, and kind of why I fell in love with yoga. Yoga taught me about evolution on both a spiritual and physical plane, you know?"

"How?" asked Bess.

"Yoga is about surrendering to a sense of flow and internal rhythm," Charlie explained. "You connect with your inner being to flow more successfully on a physical level. You are evolving inside in order to evolve outside."

"That's incredible," said Sabine. "It makes complete sense."

"You guys are very wise," said Bess. "It's great advice, it really is, but I just don't know if I am evolved enough as an individual to really pursue us as a unit. Either that, or I'm scared shitless. I mean, intelligent journalism has always been a dream of mine, and I guess true love has as well, but never as concretely. Balancing the two together seems almost impossible. Men take up a lot of time."

"Only if you let them," said Naomi. "It sounds like you are aware enough of your time and its management not to get caught up in the inevitable male domination of it. Something tells me that you would have no problem standing your ground."

"Wow," said Bess. "Thank you." She really meant it, too. She hadn't been surrounded by such warm, wise, and empathetic advice since . . . well, since never. She fought the urge to lift up her shirt and expose the tape recorder. How could she write this article when they were all caught up in the same struggle?

"I feel like I'm on *The Tyra Banks Show*," said Sabine, breaking the comfortable silence.

"I know!" agreed Charlie. "There is a whole lot of sisterhood going on at this table."

Bess laughed in relief. "Seriously! And by the way, I'm getting tipsy. Do you guys want to order some food?"

"Yes, pleaaaase!" answered Naomi. "My stomach is digesting itself at this point."

Bess motioned for the waitress. These women had incredible things to say, but she was still battling with what moving to LA really meant for her. Despite her conflicted emotions, she did feel blessed. For this interaction, for Dan, for the options she had at her fingertips. . . . Her glass was full. *Well, figuratively at least,* she thought, as she eyed the empty bottle on the table and smiled.

chapter twenty-four

Charlie & Naomi

can't believe I ate three slices of pizza," Charlie moaned, as
she and Naomi waited drunkenly for the subway. "What was
I thinking?!"

"You weren't," answered Naomi. "It was the wine talking. Besides, they were fancy pieces."

"Fancy pieces? What does that mean?"

"You know, it was a yuppie pizza joint. The pieces were small.
Three of those pieces are really only one and a half in the world of
true pizza," Naomi explained.

Charlie laughed. "I like your math, Naomi. But they were still
piled high with mounds of cheese. And don't forget the Caesar
salad and calamari."

"Why are you trying to kill my buzz?" Naomi asked, playfully
pushing Charlie away. "If you're drunk, calories don't count." She
wasn't sure if it was the drink or the company, but she felt really
good—physically and mentally—for the first time in what felt like
weeks. To be so hyperaware of everything that was going on in her
body, from the slightest muscle twitch to the mystery bruise that
she had found on her thigh, was exhausting, not to mention com-

pletely depressing. And then, to keep it all to herself . . . it was a
heavy burden. She wondered if telling Charlie about it would help.

"Another dietary gem! Okay, okay, I'll shut up about calories.
Even tomorrow when my gut hangs over my waistband during my
seven o'clock class, I'll shut up. Promise."

"Deal," said Naomi. The train approached. Once inside,
Naomi yanked off her hat. She wondered if Charlie had heard of
symptoms like Naomi's before; if she would laugh and say, *No offense, but this is clearly a case of being out of shape.* Naomi hoped
for that kind of reaction, but knew she was being naïve. There was
no way that someone as in tune with the body as Charlie would
be so dismissive. She glanced nervously at her. She was grinning
with her eyes closed, her head against the wall. She seemed a bit
drunk. Maybe this wasn't the time to bring up her troubles. Talk
about a buzz kill.

Charlie opened her eyes suddenly and faced Naomi. "When
was the last time you were in love?" she asked.

"Well, there's an interesting question. What brought that on?"
Definitely drunk, thought Naomi. She had never seen this kind of
candor from Charlie before.

"You're avoiding my question!" said Charlie.

Naomi laughed. "Yeah, I guess I am. Hmmm, the last time I
was in love. Has to be Noah's dad, Gene. We broke up like, almost
nine years ago, so . . . there's your answer."

Charlie nodded. "It's been four years for me." She sighed heavily. "Four freakin' years."

"Who was it?" asked Naomi. "What happened?"

Charlie suddenly sat up straighter and shook her head in an
attempt to realign her brain. "Oh God, look at me! Drunk girl!
Forgive me, it's that damn wine talking." She smiled shyly, reveal-
ing purple-tinged teeth.

"I'll say it's talking! You have red wine mouth. Do I?" Naomi opened her mouth wide to give Charlie a good look.

"Totally!" shrieked Charlie. "Aren't we a vision? A drunk yogi and a drunk mom, waxing poetic on love lost. It's like an episode of *Sally Jesse Raphael* or something."

"Do you remember in college how they used to air those episodes in the smoking section at the GSU?" asked Naomi. "All day long, nothing but *Jerry Springer*, *Sally Jesse*, and packs upon packs of Camel Lights. Jesus. You practically needed a flashlight to find anyone in that cloud of smoke."

"Totally!" agreed Charlie. "I never sat back there because I was such a little worker bee, but on my way to the bathroom I used to stick my head in and marvel at the level of debauchery. It was like a hormone zoo in there."

Naomi laughed. She wanted Charlie to tell her more about her former love. If she could open up to her about her heartache, then maybe it would be easier for Naomi to open up as well.

Charlie, only semi-oblivious to the awkwardness she had caused with her drunken love question, stared off into the distance, thinking about her former life. Whenever she thought about her college self, hustling to and from class and the library and studying constantly, she wanted to go back in time and give herself a hug. "Slow down," she would say. "Get to know yourself. You have all the time in the world to hustle."

"Back to the love thing," Naomi said, interrupting Charlie's nostalgic moonwalk back in time. "What happened?"

Charlie cringed at the question even though she was the one who had brought it up. Obviously, the wine helped, but she did feel comfortable enough with Naomi to peel back a layer or two. *Here goes nothin'.*

"The truth is, my heart is still kind of broken. I'm having

trouble letting go." She threw up her hands as she finished her sentence as if to say, "Sue me!"

Naomi nodded in commiseration. "Nothing to be embarrassed about, honey. Sometimes it takes a lot longer than we would like to heal. You know yourself best. Whatever you need to do to take care of you, you're gonna do."

"Yeah. He was my first big love, you know? And when it crumbled, I crumbled. Sometimes I wonder if I'll ever be open again. I've been a closed door on that front for so long that the alternative seems impossible."

"Never impossible. Just difficult." Naomi patted Charlie's hand. "I know all about heartbreak. Just imagine being broken, and then healing—only to find a miniature version of the heartbreaker eating Kix at the kitchen table every morning. It's a trip."

"Wow, I didn't even think of that," said Charlie. "That's wild. Does Noah look exactly like his dad?"

"No, not exactly. But enough. And it's crazy, sometimes the cadence of his voice is so exactly like Gene's . . . it's uncanny."

"Does Noah see his dad?" asked Charlie.

"Yeah, every Sunday. He was MIA for a very long time, and then about a year and a half ago he showed up on my doorstep, ready to make nice."

"That must have been unbelievably hard for you."

"Yeah, it was," she admitted. "But he's good for Noah. And he pays child support, which helps tremendously, you know?"

"I bet. Do you have any feelings for him still?"

"Thank sweet Jesus, no. I thank the universe every day for that. We fell apart a while before Noah was conceived and when he turned his back on us, any remote inkling of an attraction for him instantly disintegrated."

Charlie nodded. "Sounds like you're a woman of conviction.

When something's over, it's over." She wished she could be as resolute as Naomi. Maybe her influence would help her release herself from Neil's grasp.

"Oh please," said Naomi, dismissing the compliment. "I'm a wreck." She straightened in her seat and faced Charlie directly. It was now or never.

"Why, what's up?" asked Charlie.

"I've been feeling a bit off physically lately," she confessed. "I was wondering if you could shed any light on what's been happening. You know, being so in touch with your body through yoga and stuff."

Charlie put her hand on top of Naomi's, instantly sobered by the frightened look on her face. "Hey, of course. I'm no doctor, but I want to help you any way I can."

Naomi took a deep breath and described her symptoms. "Do you think this is just a case of being out of shape?" she asked, when she had finished.

"Wow, Naomi, I don't think it's as simple as that, unfortunately. I mean, if that was the case, how would you account for the headaches?"

Naomi sighed. "I know, right?" Against her will, she teared up. *Shit.*

"Hey, hey," cooed Charlie. She hugged Naomi. Her heart was breaking for her. "That doesn't necessarily mean that something horrible is happening, Naomi. It could just be a virus. Or maybe you slipped a disk in your back and your spinal cord is a bit out of whack."

"You think that's it?" asked Naomi. "I hope it's that simple. It's just that my back doesn't hurt at all, you know? Wouldn't it hurt?"

"It could be so interior that the pain hasn't progressed outward yet," answered Naomi. "Or something else I was thinking about is stress. Stress manifests itself in some really crazy ways."

Naomi nodded. "Yeah, I was thinking about that, too. I have been stressed out lately." She thought about the silly Mini-Noah saga that still, despite her best intentions to put it in perspective, bothered her.

"Yoga is great for stress," said Charlie. "Maybe you should think about coming by during the week as well. Or if you can't because of Noah, I could map you out a routine to do at home."

"Really? You would do that?"

"Of course. But in the meantime, you're going to see your doctor, right?"

"Yeah, I have an appointment next week. With a neurologist."

"Oh wow, a specialist, huh? That's probably your best bet, with the headaches and stuff."

"Yeah, I hope so."

The train pulled into Naomi's stop. "This is me!" she announced, enveloping Charlie in a tight embrace. "Thanks for all of your excellent advice." She pulled back to look at her. "I really like you, Charlie."

"Ditto," said Charlie. She smiled warmly. "And please keep me posted on everything. I mean it!"

As Naomi left the subway, Charlie thought about her symptoms. Sure, stress was sneaky as hell, but she had never heard of it having such an impact on the brain before. The headaches, sure, but the tingling? She sighed deeply. A student of hers had dealt with the same kind of sensations, and had gone to acupuncture religiously in addition to coming to yoga once or twice a week. She had gone on what seemed like an endless journey to what finally became an MS diagnosis and, shortly thereafter, medication. She was fine now; a little tired and bruised by her daily injections, but otherwise just a normal, thirty-something woman. Normal save for an incurable disease, that is.

Please let Naomi be okay, she thought. *A single mom has it hard enough. Jesus, here I am obsessing about dumb Neil, and look at the real life shit going on all around me! Why is he still haunting me?*

Why do I continue to credit him with my life change? Was it easier to give him the glory than herself? Somehow she supposed it was, in the sense that if her career tanked, she could blame him. But clearly it wasn't tanking, and her love for the practice gave her true fulfillment. *I would have found yoga on my own, without Neil.* It was time to embrace the idea that she had been on a quiet quest all along, and Neil had just been the gatekeeper—the mean-spirited centaur at the gates of her inevitable future.

On the street, she marveled at her newfound sense of self and clarity. It was as though a hundred-pound weight had been lifted from her shoulders. She sincerely hoped that her lightness would continue on into the morning, when she was fully sober.

She hugged herself over her jacket. She was that much closer to forgetting Neil entirely, just by opening up about him. She had challenged the unfair boundaries she had placed upon herself tonight, and look what had happened? It was heartening beyond belief.

She turned the key in her lock and bounded up the stairs, eager to take off her jacket and sink into blissful slumber. Once inside, she brewed herself a cup of chamomile tea to soothe her churning pizza belly.

She switched on her computer to e-mail Naomi. She wanted to let her know that she was really there for her; whatever she needed. And that's when she saw it. In her in-box, a Facebook e-mail. "Neil Saunders added you as a friend on Facebook," she read, her heart quickening at his name in boldfaced letters on her screen.

Just like that, when she had finally decided to let him go, the universe brought him back. She eyed the e-mail but could not bring herself to click on the link. Shocked and vulnerable, she switched off her computer as calmly as she could, put her mug in the sink, and climbed into bed.

Under the covers, where no one could see, she cried herself to sleep.

chapter twenty-five

Class Three

Light streamed through the studio windows and filled the space with a quiet, early-morning glow. It bled warmly into the corners, shading the wall of mats and dappling the front desk.

Charlie sat in the center of the open space, eyes closed, listening to the sheer wonder of almost absolute silence. On the ledge, she heard a soft rustle. She opened one eye to find a red robin, its tiny head darting to and fro as it opened its beak to emit a tentative warble.

The first sounds of spring. She knew it was just a tease, that at least two more months of blustery winter remained before the full unveiling of spring's glorious warmth, but it was nice to see the universe preparing.

She took a deep breath. Her long cry post-Facebook shock had released a tension that had been building for years. She had awoken on Friday morning, eyes red and bleary, with a sense of calm. In twenty-four hours, she had let go of a good four years of pain. She felt more aware of her true self than she could ever remember. It was as though she had woken from a long, tortured sleep.

She had taken down her Facebook profile and thereby erased Neil—not from her past; he would always be a part of her past—but from her future. She was at peace.

"Hellooo," spoke a timid female voice from the front room. It was Sabine. Charlie stood up to greet her.

"Hey, Sabine," she called. Sabine poked her head around the corner—her eyes sparkling from underneath her burgundy hood.

"Morning!" she chirped.

More feet on the stairs heralded the arrival of Naomi and then, a minute later, Bess. They all smiled and said their hellos—slightly shy after Thursday night's drunken bonder.

Sabine broke the slight tension. "So, who regretted that fifth glass of wine on Friday morning?" she asked.

"Oh, man!" replied Naomi. "My head felt like it was in a half nelson all day. Brutal."

"Me, too," agreed Bess. "I actually left work early. You would be surprised how meaningless celebrity shenanigans can be when you're carrying a piano on your head. I was worthless."

The women laughed in response. Bess had been terribly hungover, but she knew that her continued discomfort had much more to do with her guilt and anxiety about the article than with the tannins in the wine. She had left the bar on Thursday night convinced that she was kiboshing the article, but had woken up Friday in a state of panic about her lack of follow-through. If she didn't do the article, she was convinced she would never leave the tabloid world. It was her ticket out. Or was it? She felt like she was wrestling with a tiger.

The women unfurled their mats and sat in their respective places facing the front of the room. Charlie took her seat. She smiled at them warmly, both as their teacher and now, officially, their friend.

"Before we get started this morning, I thought it might be fitting to talk about the concept of openness." She looked at Sabine, Bess, and Naomi, referencing Thursday night without having to say so directly.

"Yoga is about opening yourself up physically, of course. You extend your muscles and open yourself both internally and externally to achieve total balance. This extension does not come easily—it is only fully achieved with practice and repetition. In life, openness is also a sort of elusive concept, especially when you are just trying to make it through the day. I often feel like there is no time for a true, selfless connection with someone. You have to train yourself to not think that way and then turn that thinking into doing. It's really hard, and harder still to open yourself up in a state of utter sobriety." Charlie cocked her head at the women as if to add, *like us, duh.*

She continued. "The concept is scary and foreign. But I also think that it's essential to a true sense of well-being. Only by taking a risk and being open in a world where almost everyone else is closed can we transcend the confines of our existence."

"I would like all of you to take the openness you experience here and apply it outside of class. I think you might be surprised at the way in which your lives will change." Charlie paused. She hoped her speech didn't come off as holier than thou or pretentious.

She segued into the beginning of class with Vajrasana. As Bess raised her arms toward the ceiling, she wondered if Charlie had special powers. Could she know about the article? Most likely not. But could she sense Bess's lies? Could she sense that she was the traitor among them? In a class of people concentrating on being "open," she felt like she was in the state penitentiary—locked up with no hope of breaking in or out. She reluctantly followed the class and transitioned into Tadasana.

As Sabine moved into what Charlie called something that

sounded like a cat releasing a hairball *(Vrka-what?!)*, and that she liked to call tree pose, she thought about what being open meant to her. Instantly, she thought of Zach. He had called her last night to cancel their date. On the plus side, he called her—not a small feat considering how easy it would have been to brush her off via text. On the minus side, their date was canceled. He had blamed it on his exhausting case, which continued to require all of his attention apparently, but c'mon. Unless it was a *Roe v. Wade* redux, how bad could it be? Everybody had to eat. He had been incredibly apologetic, and even asked her for a Wednesday reschedule, but Sabine was still suspicious. *Why can't I just go with the flow and believe him? Why does a simple reschedule send me into a tailspin of self-doubt?* She wondered if she was more terrified of Zach being a lying jerk than the unthinkable alternative—that he was nice and genuinely as bummed as she was to have to postpone their date. Her mother always said that Sabine was scared of her own power over men and that, instead of embracing her potential, she shunned it entirely. *Is that crazy lady right?* She thought of her mother's endless parade of men. Maybe she was on to something.

Oh Mom, thought Sabine. *You wise old owl.* She needed to call her mother, actually. She made a mental note, between 'learn how to roast a chicken' and 'buy Spanx.' She would never get to the other two, but she would call her mom that afternoon. *One out of three ain't bad.*

"Whatcha smiling about?" asked Charlie, suddenly standing beside her.

"I'm practicing being open," Sabine replied.

"It looks good on you." Charlie rested her hand on the small of Sabine's back for a moment and gave her an encouraging grin before walking away. Despite herself, Sabine blushed.

After a few grueling rounds of downward dog, the women thankfully sat on their mats, waiting for Charlie's next instruction. "Today, I'm going to bring in some blocks and straps," she announced. "Sounds scary, but they actually make difficult poses easier and really help you concentrate on your form."

Charlie gathered three purple foam blocks and green cotton straps from the back of the classroom. She circled the room with her booty, handing one of each to Bess, Sabine, and Naomi.

"Our first foray into the wonderful world of props will be using the block for Setu Bandha Sarvangasana, or bridge pose." Sabine stifled a laugh. Seriously, what was this one called?! That was a whole lot of syllables for something that's English translation was "bridge."

"Okay, lie on your back," Charlie instructed. "Bend your knees, bringing the soles of your feet close to your bum. Now, here is where the block comes in. Take your block, and as you lift your hips up toward the ceiling, place it beneath your sacrum."

Bess froze. What was her sacrum? She felt like an idiot. It was her tailbone, right? Or was it her brow bone? The thought of the block balancing on her forehead seemed ludicrous even for yoga, so she went with tailbone.

Naomi exhaled in gratitude. The block felt like heaven against her tired lower back. *I need to get a firmer mattress,* she immediately thought, thinking of her lumpy, years-old hand-me-down. Her parents had given it to her when she had moved into her Fort Greene apartment.

After giving their backs a pretty thorough stretching, Charlie introduced the straps for leg stretches. She demonstrated their use, looping the band into a noose around her foot and pulling her leg to its opposite side before instructing the women to do the same.

"Naomi," whispered Charlie, who—again—just seemed to materialize out of thin air like some sort of yoga prophet, "you're not falling off the Brooklyn Bridge here. Ease up a bit." She loosened Naomi's grip on her band, which was threatening to rip the plastic weave in two.

"Oh wow," exclaimed Naomi. "I didn't even realize!"

"Everything okay?" asked Charlie with genuine concern.

"Oh sure. Just one of those days."

"Already? It's not even ten AM." Charlie lowered her voice. "You feeling okay?"

"Oh yeah, fine." Naomi laughed nervously in response. She hoped that Charlie wouldn't be watching her like a hawk now in class. The last thing she wanted was to be singled out as "the sick girl." All through class, despite herself, she had been hyperaware of her body's reactions. She thought she felt normal but did she even know what normal was anymore? She couldn't relax, hence her death grip on the strap.

As the class came to an end, Charlie commended them on their progress and signaled its close with "Namaste." Exhausted, the women lifted themselves from the floor.

Charlie exited the studio as they rolled their mats and gathered their respective props to put away. She really was pleased with everyone's progress. Already, just by their third class, their growing comfort was evident.

Charlie noticed Mario talking to Felicity at the front desk. He so wasn't Charlie's type—relatively short, muscular, working class with a heavy Puerto Rican accent and an affinity for tight T-shirts—but there was something about him that made Charlie a little warmer every time she saw him. Maybe it was his unapologetic maleness in a world of hipster, emo guys in skinny jeans and Keds. Or maybe it was his tight nugget of an ass. She couldn't be sure, but something was definitely agreeing with her.

"Hello, Charlie," greeted Mario. His entire face lit up as she approached. Felicity sat back in her chair and watched their interaction with amusement. The attraction between the two of them was palpable.

"Hey, Mario," she replied. The way he looked at her made her feel naked. Not in a gross, undressing her with his eyes sort of way, but more in a Sunday-morning, postcoital, prebrunch kind of way. "Whoa, is that a Manu Chao T-shirt?" she asked, surprised.

"Yeah, you like him?"

"I loooove him," Charlie replied. "Did you see him at the bandshell a couple of summers ago? He was amazing."

"Yep, I was there. Might have been where I picked up this T-shirt. We sat outside the bandshell and had a picnic. It was the perfect summer night. The music, the food, the vibe . . . *muy bien.*"

Charlie tensed up involuntarily. *Who was "we"? Who was he having a romantic picnic with? Some raven-haired Spanish seductress?*

"Hey Charlie," he said, interrupting her paranoia. She broke out of her daze to see him extending a brown bag. "I brought you something."

"What?" replied Charlie, embarrassed and pleased simultaneously. "Oh Mario, you shouldn't have!" *Looks like the Spanish seductress is history. Bueno.*

"Please, it's no problem. Happy to do it. I was thinking of you this morning, so I made you a special Mario green tea latte. That Starbucks mess has nothing on me. Trust."

"Mario, that's so sweet of you. When did you start making green tea lattes?"

"Since I haven't seen you in weeks," answered Mario, gazing directly into Charlie's eyes. Charlie felt like her entire body might be pink. His directness made her blush from her top to her toes. And the fact that he dug the same kind of music she did turned the heat up a distinct notch.

"I miss you, so I made you a new drink," he explained. "I also got you one of those vegan muffins that you like, from that hippie joint down the street." Felicity continued to watch their interaction with glee. This was better than any of that crap her daughter watched on MTV.

"Wow, you did?" asked Charlie. "That's so sweet of you. She took the bag from Mario and peeked inside. "This looks delicious!" She pulled the latte out gingerly. "It's still warm!"

"Yeah, I just made it."

They gazed at each other for a minute as she took a sip. "This is goooood. Damn! Starbucks who?! Did you just whip this recipe together now?"

"Ahhh, no. I've been working on it for a while, hoping you would come by to try it out. But you haven't been by in so long, I had to bring it to you. Where you been?"

"I'm sorry, Mario. I've been so busy. I've started drinking tea at home in the morning. And it's so cold outside—all I want to do is get inside the studio where it's warm, you know? There's no time for hanging out."

"There's always time for a quick hello," said Mario. "Stop in and say hi—you get the Mario latte on the house. And maybe I'll have Manu Chao blasting from the speakers. Deal?"

"Sounds like a good deal to me," interjected Naomi, who couldn't help but overhear their conversation as she, Bess, and Sabine got ready to leave. The three of them had been exchanging glances as they unabashedly eavesdropped. Mario was hot for Charlie, no doubt about it.

Charlie giggled. "Yeah, it is. Deal, Mario. Thank you."

Mario grinned. "You're welcome. I gotta get back. See you soon, Charlie," he called over his shoulder as he bounded down the stairs in his work boots: *clomp, clomp, clomp*. Charlie watched him go and then turned to see four beaming faces. Sabine, Bess, Felicity, and Naomi were all wearing shit-eating grins.

"Charlie has a boyyyfriennnd," teased Sabine, as the women promptly burst into giggles.

"Shut up!" shrieked Charlie. She felt like she was in middle school. She looked at her watch.

"Shit, I have my next class in five minutes!" She ripped a chunk of her muffin off and popped it into her mouth. "See you ladies next week!" she sang as she promptly disappeared into the back room.

"Guess that's the end of that conversation," remarked Naomi. "She is in no mood to be teased, huh?"

"Yeah, she's funny about him," replied Felicity. "The attraction is so obvious, but she refuses to acknowledge it."

"She's in love denial," agreed Sabine. "Okay, I have to jet. See you gals next week!"

"I'm right behind you," said Bess. "Bye!" They took off down the stairs.

"Hey Naomi, have you had a chance to mess around with some website ideas at all?" asked Felicity. Naomi froze. The truth was that she had completely forgotten about her promise. She had been wrestling with a bear of a project all week. Between that and her body anxiety, she just hadn't had the time.

"Some ideas have been marinating," she replied, avoiding Felicity's hopeful gaze. "But I don't really have anything concrete yet."

"Of course," replied Felicity, her disappointment evident.

"But I promise, next week I'll have something. Some ideas, at the very least."

"Oh, terrific! I am just so excited about this, I can't tell you," she explained. "And grateful."

"Please! It's no big deal, Felicity. Sorry it's taking me so long." Naomi vowed to have a rough idea of where she wanted to take the website by next Saturday. It wasn't going to be easy—she had another (paying) project to finish up that week—but it would be good to get her mind off her mystery symptoms. Plus, this was a real creative opportunity for her. No client was dictating her style here. The Prana site could be whatever she wanted it to be.

Naomi put her hat on. "Okay, see you next week, Felicity. And tell Charlie I'm sorry if I embarrassed her with the whole Mario thing."

"You got it. And don't worry about Charlie. She could use a good tease. Girl takes herself way too seriously most of the time."

Naomi grinned. "Don't we all," she replied. With a final wave, she took off down the stairs.

chapter twenty-six

Naomi

As Naomi headed home, she considered the website. In her head, she was assembling the home page like a puzzle—*copy goes here, photos go here, links go here* . . . Her train of thought was interrupted by the distinct vibration of her cell phone in her jacket pocket. She pulled it out to find a text from Cecilia. "Where are you?" Maternal panic enveloped her like a dense fog. Her heart raced as she dialed into her voice mail. Three messages? *Shit.* It was all she could do to not drop the phone and just take off sprinting toward home.

Message one: Noah had broken his arm on the monkey bars. Cee was taking him to Brooklyn Hospital. Meet her there. Message two: Where is she? Noah is hysterical. Should Cee call Gene? He needs a parent. Message three: She called Gene. He's on his way. Naomi hailed a cab to the hospital in a daze. Her baby had hurt himself and she was nowhere to be found. Worse yet, Gene had been summoned to console Noah. Naomi's anxiety level was at Code Orange. *Breathe.* She looked out the window of the cab at Brooklyn going by. *Breathe.*

"Naomi!" shrieked Cecilia as soon as she set foot in the emergency room.

"Hi," she answered curtly, shrugging off Cee's attempt to hug her. "Is he okay? Where is he? What happened?"

"He's fine, Naomi," answered Gene, seemingly appearing out of nowhere. Naomi's blood began to boil. The fact that he was there before her, apprising her of the situation, made her want to scream.

"Thank you so much for the update," she snarled. Gene looked surprised and then backed away slightly. "Cee, tell me what happened," Naomi demanded.

"We were just on the playground," she explained. "Typical Saturday stuff. Noah was on the monkey bars with his friend Sophie and well . . . he fell. On his arm."

"Where were you?" asked Naomi. She knew that Cecilia had been close by, but she couldn't fight the need to blame someone for Noah's accident.

Cecilia crossed her arms across her chest defensively. "Naomi, I was right there, watching. Don't ask me questions like that. C'mon now."

"I'm sorry, Cee. I just . . . I'm just so worked up right now. You're excellent with Noah. I'm just so worried."

"I know you are, Naomi. But really, he just fell and his arm happened to get in the way. I brought him here immediately. They're setting it now."

"She called me only because she couldn't get a hold of you," Gene explained. "I'm not trying to one up you, Naomi. I'm glad I could be here."

"I know, Gene," she answered, trying to maintain a composed tone of voice. *Suddenly he knows me so well that he feels comfortable calling me out on my insecurities? Jackass.* "This isn't about who's one upping who, though. My son . . . our son broke his arm. He's in a lot of pain. I wasn't able to be here as quickly as I would have liked so I'm a bit freaked out." She exhaled, trying to release some of her anger. "All that said, I'm glad you could be here." *But am I?* she thought. Part of her wished that Gene hadn't shown up. There was something about his maintaining his inefficiency as a father that was comforting to her, and realizing that made her feel awful. It was a very selfish way to feel when Noah was the one who would suffer. "Can I go in and see him?" she asked them both.

"I think so," Cee replied. "Let's go tell the nurse that you're here."

"He really is okay," said Gene. "He's a tough little guy. I have to take off now, unfortunately. I was about to head to the airport for Paris when Cee called. I postponed my flight but my new one leaves in a couple hours."

"Really?" asked Naomi, surprised. "Thanks, Gene . . . for coming. For being here."

"It was no problem. You know, there's a reason I live nearby. Whenever you need an extra set of hands . . . I'm available."

Naomi nodded. It was time for her to accept that fact. But why was it so hard to do so? "Tell Noah that Mini-Noah and I will call him from Paris. And that I'm proud of him for being such a soldier today, please."

"Will do," answered Naomi.

"Bye, Cecilia." Gene gave her an awkward hug and took off, leaving the two women together.

"I'm sorry I had to call him, Naomi," said Cecilia. "I just felt like I didn't have a choice and the doctors needed insurance forms." Naomi nodded in response. She touched Cee's cheek. "I know. Now let's go see my baby."

Mama," whispered Noah from his bed. He looked so tiny lying there, with his little arm encased in a giant white plaster claw. Naomi's heart surged upon seeing that he was indeed okay.

"Baby boy! I heard that you were the bravest boy on the whole planet today." She sat on the bed and gingerly gathered him into a hug, careful to avoid his cast.

"I was," he answered solemnly. "It hurts."

"Oh, I know it does. Were you scared?" Noah nodded, his eyes filling with tears.

"Mama, where were you?"

"Oh honey, I am so sorry. I was in yoga class. I didn't get the message that you had hurt yourself until it was over. As soon as I heard, I ran here as fast as I could. Do you forgive me?"

"Yeah, I guess. I missed you, though," Noah replied, his lip trembling.

"I know, baby. I feel terrible about it. Was it good to see your dad, though?"

"Yeah, it was good."

Naomi brushed his hair back from his forehead. "He told me to tell you that you were the bravest soldier he had ever seen today, Noah."

Noah smiled. "Is he here?"

"No, he had to leave for Paris with Mini-Noah. He said he'll call you later." Naomi was proud of herself for relaying Gene's message without even the slightest hint of sarcasm.

"Okay. Can we go now?"

"Yeah, let's get out of here. We'll get you home and put you in bed. I'll make you a grilled cheese. Sound good?" Noah smiled weakly in response.

"And tater tots?" he asked.

"All the tater tots you can eat. A tater tot buffet."

Later, at home, Naomi tucked Noah into his bed and sat for a moment in the living room with Cecilia. She put her head in her hands. The physical and emotional stress of the day had taken its toll.

"You okay?" asked Cecilia.

Naomi opened her eyes. In all the hubbub, she had almost forgotten that she was there. She smiled weakly. "Sure," she answered. "I'm having a hard time with all of this, I guess."

"With Gene?" asked Cecilia.

"Yeah, that's part of it, I suppose. I guess I never expected Gene to be a decent dad, you know? I kind of thought that he would half-ass his way through his weekly visits with Noah and then eventually fade out of the picture. Looks like he's serious about being a part of his life."

"But isn't that good for Noah?"

"Well, of course it is!" Naomi was frustrated by Cecilia's tone. Sometimes Cecilia did this—acted like Naomi was one of her patients and not her friend. She supposed that was part and parcel of being friends with a budding psychologist, but she didn't like being dissected so obviously. "Jesus, Cee, I'm not a monster."

"I didn't mean to suggest that you were," Cee replied, hurt by Naomi's interpretation. "Of course this is difficult for you. I can't even imagine the complications."

"Sorry I snapped at you," replied Naomi. "You're right, it is so complicated. Today's events just piled on top of the whole Mini-Noah fiasco. I was already feeling a little hurt that Noah asked Gene to help with the project and didn't even think about asking me . . . and now today, my baby breaks his damn arm and guess who is there to save the day?" *Not to mention that my body is falling apart.* She wanted to tell Cee, but not now. There was way too much going on and she was so annoyed suddenly—by all of it.

Naomi massaged her biceps in an attempt to release some frustration. They ached from that morning's sun salutations. She could barely straighten them.

"Mmmm," replied Cecilia, reigniting Naomi's annoyance.

"What does 'mmmm' mean?"

"Okay, I swear I'm not pulling some undercover psychotherapy shit. I'm just talking as your friend, okay?"

"Okay," answered Naomi, fighting the defensiveness that threatened to envelop her like a shield.

"Why would Noah ask you to take on Mini-Noah if he knows that the assignment is all about taking photographs? I mean, photography is what Gene does for a living, you know? I can't remember the last time I saw you with a camera. Noah is a savvy kid, after all. From that perspective alone it makes sense for Gene to handle the assignment."

Naomi felt like Cecilia had just poured lighter fluid over her most vulnerable spot and was now dangling a burning match over it. "Cecilia, what are you talking about?" she asked, her annoyance palpable in the tone of her voice. "I design for a living. Noah knows that. He knows what a visual person I am!"

"Hey, forget I said anything," replied Cecilia, getting up to collect her things. "That was poor judgment on my part. It's obvious that you don't want to talk about this right now."

"Talk about what?" challenged Naomi. "Just because I don't have a camera strapped around my neck doesn't mean that I'm not a photographer!"

Cecilia sat back down and looked directly into Naomi's eyes. "Naomi, any time photography is mentioned, you tense up like crazy. You might think that your discomfort with it is a secret, but you're kidding yourself. I'm not saying that Noah picks up on it—I have no idea what goes on in his head—but he is a pretty perceptive kid."

"That's right!" Naomi hissed back. "You have NO IDEA. You're not a mother. You're not dealing with an MIA dad back on the scene. YOU HAVE NO IDEA." She was surprised by the intensity of her anger. She was unleashing all of her anxiety on

Cee and, although she knew that was wrong, it felt damn good to release it.

"I'm going to go now," said Cecilia, her discomfort evident. She got up and gathered her bag. "Listen, I didn't mean to—"

"Please, just go," said Naomi. She put her head in her hands. "I know I'm overreacting right now, but I can't help it. Please go." Naomi closed her eyes and rubbed her temples in frustration. She heard Cecilia close the door behind her. The apartment was suddenly—blissfully—silent. She heard the shuffle of Noah's socks on the wood floor. He approached her hesitantly.

"Mama?" he asked.

Naomi took a deep breath and sat up. "Yes, baby?"

"Where did Cee go?"

"She had some work to do." Naomi wondered how much he had heard.

"Oh. But she didn't say bye to me."

"I know, she had to run. She told me to say good-bye for her. And to give you one of these." Naomi pulled him close and kissed his ripe cheek loudly. Noah giggled and squirmed.

"Mama, can I have my tater tots now?" he asked.

"Yes you can, my friend. Tater tot buffet coming up for the bravest boy in the world! Get back in bed and I will bring them to you."

"Grilled cheese, too?"

"Grilled cheese, too." Naomi wiped her eyes as Noah scampered back to his room. She stood up, noting the ache of her hamstrings. She felt bad about being an asshole to Cee, but she really had picked the wrong time to pry. *I'll apologize later,* Naomi decided, thinking about how lucky she was to have her around. She dug around in the kitchen for the frying pan, thinking about her photography and what Cee had said. Of course, it was all spot-on.

Maybe it was time for Naomi to pick up her camera again. Especially now, when she felt so vulnerable. Her best photos always came out of her darkest moments. A few photos would be good for her. Maybe even great.

Part IV

· · · · · · · · · ·

Bahya Kumbhaka

chapter twenty-seven

Bess

Bess sat at her kitchen table, staring morosely at the small tape recorder in front of her. She pushed PLAY, suddenly bringing Sabine's slightly high-pitched voice into the room. Bess put her chin on her fist and cocked her head, closing her eyes to listen to their conversation. There was sweet Sabine, guiltily discussing the lack of creative inspiration in her life, and there she was—a rabid dog, hot on the scent of vulnerability.

I sound like Linda Tripp, Bess thought to herself, horrified at the thought. She was practically attacking Sabine, Naomi, and Charlie with her questions. Bess wondered if she was just particularly sensitive to the sound of her own voice or if she really was that much of a piranha. She suspected that it was a little of both. Subtlety was not her forte, true, but this technique was laughable. She supposed it was fine if her subjects knew they were being interviewed, but any undercover work required a more delicate touch. She made a mental note to ease up on her pitbull routine.

"I mean, do I even want to be writing anymore?" asked Sabine, her voice barely registering against the drone of the busy bar, "or do I just think I do?"

Bess sighed deeply and pushed the STOP button. *What am I doing?* She had come home from yoga, determined to make some headway on the article, but had only become more and more unsure of it as she plunged in.

It was becoming pretty obvious to Bess that these women were not the weak links she had first mistaken them for. Their sacrifices had nothing to do with the hope of landing men or decomplicating their lives for the sake of comfort. They were just trying to get by—make a living, pay their bills, maintain relative sanity in a city that never stops moving. These were struggles that Bess was all too familiar with herself. And in Naomi's case, she was trying to raise a kid, for God's sake! That was a struggle of such epic proportions that Bess couldn't even pretend to understand it.

Bess got up from the table and sat on her living room floor. She channeled Charlie and straightened her spine. "What are you going to do, Bess?" she asked aloud. Such was the beauty of living alone—you could talk to yourself with abandon.

She closed her eyes and thought about Sabine, Charlie, and Naomi. How could she write an article about their lack of creative drive, when her own hardly existed? It was a glaring hypocrisy that would no doubt taint the article. She opened her eyes and moved back to the table.

"I'm going to make a list," Bess revealed to the empty apartment. "Who these women are, what they're missing, and what they're doing or not doing about it." Bess was a big fan of lists, as a rule. Whenever she became too overwhelmed by or irrational about something, they always calmed her down and kept her eyes on the prize. She picked up her pen and stared forcefully at the yellow legal pad in front of her.

"NAOMI," she wrote in capital letters. She underlined the name with a sharp line. Underneath her name she wrote "photography." Then she wrote "graphic design." Although these two were not exactly one and the same, they weren't apples and oranges either. Next, Bess wrote "Noah" and the words "guilty about her past." Bess put her pen down and looked at her make-shift diagram. Naomi's reasons for putting her photography on pause were certainly understandable, and maybe even a little bit noble. Who was Bess to say that this was the passion that was missing from her life?

Bess picked up her pen again and wrote "CHARLIE." This was a tough one. She still had no idea who Charlie really was. She wrote "yoga" underneath her name. Here was a woman who went against the grain of her article's thesis. Charlie had switched the direction of her life to follow her dreams—she had uprooted all that she knew to take a gigantic risk. Bess thought about the Charlie that she had known vaguely in college—the driven, all-business girl who had seemed to know what she wanted out of life from the very beginning.

Now she made illusive references to an epiphany that had taken her from finance to some sort of spiritual awakening, but she had yet to elaborate on what exactly that epiphany entailed. Bess suspected a man to be at the root of such a life change, but Charlie had made no mention of such influence, and Bess highly doubted that she ever would. The obvious choice was to set her up as the example that the other women should follow, but how could Bess designate her as such when she had no facts to go on? That was the very definition of poor journalism.

And then there was Sabine. "SABINE," she wrote. Beneath her name she scribbled "writer." Sabine had said herself that she wasn't even sure she wanted to be a writer anymore. The jump from writing to editing wasn't the least bit suspect either, it was perfectly viable as a by-product of growing up and figuring out what your strengths were. Sure, Sabine didn't love her job, but she could always switch to another publishing house with a little—or a lot—of grunt work. What seemed to be a lack of follow-through creatively could simply be part of Sabine's journey.

Jesus, this article is falling apart at its seams, Bess thought. There was no meat to it at all.

She wrote her own name, "BESS," and eyed it warily. She paused before writing "journalist" underneath it. She thought about her desire to transcend her tabloid existence. On one hand, she was making a concerted effort here, with this article, to break through the ceiling her nine-to-five job created. On the other hand, this effort—the very idea of her article—was still safe. There was nothing groundbreaking about her thesis. In essence, it was just an extension of the sensationalism that she was constantly surrounded by. She had only further ensconced herself in the very jail of her career predicament.

Bess threw her pen across the room. "What the hell am I going to do now?" she asked no one. "What am I DOING?! THIS ARTICLE BLOWS!" she yelled, fighting back tears of frustration. "I DON'T EVEN LIKE YOGA!"

She got up from the table and curled herself in the fetal position on her couch, feeling sorry for herself. She closed her eyes and thought of Dan. Sweet Dan. She disliked showing him her tender underbelly in moments like this, but if he was really around for the long haul, he needed to see it. She picked up the phone to dial him, hoping that her frustration would not elicit an "I told you so!" from him.

"Hello, gorgeous," he answered.

"Ooh, cheesy," Bess replied, grimacing and smiling at the same time.

"I love cheese. I would put cheese on everything if I could. Have you ever simultaneously eaten cheese with a banana, by the way?"

"Dan! That sounds disgusting!"

"Don't be so judgmental," he teased. "It is actually quite delicious. And I know this because that is what I had for a snack this afternoon. They were the only two items in my fridge, besides salsa."

"Dude, you need to go shopping. That is just sad."

"I know! I need a little lady out here to take care of me. Someone to cook for me and to clean the linoleum in my bathroom with a toothbrush."

"Wow, that sounds so romantic. I'm on the next plane out."

"You are!? Jesus, it would be so good to see you right now, Bess. I miss your face."

Bess tingled at the thought of lying beside Dan. As of late, it was her favorite feeling in the world. Which brought her back to the article. Writing articles used to be her favorite feeling in the world. Would it ever be again?

"Why so quiet? You okay?"

"I'm okay. I'm just really at a roadblock with this damn article."

"What's the matter?" he asked.

"I just . . ." here, Bess hesitated. It was never easy for her to admit that she was wrong about something, and this article was no exception. She took a deep breath and continued. "I just don't think it's working. Please, please don't say 'I told you so,' Dan. I beg you."

"Bess, c'mon now, I would never do that." He sounded hurt by her request. "What's the roadblock about? Maybe you can take the article in a different direction."

Bess was relieved to hear him say that. There were so many perks to dating a fellow writer, and brainstorming about ideas was at the top of the list. "You think?" she asked.

"Yeah, sure. Tell me why you're stuck."

Bess explained her predicament to Dan. "How can I present

these women as drones with no creative drive, when that simply isn't the case?"

"How do you mean?"

"Not only are Naomi and Sabine still cognizant of their shelved dreams, but their everyday lives and choices aren't so far off from their original aspirations, you know? They're still swimming in the same pool, just in different lanes."

"Ooh, nice analogy."

Bess laughed. "Okay, okay, I know that was a bit of a stretch. Work with me here!"

"I am! And I like where you're going with this. What about Charlie?"

"Yeah, she's a tough one. She is the exception to the rule. Her dreams changed so dramatically. . . . She really bucked the system, instead of playing along with it, by opening her own studio. Her risk was a massive one."

"So how come she can't be the example that Naomi and Sabine idealize?" Dan asked.

"Because there's more to her story than she's letting on," Bess explained. "I mean, I think that Sabine and Naomi—and hell, even I—idolize her to a degree. But there's something to her backstory that doesn't add up. She doesn't own her decision somehow."

Bess paused, considering what she had just said. She had had such a difficult time pinpointing what it was about Charlie's demeanor that didn't quite jive, and that was it exactly. Sure, being prideful about her ballsiness wouldn't exactly be an endearing trait, but some sort of confidence from Charlie in the strength of her convictions would be nice. Bess never felt that from her. She made a note on her legal pad.

"Huh," said Dan. "I wonder what that's about. Do you think that it's just an example of how women have a harder time than men singing their own praises?"

"Maybe. But I think there's more to it than that."

"Maybe you could turn the article into a positive piece," suggested Dan. "You could focus on the pool analogy; talk about how these women are trying to realize their dreams in a different lane, so to speak."

"Look at you, loving the pool analogy! That's not a bad idea, actually. Maybe I could write about how diversified the female journey is today . . . focus on how Sabine, Naomi, and Charlie are all captains of their own destinies . . . trying to balance what their former, naïve selves wanted out of life with what their wise, weathered, thirty-something selves know to be reality: bills to pay, kids to take care of in Naomi's case, stress levels to maintain. . . ."

"Yeah, you could call the article 'Balancing Act' or something."

"Hmmm, that's a little much. But I see where you're going with that. The only problem with the new scope of the article is, who's going to publish it? *Redbook,* for chrissake?! I was hoping to break out of the women's magazine box."

"Don't be so negative!" reprimanded Dan. "I think there's plenty of room in the *Times* for a positive piece about the anti–Carrie Bradshaw gang in New York. Considering the sad state of the world at this point, I have a feeling the paper is open to some inspiring and uplifting articles. They can squeeze it in between the latest death toll from Iraq and an announcement about how gas is now going to cost $10.57 a gallon."

Bess laughed. "Oy, gas. How are you driving out there?"

"Easy, instead of eating, I drive. I'm going to pen a new diet book and share my groundbreaking technique with the rest of the world."

"You'd better be eating!" Bess said, in her best "concerned girlfriend" voice. "You know, that's a really good point about how a positive article has just as much likelihood of being published these days. Thanks, Dan, you really turned this around for me."

"No problem, sweets. I really like this version better. This way, nobody gets hurt and you don't look like a sneaky, selfish asshole. Plus, I think your thesis will have more backup in this vein. Before, you were kind of treading water."

"Tell me what you really think," teased Bess. Dan had been against the article from the beginning, but somehow Bess had convinced herself that it was because he was trying to hold her back and stifle her career. Turns out it was the other way around. Her heart surged with warmth for this man, who suddenly felt nine billion miles away.

"I miss you," said Bess. "A lot."

"Jesus, I know. I really miss you, too. Everything is just better when you're around."

"I feel the same way about you, D." Bess paused, surprised by the thought that leaped from her like a cartoon lightbulb. *Fly out there. This weekend.* "Hey . . . what are you doing this weekend?"

"You mean, the one coming up? No real plans at this point, I guess. It's Sunday, babe. I don't even know what I'm doing tomorrow."

"What if I came out? To visit?" asked Bess, hardly believing that the words were coming out of her mouth. Spontaneity was not her specialty. And the rational ramifications—she would have to miss class, obviously—did nothing to sway her need to see Dan. As soon as humanly possible. *This is what love is all about, right? Taking risks . . . throwing caution to the wind?*

"Are you serious? Really?!" asked Dan, his excitement lifting his voice a decibel.

"Yeah. I really am."

"Are you kidding me? I would love it. I've been dying for you to come out here, you know that."

"I'm not!" said Bess. "I'm going to take Friday off and come out. Leave Sunday."

"But wait, won't you miss class on Saturday?"

"I will, but that's okay. I just . . . I really want to see you." And she did. The weight of missing him overwhelmed anything else. The article, work, her class, her reservations about losing herself in him—her voice of reason was drowned out by her emotional connection to Dan. And he was so good to her, so supportive and helpful of her article and her work. Maybe she really could have it all. The creative fulfillment, love, happiness . . . ponies, rainbows, kittens. She certainly owed it to herself and to them to give it a real shot.

"Bess, this is amazing news. Book the ticket and come to papa. I cannot wait to take you all around . . . show you my life here."

So I can see how I might fit in, thought Bess. The thought of moving out there flitted through her mind without her usual defensive response. Instead of her entire body tensing at the thought, she felt fluid and calm about at least exploring the possibility. *Yoga has calmed me. Sabine, Charlie, and Naomi have calmed me. Love has calmed me.* She smiled, as the realization registered. "I can't wait to see you, Dan. I'll book my ticket and let you know the details." She thought about her dad. "Maybe I'll get there a little earlier so I can visit my parents. I could leave right after work on Thursday."

"Great idea! I can't wait to meet them. Can we look at old photos of you during your awkward adolescent stage? I'm picturing a lot of hairspray and maybe some braces with rubber bands."

Bess laughed. "Not quite. I did have braces but no hairspray. Just a weird perm." Her parents were definitely not the type to willingly bust out old albums, so at least she was safe. Better to come clean about her preteen years though, before a photo was leaked unexpectedly.

"Really!? Oh wow, I can't wait to see. There's nothing like 'tween angst to bring a couple together. By the way, I had acne and an Adam's apple the size of a basketball. A real lady's man. How is your dad feeling?"

"He's okay. It's hard to say, you know, being so far away, so I want to see for myself." Just talking about her dad's vulnerability made her nervous. "Listen, I'm gonna call them and make sure they're around this weekend. I'll call you back tomorrow and let you know what's happening."

"Okay, B. I can't wait to see you. Wait, what are your parents' names again? I want to start rehearsing my handshake into hug intro move now."

"Oh Jesus. Take it easy. My parents are not exactly the hugging kind." She laughed, imagining them being engulfed against their will by Dan's exuberance. "Michael and Anne are their names."

"Oh good, I'll get to work on my personalized poems for them," Dan teased.

"I love you, I have to goooo," whined Bess.

"Yeah, yeah, yeah, I know. Go book that ticket already. I love you, too. Talk soon." Bess hung up, somewhat stunned by the plan she had just put into motion.

She thought about her parents. She wondered if they would like Dan. She picked up the phone.

"Hello?"

"Hey, Dad!"

"Well hey, Bessie! What a treat!"

"Awww, Dad." Bess grinned involuntarily. "How are you feeling?"

"Oh, fine, fine. A little tired lately, but overall, just fine." Bess always wondered if he was telling her the truth. Talking to her mom sometimes, she sensed a different story from the one he stuck to. There was a wariness to her voice that reeked of worry.

She never said as much—Bess's parents were not the sharing kind—but Bess could sense it. When she probed and asked her mom if she was really okay, she would just brush her off, changing the subject to something innocuous like the weather. Bess often wondered what their relationship would be like if she lived closer. Maybe more real, but then again, maybe not. Her parents were master maskers.

"Listen, Dad, I think I'm gonna come out and visit you guys this weekend."

"Get out! Really! That would be terrific. Hold on, let me call your mother in here. Annnnnnnnnnnnnnnnneeeeeeeeee!"

"What, Michael? You sound like a dying animal, screaming my name like that across the house."

"Bessie's on the phone!"

"Oh! Bess!" Bess smiled at the excitement in her mother's voice.

"Bess?" she asked hesitantly, picking up the other phone.

"Hi, Mom!"

"Oh hi, honey, you sound good."

"Mom, listen, I think I'm going to come to LA this weekend."

"No! Really? Oh Bessie, we would love to see you! Do you need us to pick you up at the airport?"

"Actually, you know that guy I'm seeing? Dan?"

"Oh yes, of course," answered her mother—the hope in her voice palpable.

"I think I told you that he moved to LA for school, right? He's getting his master's in screenwriting at USC?"

"I think you may have, Bess," answered her dad. "How is he liking the West Coast? Is the pace too slow for a city boy like him?" Bess's father could never quite understand the draw of New York. *All this walking,* he would say whenever they visited.

"He likes it all right. Too much driving for him, though."

Her father laughed. "Oh, he just has to get comfortable behind the wheel."

"I can't blame him," her mother chimed in. "I just told your father the other day that the traffic here has gotten out of control. I'm thinking about getting a bike. With a basket, of course."

"So, maybe we'll come over Friday for dinner?" asked Bess, before her mother and father got into an endless conversation about the merits and drawbacks of the bicycle.

"Well, that would be wonderful," said her mother. "Will you spend the night?"

"No, we'll just go back to his place for the night."

Her father cleared his throat and Bess could sense his hurt feelings. "We wish you'd stay longer, Bess, but we understand. Maybe you'll reconsider." Bess winced into the phone. The old guilt trip.

"I don't know. Why don't we play it by ear."

"Okay, Bessie. We can't wait to see you and meet this young man. I'll let you and your mom talk now. See you soon."

"Bye, Dad, love you." He hung up the phone.

"Bess," her mother whispered. "You know that you can both sleep in the guest room."

Bess laughed. "Jesus, Mom, I would hope so. We're both a hundred years old!"

"Bess, I don't like it when you say 'Jesus' like that. It sounds crude. And I know that you're both grown-ups, but your father is old-fashioned. I'll work on him, though. And if you stay, I'll make you homemade cinnamon rolls in the morning."

"Mom, you're bribing me!"

"Maybe. It's just that we miss you, Bessie. Please think about staying over. Your father would love it."

"How's he feeling, by the way?"

"Okay . . . a little tired. He's taking his afternoon naps now without a fuss, so that's good."

"What is he, a toddler?" asked Bess. "Afternoon naps?"

"Bess, he's operating on a much smaller engine. If he doesn't get his rest during the day, it's too much strain on his heart." This was the most open her mother had ever been about her dad's health. For her to say that he needed a nap meant that he needed one and then some.

"Mom, of course, I'm sorry. Forget I said that. That was dumb. We'll stay over. Who can turn down your cinnamon rolls?"

"Oh, good! Your father will be so happy. I'll be so happy to see you, Bess. So, Friday night we'll see you! And meet Don!"

"It's Dan, Mom."

"Yes! Dan! Oh, does he eat meat?"

"Yep, he's a carnivore."

"Great, love you, Bessie. See you soon!"

Bess hung up and marveled at the fact that, in less than a week, Dan would be sitting on her parents' couch drinking a beer. Or a wine spritzer, if her mother stepped in as bartender. The last time her parents had met someone she was dating, she hadn't even been old enough to drink legally.

What was that guy's name? Alex? Aaron? No, Alex. He had come over to take her to the movies. *Sleepless in Seattle.* About halfway through, young Alex had attempted to put his hand down her pants. Mortified, she had slapped his face, right there in the middle of the theater.

Bess laughed, remembering, and returned to her computer. She had a ticket to buy.

chapter twenty-eight

Charlie

Charlie cupped her head with her hands. Her forehead pressed against her mat, its rubbery surface threatening to gauge indentations into her skin. She breathed slowly.

In for five counts, and then, on her five-count exhale, she walked her feet in toward her elbows. Her hips were at a ninety-degree angle, directly over her shoulders. With another deep breath in and out, she drew her knees into her chest as she lifted both feet off the floor.

She struggled for a moment as she straightened them and then—sweet release. Long and straight, her legs reached for the ceiling as she relished the pleasant tension of blood rushing to her head. The heat circulated through her skull. She remained upright for about three minutes and then, with her right leg leading, she dismantled her headstand.

Back on the mat, she sat in lotus position as the blood resettled throughout her body. Her head felt clearer than it had in months and the grogginess she had wrestled with all the way to the studio was now a distant memory. She closed her eyes to take in the rare moment of peaceful, contented clarity.

She heard the distinct thud of feet on the wood floor and opened her eyes, slightly alarmed. It was early morning. Had she remembered to lock the door behind her when she came in?

She noticed a familiar backside across the room, as he crouched on all fours and savored his own post-headstand clarity. Charlie smiled and waited a beat before greeting him. Wrenching someone out of a moment like that with a chipper "hello" was just cruel.

He moved into a sitting position on his mat, facing Charlie with his eyes closed.

"Hello, Julian," Charlie said. He opened one eye in response, a sly grin spreading across his face.

"Good morning," he replied. "I decided to copy you."

"How so?" asked Charlie, as she assumed the pigeon pose to stretch her quadriceps.

"I saw you headstanding and it just looked so good! I needed to do one of my own immediately."

"How did it feel?" asked Charlie, savoring her stretch.

"Heavenly."

Charlie segued into Balasana. "I know, right?" she enthused. "I was just thinking about how the headstand is like nature's version of coffee."

"If headstands needed a PR person, you would have the job, no contest."

Charlie laughed as she resumed lotus position. "Howya doing, Julian? What's new and exciting?"

"Oh, not much." He smiled coyly. "Just that I'm engaged!"

"What?!" shrieked Charlie, as she instantly sprung off the floor in excitement. "What are you talking about? Whaaaaaat?" She jogged over to his mat and hugged him, practically knocking him over backward with her enthusiasm.

"Charlie, please! You're suffocating me!" Julian teased, clearly pleased by her response.

Charlie released him from her grasp and surveyed his beam-ing face. "Get out of here! I can't believe it! What amazing news! Where's your six-carat, pink J.Lo rock?" She took his left hand to search for it.

Julian laughed. "No bling. We did get matching tattoos, though." He flipped his left wrist over to show her the small, black initials: SC. "Scott has mine on his wrist," he explained. "We're like Mariah and Nick, without the insanity."

Charlie clapped her hands in glee. "Julian, I am so happy for you! Tell me everything: where were you, how did he do it, yada yada yada."

"We were having dinner. Just a typical Saturday night, you know. We've been trying to cook more, and it was Scott's turn. He made the most amazing tuna steaks. Seriously, you have no idea. They were so fresh—"

"Enough about the tuna steaks! Get to the good stuff."

Julian laughed. "Okay, okay. So, after dinner, Scott pulls out a bottle of champagne and some chocolate-covered strawber—"

"He put the ring in a strawberry!"

"Bish, please! Hello, cheese factor! Absolutely not. And be-sides, there is no ring. Pull it together, woman!"

"Oh sorry, sorry," apologized Charlie. "Forgive me, my estro-gen is getting the better of me. Go on."

"So, he pours the champagne and sits down next to me," Ju-lian continued. "I just thought he was being sweet, you know? I honestly had no idea that he was about to propose. I mean, we had talked about spending the rest of our lives together, but never about making it legal or anything like that."

"And then what happened?!"

"He took my hand and launched into this whole spiel about how he loves me and can't imagine life without me, blah blah blah.

At this point, I was starting to get a bit freaked out," Julian explained. "Obviously, this was not just about the strawberries."

"And then?"

"He asked me to marry him!" Julian shrieked.

"Wow! Were you stunned into silence or what?"

"Hell no! I screamed like a little girl! I said yes before he could even finish his question."

Charlie couldn't help it—joy overwhelmed her. She grabbed Julian again and pulled him into an embrace.

"So then, after all the lovey dovey crap, he tells me that there's a car outside," continued Julian, as he hugged Charlie back. "We go downstairs, hop in, and it takes us to the East Village. Scott's friend Margot owns a tattoo studio, and she had stayed open late to ink us!"

"That is too cool. Wow."

"I know, isn't it? My fiancé is a thorough guy. Fiancé," Julian repeated. "What a pretentious word. *Fiancé*. I think I like *Beyoncé* better. *And this is my Beyoncé, Scott*."

Charlie laughed heartily. "This is such wonderful news! I am over the moon for you guys! We have to have a party!"

"Sounds good to me. Just let me drop a couple of pounds first. Pictures last forever!"

"Oh, please! You look amazing. I could carve a ham with your jawline," she added, stealing one of Julian's catch phrases.

Julian beamed. "Okay, okay. Twist my arm and give me good lighting. A party it is!"

"Do you know when you're getting married?"

"Probably next spring. We're going to take a trip to Vermont and do it in style. Maybe just when all the flowers are beginning to bloom . . . leaves on the trees. The whole nine."

"I love it. You are going to be a beautiful bride."

"Bridezilla! I wonder if we can get on that show. I don't think they've ever had a gay couple before. I would put any of those women to shame. *'I said I wanted lilies!!! Lilies!!! Not gladiolas!'*" Julian mimicked.

Charlie laughed. "That would be something to see. Hey, how do George and Michael feel about all of this?"

"They're thrilled. But they're refusing to wear bridesmaid dresses. George doesn't want to spend two hundred fifty dollars on a schmatta he'll never wear again. He already read me the riot act."

Charlie guffawed, envisioning the chubby little pugs in matching strapless gowns. "The nerve of him! Doesn't he know it's all about you?"

"Exactly. Don't worry, he'll know it soon enough."

He paused, getting serious for a moment. "Thanks for all of your sweetness, Charlie. I really am happier than I've ever been in my life. I love him so much." He looked down, seemingly overwhelmed by his emotions. "I just feel so blessed, you know?"

"Oh baby, you deserve all of the happiness in the world!" Charlie answered, hugging him again. "I am so happy for both of you. You give the world hope! True love can exist!"

Julian embraced her back. "Thanks, Charlie. Speaking of, what's up with you lately?"

"Zero. *Nada.* This town is drier than the Sahara for me these days."

"Charlie, that's because you're not looking for any water. You couldn't be less interested in finding a man if you tried."

"What are you talking about?" asked Charlie, slightly annoyed by Julian's statement. "My eyes are open!"

"Yeah, maybe, but the store is closed for business. It's pretty damn obvious that you're not looking for love. Or even sex, for that matter."

Charlie rolled her eyes.

"Take Mario, for example," Julian said. "That man wants to sop you up with a biscuit. He lights up at the mere mention of your name."

She blushed, despite herself.

"See, you're blushing! I know you have a thing for him, too! But"—and here, Julian lowered his voice and took on a more serious tone—"he would certainly never know that. You don't give him the time of day."

"I do so!" Charlie countered. "The other day, when he brought me tea and a muffin for breakfast, I was completely grateful!"

"Homeboy brought you breakfast!? See what I'm talking about? He is on fire for you. I bet you just said thanks and put your face in the muffin."

"What else was I supposed to do? Drop to my knees and give him a blow job?"

"Potty mouth!" shrieked Julian, feigning disgust. "No need to whore yourself out for baked goods. But you could have batted your eyes a little, maybe put your hand on his forearm. You know, work it."

"Listen, maybe my game is pathetic, that I will give you, but getting something started with Mario would be a mistake. I have to see him every day. And besides, he's not exactly—"

"Who you see yourself with?" said Julian, finishing her sentence. "I get that, but don't be such a close-minded snot about it. He's a really cool guy and a hell of a businessman."

"He is?" Charlie had no idea that Mario was such an entrepreneur. Despite herself, she was slightly aroused.

"Yes, he is, Miss Wall Street. You can take the girl off Wall Street, but you can't take—"

"The Wall Street out of the girl," finished Charlie. "Listen, Julian, don't make me feel like an asshole because I got excited about his gigs. Let us not forget that the last man I dated had no j-o-b. It was awful. A proactive man gets me all hot and bothered."

"Hellooo, I feel you! I know that. Listen, we've gotten away from ourselves here. The whole point of our conversation was to dissect the reason why you're so unapproachable around men."

"I guess I'm just scared. After Neil, I . . . well, it's just hard for me to put myself out there again. Vulnerability is not my strong suit."

"I know, honey," said Julian, as he put his arm around her. "But sometimes you just gotta take the plunge already. Neil broke your heart into a million pieces, yes. That's a fact. But you are a strong-ass woman, and now—almost four years later—it is time to move on. If that means flirting with a hot deli owner who knows how to drywall, then so be it."

"He knows how to drywall?"

"Yup. I pretended to need to know how to do it, just so he could give me a tutorial with that sexy accent."

"You slut! What about Scott?"

"Honey, please. Just because I am on a diet, doesn't mean I can't look at the menu once in a while. It's healthy," he explained.

"What's healthy?" asked Felicity, peeking her head around the corner, her jacket hood framing her pretty face.

"Felicity!" yelled Charlie. "Julian has something to tell you!" She looked at Julian, her eyes blazing with excitement for him.

"Holy shit, what is it?" asked Felicity. "You're pregnant?!"

"Even better!" replied Julian. "I'm engaged!"

"Get out!!!" yelled Felicity, rushing toward him for a huge hug. "Congratulations!"

Charlie beamed broadly as she listened to Julian proudly re-hash the story. She was so lucky to have these two as her business partners. It was a blessing, to say the least.

And as for what Julian had told her about her standoffishness—

this was not exactly news to her. For so long, Charlie had let the hurt from the Neil breakup haunt her every move. Now, when she had finally exorcised that demon, she had no idea how to reenter the world of dating, sex, lust, love—whatever.

Watching Julian's face light up as he spoke lovingly about his soul mate, however, Charlie decided that she was ready to learn.

chapter twenty-nine

Naomi

Naomi lay in bed, terrified. *What is going on with me?* She slid her hands up and down her torso. She was numb. Not totally numb—she could feel her hands on a very base level, but her skin itself felt like mannequin skin: no warmth or texture. She moved to her breasts, grabbing them as if they were made of Play-Doh. Usually sensitive there, she could barely feel the pressure of her grasp. Circling her nipple with her finger barely registered. She moved her right hand over her left forearm. *Oh, good. Normal.* She moved up its length, kneading her flesh like dough and relishing the sensation. Up to her collarbone and over her face, her hand traveled. *All normal.* She retraced her path down to her groin. Also numb. *Shit.* She traced the lines of her labia and felt nothing. *Shit. What is wrong with me? Could the universe be punishing me for not using my lady parts? Use 'em or lose 'em?* Despite her panic, Naomi smirked at the cruel lesson. She continued, traveling down her left leg. *A bit of feeling, but decidedly off somehow. Like it's asleep. Left foot? Okay. Right foot, check. Right leg—mannequin again.* She exhaled deeply, fighting the tears that welled up.

"Moooooooooom!" yelled Noah from the other room. He

came galloping in, his broken arm balanced in its sling like a bird wing.

"Careful, Noah! Don't forget about your arm, baby. You can't move around like you used to, you know." *Okay: one, two, three. Sit up.* Naomi pulled herself up to a sitting position. *Okay, good. That was easy.*

"I know, Mom, don't worry. It hurts a little."

"Does it, baby?" She pulled him close, careful not to squoosh his wing. He nestled into her.

"Yeah," he answered. "Will you make me pancakes, please?" Noah was taking the day off from school. Although his arm drama had happened two days before, Naomi thought he deserved a sick day, just because. She was also feeling neurotic about sending her broken little bird out into the world alone. They had planned to use today as a training day of sorts—showing Noah how to get around now that he was operating with only one arm instead of two.

"Noah, I . . . I don't feel so hot," she answered. Saying it out loud made it real again. She couldn't ignore the numbness, it was too much of a dangerous warning sign. Of what, she had no idea. Noah looked at her quizzically.

"Is it your head again?" he asked.

"No, not my head. My body feels a little strange. I think I may have to go to the doctor."

"Are you okay?"

"I think so, baby. I just want to be sure." She got up, swinging her legs over the side of the bed. Noah watched her carefully. *Okay, everything works.* She gingerly put her feet on the hardwood floor and stood up. *Still working.* "We'll have breakfast in a minute, okay? I need to call my doctor." Noah stood beside her.

"Okay, Mom. Can I watch TV?"

"Yes, go ahead." He scampered off and Naomi walked carefully into the living room. She retrieved her bag and dug through it for the neurologist's number. Her appointment had originally been scheduled for Wednesday, but this was an emergency. Hopefully he could fit her in.

"Hello, Dr. Dipietro's office."

"Um, hi, this is Naomi Shepard. I have an appointment scheduled with Dr. Dipietro for Wednesday. I . . . I think I'm in trouble though, and I was wondering if I could see him today."

"What's wrong?"

"I woke up and am . . . well, I'm numb. My torso, my groin, my legs . . . like a mannequin. Numb." Tears began to fall down Naomi's face as her anxiety washed over her in waves.

"Okay, I'm going to put you on hold for a moment while I check his schedule."

"Oka—" She cut her off and Naomi was suddenly immersed in smooth jazz. Did the receptionist sound panicked? She thought back on it. No. There was nothing in her voice to suggest that Naomi's explanation was anything unusual. Was that a good sign or a bad one? She wondered if she had heard the mannequin explanation before.

"Okay, Ms. Shepard?" She clicked back in. "He can see you at two o'clock today."

"Oh good. Great. I'll be there. Thank you." Naomi hung up, her gratefulness mixed with sheer terror. *This is real and it's happening to me. This doctor is going to tell me something that might scare the shit out of me.* She touched her stomach. No change. *Wait, what am I going to do with Noah? Cee?* Cee worked on Mondays, and besides—she had screwed up royally with her and had yet to apologize for it. *Gene? No, he's in Paris. My parents?* The doctor's office was on the Upper East Side. She could drop Noah off and then just take the crosstown bus. She looked at her phone for the time. Eight thirty. No problem. She wished she didn't have to alarm them with the specifics of her bumped-up appointment, but she really had no other choice. She was in a bind.

"Hello?"

"Mom?" Naomi's voice quivered.

"Nay! What's wrong?"

"Um, something really strange is going on with me. I . . . uh . . . I woke up numb today."

"What?! Numb? Numb how?"

"My torso and my legs feel like mannequin skin." The tears fell from Naomi's eyes as she explained. "I don't know what's happening to me, but I changed my appointment with the neurologist for this afternoon."

"Oh, honey." Her mother paused, careful not to further worry Naomi. "Okay, good. What time?"

"Two. Do you think you could watch Noah while I'm there? He's home sick today, because of his arm."

"His arm? What happened?"

"He broke it on Saturday at the playground." Naomi suddenly felt completely overwhelmed. Her son was functioning on one arm and she was the Amazing Mannequin Woman.

"Nay, get up here as soon as you can. We'll have some lunch and then you can leave Noah here while you go to the doctor."

"Okay, Mama." She couldn't remember the last time she had called her that, but she felt so small and vulnerable suddenly. "Thank you. I love you."

"I love you, too, baby. Listen, take a cab. I'll pay for it. I don't want you on the subway right now."

"Okay," agreed Naomi, thankful for the treat. Navigating an underground journey in this state would be a nightmare.

Set into motion by the confirmation of the day's plans, she switched to all-business mode, fixing Noah some cereal—*No pancakes today, buddy, sorry*—and taking a shower. Shaving her legs, she couldn't feel the razor against her skin. She held back her tears, and finished the job. Once out, she gulped down some coffee and zipped herself into her jeans. Getting Noah dressed with his arm in a cast proved to be a feat in and of itself. After trying to wrestle him into his sweatshirt with no success, she grabbed an old sweater of her own and put it on over his head. Perfect.

"But Mom, it's a girl sweaterrr," Noah whined.

"You can't tell," snapped Naomi. *Damn. How are we going to get his jacket on him?* She eyed it, hanging from its hook by the front door. *Am I going to have to cut the arm off?* She thought of her own jackets. She had an old North Face from her college days that might work. Ten minutes later, Noah stood before her—his bottom half that of a little boy and his top half that of a female college sophomore from the late nineties. He looked at her angrily.

"Don't give me that face, Noah. What else can we do?"

One cab ride, a peanut butter and jelly sandwich with her mother, and a crosstown bus later, Naomi sat nervously in the doctor's office, her hands in fists as she nervously relayed the symptoms of the past month. He nodded and took notes as she spoke. Naomi wished she could see what he was writing.

"And yeah, so that's where I am today. I have this weird, numbness thing going on." She looked at him expectantly.

"I want to run a few tests on you," he said, matter-of-factly. He crossed over to her and touched her torso, confirming the mannequin sensation. He checked her fingers and her toes, her reflexes, and her eyes. He took a small metal instrument and hit it, checking for her sense of vibration. He tapped her feet, her arms, and then her back, traveling down her vertebrae methodically. Fine, fine, and then—nothing.

"You don't feel that?" he asked. Was it just Naomi's hypersensitivity or could she sense some nervousness in his voice?

"No, no I don't," she answered. There were the tears again. He cleared his throat. "Am I okay?"

"I don't know yet, that's what I'm trying to figure out. Could you come out into the hallway with me, please?" She dutifully followed him.

"I want you to walk down the hall, and then stop."

"Like a supermodel?"

He cracked a smile. *Finally, a human response.* "Exactly."

"I can do that." Naomi strutted down the length of the hallway, hoping that her gait was normal. It certainly felt normal.

"Okay, good. Come back."

She returned and Dr. Dipietro put his hand at the small of her back, steering her into his office again. "Come on in."

He took a seat. "Well, we can't be sure what is going on here," he explained. Naomi chewed her lip as though it were bubble gum. "It could be a viral infection. It could also be an autoimmune disease, like Lyme."

"Could I just have a slipped disk in my back?" asked Naomi. "From yoga maybe?"

"That's a slight possibility, but not likely. Your headaches suggest otherwise. I want to schedule you for a brain and two spinal cord MRIs, so we can get a look inside. I also want you to have a couple of blood tests today."

"What else could it be?" she asked. She didn't want to say it out loud. The thing she had been avoiding since typing in her symptoms at their outset. She hadn't even said those letters out loud, for fear that that alone would make it so.

"It could be MS," he answered. Tears spilled out of her eyes. "Listen, MS is not the horrible nightmare that you think it is." He looked at her earnestly. "It's a manageable disease, and the medication available now has changed its trajectory entirely." He paused, allowing Naomi to interject, but she couldn't speak.

"I am not saying you have it. The blood tests today will tell us if it's anything else. I just want you to know that it's a possibility. Your symptoms are not textbook, but that's the thing about MS, there is nothing textbook about it. Everyone's experience is different."

"It is?" asked Naomi. She had finally pulled herself together enough to talk. "I thought that MS . . . I mean, isn't everyone with it in a wheelchair?" It was hard to breathe suddenly.

"No, no, no. For some, yes, but only a small percentage of the MS population. Some people may have only a few flare-ups in their lifetime. Some people begin with an exacerbation like yours and then progressively get worse. Some experience minor numbness at certain points in their lives that either goes away on its own or is fixable with a simple steroid injection. And the medication available today is really only a recent thing. It has changed the lives of people with MS in amazing ways, and is absolutely making a cure more than likely in our lifetime."

"MS is an incurable disease, huh?"

"Yes, it is. But it is manageable. It is not fatal." *Incurable. Disease. How could I maybe have an incurable disease? My whole life, my body has bounced back from the brink with relative ease. Now this? Am I being punished?*

"Now, Naomi, listen to me. We don't know what is wrong with you, but we are going to do our best to find out. I don't want you to focus on MS when we're not sure at all at this point what is happening."

"Will I be numb forever?" asked Naomi, her voice coming out in a squeak.

The doctor smiled. "No. This will go away on its own, but it could take several weeks. I would like you to keep a journal about your symptoms. Do you think you could do that? That will be helpful for us later on."

Naomi nodded. "If it is MS, can I have more babies?"

"Yes, you can. Actually, pregnancy is great for MS symptoms. Who knows why? Naomi, I am sorry but I have another appointment. I do wish that I could spend more time with you today, but since I squeezed you in, our time has to be short. Take my card and e-mail me if you have any questions. Or call." *Wait, what is happening? How can he just leave me after this?* He grabbed his prescription pad. "I am going to write you up for three MRIs. Call this number and set them up. They'll say they don't have appointments open, but tell them Dr. Dipietro wants you in the tube as soon as possible." *The tube?* She had heard horror stories about those.

"And here, come with me. I am going to set you up with Lauren across the hall. She is going to take some blood from you so that we can run some tests here." Naomi stood up, now numb emotionally as well as physically. Minutes later, she watched the technician insert a needle into her vein. She felt like she was watching this—all of this—from a distance. *It's not me that this is happening to. But it is.*

After she had been sufficiently poked and prodded, she left the office and walked into the cold afternoon air. The bus rumbled toward her. *I don't want to take the bus. I want to walk.* She ambled toward the park, pausing every other step to wipe the tears that continued to stream down her face. She had never felt more alone in her life.

Walking now, she mumbled a prayer to the universe for this simple pleasure. Movement—true, easy movement—was something that she had always taken for granted. *Will I be able to practice yoga anymore? Shit, will I be in a wheelchair? What will Noah do?* Her tears came faster now and she had to pause to catch her breath. *I can't believe that two weeks ago I was whining about Gene taking a dumb paper version of Noah to Paris, and now, he might have the real thing for life because I won't be able to take care of Noah myself.*

Wiping her eyes with her gloves, Naomi continued her trek across the park with her head down, oblivious to the green buds on the trees and the flowers just beginning to poke their heads out of the thawing ground.

chapter thirty

Sabine

Jesus, slow it down! Sabine realized that she had been running to meet Zach. She wasn't late by any stretch of the imagination, so even a quickened pace was irrational. She simply couldn't wait to see him. She dug in her bag for a mint. She was about three minutes away from the bar. She looked at her watch. She would be exactly on time. Such was the curse of her anal retentive tendencies. She couldn't be late, even when she was trying her hardest to do so. She also could never leave a dish in the sink when she left the house. Once, she had given it everything she had not to wash her breakfast dishes. She had forced herself to leave the house, only to make it one block before turning back around. *If a dish cleaning compulsion is the worst of my flaws, then I'm doing all right.* She looked up. She was at the bar just in time to chew the last scrap of mint and swallow.

She walked in. There he was, sipping a beer on a stool near the door. He was so . . . perfect. Dark, mussed hair, a slight scruff, a gray sweater with a white T-shirt underneath that conveyed the coveted "I'm not trying too hard, I just happen to have decent taste" message, slightly scuffed jeans, and the pièce de résistance, chocolate brown Rod Lavers. Sabine had a very strange, unparalleled affinity for brown sneakers. She had tried to figure out why after a particularly steamy encounter with a brown Adidas Gazelle on a very unattractive man at Whole Foods. The man himself did zero for her, but the shoes. The shoes! She had managed to track her obsession back to Tyler Sellers in the seventh grade. He had been Sabine's first, full-blown, "doodle his name on her notebook paper and then immediately throw it out" crush, and he had worn brown Nike Air Force Ones. Sabine wasn't sure which came first, the crush or the shoe, but now they were inseparable entities. Hence the flush that crept up her cheeks the moment she had seen Zach wearing his Lavers on the subway. And now, here she was, on her second date with him. *Will those shoes end up on my floor tonight?* She imagined them littering her living room floor. *Or maybe he'll leave them outside my door, like my neighbor's boyfriend does.*

Zach looked up from his beer. A huge smile emerged as he noticed Sabine in the doorway. Her heart sloshed around in her chest at the sight. "Hey!" he exclaimed.

She made her way toward him. "Hello," she replied, hoping her voice sounded level. He moved to hug her.

"How are you?" she asked, as she unzipped her jacket and hung it over the bar stool.

"Great, now. You look pretty."

"Thanks, Zach. You don't look so bad yourself. Whatcha drinkin'?"

"Blue Moon. It's delicious. Can I get you one?"

"I'll have a glass of wine, I think. Maybe a Shiraz?" Zach ordered it for her as she made herself comfortable. "Thanks," she said when she had settled in. She lifted her glass to toast and he did the same. "To—"

"To the longest week and a half ever," he finished. "I'm really happy to see you again."

Sabine took a sip and nodded. "Me, too. And to your case being over. Or is it?"

"It is. Our client won, too, which is a huge relief."

"Congrats!"

They smiled at each other goofily.

"How's yoga treating you?" asked Zach. Sabine had tried to mask her soreness on their first date, but eventually she had had to cop to her aching abs. Every time she laughed, her core had screamed in pain.

"You know what, I'm actually getting the hang of it! This week's class wasn't nearly as difficult."

"That's great. I've always wanted to get into yoga, but I'm afraid my flexibility level is pretty bad. I run and stuff at the gym, but I can barely touch my toes."

"No, no, I was the same way! You couldn't have convinced me that I would be able to actually enjoy it. But my teacher is awesome and I really feel like I've gotten comfortable, you know? As soon as I quit worrying about whether I was good at it or not, I started to enjoy it."

"Oh, you hadn't done yoga before?" asked Zach. "I thought you were a regular."

"No way! Why?"

"You have really nice posture," he explained. "You stand up straight when you walk. It's almost . . . regal." In the dim light of the bar, Sabine could see him blushing.

She laughed. "Really? Thanks. I never thought about my posture before." She eyed her glass of wine nervously. Zach brushed her hair back from her face. She looked up to see him staring at her tenderly.

"I'm not a 'make out at the bar' kind of guy. But I want to kiss you right now."

"Okay," agreed Sabine, her insides turning to jelly. And he

did. Soft but authoritative, aggressive but not overbearing, wet but not slobbery. Perfect. Sabine put her hand on his thigh. She pulled away and they rested their foreheads against each other. She was looking directly into his raisin jewels. "I like your eyelashes," she whispered.

He laughed softly. "Thanks. I like yours, too." They stayed like that, foreheads together, for a minute more, before Zach sat up straight and smiled. "Want to get something to eat?"

No, I want to take you home and rip your clothes off. "Okay," agreed Sabine. She was further from being hungry than she had ever been in her life, except maybe once, when she had promptly spiraled into stomach flu after ingesting a salad swimming in Ranch dressing. She had never been able to look at that condiment the same way since.

Zach settled the tab and they walked hand in hand to a little Italian joint down the street. A bottle of wine and a few shared nibbles later, Sabine was tipsy and irrefutably horny. Every time his knee brushed hers under the table, she felt jolted by an invisible electric current.

"You want dessert?" he asked, as the waiter cleared their plates.

"No," Sabine replied. "I want to take you home." She was surprised by her forwardness, but she couldn't help it. She wanted him. Now.

"Check, please!" Zach yelled to the waiter. He stroked her jaw and smiled. Sabine thought about what his chest would feel like against hers. *Warm.*

Upstairs, in her apartment, Lassie lurked in the kitchen, peering out from behind the counter with curiosity. His little cat eyes didn't often see Sabine in such a compromised position. She and Zach were shirtless, pawing each other like wild tigers.

"You feel so good," Zach murmured. "Jesus."

"Mrmrmrm, mrmrmm," Sabine mumbled back. He felt better than she had ever imagined he would. All those months of subway longing, and she had never thought that her imagination was right on the money. She unbuttoned her pants.

Zach sat up suddenly at the sound of her zipper making its way down. "What?" she asked. She knew that they had talked about taking it slow, and in principle she did agree, but this felt too good. To stop now would be a crime against humanity!

"Sabine, I . . . I can't. I want to, believe me, but I just don't think it's a good idea. I think it's too fast."

Sabine sat up, too, suddenly longing for her shirt. "Zach, I mean . . . I understand your point, but come on! Don't you like this?"

"Sabine, I love this. You feel amazing. You're beautiful, believe me. My feelings for you have nothing to do with not wanting to have sex tonight. Trust me."

"Then what is it?" Sabine was embarrassed and annoyed simultaneously.

"No, that's not what I meant to say. My feelings for you have everything to do with not wanting to have sex tonight. I like you. I want to take it slow." *What the hell?* She wondered if he had a tiny penis. She hadn't really felt any sort of tell-tale lump when they had been wrestling on her couch. *What if it's the size of a jelly bean? I knew there was a catch!*

She attempted to regain her composure. Yelling at Zach about the validity of his manhood was not a good idea. That she knew. "Okay. I mean, I guess I understand where you're coming from." But she didn't. Something wasn't kosher here. What kind of guy denied himself sex? "Do you want to talk about it?"

"There's really not so much to talk about," answered Zach. "I've made the mistake of having sex too soon before, you know? I just think we should wait a bit. I mean, we have time. I'm not going anywhere. . . . Are you?"

Just to bed alone, jackass, thought Sabine. She was surprised by the intensity of her anger. She really liked Zach, too, obviously. She just thought that the waiting thing was a load of horseshit. She couldn't help but feel that there was more to the story than Zach was letting on. Was he grossed out by her stomach roll?

"No, I'm not going anywhere," she finally answered. She grabbed her shirt off the floor and slipped it on over her head. After she pulled her head through, she added, "Except to bed."

"Do you mind if I stay over?" asked Zach. "I really want to sleep in your bed with you. Feel you." He laughed. "Do I sound like such a mangina right now, or what?"

Sabine laughed. "Sort of."

"Seriously. Wow. 'No sex but can we snuggle?' Who am I right now? I'm sure you're pretty over me at this point. Sorry I'm acting like such a weirdo. I just . . . I want to try to do things differently this time," he explained again, but it still sounded like he was holding something back.

"It's okay," Sabine answered, softening slightly. His humility was endearing, even though she still didn't get it. "You can stay over if you want."

She gathered her things and gave Lassie a pet as she deposited them in her hamper. She washed her face and brushed her teeth, still dazed by what had just happened. She emerged to find Zach lying on her bed in his underwear. Long and lean. *Okay, so he's not a total chick,* she thought. She eyed his crotch. *How could someone this tall have a jelly-bean dick?* "You can use my toothbrush if you want," she offered.

"Thanks." He got up and walked into the bathroom, giving her butt a little swat on his way in. Sabine took off her clothes and pulled a tank top over her head. She climbed into her bed and shut out the light. Her mind was racing. Her libido, which had been a raging inferno just an hour before, was now reduced to a blown-out birthday candle—a stream of flimsy smoke trailing from its tip. She turned on her side. *Is he really going to spoon me?* she wondered. She just wanted him to go home.

Zach climbed into her bed beside her and answered her question immediately. With his arm over her and his chest to her back, she did feel warm and protected. But she also still felt uneasy. How could he be so capable of going to sleep beside her when her braless breasts were just a grope away?

"Good night, Sabine."

"Night," she replied. *Dummy.*

Moments later, Zach was asleep, his breath heavy in her ear. His arm suddenly seemed to weigh a million pounds. She didn't want to snuggle, damn it! She gingerly removed the offending limb and he rolled over in response. *Ahhh, freedom.* She stared at the ceiling and rehashed the night's events. Had she inadvertently used her finger to scoop food onto her fork instead of her knife? Was her muffin top particularly offensive in her jeans? They were a little snug. Had he smelled the emergency, anxiety-provoked cigarette she had smoked that afternoon on her breath? Had she gotten spaghetti sauce in her hair? She sighed deeply. There was no point in torturing herself any longer. She wondered if dating was even worth it. All of the drama, and for what? When it was just her, she could do whatever she wanted. She didn't have to shave, she slept like a baby, she could eat cereal for dinner with no judgment. . . .

She listened to Zach's breathing in the darkness and felt his body's warmth two feet away. Despite her anger, it was a nice feeling to have him in her bed; and one that trumped cereal any day of the week. She closed her eyes and drifted off, her doubt temporarily silenced by sleep.

chapter thirty-one

Bess

Bess squinted as she stared out her little porthole at the tarmac. LAX loomed, sun-dappled in the near distance. She was here. Even through the plastic window, she could feel the sun warming her face. She had left 20 degree slush-land and now, just six hours later, was about to break out her flip-flops. She sat up as straight as she could in her cramped seat and stretched her arms to the ceiling. Despite the red-eye and her close quarters, her body felt good. Yoga was working. And in more ways than one—while she was packing, she had pulled out a tank top that hadn't seen the light of day in years because of her dreaded bra-bulge. She had tried it on, just for the hell of it, and had been shocked and surprised by the results. The bulge was no longer a bulge. It was more like a slight swell. Naturally, she hadn't taken it off since.

As they pulled into the gate, Bess's heartbeat quickened. She couldn't wait to see Dan. She had never been picked up at the airport by a boyfriend in her life, but had always secretly dreamed of it. In the movies—how they always flew into each other's arms with abandon, her hair blown back by a wind machine and he carrying a bouquet of fresh wildflowers . . . Bess's inner girly girl always swooned at the sight. Not that she would ever admit it. *I have a reputation to uphold,* she thought, as she stood up to yank her bag out of the overhead compartment.

As she left the plane, she practiced her deep breathing. *Bess, get a hold of yourself! Jesus, you just saw him less than a month ago. Take it down a notch.* She wondered what her insane level of excitement was all about, really. Probably the fact that this was a huge trip for her—a huge trip for them. Whether she openly admitted it or not, this trip was about her feeling out LA as a possible new home, not to mention that he was meeting her parents. The fact that she had even gotten on the plane realizing her true intention was huge. Two months ago, the idea of relocating was ludicrous to her. It had been the combination of love, yoga, the article, and the women themselves that had opened up her mind to the possibility that she could chase her heart while accomplishing her goals.

At baggage claim, she searched as subtly as she could for Dan. *Where is he?* she wondered. *Did he forget that today was the day? Shit.* She scanned the area and turned around to do the same on the opposite side. There he was, grinning his lopsided, goofy grin and holding a single balloon. "Hi, lovely."

It was all Bess could do not to burst into tears. The anticipation of seeing him and now, actually seeing him, was the equivalent of an emotional punch to the gut. "Dan!" she squealed and hugged him tightly. "Hi," she whispered into his neck.

"Hello, my love. It's so good to see you. Damn." Dan released himself from her grasp. "To see you *here*. In LA!"

"I know. It's a trip, right?"

"Literally and figuratively," Dan added.

"Hardy, har, har. Mr. Clever!"

Dan pulled her back into an embrace. "You smell good. Like airplane peanuts and hyacinth."

"Mmmm. delicious. Let's get out of here!" She pointed to her carry-on bag. "I'm ready to roll."

"You got it," answered Dan, taking its handle. "But take your balloon, damn it!"

Bess grabbed its string. "Thank you for this. It's a nice touch." She tilted her neck to gaze up at the pink sphere. "What does it say?" She tugged sharply at it to bring it down to eye level. *IT'S A GIRL!* had been manipulated to read *IT'S A MY GIRL!* Bess laughed. "You are ridiculously clever and cute." She kissed him firmly on the mouth.

"Well, thank you," Dan replied with a satisfied grin. "I thought that was way better than the whole recycled red rose experience." He took her bag. "Now let's get the hell out of here before the paparazzi swarm."

Driving down Sunset Boulevard, Bess gazed out the window and relished the sunlight already browning her pale, New York–winterized arm. Being in LA brought back so many memories of her adolescence. *Can I really make a new start here?* she wondered. Adolescent Bess really wasn't that much different from Adult Bess. Yes, she had grown up in LA, but the whole experience had never really seduced her. No fake ID, body glitter, beach blanket bingo, or beer bong moments for her. It had been all about school. And journalism. Maybe one or two boy-related slips, but they never lasted long.

"You know, it's crazy, Dan. I'm sitting here staring out the window, thinking about growing up here, and I realize that there was nothing truly Californian about it—at least in the general sense."

"Whaddaya mean? Because you were such a nerd?" Dan smiled.

Bess laughed. "Yeah, I guess. I mean, the only time I came to Sunset was to buy CDs."

"You never OD'd at the Viper Room? Or snuck into any of those hellacious clubs?"

"Nope, not ever. I barely went to the beach."

"Do you regret it? Does part of you wish that you had embraced your inner Paris Hilton?"

"Not at all. At least I don't think so. I mean, I honestly can't remember wanting to do the sunny California, surfer girl type shit. It just didn't appeal to me."

"Were you the class freak?"

Bess ruminated on the question for a minute. "No, I don't think so. My looks saved me from that superlative."

"Yeah, you might not have had an ounce of California in you, but you definitely look the part. My hot, blond, beach bunny."

God, I'm only an hour into the trip and already I'm having flashbacks, she thought. *Would living here again submerge me in the past? Or would it give me a chance to enjoy the things about LA that I basically ignored growing up?*

"You okay?" Dan asked. "Your brow is all crinkled up like you're deep in thought."

Bess relaxed her face and immediately thought of Charlie. She loved it when she massaged their faces at the end of class. She'd be lying on her back, with her eyes closed—certainly feeling relaxed—and then Charlie would knead her forehead and jawbone gently. Bess had no idea that she held so much tension there. "I'm great, Dan. Sorry, it's just that being here brings up all these questions and memories. It's pretty wild."

"I bet. Listen, we'll get back to my house, you'll take a shower—"

"I'll jump your bones," interrupted Bess.

Dan guffawed. "Jump my bones! What is this, 1989?"

Bess gave him her best vixen smile and dug in her bag for her sunglasses. Why hadn't she put these on before? It was part of the LA uniform. Minutes later, they parked on the street in front of his apartment. "Here she is," Dan announced. "Home sweet home."

"I can't wait to see it!" gushed Bess. "Is your roommate home?"

"Alas, no. My good man has taken one for the team and gone elsewhere for the entire weekend. The palace is ours."

"You're kidding me! He didn't have to do that. I feel like an asshole for kicking him out."

"But you're also sort of psyched, right?" asked Dan as he climbed out of the car. "C'mon, let's be real." He grinned at her. "We can make all the noise we want now."

"Walk around naked," added Bess, as she grabbed her bag from the trunk.

"Use his sex swing," added Dan. He took her bag from her hands.

"Get out! He has a sex swing?"

"Dirty girl! No, I'm just yanking your chain. Let's get in there already. Follow me."

In bed, Bess lay on Dan's chest, relishing her bliss. "I like your place," she said. With three bedrooms, a living room, a bathroom and a half, and a kitchen with an island, it made her apartment in New York look like a dressing room at Target.

"Yeah, the third bedroom makes a cool office, right? When I first moved in here I was like, there's no way we're going to be able to use all this space! But Jesse looked at me like I was nuts. He's never done the whole New York, live in an apartment the size of a bathroom thing."

"Lucky man," said Bess.

"Is he, though? I think everyone should have to endure the abuses of New York real estate at least once in their lives. Puts some hair on the chest."

"If you're implying that New York men are particularly manly, you are out of your mind."

Dan laughed. "Point taken. Maybe it just puts hair on women's chests, then."

Bess pinched his thigh.

"Oww!" he shrieked. They burst into contented laughter. "You know, if you moved here, we could get a place just like this, for like, half of what you pay in rent now."

"I know that, Mr. Trump. Thanks for the real estate sell."

"I'm just saying," said Dan. "We'd be living together, but not living on top of each other a la New York."

"I know, I know. And we'd go for hikes every day in the morning and swim in the ocean at night. It never rains in sunny California, blah blah blah."

"You sound like such a New York cliché right now," said Dan, visibly annoyed by her brush-off.

"I'm sorry, Dan. I do think that LA is beautiful, I really do. And the idea of moving here does not repulse me."

"Really?!"

"Slow down there, sparky. The slightest bit of overexuberance from you could send me into an anti-LA spiral. I'm taking baby steps, here."

"Okay. I will be as unenthusiastic as possible. One step up from an amoeba."

Bess laughed. "Dan, I am starving! Do people eat brunch here?"

"Sure they do. Egg whites only though, across the board. Carbs cost three dollars extra an ounce."

"Seriously, do you have a favorite spot? I'm about to eat your comforter."

"Yes, my little love crumpet. It's down the block a bit. Put on some clothes and we can be there in thirty minutes max."

"Oh, good." Bess leaned over and gave Dan a kiss. "Magic words. Let's go." She rolled out of bed and searched the floor for various articles of clothing. She reassembled her outfit and washed her face. *Yikes,* she thought, gazing at herself in the mirror. A long flight was always brutal. You board the plane looking like the travel-ready version of yourself, but then disembark as Keith Richards. She patted on some eye cream in an attempt to de-puff.

"You ready, Bess?" yelled Dan from the living room. Bess turned out the light and made her way to him, her stomach growling violently.

"Yep. We can walk, right?"

"Walk?" Dan asked. He looked at her like she had just told him to go fuck himself. "Bess, no. Walking is a no-no."

"But didn't you say the place was just down the block?"

"Yeah, so? That's not how we roll here."

"It is today," retorted Bess. "Let's walk, come on. It will be nice to get some fresh air."

Dan looked at her in horror. "Really?"

"Really. Come on!" She led Dan out the front door and into the warm sunlight. A slight breeze ruffled the leaves of the palm tree in the front yard. "I can't believe this," said Bess to a pouting and shuffling Dan as they made their way to the restaurant. "When I left New York last night, it was freezing and damp and just generally winter sucky. Now, I'm in flip-flops and getting sunburned." She shook her head in wonder. "I had forgotten about what a difference nice weather makes. I'm actually smiling! Smiling, outside, in March!"

She looked at Dan, who had accepted his walking fate. He smiled back and took her hand. "I can see that, Bess. It looks good on you."

$\int$ o, are you excited to meet my parents tonight?" asked Bess at lunch, her french fry halfway to her lips.

"I really am. I think I might even be nervous." Dan chewed a bite of his omelet and swallowed, watching Bess's reaction. "What if they don't think I'm good enough for their precious baby girl?"

"Oh God, please. My parents love me, but there's no 'precious baby girl' thing going on. I'm sure they'll like you, if you act like a gentleman." But would they? And if they didn't, would they even tell her? They were so low key about everything. Or at the very worst, passive-aggressive low key, which would mean a response like: *He's nice,* followed by silence.

"I am always a gentleman! Should I get your mom some flowers or some wine?"

"Hmmm. Wine, I guess. My mom's a fan of the wine spritzer, so maybe a white."

"Got it." Dan gazed at her. "Do you look like your parents?"

"I do. Mostly my mom, though. We're both blondies."

"Ooh, a MILF."

"Gross! Dan, she's . . . shit, how old is she? Oh, sixty-four." Sixty-four felt like a big number. Next year she could get the senior discount at the movies. And her dad was three years older. Sixty-seven. How did this happen?

"What would you be doing tonight if you weren't sipping wine spritzers with my parents?" she asked, eager to change the subject. "Out at some bar, ogling women with plastic breasts?"

"No way," said Dan. "Most of the bars out here sort of suck. When I get together with people, it's usually at someone's house."

Bess considered his statement. *How depressing. The people here suck so bad that the bars aren't fun?* She ruminated on it for a minute. *But wait, when's the last time I went to a bar in New York and had the time of my life?* She had had fun the other night with Charlie, Naomi, and Sabine, but that's precisely why. She was with *them.* She wasn't looking to meet people, she had come with her posse already assembled. "Dan, are we officially old?" she asked.

"Why, because we hate bars now?" He smirked. "Yeah, I guess so. But somehow I don't mind it that much, you know? I mean, maybe if I were single it would be more of a bummer, but I'm with the most amazing woman in the world. There's just no need for the whole bar scene."

"How come you always say the perfect thing?" asked Bess. "You're lucky I don't straddle you right here as a reward."

"What's stopping you?" Dan gave her his best sexy look.

"Ooooh, sexy." *I really love him,* she thought. *He makes me inordinately happy. Why do I live a zillion miles away?*

Bess took a sip of her drink and surveyed the smallish crowd. Brunch in New York always meant at least an hour wait. You'd be dying for just a drop of caffeine, just a bite of bacon, just a place to sit your weary, hungover ass and . . . nothing. No matter how fair the system supposedly was, inevitably someone who had arrived after you would sit before you. You would see it happening, but be too weak to protest the injustice. Bess had actually been a brunch fanatic once upon a time, but New York had silenced that passion about two years in. It just wasn't worth it. Here, though, she could brunch to her heart's content—a huge selling point.

"You ready to go?" asked Dan. He placed some money on the table and they made their way back outside.

"Oh shit," said Bess, rubbing her belly. "I really wish we had your car here."

"See! I told you!" yelled Dan. "Hilarious. Too bad sista, we're walking home. Strap on your sneakers."

"Gahhhhhhh," Bess whined. "I'm too full to walk."

Dan laughed. "You are too much. Let's go. As soon as we get to my apartment, we'll jump in the car and I'll take you on a scenic

LA tour. We have time, right? When do we need to be at your parents' house?"

"Around seven. We've got plenty of time for a tour." She grabbed his hand and they strolled home, the sun freckling Bess's shoulders.

The day was pretty magical—blue skies, seventy-something degrees, relatively traffic-free drives along the coast and up winding hills, strolling down Rodeo Drive and making fun of the women's face-lifts and boulder breasts, even a celebrity spotting or two.

Before Bess knew it, they were at the grocery store, picking up the wine. Inside, she practically wept with delight. The aisles were so big! The produce was so fresh! And the lines . . . what lines!? LA was growing on her, there was no doubt about it.

Back in his car, Bess started to get nervous. "Are you sure you're okay with spending the night?"

"Bess, for the hundredth time, it's fine. Really. As long as we can sleep in the same bed and your mom cooks us up a hungry man breakfast in the morning, I am golden. Please stop worrying."

"Okay, sorry. I need half a valium or something." She reached into her bag. "I have one on me, I'm going to take it, okay?"

Dan glanced at her sideways. "Shit, really? You're that nervous about this? Okay, Bess, if you think it will make you feel better. Just don't go facedown into dinner after your first spritzer, okay?"

Bess laughed. "Not to worry, this is a super-low dose. It's probably just a sugar pill, but I take it when my anxiety reaches the breaking point. Works like a charm."

"Do you get really anxious often?" asked Dan, surprised.

"Sure, don't you?"

"No, not really." He paused.

I hope he doesn't think I'm some sort of pill-popping psycho.

"Dan, it's no big deal! It's just a pill."

"Bess, I could give a shit about the pill. I just can't believe that I don't know my girlfriend has anxiety issues. Why haven't you told me about this before?"

"I don't know. I mean, it's not exactly something that comes up in casual conversation." She looked out the window, recognizing the street as her own. "Turn right here."

Dan was silent. "Dan, come on, what's wrong? I don't tell you everything about me, that's just not my style."

"But I want you to, Bess." He slowed the car. "Is this it?"

Bess smiled at the sight. There it was—the house she had grown up in. One story high, it really was no different from the other ranch-style homes in the neighborhood. It was only when you looked closely that you could tell that she had lived there. In the front walk, on the left-hand side at about the middle of its length, were her initials. And the far right pillar of the front porch had grooves carved into its wood, from when Bess had gone through her *Gilligan's Island* phase. She had pretended to be on a deserted island—waking up each morning and notating it with a steak knife. That hadn't even lasted a week though—just six days.

She turned to look at Dan, wondering what it looked like through his eyes. He was frowning. "Bess, of course I don't want you to feel like you have to tell me everything, but how are we going to work if you're holding back on the important stuff?"

"Dan, I'm sorry. I love you and I'm sorry. It's really not such a big deal. Now, look outside! This is where I grew up! Can you believe it?"

Despite himself, Dan smiled. "Little Bess used to play in this yard!"

"Yep." She reached over and kissed him. "Come on, let's go in."

Out of the car, with wine and flowers in hand, they strolled up the walk. The door opened. "Bess!" exclaimed her mother.

"Mom!" Bess ran to her, suddenly overcome by the need to hug her. She looked the same except somehow smaller, as though the years were shrinking her.

"Oh Bess, you look beautiful." She took Bess's face in her hands. "My pretty girl."

"Bess!" boomed her father, bringing up the rear. Instantly, Bess's heart flopped in her chest at the thought that he might look much older and more frail than she had imagined. He pulled her close before she had a real chance to look at him. Peeling herself out of his embrace after a moment, she took him in. A little smaller, with a little less hair, but the same dad. She fought back tears of relief.

"Mom, Dad—this is Dan." She turned to pull him into the circle.

After a dinner of barbecued chicken, steak, and salad on the back porch, Bess sat with her dad on the couch inside while Dan fulfilled his dream of sifting through her old photos with her mom.

"You feeling okay, Dad?"

"Bess, I'm feeling okay. I get tired more easily these days, but I can't tell if that's just because I'm old or it's because of my heart." He laughed. "The operation wasn't so bad, you know. It's pretty wild to have this thing protruding out of my chest, though." He fingered the pacemaker just above his heart.

"Makes it hard to wear tank tops huh?"

"Ha! Bess, that's funny. Exactly. My tank top days are over, I'm afraid."

They settled into the couch contentedly. Bess sipped her spritzer.

"Bess, this Dan is a nice guy."

"Really, Dad? You like him?" It felt so good to hear him say that. Better than she thought it would.

"I do. He seems to be crazy about you, and that's really all I care about. Well, not all I care about. I wish he had a job."

"Dad, he did have a job. Now he's in school pursuing his passion. I'd rather be with somebody who is doing what he really wants to do than with a man who is trapped in a job he hates."

"Fair enough, I suppose. That's just what a dad does, you know. Worry about who's going to take care of his girl. Who and how."

"Dad, I don't need a man to take care of me! C'mon now! This is not 1952. I make damn good money on my own."

"How is your job, by the way?" He looked at her with a bemused expression on his face. "You still trying to get out of there?"

"Every day. I'm working on something now that I think might work. It might be my ticket out of tabloid hell."

"Oh yeah? You want to tell me about it?"

For some reason, she didn't. She needed a break. "Not yet, Dad."

"Okay, Bessie. Fine with me. You know what you're doing."

"Most of the time." She smiled up at him and grabbed his hand.

Did you get your period in this room?" asked Dan, as they snuggled underneath her floral bedspread.

"You know what? I don't know." She thought back. "I think I was at a friend's birthday party, actually. At Sunshine Skate Club. It was horrible. I had to skate with a wad of toilet paper in my underwear."

"Ewwwww," teased Dan. "I really like your parents. They're pretty adorable. And boy, do they looooove you."

Bess smiled in the dark. "Yeah, they do, don't they?" She paused. "You know, Dan, about what you said earlier. About me not telling you things?"

"Mmm hmmmm."

"I'm going to try harder to let you in. Fully. It's hard for me to be so open, you know? I guess I'm scared about coming across as weak or something."

"Bess, I would ne—"

"No, Dan, I know. I truly know that. So I'm going to try. Just be patient with me, okay?"

"Okay. I'll be patient. Not to change the subject, but did your parents like me or what?"

"They really did. They do." Before they had gone to sleep, Bess's mother had pulled her aside. *I like him a lot, Bessie. He's good for you.* Bess had been unexpectedly moved by her mother's openness. Age seemed to be mellowing her, and her father, in a lovely way.

"Yes!" He did a victory pump in the air with his fist. "Shew."

"Dan, I have to tell you something, but I don't want you to get overexcited and act like a nerd."

"No nerdiness, I swear. I'll channel my inner Jack Nicholson. What's up?"

"I like LA," she admitted. Dan remained stoic. "A lot more than I thought I would," she continued. Still nothing from Dan. "And I like being able to see my parents. I think maybe I might be willing to move out here if I can find a job." Nothing. "Hello? Dan?! Anything?"

"You told me I couldn't act like a nerd!" he protested. "I am trying my best to remain cool under these circumstances."

"Okay, I take it back, act like a nerd."

"Yeahhhhhhhhhhhhhhhhhhhh!" Dan howled, pulling her to him. "Woot wooooooooooot!" He moved his arms in a circular motion in a pathetic attempt at the cabbage patch.

"Okay, that's enough!" laughed Bess. "More than enough." She hugged him close. "I just wanted you to know, okay? What I was thinking."

"I'm glad you told me, Bess. Obviously, your moving here would be the best thing that could happen to me. I don't expect any sort of definite answer from you right now, I hope you know that." He released her from the hug and looked in her eyes. "I'm just so happy to hear that you're considering it."

"Baby steps," whispered Bess, arching her neck to kiss him.

"Baby steps," he whispered back, squeezing her tight.

chapter thirty-two

Class Four

Naomi sat on her couch on Saturday morning as Noah watched his favorite cartoon, hoping that Cecilia was coming. They hadn't spoken since her inappropriate explosion the week before, and so much had happened. Their argument about Gene seemed so silly now, not to mention so long ago, that Naomi wasn't sure how to apologize without bringing up her more recent troubles. She hadn't spoken to anyone about them, other than her parents and, briefly, Charlie. She wasn't sure she was ready to open up further. She knew that Cee would be a wonderful ally, especially since she would no doubt need her more then ever if her MS was real, but there was something easier about living in her bubble of denial for the time being. After the doctor's appointment, she had scheduled her MRIs for the following Monday and returned to her life as before—taking care of Noah and his broken wing, and working on her projects. At night, in bed, was the only time her fear was inescapable.

A timid knock at the door made Naomi's stomach seize up. *Oh, thank God,* she thought. She had been envisioning Noah having

to occupy himself at the studio while she took her class, and the
vision wasn't pretty. She stood up to answer the door.

"Hey, Cee," she said, as she let her in. Cecilia seemed to be
deliberately avoiding her gaze.

"Hi, Naomi," she replied curtly. "Hey, Noah," she added as
she brushed past Naomi and into the apartment.

"Cee," said Naomi, touching her arm. "I am so sorry for the
way I behaved last week. I was out of line."

Cecilia's face softened. "Thanks for apologizing. I appreciate
that."

"I completely overreacted," explained Naomi.

"You really unleashed all of your frustrations on me," added
Cecilia. "Don't shoot the messenger, you know?"

"I know, believe me. I've felt like such an asshole all week."

Noah looked up in alarm. "Mom!" he exclaimed. "That's a
bad word."

"I know, baby," she answered. "I'm sorry. Pretend you didn't
hear it, okay?"

Noah got up, shaking his head in disapproval before announc-
ing that he was going to the bathroom.

"Tough critic," Cecilia said, laughing as he scampered away.

"Seriously. He's my own little word policeman. Anyway, I do
feel terrible about it all. I'm sorry I didn't come down and apologize earlier." *I've been a little preoccupied with the idea that I might
have an incurable disease.*

"It's okay," said Cecilia. "I just worry about you, you know?
All of these emotions you repress . . . they'll eat you alive if you
don't at least acknowledge them." Cecilia moved to the sofa to sit
down and Naomi followed.

"You are absolutely right," Naomi agreed. "And everything
you said about my photography is true. I . . . well, it's complicated." *Especially now.*

"I know. You should think about seeing someone. To just talk stuff out, you know? You don't have to handle all of this by yourself."

"You're right. I've been thinking about it." Naomi sighed. "But I've also had a lot of other stuff on my mind lately."

"Hey, you okay?" As if on command, Naomi's eyes welled up with tears.

"Shit, Naomi!" Cecilia moved closer to her on the couch and grabbed her hand.

"Um, I guess I, well . . . I've had some health stuff going on."

Cecilia looked at her earnestly, the worry dancing in her dark eyes. "Like what?"

"Well, to make a very long story short, I might have MS?" It came out like a question instead of a statement.

"What? MS? Oh my God. Naomi, what's been happening?"

Naomi rehashed her story as rationally as she could through her tears. Talking about it still reduced her to a slobbery mess. When she was finished, she looked around the room, thankful that Noah hadn't wandered back in. She hadn't told him anything—just that she hadn't been feeling well. If MS was impossible to understand at thirty-two, how could it possibly make sense to an eight-year-old?

"Oh, baby," murmured Cecilia. She wiped her own eyes. "I am so sorry for all of this. What a nightmare. How are you feeling physically?"

"Still numb around my midsection, but it seems to have lessened a bit. My fingers feel the strangest now. Their tips are numb."

"Are you able to get around okay?"

"Oh completely, thank God. I'm not encumbered in any physical way with these symptoms, you know? Mentally is a whole other ball of wax, though. I can't blow my nose without worrying that my brain will explode."

"I cannot even imagine. Does Noah know?"

"No, I haven't told him anything specific yet at all."

"Of course. What would he do with that information?"

"Exactly. Hey listen, sorry my delivery was so messy. I haven't quite mastered the art of talking about this yet, as I'm sure you can tell."

"Naomi, please. If you ever apologize to me again about your emotions I will smack you. So, how can I help you? What can I do?"

"Thanks, Cee. Nothing right now, I don't think. Noah will be in school while I'm getting my MRIs on Monday, so there's no problem there. I may need your help later, though. Yours and Gene's."

"Have you told him?" asked Cecilia.

"No, he's in Paris. I will when he gets back, though. Depending on the situation. Talk about letting him in, right? God, I was freaking out about a paper doll two weeks ago and now . . . well, the universe works in mysterious ways, doesn't it?"

"You've got that right. Whatever you need from me, just let me know. I love you and am here for you and Noah one hundred percent. And you know, if you decide that you want to speak to someone with MS, my friend Susan would be a wonderful source."

"Oh yeah? She knows about MS?"

"She has MS. Was diagnosed back in 2000 I think."

"Are you kidding me? I had no idea! She is completely normal. Whatever normal means. Wow, that is really inspiring."

"Yeah, she's amazing. She takes her medication and goes about her business. No drama about it whatsoever."

"Oh man, I have to go!" Naomi realized with a glance at the clock that she had only ten minutes to make it to class. "Thank you, Cee, for everything. Talking about it with you just made me feel so much better." She grabbed her coat and her camera. "Did I tell you that I'm taking pictures for the Prana website?"

"Get out! I think that's a great idea. Are you sure you're ready?"

"Yeah, I am. I'm designing the website for them, so I thought I might take a couple of shots of the space and the people, you know? Just to give it a personal touch."

"Naomi, I love it," encouraged Cecilia. "I really do."

Naomi hugged her, suddenly overwhelmed with gratitude for her friendship.

"Wait—hellooo?! I don't know anything about this mystery man in your apartment! What's the story, you minx?"

Cecilia blushed. "He's pretty great, Naomi. I met him out in the neighborhood." She paused mid-story and looked at the clock. "You better go, though! You're going to be late for class."

"Okay, but will you tell me about him later?! Please?" begged Naomi. "I want to know everything."

"Will do."

Naomi arrived at the studio feeling lighter than she had all week. Opening up to Cee felt like losing fifteen pounds.

"Hey, Felicity," said Naomi, as she took off her jacket as quickly as she could. She could hear Charlie's voice coming from the studio. "Class has already started?" she whispered.

Felicity nodded. "Get goin'," she chided with a smile.

Naomi crept in as sneakily as she could. She made eye contact with Charlie and attempted a silent apology.

"Hey, Naomi," said Charlie. Sabine turned to smile at her in welcome. *Where was Bess? Curious.* "I was just talking about those lightbulb moments in life. You can be going about your business, pretty content with the setup you have, when all of a sudden: bam!

You make some sort of new discovery about yourself, or your perception is forced to change so abruptly that it feels as though the wind has been knocked out of you. It's a form of reawakening, really. Marcel Proust once said, 'The real act of discovery is not in finding new lands, but in seeing with new eyes.'" Charlie paused. "I think that's a pretty accurate metaphor for self-actualization—this whole idea of 'new eyes.' I want you to think about reawakening today as we practice. Think about the self-imposed constraints that are holding you back—in yoga and beyond."

As Sabine followed Charlie into Tadasana, she thought about the whole idea of fresh perception. Unintentionally or not, she did hold herself back a lot of the time. Take Zach, for example. Wednesday night had really thrown her for a loop. She wanted to believe that he really liked her, but couldn't help but think that he didn't. If a guy liked you, he wanted to sleep with you. Right? Or wrong? She had been obsessively rehashing the night's events since; so much so that she could barely function at work. It was ridiculous. Zach had called her Thursday, to ask her out for the weekend, but she had made up some excuse as to why she couldn't. *Why did I do that? I like him.* She had thought she was taking a stand by playing hard to get, but in reality she was just playing a silly game instead of confronting her feelings. Zach had been understanding, and had even gone so far as to schedule a date for the following Saturday, so obviously he did like her. . . . *Why am I being such a jackass? No, you know what, I need a week to calm down. I really do. Knowing that might be fresh enough in terms of perspective, at least for now.* She took a deep breath in.

Charlie realigned Naomi's shoulders. She hoped she hadn't sounded too "woo woo" up there, talking about reawakening. Up to this point, she had really had only one complete reshuffle of all she had deemed inherently "Charlie." Now she was experiencing another as she shed the memory of Neil like molting snake skin.

It felt right, but that didn't mean that it wasn't scary. Redefining yourself took patience. She hoped that yoga was helping Bess, Naomi, and Sabine redefine themselves in a similar way. They had all been so quick to classify themselves as "nonyoga" people at alumni night. Bess had been particularly hard to get to open up. Charlie missed her today. She wondered if she was getting any yoga in LA. Most likely not. Regardless, it was clear that Bess had made some progress. Charlie hoped that all of them saw themselves, and yoga for that matter, differently now.

She took them through their sun salutations, happily noticing their increased confidence with the sequence. Sabine was almost graceful as she swooped to the floor. Naomi's brow was smooth instead of scrunched like an accordion. The Saturday before, Charlie actually had to readjust her face—smoothing out her forehead as she assumed a posture. This morning, there was not a furrow to be found. *I wonder how's she's feeling.*

Naomi's arms wobbled as she propped herself up by her wrists in an upward facing dog. Her back muscles burned a bit from the arch she had been holding under Charlie's instruction, but it wasn't an entirely unpleasant sensation. She was happy just to "feel" anything. Her appreciation for her muscles—for a body that "worked"—had never been so great.

"As you inhale, try to get your legs off the floor," encouraged Charlie. "Very good. Today we're going to attempt Urdhva Dhanurasana, or wheel pose. It's a back bend, really." She led them through their prepositioning. "Now press your inner feet into the floor," she continued. "As you exhale, push your tailbone up. Pull in your tooshies and lift them off the floor. Keep your thighs and inner feet parallel. Very nice, ladies.

"Take three deep breaths here. In for three and out for three." Naomi followed the count, noting the way she relaxed more fully into the stretch when she paid close attention to her breathing.

The blood pooled in Sabine's head as she held the position. She couldn't remember the last time she had been in a back bend, but she suspected it might have been at a slumber party circa 1987.

"Excellent! Now release," said Charlie. "Lie on your backs and regain yourselves for just a moment." Sabine inhaled deeply. Her shoulder muscles were screaming at her.

"Okay, we're going to repeat the wheel three times," Charlie continued. Sabine closed her eyes and mouthed "motherfucker" silently before launching back into the sequence.

Fifteen minutes later, after they had cooled down and uttered their requisite *Namaste*s, Sabine felt differently. Her muscles were still jelly, sure, but she felt powerful nevertheless. Her head felt clear and her body lighter. She noticed the same kind of dazed, contented expression on Naomi's face. If she didn't know any better, Sabine would think that they were all in a postcoital haze.

Not postcoital, she thought to herself as she hoisted herself up from her mat. *Postyoital, maybe?* She smiled at the thought. *Yo-ital.* Sounded like a new brand of yogurt.

"Do you know where Bess is?" Sabine asked Charlie as they put their mats away.

"Oh yeah, she e-mailed me this week saying she wasn't going to make it today. She's in LA."

"Really?" asked Naomi. "That's great for her. She went out to visit her man, huh? I wonder if she is giving the whole moving thing some more thought."

"Sounds like it," said Charlie. "I hope she eases up on herself a bit. Moving out there doesn't mean that she's giving up her identity, you know? She's just taking a risk."

"True," agreed Sabine. "But I don't think risk-taking comes naturally to our girl Bess."

"I know!" said Naomi. "She is tightly wound, that's for sure."

"Although when Dan was in town, she was positively fluid," said Charlie. "I've never seen her so relaxed in class."

"Homegirl is dickmatized!" exclaimed Sabine.

"Wait, what!?"

"Sorry to be so crass, it's just that I have been waiting and waiting to use that word in the proper context! The guy who writes one of the gossip websites I'm addicted to coined it, I think."

"Which website?" asked Naomi, grinning. "That is a great word."

"Dlisted? You know it?"

"I do!" interrupted Julian, overhearing their conversation from the front desk. "That guy is funny as hell."

Sabine nodded in agreement.

"Speaking of websites, I've come up with some ideas for Prana," said Naomi, reducing her voice to a whisper.

"Oh, cool!" replied Sabine. "Like what? And why are you whispering?"

"I dunno. I guess I'm sort of nervous. I'm gonna go talk to Charlie, Felicity, and Julian now," answered Naomi. It was strange—this is what she did for a living, and she rarely, if ever, experienced any sort of nerves with her other clients. She had a job to do, and she did it. But there was something about this assignment that made Naomi a bit wary, and it had nothing to do with her vulnerable emotional state. She suspected it had something to do with the fact that she was completely in charge of the site's artistic direction. Charlie and Felicity had placed it in her hands, no questions asked, no artistically displeasing requests. It was liberating, but a bit scary. She took a deep breath and walked over to the front desk to chat with Felicity. Sabine trailed behind her.

"Hey, lady," greeted Felicity. "How are ya?"

"I'm well," Naomi answered. "A little bit pooped, though. Charlie worked us today."

"I know, I peeked in earlier," said Felicity. "You all have really come a long way since your first class. It's kind of amazing."

"Really, you could tell?" asked Naomi.

"Absolutely. I'm impressed."

"Well, thanks," said Naomi. "Charlie is a wonderful teacher. Listen," she continued, "I have some ideas about the website."

"Oooh, goody!" Felicity exclaimed, clasping her hands together with glee. "Tell us, tell us!"

"Tell you what?" asked Charlie, suddenly beside them.

"I've been thinking about the website," repeated Naomi. "I'm thinking that it should walk the line between personal and professional. You know, a really sleek, open design that mimics what you've done with the studio, paired with some great photos of you guys and the space. A mix of black-and-white and color photos."

"That sounds perfect!" said Felicity. "I like what I'm hearing. Nothing too over the top."

Julian nodded his approval.

"Yeah, I also love that you're staying away from the whole hippie-dippie scene," said Charlie. "I've seen a lot of yoga websites that look like acid flashbacks."

"Or sites that are way too cool for school," said Sabine. "You know, those stark, SoHo, Gwynnie and Madonna joints? Ugh. Those sites are so uninviting."

"Who's going to take the photos?" asked Julian.

"Well, I thought I might," answered Naomi. She studied the floor, annoyed by her own nervousness. She forced herself to look up.

"Naomi, I think that is an excellent idea," said Felicity. "I love it."

"And I thought I would just set up a link on the site that took viewers to a page about your hair products," Naomi added. "Your page will have the same look, but it will be all about the hair."

"When is it not all about the hair!?" shrieked Julian, as Felicity beamed. "I love it, I love it, I love it!"

"I do, too," agreed Charlie. "It sounds perfect. What can we do to help?"

"Well, I thought I might hang around and take some candid photos today," replied Naomi. "Just to get a feel for the light in here." She pulled her camera out of her bag. She was still nervous about taking photos, but somehow this felt right. The way that everyone had responded to her ideas made her feel confident and capable, like a woman who made her own rules. Like a woman who wasn't consumed by worry about her health.

She stood up and looped the camera over her head. It felt so familiar to be wearing it again, but also somehow completely different. "Okay, just go about your business," she instructed Felicity, Charlie, and Julian. She peered through the lens.

"Julian!" she exclaimed. "Be natural!" The women burst into giggles as they noticed Julian's arm popped in an attempt to highlight his muscles as he leaned against the counter.

"Sorry, sorry!" he replied. "I can't help it! It's in my blood. You're lucky I kept my shirt on. It took everything in me not to disrobe."

"Thanks for that, Julian," said Felicity. "You truly are a man of great sacrifice."

Julian reached across and caressed her cheek in response. *Snap*, went Naomi's camera. That was the kind of moment she wanted. She held the camera to her cheek, relishing the feeling of becoming one with it again.

chapter thirty-three

Charlie

Charlie approached the register nervously. It was official, she had a crush on Mario. She supposed she had always been aware of it, but the conversation with Julian had really brought it to the surface, like some kind of suddenly buoyant treasure chest that had been buried under the sea floor for hundreds of years. She hadn't actually seen Mario since she had accepted her crush, which was always how these things went. The minute you wanted to see a guy, he disappeared, but when you weren't into him, he was everywhere.

She rounded the corner of the aisle to get a peek at him. He was cleaning the coffee machine with studied concentration. Even squished, his face was beautiful. She took a deep breath. *It's still just Mario*, she reminded herself. *You know him. There's no reason to get all silly about it.* He paused, looking up. His face broke out in an enormous smile upon seeing her there.

Okay, I'm silly. Dizzy even. She smiled back.

"Good morning, Charlie!" Mario exclaimed, practically leaping over the counter to embrace her.

"Hey," she replied. Suddenly, she felt like they were reenacting a scene from *Grease*, with her as the virginal Sandy and Mario as the dangerous Danny Zuko. She stifled a laugh. "How's it going?"

"Life is good, can't complain. Just trying to get this mess off the coffee machine; spiff it up a bit. You look beautiful this morning, as always."

Charlie's face warmed. "Thanks, Mario." She felt awkward. Before, when she was happy to float along in her river of post-Neil asexuality, Mario really hadn't fazed her. But now, back in the game so to speak, she was frazzled by his mere presence. She was sure that the hair on her arms was standing up beneath her jacket. What should she say next?

Mario saved her. "And you? What's going on with the studio?"

"Studio is good," answered Charlie. "Business seems to be picking up." She fingered the packs of gum below the register. "One of my students is designing a website for us."

"Nice! That's something that will really make a difference. Web presence is key. That's the first thing I did for my other business."

"You have another business?" asked Charlie. She remembered Julian telling her about Mario's entrepreneurship empire, but she couldn't pinpoint what it was that it entailed. Or did Felicity tell her? Funny how, thinking back, it was so obvious how eager both of them were to get Charlie to admit to her feelings for Mario—always bringing him up or asking her to pick up something for them at the deli.

"Yeah, my brother and I run a catering service," he answered proudly. "Mostly upscale Puerto Rican food."

"That's incredible! I had no idea that you were a chef."

"Well, my brother is the better chef, by a long shot. I got into it at first just for the business angle. I thought he could do really well for himself. And he really has, too. It's great to be a part of it."

"That's wonderful, Mario. Are you booked every night?"

"Oh no, we both have other jobs. I'm here and my brother also owns a small restaurant up in the Bronx. We mostly book gigs on weekends. And then, you know, I have my band, too. It's been harder and harder lately to get it all in, you know?"

"You're in a band?" How was it possible that she had known this man for so long, and actually not known him at all?

"Yeah," replied Mario, somewhat bashfully. "It's just a bunch of middle-aged guys messing around on some instruments, really. But we have a lot of fun. You should come see us sometime."

"What instrument do you play?"

"Guitar."

"Wow, I'm really impressed."

Now it was Mario's turn to blush. "Thanks. You know, we have a gig coming up next month in the neighborhood."

"I'll definitely come," said Charlie.

"Really? Maybe we could grab dinner afterward or something," he added. The intensity of his stare made her knees tremble. She clutched the counter for support.

"Yeah, that would be nice."

Mario looked over her shoulder. "Oh hi, how can I help you?" he asked the customer behind her.

Charlie turned to let the customer pay. Her heart plummeted to her feet as she realized who was standing behind her. There, holding a canister of coffee and a roll of paper towels, was Neil.

He looked at her, dumbfounded. "Holy shit!" he exclaimed. "Charlie! Hi!" Charlie swallowed deeply, desperately trying to moisten her Sahara-like mouth.

"Hi," she squeaked in response. He looked the same—sort of. He had cut his hair and shaved the shadow that once had enveloped his face like a bristly cloud. He had also changed his glasses. Before, they had been thick-rimmed, "look at me, I'm a hipster intellectual" glasses, but now he was sporting a much more conservative pair. His entire countenance was actually that of a much more conservative man. Neil, the former chess-playing, wheatgrass-swilling, Bhagavad Gita–reading atheist now officially looked like someone who Hamptoned on the weekends and had a subscription to Netflix. He was a bona fide yuppie. The change was alarming.

"You look great," he said, taking Charlie in. She wondered what he must think of her makeup-free face, her wild hair, and her puffy jacket. For so long, she had planned this reunion in her head. In it, of course, she had been the embodiment of spiritual fulfillment and easy grace, not a frazzled, winter-clad Bushwicker, flirting mercilessly with the deli guy.

"Uh, thanks." Charlie felt Mario's eyes boring into the back of her head. "Neil, this is Mario. Mario, Neil."

"Hey man," said Neil, extending his hand.

Mario tensed in response, as he grasped it to shake. "Hello," he replied frostily.

"So Charlie, how have you been?" asked Neil. "God, I can't remember the last time I saw you."

Charlie remembered it all too well. They had broken up, and Neil had been sleeping on a friend's couch. He had gone to collect his things one afternoon, thinking Charlie would be at work. Instead, he found her basically right where he had left her—curled in the fetal position on her couch with a blanket wrapped tightly around her. They had fought, again, and then, with a trash bag full of his belongings, he had taken off.

"Me, either," replied Charlie. If he wanted to play dumb, she could understand that. She studied his face. She had no sexual response to his presence. Zero. It was an incredible realization. "What are you doing in Bushwick?" she asked.

"I live here now. Down the street actually." He looked down, avoiding her eyes. "I'm, um, engaged," he explained. "We moved here about a month ago." Despite her joyful moment earlier at the realization that Neil no longer held any resonance for her, this stung. More than it should.

"Oh!" she replied, as convincingly as she could. "That's great! Congratulations."

"Thanks," Neil answered, obviously relieved by her good-will. His reaction annoyed Charlie. Why would he think that she would be anything but happy for him? He might have changed his look, but his ego remained the same: monstrous.

"What brings you to these parts?" he asked, feigning a hor-rible Southern accent in a failed attempt to be cute.

"She lives here, too," Mario interjected. "She owns the yoga studio upstairs." Charlie looked at Mario, trying to communicate her appreciation with her eyes.

"Get out!" said Neil. "That's awesome! And such a change for you." He looked at Mario. "Charlie used to run Wall Street with her eyes closed." It was all Charlie could do not to scratch Neil's eyeballs out. Even though he was only including Mario in the con-versation, there was an edge of condescension to his voice that she remembered all too well.

"Yeah," she replied. Volunteering any more information about herself felt like a waste of time.

"You're never going to believe this," said Neil, naturally happy to turn the focus of the conversation back to him, "but I'm getting my MBA!"

Charlie practically choked on her tongue. The guy who gave her endless crap about her lifestyle for the entire two years that they dated was now replicating it for himself! The irony was out-rageous. Charlie could not believe it.

"What!?" she practically shrieked. She wanted to add, *You*

moronic poseur, you asshole blowhard! The same guy who pretended to shun all that was remotely materialistic; the same guy who rolled his eyes any time Charlie talked about a merger or expressed interest in going out to a restaurant that involved table service . . . this guy was pursuing a career in finance? His new image suddenly made complete sense.

"Yeah, I know, right?" he responded. "Big change."

Charlie looked at him. The epiphany she had been waiting for was finally here—transforming her in this deli. Neil was an insecure guy with no sense of self. Whatever he was doing was a reflection of the latest trend. Living on the Lower East Side in his twenties, it was deemed cool to work at a restaurant, smoke weed, do yoga to fool chicks into thinking you had a sensitive side, and talk about philosophy. Now that he was in his thirties, it was time to move to Brooklyn, get engaged, and pursue an MBA. Neil did not possess a shred of authenticity in his entire body. He was a joke.

"I'll say," she said. "Listen, it was good to see you. I've got to run. See you around, I guess. Good luck with everything."

"Uh, yeah, you too," said Neil, perplexed, no doubt, by her sincere lack of interest.

"Bye, Mario," she said. "Come up to the studio and let me know about your gig, okay?"

"You got it, Charlie."

She left them both there—the old and the new—and gulped in the fresh air outside. She could feel spring coming. Already, the cold was less bitter and there was a hint of balmy warmth in the breeze. Very slight, but definitely there. Soon, winter would end and spring would begin—ushering in a whole new beginning.

So much had been healed for her in that brief exchange with Neil. The pain about the breakup, although finally on its way out, had been lingering at the fringes of her heart, despite her attraction to Mario. Now the broom of reality had swept it out.

She couldn't believe that she had thought him to be the impetus for her life change. She had more spirituality and authenticity in her baby toe than he had in his entire family lineage. It was unreal.

For a long time she hadn't been giving herself credit for changing her life so dramatically. She had been giving that credit to him! And why? Maybe it was easier to fall back on that when running the studio proved difficult. If she didn't own her life path, then she didn't have to take responsibility for it when it got messy or unpleasant. At the same time, when things were going really well, when her life brought her tremendous joy—whether from the practice of yoga itself or from realizing that she truly loved her coworkers or from breaking through a boundary with one of her students—she, in effect, was giving that credit to someone else. To Neil, of all people.

Charlie stopped short in the middle of the block. She closed her eyes and listened. A bird was chirping. The first she had heard in what felt like forever. Change was coming.

No, Charlie thought. *Change is here.*

chapter thirty-four

Bess

"Have a good night, Rob," called Bess as he left the office. "Don't stay late!" he reprimanded over his shoulder.

Bess took in the silence of the now-empty office. She looked around, making sure that she was alone. She saw a light on in her boss's corner office. She swore she had seen her leave for the night, but maybe she had returned, anxious to capitalize on the latest starlet's unfortunate crotch-flashing incident.

Bess got up from her chair and strolled casually by, glancing to the side as nonchalantly as she could. If she was in there, Bess certainly didn't want to attract any attention to herself. The last thing she wanted to do tonight was engage in bullshit banter about the spring fashion collections.

She glanced in to find Esme, the cleaning lady, dusting the window ledges. "Hey, Esme."

"Hey, Bess," she replied, turning the trash can upside down to empty its contents into her cart. Bess didn't know how long Esme had been cleaning these offices, but she suspected since the dawn of time. She knew everyone. It was one of Bess's goals to stay late and get drunk with Esme one night and pump her for insider information. The woman had to be a vault of blackmail-worthy gems.

Not tonight, though. Bess had important business to take care of. She returned to her desk. She watched Esme leave the office, dragging her cart behind her. She rattled down the hall and made a left. Moments later, Bess heard the telltale *ding* of the elevator opening. The coast was clear.

Bess gathered her notepad and pen and approached the office—now clean as a whistle thanks to Esme's skilled expertise. She tiptoed to the chair. She felt like Velma in *Scooby-Doo*.

She settled herself on the ridged leather of a chair that she was sure cost more than three months of her rent. It was a lot more comfortable than the sad contraption she sat on. She spun around once for good measure, taking in the view as New York City went by in a blur of lights.

Facing forward, she opened her notepad to review her scribbles. She uncapped her pen. She cleared her throat. "Here goes nothing," she whispered. As she dialed the number, her palms began to sweat. She remembered a former boyfriend that had been repulsed by her overactive sweat glands. He had called her lava hands. She had broken up with him shortly thereafter.

As the phone rang, Bess tried some yoga breathing. She inhaled as deeply as she could and then let it *whoosh* out in a rush. Mid-*whoosh*, Kathryn picked up.

"Hello, City Section," she answered. Bess desperately tried to cover her *whoosh* with a cough.

"Hello!?" Kathryn barked.

"Oh, sorry!" said Bess. "I have a little bit of a cold. Kathryn, it's Bess."

"Bess?" asked Kathryn, towing the line between pretending to know who Bess was and actually having no idea.

"Yeah, we met through Jason at one of his get-togethers? About six months ago or so?" Bess prayed that Kathryn had a decent memory. In truth, they had spoken for about four minutes, and that estimation was generous. "I work at *Pulse*? We talked about Britney Spears's weave?"

Kathryn laughed. "God, I have that conversation way too often, sadly. Bess, I can't say that I honestly remember you, but I'll buy it. What's up?"

"Well, I have a piece to pitch. I'm hoping it's a natural fit for the City Section. Is this a bad time?"

"No, no, it's fine. Go on," encouraged Kathryn.

"So, it's about a yoga studio in Bushwick," Bess said.

"I like that. Bushwick is the new Prospect Heights, Prospect Heights is the new Carroll Gardens . . ."

Bess laughed. "Exactly. So, the article is about four, thirty-something, single women in a six-week Basics class. In a nutshell, ten years after college graduation, they're all on a quest for balance in their lives. You know: work, passion, love, yoga, happiness . . ."

"Um, not to sound like a dick, but the City Section is not *Marie Claire*, Bess. All due respect to my sisters, but this sounds like every other women's magazine puff piece I've read in the past six months."

"No, I swear, it's the women themselves that make this article special," Bess explained. "Their quest for balance and self-actualization is new and fresh. My article does not define 'having it all' in any kind of stereotypical way. It's about the individualistic nature of that goal set against the backdrop of today's New York. The point is that 'having it all' for women today, especially urban women, is becoming more about being able to express and utilize different facets of ourselves. It means having the drive to fulfill ourselves creatively while supporting ourselves and hustling the way city life requires us to. These women are inspirational—this is the type of balance that all women strive for on some level—or at least, they should."

Bess noticed that her heart was beating quickly as she talked. She was more passionate about this than even she had realized. She truly believed in it. It wasn't about her byline anymore, it was about a piece that she thought might really make a positive impact on its unsuspecting reader—the same way Charlie, Sabine, and Naomi had made an impact on her.

"Shit, that sounds good. Girl power!" Kathryn yelled. "Hmmm. It might be tough to get this past my editor, who's a man, thank you very much. I mean, I see the validity in your piece, but he might tell me to take a hike. . . . Can you promise me an emphasis on Bushwick and details about its revitalization?"

"Absolutely," answered Bess. "I'll weave it in like Britney's hairdresser."

"Ha! That's a good one. You know what, we do have space. Let's run it. Can you have it to me within the week? If I like the finished product, I'll run it in next Saturday's paper."

It was all Bess could do not to scream. "Done."

"All right, cool, I gotta run," said Kathryn. "Just e-mail it to me as a Word doc by Wednesday afternoon, latest."

"No problem," said Bess. "Thanks a lot for the opportunity."

"Not at all," she answered. "Your idea sounds very relatable. I'm looking forward to reading it."

"Thanks so much! Bye!" said Bess as she put the phone back in its cradle.

She took a few liberty spins in the fancy chair. She couldn't believe it! Her article actually had a shot at running in *The New York Times*! She had been visualizing this moment for so long. She faced the window and took in the New York skyline. She had used her boss's phone to make the call so that she could actually see New York supporting her; her own cubicle had no windows. The city never failed to impress her, even after being here for more than ten years. Its sheer immensity always made her agape with wonder—the same way it had made her feel the very first time she soared above it. *I will really miss this place if I move to LA,* she thought, staring out at the gigantic buildings with their randomly lit windows. New York was one of a kind. She circled back and got up from the chair. She wondered if it had always been her boss's dream to end up as editor in chief of a vapid celebrity rag. She guessed not.

Sure, her boss was living a glamorous life that almost anyone would applaud and envy—wealthy, powerful, a mother of two with what appeared to be a loving husband—but maybe, in the back of her mind, she had a dream to be a pianist . . . or a painter . . . or even a kung fu master. Who knew? The possibilities were endless. By day she ran a magazine and took care of a family, but maybe late at night, or early in the morning, she made time for whatever it was that truly inspired her and made her feel whole: the juggling act of every woman was not to be trivialized.

Bess returned to her own desk, gathered her jacket, and switched off her computer. She had pitched to the *New York* freakin' *Times* and it had worked. To say that she was psyched would be a tremendous understatement. She would buy a nice bottle of wine on the way home to celebrate and then call Dan immediately. She was so grateful to have him in her life. Without him, the article would have sputtered and died before she had even given it any gas.

On the street, she hurried to the subway, anxious to get home to call him. Speaking to him in transit always felt so rushed. She liked to be stationary when they spoke, so she could concentrate fully on him and not on the jerk riding her ass on the side-walk.

Holy shit, she thought, *I'm sweating!* She unzipped her jacket and unwound her scarf, noticing similar looks on her fellow ur-banites.

Spring was on its way! At last!

chapter thirty-five

Naomi

Naomi sat in front of her computer, staring at her screen. She had finished the layout for the Prana website and really liked the way it was coming along. It was warm and inviting, just like the studio itself. The technology was fresh without feeling intimidating. She liked the rollover that led to Felicity's hair products the best. She had fashioned a black-and-white illustration of a Buddha with an Afro, smiling broadly. Click on the Afro and voilà—you're in hair heaven.

It was the copy that was eluding her. Naomi was many things, but a writer was not one of them. Although she didn't usually provide copy for her clients, she really wanted to deliver the full package for Prana. She had perused other sites for inspiration, but it was futile. She put her head in her hands, thinking of the studio, the students . . .

Sabine! She had completely spaced on Sabine's talents. She was perfect for this, and she was sure she would welcome the opportunity to flex her scribe muscles. She clicked into her e-mail and began to compose her plea. As she began, her buzzer shrieked.

What? she thought, stunned by the interruption. It was the middle of the afternoon. Who would be buzzing her? Maybe it was a Jehovah's Witness. She continued typing, hoping that was the case. The buzzer shrieked again.

"Shit," she mumbled, noting her pajama pants and coffee breath. She got up to find out who was bothering her. She pressed her intercom button. "Yes?" she asked.

"Um, Naomi?" a timid voice crackled.

"Shit!" Naomi said for the second time. It was Gene.

"Gene?" she asked, hoping that the UPS guy's voice bore an uncanny resemblance to her ex's.

"Yeah, hi! Can I come up?" Naomi so did not want him to invade her space at that moment, but she didn't seem to have a choice in the matter. To deny him entrance would be bad manners. She pressed the button to open the door.

Once again, I am in my pajamas. It was a good thing she wasn't attracted to him anymore. Any chance of seducing him looking like this was out of the question. She cringed as she heard him clomp up the stairs. She was sure he would reek of Paris— cigarettes, Côtes du Rhône, models, and hashish. She, on the other hand, reeked of Mommyhood—milk, Cheerios, and coffee. Intoxicating.

The knock on the door erased any hope she had of brushing her teeth. She took a deep breath and opened the door. Gene stood outside it, the very picture of European sophistication: worn jeans, a perfectly softened cotton tee, a slim-fitting, buttery leather jacket, a patterned cashmere scarf, and a knit cap that cradled his pretty head. She wondered how many women he had slept with during fashion week and then immediately felt bad for Mini-Noah. She hoped Gene had made him some mini-blinders.

"Hi, Naomi."

"Hey, Gene." She opened the door farther to let him in. "How was Paris?" *I hope it was fun. I might have multiple sclerosis. Can I get you some coffee?*

"Oh, you know, the usual bullshit," answered Gene, pulling the cap off his mess of dark curls—the very same curls that cupped Noah's beautiful head. The kid had good genes, what could she say? "Fourteen-year-old models, near overdoses, champagne morning, noon, and night."

"Sounds like torture."

Gene laughed. "I know, 'poor me,' right? But I'm telling you, Naomi, the scene is getting tired. I don't know if it's me being older or what, but I'm pretty sure, finances allowing, that this is my last year."

"Are you serious?" asked Naomi.

"Yeah, I think I am. Send out a news bulletin—Gene Hoff is officially an old man."

"Wow, that's really some news," said Naomi. "Being old isn't that bad, I promise. You can wear your pajamas all day and not give a shit. *Should I tell him? I know I have to . . . eventually, but it feels too soon. Why does he need to know? I know, I know. I need his help with Noah.*

"I hope that's not the only perk of adulthood," Gene teased. "Because I distinctly remember that being a perk of adolescence as well."

"You have a point. It's not. I guess I just mean that there's a comfort in accepting your age, you know?"

"I do know. I'm telling you, Naomi, the best part about Paris was this silly little cardboard guy." He reached into his bag and pulled out a manila envelope. He shook it, and Mini-Noah came tumbling out onto the couch, intact and actually looking as good as he had when he left the country, all things considered. "Look,

I made the little dude a cast!" He picked up Mini-Noah with his thumb and forefinger to show Naomi. Sure enough, a tiny white cast had been attached to his tiny cardboard arm.

"You're kidding me!" exclaimed Naomi. "The cast is a great touch." She paused. "By the way, thanks for being there for Noah at the hospital. I know I behaved pretty badly when I saw you there, but I really was grateful."

"Hey, I understand. I would have a hard time trusting me with the whole dad thing, too. I've changed though, Naomi. Honestly. I . . . I really love that kid, you know? I would do anything for him."

"I think I know that now," replied Naomi. "You just have to be patient with me, if you don't mind. It was just him and me for so long, you know? To have you come sailing back in . . . it's not the easiest pill to swallow."

Gene nodded. "I know."

Naomi picked up Mini-Noah and examined him. "So, you actually had fun with this guy? I couldn't decide if the project sounded adorable or like a giant pain in the ass. The science fair of 2006 comes to mind."

"Noah had to enter a science fair when he was six?! What did he enter, a stool sample? Jesus, that's a little young, isn't it?"

"Totally," answered Naomi. "I'm convinced these projects are just the government's way of punishing us for procreating. We made a model of the solar system. It was beyond complicated and I think it shaved about two years off my life."

Gene laughed. "I am telling you, Mini-Noah and I had a blast. After hearing your science fair woes, I feel bad. Almost like I'm rubbing your nose in our cardboard-human love affair."

Naomi smiled. She had forgotten how charming Gene could be. "Don't feel bad. You shouldn't have to keep your new romance a secret. So, you had fun taking him all over town?"

"I really did. The pictures I took are hilarious. Here"—he pulled another envelope out of his bag—"have a look!"

"You already got them developed?" asked Naomi, surprised once again by Gene's sense of responsibility.

"Oh yeah, it was nothing. I have a color printer at home, so I just hooked it up."

Naomi took the photos and began to flip through them. "These are fantastic!" There was Mini-Noah in front of the Eiffel Tower, on the edge of a fashion runway, drinking red wine with Johnny Depp. Wait, with Johnny Depp!?

"Um, excuse me!" she practically shrieked, pointing to the photo with a wavering finger. "Is that who I think it is?"

Gene nodded sheepishly. "It's Johnny."

"Hello, I know it's Johnny! Holy cow, how do you know him?" Naomi stared longingly at his perfectly chiseled face. He was pretending to be engrossed in a chess game with Mini-Noah. The way the board had been set up, it looked like Mini-Noah was about to pulverize Depp.

"He bought a few photographs of mine back in the day," Gene explained. "We sort of became buddies. I always try to see him when I'm in Paris. He got a real kick out of Mini-Noah."

"This is unbelievable!" She shook her head in wonder at the life that Gene led. As she looked down, she noticed a piece of cereal stuck to her breast. *Ah, the irony.* Gene was hobnobbing with Johnny Depp and she was a human cereal bowl.

"You think the pictures are okay? That Noah will like them? It really was so important to me to do a good job by him."

"Gene, I know he'll love them. No one in his class is even going to come close with their minis. It's no contest."

Gene smiled broadly. "Thanks, Naomi. I'm so psyched to show him. I was thinking I would take one more photo here, if you don't mind."

"Here? This is hardly Paris. Why?"

"Well, Mini-Noah lives here, you know?" answered Gene, suddenly looking so much like Noah that Naomi's heart broke a little. "He went on a trip to Paris, but he comes home to his mom when it's over. Just like the real Noah."

"Oh, is that how it works?" asked Naomi, touched by the gesture, but also hoping that Gene did not want her actually in the photo.

"Yep, it's my creative vision," Gene teased. "I thought I'd lay Mini-Noah in Noah's bed and take a shot of you kissing him good night."

"Oh no, Gene, I am in no shape for pictures! I look like death. The photo might scare the kids."

"Are you kidding me? You're Noah's beautiful mommy. I know he'd want you included in the montage. C'mon, pleeeeeeeeeee-aaase?" Gene begged.

"Oh man. You are good. I guess I can do that. Just let me try to contain my hair for chrissake."

"Yes!" said Gene, pumping his fist in victory. "This is going to be fantastic. He sprung off the couch with Mini-Noah in tow, headed for Noah's room.

Naomi retreated to the bathroom. She smoothed some of Felicity's pomade over her strands in a halfhearted attempt to style it. She thought about the day before—the confinement of the MRI tube and the haunting, spaceship noises it made as it scanned the interior of her skull. As she sat in the waiting room beforehand, shivering in her hospital robe and flimsy socks, she had thought about how she would tell people, particularly Gene. It was hard to conceptualize an easy way to drop such a bomb. She had decided to just make it as casual as possible—no fuss, no muss—but now, in the moment, that was much easier said than done. "Just tell him, already," she said to her reflection in the mirror.

"Okay, I'm ready for my close-up," she announced, as she entered Noah's room. Mini-Noah lay on his pillow, but Gene had positioned him so that just his tiny cartoon head poked out from underneath the blanket.

"Perfect!" exclaimed Naomi. "That is too funny."

"I know, you would not believe how much fun I had with this ridiculous paper doll. Okay, so just lean over the little guy and give him a good night kiss."

"But what about the light?"

"Already took care of it." He pointed to the drawn blinds. "I thought I'd shut off the overhead light and just switch on his bedside lamp—kind of frame your profile a bit."

"Sounds good." She let Gene do his thing and then leaned in for the kiss. Gene shot away in the corner with his digital camera.

"Looks fantastic! That's a wrap. Here, Naomi, have a look."

Naomi approached him. "Hey, that is nice." Her profile looked pretty. "Cool shot, Gene."

"Thanks. I'll print this out later," said Gene, switching off the camera. "Have you been taking any pictures lately?"

Naomi immediately tensed up at the question. If only Gene knew how intertwined her photography was with her memories of their life together. He had no idea that she had abandoned photography as soon as they had broken up.

"Oh, I take shots here and there," she said, as nonchalantly as she could. "Mostly of Noah, you know."

"You always had such an amazing eye. You taught me so much. I probably never told you that when we were together—mostly because I'm an asshole. But you really did."

"Really?" asked Naomi, touched by his honesty. "Yeah, we

did some good stuff together." Feeling awkward suddenly, Naomi fluffed Noah's pillows and smoothed his comforter.

"I started taking some photos again recently," she offered—surprising herself with the ease of her revelation.

"Oh yeah? Excellent. Of what?"

"I'm taking this yoga class on Saturdays in Bushwick. They've asked me to design their website, so I figured I might as well take some shots of the staff and the studio to weave in."

"Yoga! Nice! That is really cool. Have you been taking some candids and stuff?"

"Yeah, trying to capture the essence of the studio itself," explained Naomi. "The people there are so cool. . . . And the space is so inviting. There's nothing even remotely pretentious about it."

"Wow, you're the right woman for the job then. Your photos were always so pure—not an ounce of ego in them. They're so special. I mean, I don't mean to be a total kiss-ass, but . . . I just have a lot of respect for your eye. For you."

Naomi was taken aback by Gene's gush of kindness. A small part of her wondered what his angle was, but she decided to ignore her cynicism and take the compliment, just this once. "Thank you, Gene. You know, actually . . . I need to talk to you about something."

"Sure," said Gene, nervousness clouding his perfect face. "What's up?"

"Some health stuff came up while you were gone. With me, not with Noah. I, uh . . . I may have MS."

"Oh no, Naomi. Wow. Are you okay? When will they know? Shit, I'm asking too many questions. Forgive me."

She went on to give him the condensed version of the story. The headaches, the flare-up, the doctor, and the MRIs.

"Nay, I'm so sorry. This is terrible news. How have you been dealing?"

"Eh, each day is a little easier. Or, well, some days are easier than others. It helps that my symptoms are going away." Out of habit she touched her stomach. The numbness was pretty much all gone, save for a lingering tingle here and there.

"You're an amazing woman, Naomi. You always have been. I don't know how I would deal if I was hit with something like this. But you, you just get on with it. It's inspiring as hell."

"Gene, it's not like I have a choice, you know? I have a son and a career and a life that needs me. Even so, I have my sad, 'why me?' moments. They're just not public."

"You know, you can make them public with me. I want to help. With Noah, with you, with anything. What can I do?"

"Right now, I'm all right. We're all right. But next Monday, could you pick Noah up from school? I have a doctor's appointment."

"Of course. Done. Does he know anything, by the way?"

"No, I've decided not to tell him until I have a better idea of what's happening. He just thinks I have a nasty cold. Or at least he's pretending to buy it. He's a smart kid, so who knows what he picks up on." Naomi was looking forward to Monday, only because that would mean some clarity about the MRIs and the chance to really talk to Noah about what was happening. She hated being so secretive with him, but she didn't feel as though there was an alternative at this point. *Just a few more days.*

"That's probably wise," said Gene. "Tough on you though, I'm sure."

"Yeah. But what can I do?" They smiled at each other. Naomi looked at the clock and gasped.

"What's the matter?" asked Gene.

"I have to pick up Noah at school in twenty minutes!" she explained. "Where did this afternoon go?"

"Oh, okay, let me get out of your hair," said Gene, moving out of the bedroom and gathering his things. He slid Mini-Noah back into his envelope. "Here, you can give this to Noah," he said, handing her both Mini-Noah and the photos. "I'll give him the one of you and the mini when I see him on Sunday."

"Wait!" said Naomi. "What am I doing? Why am I rushing around like a lunatic? You should pick Noah up. He would love it."

"Really?"

"Sure, go ahead," said Naomi. "Take him out for a cookie or something and tell him about Mini-Noah's adventure. He is going to be so thrilled about the photos."

Awkwardly, Gene moved to embrace her but then thought better of it. "Thanks a million. I'll have him home by four, promise."

"No problem, Gene. And thanks for being so supportive. It means a lot that I can lean on you."

"Naomi, I am so glad you came to me about this. Whatever I can do, please let me do it." He hugged her then, pulling her toward him before she could make it awkward. It felt nice to be hugged by someone who wasn't a female or four foot eleven.

"Okay. I will." She swallowed the lump in her throat.

Gene closed the door behind him and left, clomping his way down the stairs the same way he had come up them.

Naomi exhaled and sat on the couch. What a strange afternoon. A very nice afternoon, but a strange one. Gene had changed so much. And so had she.

She thought about her looming doctor's appointment. Whatever the MRI revealed, she knew she would be able to handle it. And although her maybe-MS was a nightmare on so many levels, it had shaken her out of her self-sufficient to the point of insanity coma. For the first time in what felt like forever, Naomi was open to help, and she actually felt stronger as a result. It was amazing how the universe delivered its lessons. Or maybe she was the amazing part—*is it okay to call myself "amazing" or is that obnoxious? Oh hell, why not*—for trying to see the positive in such a negative. Either way, the cloud was lifting, and for that she was infinitely grateful.

chapter thirty-six

Class Five

Charlie lay on her mat like a lazy cat, relishing the sun that filled the studio with buttery morning light. She hoped that the recent warmer weather was not just a tease and that spring firmly had its foot in the door.

"Mornin', Charlie," called Felicity, as she arrived. "Look at you, soakin' up the sun!" she said, poking her head into the studio as she disrobed. "It is somethin' out, isn't it?! Hope it's here to stay."

"You took the words right out of my mouth," agreed Charlie. "If this is just a tease, I will be sorely disappointed." Charlie got up from the floor and rolled her mat up.

"How's tricks?" she asked Felicity, approaching the front desk.

"Good, good. Can't complain. Hey, listen, I wanted to apologize for something."

"Oh no, what did you do?!"

"No, seriously. I gave you such a hard time about your Saturday Basics class when you were starting it up. I was stuck in business mode—couldn't see the forest for the trees."

"Oh, it's okay, Felicity," interrupted Charlie. "It wasn't exactly a sound business proposition."

"No, I know, but those women are so lovely. And I can see them really opening up to yoga in a way that I don't think being part of a larger class would have allowed. You were right to create such a haven for them."

"Hey, thanks, Felicity. I appreciate that." She really did. Felicity was not one to bullshit, that was the truth. For her to go out of her way to admit she was wrong was a really big deal.

"And now, with Naomi creating the website, it's all good. All of it. And you . . . you look like a different person since you started teaching this class."

"What do you mean?"

"You look good," explained Felicity. "Relaxed, open. Accessible in a way that you were not two months ago. If I didn't know any better, I would swear you were in love." She smiled coyly at Charlie.

"I'm not in love! But I am happy. I feel freer than I have in a very long time."

"You're over that creep finally, huh?" Felicity put her warm hand on top of Charlie's. "Sometimes it takes a village?" she asked knowingly.

"It really does," agreed Charlie. The woman had a sixth sense. Whatever was bothering you, she knew. Charlie was sure that she was an amazing mother.

"I'm proud of you, Charlie," she whispered. "You took your time and fought that demon on your own terms. I did the same thing with my ex-husband. Took me a minute, but when I let him go, I felt like a million bucks for doing it my way. Giving myself permission to mourn the death of that relationship might have been the smartest thing I've ever done."

Charlie hugged Felicity fiercely. "Thank you, Felicity. That means a lot. You sure are sweet this morning," she added, releasing Felicity from her embrace.

"I can't help it. Spring brings out the sweetness in me." She winked at Charlie.

"Good morninnnnng," greeted Sabine, breaking the women out of their love fest.

"Hey!" replied Charlie, genuinely thrilled to see Sabine's rosy-cheeked face. "How are you?"

"I'm well! How could I not be? Spring is practically knocking at our doors!" She had decided to focus on the weather rather than her love life. The weather was getting better every day and promised good things to come. Her love life, not so much. She was supposed to go out with Zach tonight, and the time away from him had only made her more confused. It didn't help that she had talked to him only once.

"Happy spring!" sang Naomi, shuffling into the studio next. It was much easier to focus on the positive when the sun was shining and the birds were chirping.

"I know, isn't it amazing out?" asked Sabine. "You can feel it coming, right?"

Charlie smiled at their enthusiasm. They were like two little squirrels, scurrying up and down tree branches with unbridled glee.

"Mornin'," echoed Bess—the last to arrive.

"Bess!" Sabine yelled. "Welcome back!"

"Yeah," echoed Naomi. "We missed you!" She walked over to give Bess a hug.

Bess hugged her back. "I was in LA, visiting Dan. Sorry I didn't let all of you guys know. It was sort of a last-minute decision." She laughed. "Because, you know, spontaneity is my forte." She realized that Charlie, Naomi, and Sabine did know her well enough by now to know that it was anything but.

"Is everything okay?" asked Charlie.

"Everything is great. I had such an awesome time out there—"

"Holy shit, are you moving there!?" squealed Sabine.

"Take it easy!" said Bess. "I don't know what I'm doing. But I do know that I had a much better time in LA than I expected to. I ended up talking to a couple of friends in the business out there, just to see what was what. I think I could work out there if I really hustled." *And this article is well received.* She had been working on it all week and really liked where it was going.

"I think it's awesome that you went out there," said Sabine. "You opened yourself up to the idea of moving, and were surprised by what you found."

"Yeah, it's amazing what happens when your attitude shifts," added Naomi. *I'm trying, I swear.*

"I introduced him to my parents!" Bess blurted out.

"Get out!" exclaimed Sabine. "That's huge!"

"Yeah, it really is," agreed Bess. "But it worked."

"When's the wedding?" teased Naomi. "You need a ring bearer? I'm happy to offer Noah's services."

"Let's move into the studio, shall we?" interrupted Charlie. She felt a bit uneasy. She wanted to open up to them about Neil, but her previously established ideas about boundaries and the perils of crossing them haunted her. On the other hand, their talk of attitude changes was right on. If she didn't break through her own boundaries, she would forever be restrained by them.

She surveyed their warm faces from the front of the room and decided to go for it.

"Hi, everyone," Charlie said.

"Hiiii," they sang back.

"I wanted to start off today's class a little differently," she explained. "Something happened to me this week that I feel might resonate with all of you. I . . . I ran into the former love of my life, and the universe rewarded me with this . . . this . . ." She searched for the right way to phrase it. "This life-affirming, closure-inducing epiphany of epic proportions."

"Wow," whispered Sabine.

"Yeah, wow," said Charlie. "I know, it sounds kind of mind-numbingly dramatic, but it really did change so much for me in such a positive way, most especially the whole concept of timing."

"I don't want to take up too much of class with my story, so maybe we can begin some stretching exercises while I tell you about it," said Charlie. "Everyone come up onto their hands and knees. We'll do a couple of rounds of cat-cow." This setup was good actually. Now she could share her story without having to face their expectant stares. She was still the teacher this way.

"Okay," said Naomi, as she pulled herself up onto her knees. "But I still want to hear this story. Don't stop now!" She was so happy to see Charlie opening up. It felt like a gift.

"Yeah," echoed Bess. "On with the show!"

"Okay, simmer down, I'm gettin' to it," replied Charlie. "Inhale deeply. And as you exhale, be sure to draw your navel to your spine. Nice, Sabine. So, about this former love of my life," Charlie continued, as she circled the studio. "Our relationship was pretty textbook really. I was young and naïve and he was an asshole." Bess laughed in response as she arched her back.

"He was into Buddhism and spirituality in a way that I just wasn't," Charlie continued. "I was working on Wall Street and hustling my ass off to fulfill what I thought was my legitimate dream. We were complete opposites, but something about that appealed to me. Work was making me very unhappy, and he was a hundred-eighty-degree switch from that world.

"Nice, ladies, two more. Make sure you drop your belly, Naomi," said Charlie, momentarily breaking from her story.

"At any rate, to make a very long, painful, and predictable story short, we broke up under the guise that 'I wasn't spiritual enough for him,' and some hot, young twenty-one-year-old was instead."

"Are you kidding me?" asked Sabine. "Just because you had a job and weren't wearing crystals around your neck, you weren't spiritual!? Give me a break."

Charlie laughed. It was nice to have this sort of support. "Exactly," she replied. "But I couldn't see his ridiculousness at the time. His words haunted me. So much, in fact, that they led me to yoga. Very good, everyone, last exhale. At first, I didn't take to the postures as naturally as I would have liked, but I loved it. And with that love, I began to see just how much my day job was sucking the life out of me. I struggled with it for a while, but then decided that I wanted to make the switch. I wanted to be a yoga instructor. I left it all behind. Quit my job, got a smaller apartment, sold my furniture and a lot of my clothes. You name it, I did it."

"That's pretty amazing," said Sabine.

"Eh, it's not so amazing. Okay, take a child's pose. Nice. See, I was in love with yoga, but I was also still in love with Neil. In my mind, he was solely responsible for changing my life so dramatically."

"How?" asked Bess, her voice muffled.

"I thought that I never would have found yoga if he hadn't challenged my spirituality. In part, I felt like my new life was a little bit about proving him wrong. I was giving him all the credit."

"Can we sit up for a minute?" asked Naomi. "I really want to hear you."

"Uh, sure," answered Charlie. "If that's okay with everyone else."

"Absolutely," said Sabine. "Naomi, you read my mind." The women all sat on their mats, waiting expectantly to hear the rest of Charlie's tale.

"For years, I lived under that assumption. I was beyond happy with my decision to change all that was familiar to me, but I couldn't shake the feeling that he was responsible. Lately though, I began to break out of that bubble. I was releasing him, finally. And then, naturally, I ran into him."

"That's always the way it happens," Bess volunteered. "Just when you're over someone—there they are. It's like the universe is testing you."

"Exactly!" agreed Charlie. "Seeing him, now, was such a gift. I truly saw him for what he was and was able to give myself the credit that I had been masochistically denying myself for so long. He was just a rung on the ladder to my self-awareness, you see," Charlie explained. "I am my own inspiration." She teared up, saying it aloud. She paused, regaining her composure. "I just wanted to share this with you all. You are all such wonderful women. I really think our class has opened me up. Our friendships have opened me up. So I wanted to share this with you and then thank you."

"I want to hug you so badly!" exclaimed Sabine. "What a wonderful story."

"And one we can all relate to," added Naomi.

"I don't care, I'm hugging her!" said Bess, crossing the room to embrace her. Charlie's story was such a perfect addition to the scope of her article.

Charlie hugged her back. "Thank you," she said. "All of you." She smiled broadly.

"Okay, enough of this!" said Charlie. "Class will begin now," she said. "Officially. Everyone, press up into downward dog," she instructed.

As Naomi flowed through her postures, she thought about Charlie's story. It was so nice to hear about the "real" her. Her confession had set the stage nicely for Naomi's own reveal. *But am I up to it? Do they really need to know?* She wiggled her finger-tips. Still numb. They were the only remaining evidence of her episode. Naomi had read that sometimes, symptoms from a flare-up never disappeared. The idea of never again feeling Noah's soft skin against her fingertips took her breath away.

Bess eyed her mat as she moved into downward facing dog. She thought about how much her article had changed—how much she had changed—since this class began. She had come in with such evil intentions. In a way, she supposed she had been hold-ing these women responsible for her unfulfilled dreams as a jour-nalist—using them as innocent pawns in an attempt to make her name known. It wasn't until she took a step back and looked at the bigger picture—the truer picture that painted them all as women trying to maintain a balance between what they had to do and what they wanted to do—that she was able to consider the article from a different angle.

At the end of class, they all lay on their mats, eyes closed, emo-tionally and physically exhausted. Charlie's story had set the tone for a grueling mind/body hour and a half.

"Allow your feet to fall apart," instructed Charlie. "Spread your toes wide. Relax into your mats," she encouraged. She dimmed the light and circled the room, stretching each of their legs and arms softly and rubbing their heads. When she finished, she asked them to slowly roll up to the seated position.

"Thank you so much for your compassion and empathy to-day," Charlie said. "It means so much to have such an incredible support system. I hope that my story filters into your openness about yoga and, really, life as a whole. I'm learning so much lately, that I can't help but share."

"We're so glad you did," answered Naomi.

"Namaste," said Charlie, smiling.

"Namaste," they echoed.

Charlie stood up, slightly embarrassed but mostly so grateful. There was a reason these women had come into her life as she transitioned into this next, post-Neil phase. They were excellent guides.

Bess stood up and began rolling her mat. "That was like therapy!" she announced.

Naomi laughed. "Completely. Mind and body therapy."

"Should I add a new class to the schedule?" asked Charlie. "Thoga?"

Sabine clapped her hands in excitement. "Thoga! That's excellent. What about Yogapy?"

"Also good," said Bess.

Naomi interrupted their conversation. It was now or never. "You guys, I need to tell you about something."

Sabine, Bess, and Charlie turned to face her, noting the seriousness of her tone. "Naomi, sure. Go ahead," said Bess.

Naomi took a deep breath and rehashed her MS-or-maybe-not-MS story. She had gotten much better at telling it. Practice was a natural editor. She no longer battled her own sobs when she spoke about it, either. The more she told her tale, the more rational she became.

"What a shitty break," said Bess when she was finished. "Wow, Naomi. I am so sorry."

"Me, too," agreed Sabine. She fought back her own tears. Why did things like this have to happen?

"When do you get your MRI results?" asked Charlie. She had been wondering about Naomi's health since their subway ride together, but hadn't wanted to intrude on her privacy. She had been hoping and hoping that Naomi's tingling was nothing; just stress-related moments of weirdness, but something inside her knew better.

"Monday. I'm nervous, of course, but I'm also looking forward to some sort of news. This limbo business is tough for a control freak like me!" Naomi laughed. "I can't believe that I can joke around about it now. A couple of weeks ago, I couldn't even say hello to someone without bursting into tears."

"Naomi, do you want me to come with you on Monday?" asked Sabine. "I'll take off of work."

"You're sweet. No, that's okay. I can handle it."

"Naomi, whatever you need, please just ask," said Bess. "I mean it." The reporter in her had immediately thought about how interesting the MS angle would be in her article. The friend in her had put the kibosh on the idea before it grew any bigger.

"Thanks, guys, I will. Right now, it just feels good to talk about it." She smiled at them. "Can you guys believe that next week is our last class? Is that nuts or what?!"

"I really can't," replied Charlie. "The time has flown. It makes me a little bit sad."

"Me, too," agreed Sabine. "You know what? We should have a brunch party after class next week!"

"That is a great idea!" said Charlie. "I like that. Everybody could bring something. Bagels, lox . . ."

"Danish!" added Bess. "I love it."

"And I'll unveil the website!" added Naomi. She looked to Sabine. "Sabine, do you think you could have the copy to me by Tuesday?"

"No problem," said Sabine. "I'll get cracking this afternoon."

"Really?!" exclaimed Charlie. "The website is going to be ready next week? Naomi, are you sure? With all that you have going on?"

"Positive. It's a great distraction, actually."

"Okay, but only if you're sure. I'll have Felicity and Julian come."

"And George and Michael," added Sabine.

"The whole family," said Bess. Her article was running in Saturday's paper. It was perfect—or was it? Suddenly, she was scared. She thought it was something they all would love, but was she being naïve? Should she tell them all about it ahead of time or let it be a surprise? She made a mental note to consult with Dan. He would know the right thing to do.

"Great plan," said Charlie. "I'm really looking forward to it." She paused and then, to everyone's surprise, hugged each one of them separately.

Slightly stunned, they hugged her back. In five weeks, their ice queen teacher had melted into a snow bunny. Call it what you want—thoga, yogapy, whatever—it was working.

chapter thirty-seven

Sabine

Sabine exited the train with her head down, lost in thought. *How could Naomi have MS? How does a healthy woman just go about her business and then—pow—wake up totally numb?* To think that whatever it was that was hurting Naomi had been lurking in her body; silently waiting for its moment, was terrifying. And so unfair. *I have to get a physical, immediately.* Sabine cringed, realizing that she didn't even have a doctor doctor—just a gyno. *Stupid.*

Suddenly on the street, she looked up to get her bearings. Was that? Sabine's heart plummeted in a mix of excitement and nausea. It was Zach. Well, the back of his head anyway. And he was with a woman. Sabine quickened her pace.

She wanted to get a better look at the back of their two heads. Could she really be trusted to pick out the back of his head in a lineup? Naturally, she knew the answer to that question before she even finished it. Thanks to months of subway stalking, she could pick out his backpack in a lineup if need be. She would know him anywhere—front, back, side to side. She peered at the shoulders, the thin hips, the corduroys, the peacoat . . . the brown sneakers, the hair. It was Zach.

Sabine watched him interact, or at least his back interact, with the woman beside him. She was blond and petite. *Two strikes.* Her hair was longish, reaching just below her shoulders, and wavy. Her jacket was of the puffy variety, in a soft gray color. It covered most of her, but Sabine could make out her legs, clad in dark, skinny jeans and a pair of ankle boots. Sabine considered the outfit. It was Saturday morning. She pulled her phone out of her bag to confirm the time. Around 11 AM. Who wore ankle boots and skinny jeans to go for a casual walk on a Saturday morning? No one, that's who. *This is a morning-after situation.* Sabine's heart crumpled like a lunch bag. She stopped in her tracks and watched them as they continued down the street. They made a right on Fourth Street. Brunch, no doubt.

Sabine suddenly wanted, more than anything in the world, to be in her bed. This was way too much emotional drainage for a Saturday morning. She ran/walked the rest of the way, practically knocking over a baby stroller the size of a small SUV and an old lady. In the door, up the stairs, out of the jacket, into bed.

"Ahhhh," she murmured, pulling the comforter over her head. She felt Lassie's tiny paws tiptoeing around her body. He was certainly familiar with Sabine's hiding under the covers after a shitty day, but the fact that the sun was up threw his tiny cat brain for a loop.

Sabine closed her eyes inside her cocoon. She tried to make sense of how she felt about what she had seen. She wasn't exactly sad . . . it was more a mixture of disappointment and anger. And not necessarily anger toward Zach—he was certainly allowed to date and sleep with other women, especially considering how she was treating him—it was more anger toward the predictability of the whole system. The dating system and, furthermore, the whole men/women/New York City dynamic.

If you were single here, you just had to accept certain codes.

There was always going to be someone who was better looking, smarter, funnier, cooler, better dressed than you. That was a given. This was New York City, after all. Because of said code, a single person really had no firm ground on which to stand. Dating someone insured nothing in terms of exclusivity, and actually could be further fuel to the skirt-chasing fire. If a guy could "get" you, why couldn't he "get" the hot chick at the bar? Or the girl at Starbucks?

Sabine's head emerged from her fortress of solitude. She knew single women could, and often did, behave similarly, but somehow it wasn't as gross when they did it. Well, actually no, it could be very gross, but it was never as maddening. Sabine wondered why. It just wasn't as animalistic, somehow, when women made sex a sport. It seemed more to be about female empowerment than sex for the sake of sex. Sabine sat up. Nothing made sense, especially if he was not sleeping with her, but he was sleeping with this blond person. She felt like Carrie Bradshaw on crack. All she needed was a laptop and a ridiculous outfit and she would be all set. Maybe some men's boxers, suspenders, and a pair of stilettos. With a sports bra. Lassie approached her, cocking his head in concern.

"Don't worry, I'm not losing my mind, Lassie," said Sabine, as she scooped him into her arms and buried her face in his calico fur. *I wonder if they met on the subway.* Sabine hated to admit this, but maybe part of her was secretly relieved that Subway Crush a.k.a. Raisin Jewels a.k.a. Zach was a cad. Believing that he was actually someone with potential was somehow scarier than thinking he was a penis-driven jerk. *I can't believe that I am obsessing about this when a good friend of mine just told me she might have MS. Jesus, what is wrong with me?! Am I the most self-centered person on the planet? Who cares?* She sat up abruptly and threw her covers off, startling an annoyed Lassie. "Enough already, Sabine!" she said aloud.

She eyed her phone, picked it up, and dialed her mother. Sabine wasn't sure if she would even tell her about what was going on with Zach or with Naomi, but she knew that just the sound of her voice would make her feel better.

"Saby!" her mother cooed into the phone, picking it up on the fourth ring.

"Hi, Mama."

"What's wrong?"

"What do you mean, 'what's wrong'?" asked Sabine defensively. Even though her mother was right, something about her self-assuredness was irritating.

"You sound like someone ran over that damn cat. Wait, did someone run over that damn cat?!" Sabine's irritation meter was officially at its limit. Her mother's chipperness about the prospect of Lassie's death was the last thing she wanted to hear right now.

"Listen, I'm gonna go, Mom."

"Wait, wait, wait! Honey, I'm sorry. Forgive me. Hold on a minute." Sabine heard her speaking to what was no doubt a table filled with her girlfriends for Saturday brunch. "Gladys, order me the fruit plate and a side of Canadian bacon," she commanded. "I'm going outside to talk to my *shana maidela*." Sabine smiled, thinking of her mother's friends nodding sagely in response to her announcement.

"Doesn't the bacon cancel out the fruit?" asked Sabine, when her mother was safely outside the restaurant and she had her full attention.

"Don't be fresh. I like the combination. I just have a couple bites of the bacon. Sabine, you should see my thighs, by the way. This Pilates business really works."

"So, what's doing?" asked Sabine.

"Me, I'm fine. Same Saturday as always. Saby, are you okay? You sound down. And you rarely call me on a Saturday morning. Did some schmuck do something stupid?"

"Not really. Well, at least not intentionally."

"Is this Subway Crush?"

"Maybe."

"You don't want to tell me, but you call me to talk about it? Sounds a little silly, Sabine."

"Sorry, I sort of just wanted to hear your voice, Mom."

"Sweetie, I understand. If you want my voice, that's what you'll get. If you don't want to talk about whatever this idiot did, we don't have to." She paused. "Although, if he isn't treating you like the goddess you are, kick him to the curb. You know, we get all these reruns of that talk show, what's it called? *Ricki Lake*? From the nineties? Anyway, we get them here on channel eleven, and every single one of her episodes is about these women 'kicking men to the curb.' I had never heard that expression before! I like it. And between you and me, Ricki needs to kick her stylist to the curb. Her clothes do nothing for her figure!"

Sabine laughed. "Mom, it was the nineties. Nobody wore anything flattering."

"Oh, right! That was when you came home from college wearing that frosted brown lipstick that made you look like a corpse! That was terrible, Sabine."

"He's not treating me badly," Sabine offered, changing the subject before it spiraled into a discussion about the wherefores and whys of Sabine's fashion history. "He's treating me sweetly . . . but I don't know what to do with it, I guess. Or, at least he *was* treating me sweetly."

"Are you pulling this 'tough girl' business?" asked her mother. "God forbid a man should treat you with some respect, Sabine."

"Well, maybe a little 'tough girl,' but not really. We're supposed to go out tonight . . ."

"Saby, I don't know the whole spiel obviously, but I'm wondering if you're still pulling this 'bad guy' crap. If he's too nice, or too much of a gentleman, you're over it. I wonder if you're looking for flaws in him that don't exist, just so you don't have to put yourself out there."

Sabine thought about the blonde. She wasn't making that up. True, she could be a cousin or something, and this was a free country—he could date whomever he wanted—but it was justifiably unsettling. "What if you're wrong, Mrs. Know It All?" asked Sabine. "What if he's an asshole and that's why I'm upset?"

"How can a nice Jewish lawyer be an asshole? Oh wait, I just answered my own question. Maybe you are right, Saby. The point is, how do you know? You've been seeing him for only a minute. Give it some time. You always jump the gun! Anyway, listen, I have to dash. I am starving and I know my girls will attack my bacon like vultures if I'm not around to claim it. Think about what I said and I'll call you later. I love you, Sabine."

"Love you, too."

Sabine hung up the phone and reached into her bedside table drawer for her journal. She had been so religious about keeping one for such a long time, but in the past year she had fallen off the self-reflection wagon. It wasn't that she didn't have time for it, it was just that dealing with her emotions was often harder than ignoring them completely. You couldn't lie to your journal.

Sabine rolled out of bed and moved to her desk. She grabbed a pen and turned to a fresh page, writing the date with care. With a deep sigh, she began. She wrote about yoga and Zach and work and writing and Naomi, along with anything else that came to her mind. At one point, she stopped. Her hand hurt. And her sweaty yoga clothes—stale and scratchy—felt like a straightjacket. She shook her hand and ripped off her sports bra. *Jesus, that feels good.*

Back in her shirt, she resumed her writing. It felt good to get it out. There was so much in her head! The Zach fiasco had inspired her session, but that was just the tip of the iceberg. Finally, she finished. Her hand throbbed. She looked at the clock. It was almost six! She couldn't believe it.

She got up from her desk and stretched to the ceiling. As she did so, she got a whiff of her underarms. "Shower time!" she exclaimed in a mixture of disgust and testosterone-fueled pride.

There was something about not showering that made her proud of herself. It didn't happen often, but when it did, Sabine viewed it as a deliberate "F you" to society's rules of femininity. Ninety-nine percent of the time, she followed those rules willingly, but when she didn't, she felt sort of like a badass. A dirty, smelly badass, but still.

In the shower, Sabine thought about Zach and the date they were supposedly going on that night. Was he really the kind of guy that had two women in one weekend? What was all that crap about how he couldn't sleep with her because he cared so much about her? Was it all a load of bullshit like Sabine had imagined?

She turned off the shower and wrapped herself in a towel. *I'm starving,* she thought, as she wrung out her hair. She hadn't really eaten anything since . . . shit, she wasn't sure if she had eaten all day! *Who am I?* She had always despised those women who claimed they "forgot" to eat. Who forgets to eat? People who "forgot" to eat were the same people that ordered a salad for dinner, hold the chicken please! With the dressing on the side. The only thing they had forgotten was how to eat like a human being.

Sabine emerged from the bathroom to find Lassie gazing at her expectantly. "You're hungry, too, huh?" she asked, watching his ears perk at the mention of food. She did a quick full-body moisturize and pulled on her favorite sweatpants and T-shirt.

In the kitchen, she fixed Lassie his dinner and pulled her trusty dossier of takeout menus off the top of the fridge. As she decided between Chinese and Japanese, her phone rang. Her stomach dropped. She picked it up to see who was calling, halfway hoping that it was Zach and halfway hoping that it wasn't. It was.

She let it go to voice mail. She just didn't feel like dealing with it—with him. Still, she was curious about what he would say. "Uh, hey, Sabine, it's Zach. I just woke up from a long nap. The chick I banged last night left after a late brunch and I was sooo tired. Anyway, now I'm up—and just want to cuddle. Call me so I can pretend I really like you just so I can screw with your head some more." Sabine wondered how much simpler life would be if everyone just said what they meant all the time. The red light blinked angrily on her phone. Voice mail time!

Sabine picked it up to listen. "Uh, hey, Sabine. It's Zach. How are you? I, uh . . . I think we talked about going out tonight. Was wondering if you were still up for it? Give me a call. If you can. Uh, okay, bye—hope you're well."

Sabine pressed seven to erase the message—regretting it approximately twenty seconds after doing so. This was the second dis from her. If she ignored his message, he might never call her again. And who could blame him? She put the phone down and thought about calling him back. He didn't sound like a jerk in his message . . . he sounded kind of sweet and intimidated, actually, but the fact remained that she had seen him with someone else. As her mom would say, *If it walks like a duck and talks like a duck . . .*

She picked up the phone. She had decided on sushi suddenly. Ordering Chinese would have felt a bit cliché. Single girl in the city gets her heart broken, drowns herself in sesame noodles. She'd heard it before. Hell, she'd done it before.

As she waited for the food to arrive, she lay on the couch, staring at the ceiling. This Zach wrinkle was a bummer, no doubt about it, but in a way, she was strangely relieved by the fact that it was over before it started. If he was truly all those wonderful things that she wanted him to be, she would have had no choice but to fall in love with him. And then her entire life would be flipped around. Everything would change. She would no longer be the top priority. She would have to share things, like her rotisserie chicken.

"I don't think I'm ready for that quite yet," she mumbled into Lassie's fur. Or maybe she was, and was telling herself these things to avoid getting hurt, to avoid taking a risk. Risks were not her forte. She stared at the ceiling, bored by the subject already.

Her buzzer rang suddenly—piercing through her melodrama like a fog horn. She jumped off the couch in a ravenous burst of energy.

Later she would return to her favorite subject—her—but now she would eat.

chapter thirty-eight

Bess

It was 8:30 AM and Bess was on her fourth cup of coffee. She had been up since five. All weekend she had been working on the article and now it was Monday morning. She had been writing nonstop, and enjoying every minute of it. She liked the succinctness of it, and the way that—just like yoga—each paragraph flowed directly into the next without any jarring starts and stops. She had now read it over four times and was confident that it was the best thing she had ever written.

The problem now was the question of whether or not to tell Sabine, Naomi, and Charlie about it before it came out. She had wondered about the possibility that she might be violating some gigantic journalistic code of ethics, but a call to one of her fact-checking friends had confirmed otherwise. She was all set on that front, but there were so many pros and cons to the dilemma. She knew her article painted them in a lovely light—so the surprise would most likely be a nice one for them—but on the other hand, she had been scheming to write this all along without any of their knowledge. They could end up feeling victimized and resentful.

After all, they were her friends now. She didn't want to offend them—or shock them. It was a serious crap shoot.

Bess put down the cup of coffee. The caffeine had her heart pumping overtime. She held up her hand and watched it shake without her consent. *Time to eat something.* She walked into the kitchen and opened the fridge, only to discover a can of diet soda and a dead head of lettuce. *Nice,* she thought, tossing the lettuce in the garbage.

"Okay, I'll go out for a bagel," she announced. She hoped that she wouldn't have to deal with any awkward run-ins with anyone from work. She had called in sick to finish her article. Bess looked in the mirror. She looked like a corpse. "Well, at least I don't have to worry about being busted," she mumbled. Anyone she ran into would have no problem believing she was ill.

She sat down on the couch, suddenly exhausted by the idea of getting dressed and going out. This was when she wished she had a personal assistant like the idiots she wrote about. She would communicate with her via hand signals. No, make that him. She wanted a young guy that she could boss around. Girls gave too much lip. Two fingers would mean a toasted pumpernickel bagel with low-fat veggie cream cheese. Three would mean "Add a to-mato but make sure it's not mealy!"

She looked at her phone, suddenly missing Dan violently. He was just the person to ask about her tell/not tell conundrum. She decided to call him, despite the early California hour.

"Hello?" grumbled Dan's sleepy voice into the phone.

"Hiiii," Bess whispered. "Rise and shiiiiiiiiine!"

"Bess, Jesus, it's 6 AM here. Is everything okay?" Dan's voice was thick with both annoyance and concern.

"I know it's early. I'm sorry, but I really needed to hear your voice."

"It's okay," answered Dan, his tone warming. "Here I am."

"And also ask you a teeny tiny question," added Bess.

"Let me guess: it's about the article."

"Why, however did you know that?" Bess had been yapping Dan's ear off about the article since she had left LA.

"Go ahead."

"Listen, should I tell them?" asked Bess. "Should I let Charlie, Sabine, and Naomi know about this article? Or should I just let it be a surprise?"

"Wait, I thought we agreed that you don't need to tell them first. I mean, it's a wonderful article—kind of like a tribute to them, really. I don't see why they would be upset."

"Well, yeah, the last time we spoke about it, we agreed to let it be a surprise," replied Bess. "But now I'm having second thoughts. What if they feel ambushed and they hate me?"

"Why would they feel ambushed?" asked Dan, genuinely baffled. "I've read the article around seventeen thousand times, Bess. It is a really positive piece. Anyone would be honored to be depicted in such a way."

"Wait, are you saying that it's a puff piece?"

"Bess, Jesus, no!"

"Dan, what's the matter?"

"To be honest, I'm a little bit over this damn article. It's all we ever talk about. I don't know how many times I can reassure you that it's an excellent piece. I mean, enough already."

Bess was silent for a minute, considering his point. He was right, that was all they talked about. "You're right, Dan. I'm sorry I'm being such a freak show. It's just that your opinion means so much to me—"

"I know, Bess. I want to be included, I just am a little bit over it at this point. I also don't want you driving yourself mad about it."

"I think you might be a wee bit too late on that one," said Bess.

Dan laughed. "Tell me about it. But that's part of why I love you, I guess. You're so passionate about things that really mean something to you."

"Is *passionate* another word for *crazy*?"

"Maybe, but don't you think it sounds better?"

"Definitely. *Passionate* makes me sound like a bipolar Mediterranean beauty that welds intricate sculptures out of steel."

"That's rich," said Dan, really laughing now. "I like that visual."

"So, Dan? You really think I should let it be a surprise? You don't think Charlie, Naomi, and Sabine will feel like they were taken advantage of?"

"I really don't. Even if they're a little bit taken aback at first, I think that discomfort will quickly give way to warm fuzzies."

Bess exhaled deeply. "You give me warm fuzzies."

"I know something else warm and fuzzy I can give y—"

"Ewwww, Dan!" teased Bess, happy to be laughing with him. "Dan, seriously, I'm sorry I've been such a maniac. I'm going to turn it in today, and I promise I won't mention it again until Saturday, when it comes out and ruins my friendships with these three amazing women."

"Bess! I am telling you—nothing will be ruined. It's a wonderful piece and a testament to their strength and complexity. Plus, it's in *The New York* freakin' *Times*, man!"

"Damn right it is! You can't hate on the *Times*."

"No, you cannot," agreed Dan. He yawned.

"Okay, I'll let you go back to sleep. Dan, I love you. Thank you for putting up with me."

"I love you, too, Bess. Now, turn in that damn article and get some sleep yourself."

"I will. Bye, Dan."

"Bye, Bess."

She hung up and composed a note to Kathryn. Before attaching her piece, she paused for a moment, visualizing everyone's reaction on Saturday. She put herself in Sabine's, Charlie's, and Naomi's shoes and imagined someone writing in the same tone about her without her permission. Would she be okay with the result?

I would, she thought. *I really would.*

She attached the article and pressed SEND. The deed was done. Now it was time for that bagel.

chapter thirty-nine

Sabine

Sabine clomped up the subway stairs after work on Monday evening, breaking a slight sweat in her heavy jacket. She was excited to finish the website copy. It was no novel, but at least it was some sort of writing.

As she rounded the corner to her apartment, she considered the tone she had decided to take. She obviously couldn't rely on her humor—yoga was many things but funny was not one of them. She also hadn't wanted to veer too far in a spiritual direction. A little was good, but nothing too over the top. She had ended up somewhere in the middle, and hoped she had Prana's vibe correctly. When she sat down to write on Sunday morning, she had tried to remember how she had felt, walking into the studio as a virtual yoga virgin just five weeks ago. Although she had been intimidated by the idea of yoga, the studio itself—along with Charlie, Felicity, and Julian—had really eased her anxiety. It had been important to Sabine to translate the nonjudgmental attitudes of all of them in her copy. She was pretty sure she had done it. At least she hoped she had. She would go over it again tonight and edit with a fresh eye.

Deep in thought, she realized she had come to her stoop. She searched in her seemingly bottomless bag for her keys, cursing its lack of pockets.

"Hey," she heard. She looked up, confused. Was someone talking to her? There, at the top of her steps, in all of his handsome glory, was Zach.

"Whoa!" she exclaimed. "Hey!" She paused for a moment, momentarily frozen in place by the shock of seeing him there. "What . . . what are you doing here?" she asked.

"I'm stalking you," Zach replied, flashing a toothy grin.

"Oh, that's comforting," Sabine replied.

"No, I'm not, I promise," he said. "I came by to see if you wanted to grab a drink or something. I rang your doorbell and no one answered. Then I called your cell phone and it went straight to voice mail. I had a feeling you might be on the train, so I figured I'd wait a bit."

"What if I was upstairs with a guy?" asked Sabine, climbing the stairs to sit beside him. "And I never came down? Or what if I came down with him?"

"That was a chance I was willing to take. Better to know what your deal was than not to know at all."

"What do you mean?"

"You never called me back. And I called you twice. What happened to that date we were supposed to go on?" He looked her in the eyes, earnestly.

Wow, thought Sabine, her resolve turning to goo. *No, Sabine! Don't get lost in his raisin jewels and forget about Blondie!*

"Oh, uh . . . sorry. I've been busy and . . ." Sabine paused midsentence. She could either play it cool and lie about her reasons for avoiding him or take a chance and tell him the truth. If she told him the truth, she would be putting herself out there. She thought about what Charlie had spoken about in class on Saturday and went for it.

"Actually no, wait. That's not true. I haven't been that busy. I'm confused."

"Huh? What do you mean?"

Sabine took a deep breath before continuing. "That whole 'no sex' thing the last time we hung out. It really messed with my head."

"I thought I explained myself about the sex. You told me you understood, but I guess that's not the case."

"I know you said you didn't want to have it because you liked me, but it ended up making me feel like you didn't *want* me."

They sat in silence for a minute, listening to the birds chirp excitedly about spring's imminent arrival.

"And then something else happened," offered Sabine.

"What?" asked Zach, a look of concern clouding his raisin jewels. "Are you okay?"

"Oh yeah, I'm fine," answered Sabine, resisting the urge to pat his hand. Any physical contact at this point was a bad idea. "I saw you with another chick," she blurted out.

"You did?! When? Where?"

"Walking down the street together last Saturday morning, when I was coming home from yoga," said Sabine. "I only saw the back of you, but I dunno . . . it looked suspicious."

Zach put his head in his hands and exhaled. "Yeah, that was me."

"Had she stayed over the night before?" she asked, her voice shaky with sadness. She had so wished that Zach would either deny it had been him or tell her that it was his cousin. His response to her question indicated that that, unfortunately, was not the case. "I mean, we don't even know each other, so I realize that it's silly of me to feel any sort of rightful claim on your love life whatsoever. But it made me sad, seeing you like that. And then angry. So when you called, I figured I would get out now, before I got hurt. It seemed easier to ignore you."

"Let me explain," said Zach. "That was not a morning-after situation, that I swear to. Okay?"

"Okay," answered Sabine.

"But I was with my ex-girlfriend and we were going to brunch," he continued.

"Please don't tell me you're 'on a break,' " she whimpered. She needed another one of those like she needed a hole in her head.

"I'm not. We are broken up. It's over and it has been for a few months now."

"Then why are you going to brunch together?" Sabine was a firm believer in the fact that old lovers could not, in fact, be friends. It was impossible, in her book. Someone always had an agenda.

"She's having a tough time with it," he explained. "And I don't mean to sound like some narcissistic asshole. I don't think it's about me at all, really, I just think she has trouble being single."

"Oh, she's one of those?"

"One of what?" asked Zach, annoyed by Sabine's assumption.

"Sorry, I don't mean anything by it. I just mean that I know women like that. Women who have trouble being alone. I'm not . . . I'm not one of those women."

"I know," said Zach. "That's one of the reasons I dig you so much."

Sabine turned to him and smiled. "You dig me?"

"I do."

"Is she going to be a part of your life indefinitely?" asked Sabine.

"No," answered Zach firmly. "You're the first girl I've really liked since we broke up, hence my wanting to wait to sleep with you. Even though I want to . . . badly. It's all I can think about most days." Sabine blushed. *That's more like it.* "I asked her to brunch so I could tell her about you."

"You did?"

"Yep. She didn't take the news so well."

"I'm sorry this is so complicated for you," said Sabine, giving into her impulse and grabbing his hand.

"Hey, life is complicated," said Zach, squeezing her hand in return. "I promise that's the whole truth and nothing but."

"Your story wasn't the one I was expecting to hear, but it makes me feel exponentially better. Thanks for being so honest with me."

"You're welcome. Sorry I stalked you."

Sabine laughed. "That's okay. Sorry I ignored you."

"Yeah, what's up with that?" asked Zach, moving closer. "You're cold as ice!"

"Hardly." Sabine moved in closer to him, and suddenly they were kissing. A long, beautiful, soft, sweet but not too sweet, just the right kind of kiss.

"You look beautiful," said Zach. "I missed your face."

"Yeah, right. Aren't the bags under my eyes gorgeous?"

"No bags," said Zach, touching her cheek. "How was class on Saturday, by the way?"

"It was great. The women in my class are really excellent people. They make me proud of my gender."

"Wow, that's a really cool thing to say," said Zach. "I can't remember the last time I was proud of my gender." He paused to think. "Oh, maybe Obama. He makes me proud to be a black man."

"But you're not a black man!" shrieked Sabine.

"I'm not?!" asked Zach, feigning surprise. He laughed.

"Listen, I'm working on the copy for the studio website, so I better get going." A huge part of her wanted to just stay right there, on her stoop snuggling with Zach, but she had to get her work done.

"Studio website?" asked Zach.

"Yeah, one of the women in our class is a web designer, so she's designing a site for them. She asked me to write the copy."

"Very cool. Okay." He stood up and grabbed Sabine's hands, pulling her up to face him. "Can I see you soon?"

"Yes," answered Sabine.

"When?"

"Well, I want to turn the copy in tomorrow. What about to-morrow night?"

"Works for me," said Zach, pulling her toward him for a hug. "Maybe I'll cook you dinner."

"That sounds nice," Sabine murmured into his neck. God, he smelled good.

She loosened her grasp and tilted her chin to kiss him good-bye. "See you soon."

"Yeah," said Zach. "Soon. I'll call you tomorrow. I don't want you disappearing again."

Sabine smiled and waved good-bye. *No need to worry about that,* she thought, as she closed the front door behind her. Safely in her apartment, she retrieved her phone from her bag and scrolled through to the M's.

"Hello?" her mother answered.

"Hi, Mama," Sabine replied.

"Sabine!" she shrieked. "Where have you been? I thought you were dead."

"Mom, it's only been two days since we last spoke," explained Sabine, already exasperated.

"Two days is a long time," her mother replied. "I thought to myself: well, she's either dead in a ditch somewhere or she's in love. Obviously, you're alive, so I take it you worked things out with the subway Romeo?"

Sabine laughed. "Mom, if you thought I was dead, why didn't you call the police?"

"How do you know I didn't? Okay, okay, I didn't really think you were dead. But I was worried. Don't do that to your mama, okay? I'm old and feeble. I need a check-in."

"Mom, you're more sprightly than a four-year-old. Feeble, my ass."

"Well, you do have a point," her mother admitted. "Did I tell you that I started Rollerblading?"

"You did not! Mom! Jesus! I hope you're wearing a helmet for God's sake."

"I am, don't get your panties in a wad," she replied. She lowered her voice. "Honey, my new boyfriend is forty-four! I'm officially a cougar!"

Sabine laughed. "Wow, Mom! That is pretty impressive. Is he your Rollerblading inspiration?"

"You got it. Let me tell you, the sex—"

"Mom! That's okay, I got it," replied Sabine, cutting her off mid-sentence. It was bad enough to admit that your mother's sex life was more active than your own. Details were unnecessary.

"Fine, be a prude, Sabine. Listen, you never answered my question."

"What question?"

"Don't be coy, missy. How's the Subway Crush? Is he worthy of the most beautiful, funniest, smartest, most sophisticated woman in the world?"

"And who is that?" asked Sabine, grinning into the phone.

"You, my bean," she replied. "You know I worship you."

"Thanks, Mom. And yes, he seems worthy. I took some time to

think about things and ignored him for a bit. When I came home from work tonight, he was sitting on my stoop. We had a good talk and . . . I think things are going to be okay between us."

"Oh good! You sound so much better than you did on Saturday. Talk about a sourpuss. Does he still have a job? Is he good in bed?"

"Jesus, Mom, relax with all the questions! He's a really great guy."

"Oh honey, sorry for all of my nosiness. You know I can't help it, it's in my blood."

"I am good, Mom." She briefly considered telling her mother more, but decided against it. She wanted to keep the details to herself. For a while at least.

"Good, honey. You sound happy. I like when you sound happy. What else is going on? How's the writing?"

"I'm actually working on a project right now." Being able to say that was such a gift, as opposed to her usual noncommittal, vague response. It made her just as happy as talking about Zach.

"That's terrific!" exclaimed her mother. "Tell me about it."

"You know that yoga class I've been taking?"

"Absolutely."

"Well, one of my classmates is a graphic designer. She's designing the website for the studio, and she asked me to handle the copy."

"Bean, that's great news! Are you enjoying it?"

"I really am. I'm about three quarters of the way through at this point," she explained. "I just have to work out some kinks about some hair product descriptions."

"Hair products? I thought this was a yoga website."

"It is, but one of the owners creates her own hair products. We're linking to her line."

"I don't understand all of this web jargon, but it sounds like a great opportunity. I'm so proud of you, Sabine. You're really in charge. Work, writing, a man, a nice dose of self-respect . . . you're juggling all the good stuff."

"Thanks," said Sabine, surprising herself by tearing up at her praise.

"I have to go now. Got a dinner cruise date with Ron."

"Ron? He sounds like a porn star."

"Maybe he is! Wouldn't that just float your boat!?"

"Moooooom! Gross."

"I love you so much, Bean. You're my hero."

"Thanks, Mom. I love you, too. Have fun!" Sabine hung up the phone and gazed out the window, watching the sun set over the city, turning the sky into cotton candy as it inched its way down.

chapter forty

Naomi

Naomi stood at the bottom of the stairs of her brownstone. The journey to the inside of her apartment seemed impossibly arduous. She sat and rubbed her puffy eyes. She had been crying since 1:42 PM, when her doctor had told her that it was "probable MS." *Probable because of the three lesions in your brain and the large one at the base of your cervical spine. Probable because their location is concurrent with early MS. Probable because we can't tell you it's definite until you have a second episode.*

"And when will that happen?" she had asked. "This elusive second episode?"

"We have no idea."

"NO IDEA?"

"It could be three weeks; it could be five years; it could very well never happen at all. We just don't know."

Even with all of the MS research she had done on her own, Naomi was still stunned by the unjust unpredictability of this crazy disease. *You're a planner? Too bad. You want a real answer? Too bad.* Your real answer is delivered only via an episode that renders you immobile for—hopefully, if you're lucky—a few days or weeks, or, like her mother's friend Elizabeth, takes your sight in one eye for a month. You may get your mobility or your eyesight back, but there is no assurance of that. Nobody knows.

"The good news is, if you do have it, it's early. And the medicine available today can really alter its course," explained her doctor. Naomi could barely see his face through her tears.

"What kind of medicine?"

"There are a few kinds. *Blah blah blah blah.* Needles. Every day *blah blah blah* or once a week *blah blah blah.* There are side effects but they're manageable." *How is a disease manageable if you have to stick yourself with a needle every day? That's manageable? What's unmanageable? Imminent death? That's the quantifier?*

Before the appointment was over, Naomi had scheduled a spinal tap for the following week. This was another way to *maybe* determine MS before another episode walloped her (or didn't). Again, here, the vagueness was infuriating. Around eighty percent of people who had MS had a positive tap. *But wait, don't get too excited if yours is negative!* Twenty percent of MS patients have a negative tap. What was the point really?

I guess, in a perverted way, I hope I get a positive tap. At least then I would know, or sort of know, and the idea of medication wouldn't seem so ludicrous. Okay doctor, whatever you say. Oh, that's $6,000 a year for meds? With no formal diagnosis? Sure, here's my check. Naomi wondered if she was so antimedicine because living in denial of the MS was a hell of a lot more pleasant than facing it every day with a big fat shot in the ass.

Naomi heard the window being raised upstairs. She'd been spotted.

"Mom, whatcha doin'?" called Noah from above. He lifted the screen and stuck his little head out. Naomi could hear Gene reprimanding him. She composed herself as best she could. She had to tell her little man today. "Baby, get your body back in that window!" she yelled. "Right now!" She heard the screen slam shut.

"Sorry, Naomi!" yelled Gene.

Turning to make her way in, she heard galloping down the stairs inside and smiled. Nothing was better than Noah's excitement to see her every time she walked through the door.

"Moooooooooom!" he yelled, scrambling down the stairs to hug her. He smelled like peanut butter and orange juice.

"Hi, baby," said Naomi, nuzzling his neck. "Careful of your cast!"

"How was the doctor?"

"Hey, Naomi," greeted Gene, coming down the stairs after him in his jacket. "You okay?"

No. "Oh yeah, fine. Listen, thanks for picking Noah up today."

"No problem. Anytime." He locked eyes with Naomi, not buying her story. Anyone could see that she had been crying. "You give me a call if you want to." She supposed she had to tell him, but not anytime soon.

"I will, Gene. Thanks."

"Bye, Noah. See you Sunday."

"Bye, Dad!" They hugged and Gene waved once more before walking away. "What happened at the doctor, Mom?" Noah asked again.

"Well . . . some stuff is going on with me." Although she was trying with every ounce of her strength not to cry, a tear slid down her cheek.

"Mom, what's wrong?" He put his warm hand on hers.

She took a deep breath. "I might be sick. The kind of sick that doesn't go away, like a cold. You always have it, but some times are much worse than others."

"Oh." Noah's brown eyes swam with concern. "Like Morgan's mom? She has cancer."

"Sort of like that. But this sickness isn't life-threatening. It's more like a huge inconvenience. And sometimes I might not be able to walk or see or talk as well. It's a disease that affects the nervous system."

"Oh, so your spinal cord?" *Suddenly my kid is Jonas Salk?*

"Yes, exactly. It's called multiple sclerosis. And, excuse me, how'd you get so smart?"

"Mom, I'm not a babyyyyyy."

She pulled him close, careful not to jiggle his cast. "Anyway, we're not sure if I have it yet. I have to get a spinal tap next week."

"That doesn't sound fun."

"It won't be."

"Will it hurt?"

"Not so bad, I don't think."

They sat in silence for a few minutes, Noah's hand still clasping hers. The sun filtered through the budding leaves on the trees and above them two birds sang to each other. Mr. Smithers walked his fourteen-year-old lab, Mikey, past them.

"Hey, Noah," he grumbled. "Gonna be baseball season soon, huh?"

"Yeah," answered Noah noncommittally. Mr. Smithers continued on his way, unphased by Noah's lack of enthusiasm.

"So," said Naomi.

"So," repeated Noah. "I don't think you're sick, Mom. You don't look sick."

"I know, and we're not sure yet if I really am. But the fact is that I might be. I wasn't going to tell you until I knew for sure, but I thought I should go ahead and let you know. You're a big boy."

"Yes, I am," answered Noah solemnly. "I love you."

"I love you, too, Noah."

He hugged her fiercely with his free arm, surprising her with his strength.

chapter forty-one

Final Class

"Mornin', sunshine!" cooed Julian as he strolled into the studio. Charlie looked up from her mat. She had come in early to do some stretching before class. She couldn't believe that this was it. How could six weeks have passed so quickly, yet so much have changed? It boggled her mind.

"Hey, hot stuff," she replied. "How are you on this beautiful Saturday?"

"Me and my boys are excellent." As if on cue, George and Michael came running in. George skittered directly over to Charlie and began licking her leg with sloppy gulps.

"Someone is in a good mood!" Charlie remarked, scratching him lovingly behind his ears. Michael approached from her other side, wanting to get in on the action.

"I know! George and Michael are in rare form today. I think it's spring. They might not technically have their balls anymore, but their instincts are spot-on."

Charlie laughed. "Julian, can you believe that this is my last class with Bess, Naomi, and Sabine?"

"I really can't. It seems like just yesterday I was bitching you out for signing up such a small class."

"Doesn't it? It's nuts."

"I'm psyched to see the website," said Julian.

"Helloooo," called Felicity, entering the studio. "I brought bagels! The devil's carbohydrate." She put down her bags. "Today is the day! I can't wait to get my hands on that website."

"I know, we're excited, too," Charlie replied. "As soon as class is over, we'll have a look."

"A look at what?" asked Sabine, entering next. She put down her bag of champagne and orange juice and beamed at them. Her date with Zach had gone incredibly well. She was still coasting on the high.

"The website," answered Charlie. "Are you happy with the way your copy turned out?"

"I really am. It's tight."

"Nice," said Julian. "Okay, I'll let you ladies get to it. See you after class." He swatted Sabine playfully on her behind as he and his canine entourage left the room.

Naomi and Bess arrived next—Naomi with her laptop and pastries in tow, and Bess with a bag of newspapers and fruit.

"What's with the newspapers?" asked Sabine.

"All will be revealed after class," answered Bess, with what she hoped was a coy grin and not one of acute anxiety. She was a nervous wreck. What if they all ganged up on her and clobbered her to death with yoga blocks?

"Ooh, mysterious," joked Naomi.

After disrobing, they all took their respective places on their mats, the gravity of this last class weighing on all of them.

"I can't believe this is it," said Charlie. She looked at all of them with pride. "We have all come so far here. Yoga and life-wise."

"Yogapy," said Sabine.

"Exactly," agreed Charlie. "You know, it's interesting. I always thought of yoga as the ultimate balancing act, but never before have I seen it transcend boundaries in such a way. All of you," she paused, "no, all of *us* have really taken the practice outside the classroom. Our work here has inspired balance and movement in other very important areas of my life, and I want to thank you for that inspiration."

"Me too," said Bess. "I've learned so much from all of you."

Sabine and Naomi nodded. "Me too," they said simultaneously.

"So with that said, let's begin our last class together," said Charlie. "I know I haven't opened class with *Om* before, but I really feel it's appropriate now, in this moment. In essence, *Om* is a sound that represents the union of mind, body, and spirit. It truly is what yoga is all about, and also what our journey here and outside the studio has been about these past six weeks. If you would, please join me."

"Ooooouuuuummmmm," chanted Charlie. The ladies followed suit.

Bess thought about just how much her attitude toward yoga had changed since class had begun. Six weeks ago, she would have rolled her eyes and refused to participate. She could see now just how self-conscious she had been.

As they flowed through class, it was all Sabine could do not to burst into tears of happiness. Yoga no longer intimidated her. A lot of things no longer intimidated her. She was writing again, and she was opening up in a way that she had never been able to do before. She had so much to be grateful for. It truly was astonishing how her entire perception had changed.

In cobra, Naomi felt her chest muscles expand. She thought about her brain and those small, seemingly innocent white circles that her doctor had shown her on her MRI. What was happening in there? Were her lesions multiplying right now, as she moved into downward facing dog? How could she feel so good if that was the case? If her nerve signals weren't firing correctly, then how come she was able to enjoy yoga? It was one thing to be aware of your body through exercise, but another entirely to be hypersensitive for all of the wrong reasons. *It's going to be so hard to find the balance between body consciousness and my well-being now.* She segued into warrior I and faced the front of the room with determined confidence. *But I will try. Every day I will try my best. And that's all I can do.*

At the close of class, Charlie made a suggestion. "I was hoping you guys would be into trying handstands today," she explained. The women cringed. Was she nuts?

"I don't expect you to get up there, but I think if you try it, you might surprise yourselves."

Bess, Naomi, and Sabine looked at each other for affirmation. "We'll try it," said Naomi, speaking for all of them.

"Good," said Charlie. "Take your mats over to the wall. Now, I'm going to demonstrate for you. Make like you're going into a handstand, one leg in front of the other, like so." She got into the position. "Then, just ease your weight onto your hands and kick up. One leg at a time." She showed them how, rocking back and forth a few times before her long legs went up, perfectly vertical, and then rested against the wall. She released the position. "Have a go," she said.

Sabine felt kind of like a fool, but she went for it anyway. Each time she went down on her hands, she had trouble remembering what to do with her legs. She would come right back down, her feet landing with a resounding thud.

Bess had the same issue, but found the whole thing comical.

Six weeks ago I would have been cursing Charlie's firstborn for making me do this, she thought to herself. Now she just found her lack of balance endearing. She would get it eventually. What was the rush?

Naomi rocked back and forth a few times, feeling her legs go higher with each attempt. On her fourth try, she went up, the blood rushing to her head. It felt good. She closed her eyes and imagined those little white bad guys becoming dissolved by a rush of healthy red blood. Biologically, it made no sense, but the visual soothed her. As her feet rested against the wall for support, she heard clapping. She opened her eyes to find upside down versions of Charlie, Bess, and Naomi, smiling and laughing.

"Awesome, Naomi!" said Charlie.

"You are a goddess!" echoed Sabine.

"I hate you!" shrieked Bess.

Laughing, Naomi lowered her legs. She turned over. "I can't believe I did that!" she exclaimed. "I feel like a rock star!" She couldn't wait to tell Noah.

"You are a rock star," said Charlie.

Charlie returned to the front of the room and walked the women through their cooldowns. It was difficult for all of them to relax however, knowing the party was moments away.

As they sat up to face Charlie, she smiled at them. "Well, no need to close with some sentimental statement," she explained. "We can get mushy over bagels."

"And mimosas," said Sabine.

"And mimosas," echoed Charlie. "Namaste, beautiful ladies." She bowed her head.

"Namaste," they replied, relishing the importance of what was technically their last yoga good-bye.

"Party time!" yelled Sabine.

The women laughed and jumped up from their mats, scrambling to get their supplies. They left the studio to find Felicity and Julian hovering over a setup of bagels, Danish, fruit, and mimosa supplies.

"We figured we'd help out," said Julian. "Also, I was starving! I can't be surrounded by this many carbs and keep it together!"

"Ooh, this looks delicious!" said Charlie.

"Wait!" yelled Bess, a little bit too loudly. She had to show them the article immediately or her head would explode.

"Whoa, what's up, honey?" asked Felicity. "You okay?"

Bess took a deep breath. "I am. But I have something to share with you all." She retrieved her bag of papers. "Just let me explain first." She surveyed their faces before continuing. "I wrote an article for the *New York Times*," she explained.

"Bess!" interrupted Sabine. "Wow, I—"

"No, wait. Please," said Bess. "The article is about this class." She watched their faces clench in response. "But it's really a beautiful article, if I may say so. It's about, well, it's about women and their struggle to balance everything in their lives." She looked at Julian. "Sorry, Julian."

"No problem," he replied.

"I used this class as an example. Really I used all of you as an example," said Bess.

"Did you use our real names?" asked Naomi, clearly concerned.

"I did. But not your last names. And Charlie, I definitely mention the studio, but I thought you might welcome that publicity."

"I dunno, Bess," said Sabine. "It's sort of messed up that you used us without our permission."

"I know, I know," answered Bess. "But you should know that my original intention for the article was not as pure. I came into this class as this bitter, angry journalist who wanted to blame everyone else for my lack of success. I thought I was going to write about the lameness of the modern urban woman. The lack of follow-through on their dreams . . . the reluctance to take any risks . . . the focus on others instead of themselves as a bad thing."

"Wow, sounds like a nice article," said Felicity, her voice heavy with sarcasm.

"But that's the thing!" said Bess. "That's not the article that I ended up writing at all. As I got to know each one of you better and became more comfortable in my practice, my whole outlook changed. My previous idea was rooted in so much negativity and I was projecting my worries about my own life unfairly onto all of you. Class made me realize that. You guys made me realize that. So the article changed. I really think you'll like it."

"What section is it in?" asked Naomi.

"City," answered Bess. "It's very short, really. No offense to the Metro section, but I doubt many people will read it."

"True," said Julian. "I'm a Styles Section man myself."

"You don't say," said Charlie. She faced Bess. "Well, I have to say that I'm not entirely sold on the idea, and something about the fact that you went behind our backs to do this doesn't sit well with me. This is my business, you know? Julian, Felicity, and I have poured our hearts and souls into this place, and to have it be the focus of an article without our permission seems grossly unethical on your part."

"Not to mention your intentions in the beginning, Bess," said Julian. "Who were you to consider yourself more evolved than any of these women? To be so patronizing and ugly, it's pretty unforgivable."

"But that's just it," explained Bess. "I was an asshole coming into this, no question. But through the friendships I've made here and the way that yoga makes me feel—open, less aggressive, more aware—I've changed. The article reflects all of that, I promise you."

"You don't even want to know what I will do to you if this article pisses me off," said Felicity. "Seriously."

"Bess, if you mentioned my MS, I will never forgive you," said Naomi. "For you to take that information as your own, without my permission—"

"No, no, of course I didn't, Naomi. There is no mention of that or anything too personal in the article. I tried to keep you all as anonymous as possible."

"Other than the fact that you used our real names, of course," snapped Sabine. "I might not love my job, but I certainly need it. You're not going to get me fired, are you?" Her boss was notorious for reading the paper cover to cover every day. How many Sabines in book publishing could there be?

"I swear, I won't. Please, will you all just read the article so you can answer these questions yourselves?"

"At this point, I am damn curious," admitted Charlie.

"Me too," said Sabine.

"Okay, have a look," said Bess. She passed out the paper to all of them and walked into the studio to pace. *Please, please, let them like it,* she said to herself.

The minutes passed like hours. Finally, Charlie poked her head in. "Hey Bess," she said.

Bess looked up nervously. "Yeah?"

"It's fantastic!" said Charlie, with tears in her eyes. "I am so touched!"

"Me too!" yelled Sabine, rushing in to give her a hug. Naomi and Charlie followed, and soon they were all entwined in a gigantic, four-way embrace.

Tears streamed down Bess's face. She was overwhelmed with relief and happiness. Never had something been so important to her before. The respect of these women meant the world to her.

"Bess, it is so well done," said Naomi. "Thanks for that."

"Do you really think we're that special?" asked Sabine coyly.

"I do," answered Bess. "I really do. I mean, we're all just getting by, you know? We're doing the best we can, every day."

"Bess, this is the best publicity ever!" shrieked Julian. "Business is really going to pick up! Boy, did you save your own ass."

"Yeah, this all could have gone horribly wrong, but you did Prana right," said Felicity, embracing her next. "I think it's really going to make a difference in our business."

"We're going to be rich!" exclaimed Julian, dancing around as George and Michael skittered across the floor.

"I wouldn't go that far," said Charlie. "Now, let's eat!"

"Wait! One more thing!" said Naomi. "The website!"

She turned on her laptop. "Okay, here it is," she said, as it came up on the screen. "Now remember, this is just a first draft. Sabine and I are more than happy to go back to the drawing board if you absolutely hate it."

She walked them through the site, clicking through the links one by one. *Ooh*s and *ah*s filled the room. When she was done, she faced them.

"Naomi, the website is perfection," cooed Felicity. "It is perfectly Prana."

"It really is," said Charlie. "From the pictures to the copy to the clean, open layout—"

"It's genius," said Bess. "Truly beautiful."

"You like it?" asked Naomi, beaming. "Really?"

"Really," said Julian. "I think I need to give you a hug."

"And Sabine, the copy is incredible. Warm, funny, open . . ." said Charlie. "Just like you."

Sabine beamed. "I'm so glad you like it."

"And the way you wrote about my products!" added Felicity. "I might need to hire you full-time."

"I can launch the site right now, if you like," said Naomi.

"Really?" asked Charlie. She looked at Felicity and Julian, who gave their nod of approval.

"Wait, wait, get the champagne!" said Bess. Sabine grabbed a bottle and prepared to uncork it.

"Okay, Naomi—one, two, three!" As Naomi officially launched the site, the champagne cork went flying, the bubbles erupting in a torrent of frothy white.

"L'chaim!" yelled Sabine.

To life.

Three Months Later

W here are you goingggg?" whined Zach, as Sabine crept out of bed as stealthily as she could. He reached out to pull her back in. She submitted, relishing the warmth of his bare chest against her cheek as she snuggled in for one last hug.

"I told you, I'm going to Prospect Park today to see Charlie, Bess, and Naomi. Do you listen to me?"

"What?" teased Zach, pretending he hadn't heard her.

"Very funny." She squeezed him. "I'll be back later this afternoon."

"Didn't you just see them yesterday for class?"

"I did, but this is different. This is a park picnic. Bess organized it. I think she has something big to tell us or something."

"Maybe you're all on the cover of *People* magazine or some shit. *Surprise! I wrote a tell-all about each and every one of you! But it's super nice, so don't be mad.*" Zach had never really gotten onboard with Bess after her initial article about them all. He thought that she had been out of line.

"Zach, don't be a dick." Sabine rolled out of bed and surveyed herself in the mirror. To shower or not to shower, that was the question. She took a closer look and gave herself some props. Her abs were definitely tighter. *Thanks, yoga.* After the women had ended their Basics class, they had decided to return to Charlie's open class on Saturday afternoons. The double whammy of Bess's article and the Prana website had increased the student population very respectably. Sometimes, the class was so crowded that the most they could hope for was an inch between yoga mats.

No shower, thought Sabine. It was the middle of June and she would be sweating like a hog in the park anyway. A little deodorant and a hat to keep the sun off her face would do the trick. Sabine had always been a sun worshipper, but lately, her face was telling the tale. She had a weird sun spot situation happening on her upper lip that bared too close a resemblance to a mustache. Her reckless tanning days were over.

"See you later, babe," she whispered in his ear. He smiled and mumbled good-bye. Sabine shoved her hat in her bag and trotted out of the apartment, praying that the subway gods would be kind to her.

"Noah, slow down!" yelled Naomi. He was in front of her on his bike, his long legs pedaling at the speed of light. She had bought them both bikes in May, and they had been having a blast on the weekends, taking the Brooklyn streets by storm. Their first few rides had been unbearably tense for Naomi—between her worries about her own balance and Noah's tendency to show off, she was constantly afraid that one of them would break their neck, despite their first-rate helmets. Over time however, she had eased up. Noah was a natural and she, well . . . exercise held new meaning for her now. Having that kind of positive control over her body—to really appreciate the fact that her brain was telling her legs to peddle and that's exactly what they were doing—was reassuring. Noah slowed his pace and she eased up beside him. He looked over and reached out to touch her arm.

"Careful!" she teased. His cast had come off months ago, but she wasn't taking any chances. He stuck out his tongue at her. "Race!" she shrieked, taking off in front of him toward the park entrance.

"There's Dad!" yelled Noah, passing her. She smiled. Gene was waiting for them, his own bike resting on his kickstand beside him.

"Easy, Lance Armstrong," he said, as Noah circled him like a shark. Noah stopped his bike and jumped off it, enveloping Gene in a bear hug. Naomi marveled at her lack of jealousy at seeing Noah so ecstatic. The past months had been amazing for her in terms of relinquishing her grip on him. Gene had really proved himself, too—making himself available whenever she needed his help, with no complaints. "Hey, Naomi," he said.

"Hey, Gene. Thanks for coming today. I should be done in a couple hours or so."

"No sweat. Who's going to your picnic?"

"My yoga ladies. We're taking it out of the studio for a change. We haven't really caught up in a while, so it'll be good to see them."

"Very cool. We'll meet you back at the house around four or so, if that's okay. I thought I might take Noah over to the Brooklyn Museum."

"Sweet!" Noah enthused. "I like that place."

"Perfect," said Naomi. "You guys have fun. I love you, Noah. Be good!"

"I love you, too, Mom." He hopped off his bike to hug her and let it crash to the ground, despite Naomi's constant reminding him to take better care of it. She shook off her annoyance. *Boys will be boys*. She hugged him back, waved, and took off, anxious to find out Bess's news.

I dunno, what do you want to do tonight?" asked Charlie into her phone. The sun felt amazing on her bare shoulders. June in New York could make you forget about the interminable winter in just an instant. This was that instant.

"Maybe I should cook you dinner," answered Mario. "Something delicious. We can eat outside on my deck." Mario was a lucky man. A Brooklyn apartment with a deck was the equivalent of winning the lottery as far as Charlie was concerned.

"That sounds good. I have to teach two classes in the late afternoon, but I could be showered and at your place by seven thirty or so." Mario lived very close to Prana and, consequently, very close to her. Geographic compatibility was only one of the many reasons they were enjoying each other. As promised, Charlie had gone to see his band play soon after the infamous Neil run-in at the deli, and the rest had been history. She even had him trying yoga.

"*Bueno*," he answered. "Have a good time with the girls. Can't wait to feed you later."

Charlie laughed. "Okay, Mario, see you soon." She picked up her pace, noticing the distinctive feel of sweat beginning to bead up on her brow.

B ess rearranged her blanket for what felt like the ninety-seventh time. She had brought some fruit, cheese, tuna salad, and some crackers. Surveying her spread, her stomach growled. She wanted to eat, but her nerves were off the charts. She wondered how Charlie, Naomi, and Sabine would react to her news.

"Bessss!" yelled Sabine, approaching her on the grass. "Hello, mysterious vixen!" she said, hugging Bess in greeting. "Tell me first, before anyone gets here. I won't let on."

"No way, lady," Bess replied. "Besides, it's not that big of a deal. I think I might have blown it a bit out of proportion." Actually, it was that big of a deal, maybe the biggest deal of Bess's life thus far, but she was embarrassed by how much she had played it up. "How are you?"

"Well, I just left Zach at home . . . and am loving this weather! Isn't it amazzzzinggg?"

"It really is. Feeling sunbeams is a top-five sensation."

"Shit, I almost forgot," said Sabine. She pulled her hat out of her bag. "Protection," she announced, plopping it on her head.

"Wow, look at you!" said Naomi, walking her bike up and laying it beside them on the green lawn. "You look like a Palm Beach diva!"

"Through and through!" answered Sabine. She stood up to hug Naomi.

"Hey, Bess!" Naomi sat down and hugged her as well. "It's great to see you."

"Not covered up in huge jackets," added Bess. "In tank tops, no less."

"And may I just say that we are all looking *tres jolie*," observed Naomi. "Yoga is treating us right."

"Holla!" replied Sabine.

"Are you guys hungry?" asked Bess. "I brought some snacks."

"Ooh, I'll have some fruit," said Naomi. She picked a pineapple chunk out of the bowl. "Yum."

"Hey, ladies!" said Charlie, jogging over to the blanket. "Sorry I'm late."

"Could Mario not bear to have you leave him?" teased Naomi.

"A hundred bucks says he wanted to make you some bacon and eggs for breakfast."

"Very funny," replied Charlie, in between kissing them all on their respective cheeks. "For your information, I stayed at home last night."

"Really? How come?" asked Sabine.

"I'm organizing a retreat! I'm so excited about it. One of Julian's friends is the manager of this gorgeous hotel down in Puerto Vallarta, and she is pumped about getting a yoga retreat package started. She's asked Julian and me to sign on as the official instructors."

"Get out of here!" shrieked Naomi. "That is awesome! Puerto Vallarta is supposed to be incredible."

"When is it?" asked Bess.

"It's right before Thanksgiving. Wednesday to Wednesday."

"That is too perfect," said Sabine. "You cleanse your body and your mind right before diving into a tryptophan coma. I like it."

"You know, I could get you guys a discount if you were interested," said Charlie, with a sly smile. "I already asked her if I could hook up a few star pupils, and she was amenable to twenty-five percent off the package price."

"No way!" said Naomi. "Oh wow, how lovely would that be? Yoga in Mexico!? In November?"

"It would be even cheaper for me," said Bess. She was so nervous to reveal her "big secret" but this segue was ingenious.

"How so?" asked Charlie, slicing off a piece of cheese.

"I'm moving to LA!" replied Bess.

"Wait, what!?" said Sabine. "You're moving out there to be with Dan?! Bess, that's so exciting!" She jumped up to hug her.

"It is exciting!" agreed Naomi. "But what about your job? What are you going to do?" Naomi paused. "Look at me, Ms. Buzzkill. Sorry, Bess."

"Oh no, are you kidding me? Of course you should ask that question. I'm equally excited about that as I am about the Dan factor."

"Holy shit, what are you going to be doing?" asked Sabine.

"Writing for the Style section of the *LA Times*," Bess answered. "I know, it's not exactly war-torn Bosnia, but I've been told that the position has legs. A year or two there, with a couple of free-lance projects under my belt, and I'm in pretty good shape. It's a great foot in the door situation."

"I'd say that you were in excellent shape," said Sabine. "Bess, I am so happy for you! This is huge news!"

"It really is," agreed Charlie. "How did you decide to just go for it?"

"You know, I think it was just a gradual process," she answered. "I started to open up my mind to the idea of moving there and then slowly but surely, it became less of a sacrifice and more of an opportunity. Plus, I'm actually excited to be closer to my parents. I never thought those words would come out of my mouth, but there they are."

"I think that this is going to be fantastic for you," said Naomi. "For both of you. And by the way, I am really into this Puerto Vallarta retreat idea. I think we should do it."

"Look at you, Miss Moneybags!" teased Sabine. "How are you feeling by the way?"

"Good, good. I'm still thinking about the medication and, in the meantime, reaching out to whomever I can talk to. I'm also doing acupuncture and have modified all the fun out of my diet. I feel good, I think."

"And your doctor is okay with your not being on the meds?" asked Bess.

"I mean, he's not jumping for joy about it, but he can't make me take them, you know? I'm getting another MRI in a month, to see what's cooking in my brain, and we'll take it from there. After my negative spinal tap, I just couldn't get on board with the meds so soon. It felt so rushed and panicky to me. At least, most days I think that. Other days I think that my fondness for denial is going to bite me in the ass." She sighed heavily. "Oh, it's so boring! Honestly, I'm sick of talking about it. But thank you, guys, for asking."

"How's business?" asked Charlie.

"You would not believe how much shit I have going on right now. Ever since the Prana website, it has been gangbusters."

"Naomi, that's terrific!" said Bess. "What are you working on?"

"Well, one of Felicity's friends was really impressed by my work for her hair products. She's one of these super-mom, Park Slope bloggers." The group collectively groaned. The stereotype was all too true. Brooklyn's sidewalks were overrun with that very cliché—clog-wearing moms pushing their gigantic strollers and nibbling their gluten-free, dairy-free, everything remotely tasty-free energy bars.

Naomi laughed. "She's not so bad, really. I mean, she practices what she preaches at least. She designs this eco-friendly clothing line for kids. Really cool stuff, actually. I mean, Noah wouldn't be caught dead in it, but that's just because he's taking fashion tips from his rock-star daddy as of late." She grinned and rolled her eyes. "Anyway, she needs a website, so she called me. It's going live this week with photos I took of her kids in the clothes."

"Naomi, I am psyched for you," said Bess. "I'm sure her site is going to draw loads of traffic."

"And then who knows where you'll go!" said Sabine. "You're about to blow up."

Naomi smiled. "Thanks, guys. I'm pretty excited about it." She took a swig of her water. "Sabine, how's your writing class going?"

"It's going pretty well, I have to say. Just meeting with other writers once a week, critiquing and being critiqued . . . it feels good. And with someone else cracking the deadline whip, I actually listen."

"No more tweezing breaks?" asked Bess.

"No! I'm a focused machine. Don't they look thicker, by the way?" She furrowed her brow in an attempt to show her brows off.

"They do!" Charlie replied, examining them close-up. "I like 'em. Very sophisticated."

"French woman drinking a cappuccino and smoking a cigarette in some combination of navy and black sophisticated?"

"Exactly," answered Charlie.

"Look at us!" yelled Naomi. "Can you believe it!? Summer is here, babies!"

"Hallelujah!" said Sabine. "Damn, Bess, you're gonna have summer all year long in LA, aren'tcha?"

"Pretty much," she answered. "Can't say I'm not looking forward to that."

"So when are you moving out there?" asked Charlie, digging a strawberry out from under a piece of cantaloupe. Bess lay on her back to relate her moving plan, and Sabine—seeing prime pillow real estate in the form of Bess's stomach—lay her head back on it and adjusted her hat accordingly. Naomi, noticing the way the shadow of Sabine's straw brim dappled her chest when the sun hit is just so, pulled her camera out of her backpack gingerly.

As the morning turned into afternoon, the four of them remained on their little blanket island—relishing the blissfully warm, fresh air and each other with equal enthusiasm. Who could say for sure what the future had in store for them, but right then, on that perfect summer day in Brooklyn, life was pretty damn good.

acknowledgments

First and foremost, thank you to my parents, Sue and Ethan Fish-man. Mom, it is from you that I learned to love the written word. And Dad, thank you for "summer school" and teaching me to never give up. Thank you to my brother, Brenner Fishman, for be-lieving in me; my grandmother, Edna Horan, for making me the most popular granddaughter at the library; and my grandfather, Steve Fishman, for inspiring me with his curious mind. Thank you also to the rest of my family—your love and support mean more to me than I can possibly express.

Thank you to my wonderful, wise editor, Jeanette Perez. Without you, this never would have happened, and I am beyond grateful. Thank you to Carrie Kania and Michael Morrison for giving me a shot.

Lastly, thank you to all of the fantastic women in my life. Your strength, grace, and balance serve as constant inspiration. If you see just a flicker of yourselves in these pages, then I am doing al-right. You were the source, after all.